Alchemy Unlimited

"Fine, fanciful, farcical . . .
One of the most original fantasy novels
I've seen in years,
in both concept and execution."
Lawrence Watt-Evans, author of *The Misenchanted Sword*

"What did the Spanish Inquisition
do with the demons it exorcised?
At last we learn the answer!"
Piers Anthony

"Unusually well crafted"
Locus

"Amusing, engaging, pungent"
Roger Zelazny

"Wonderfully inventive"
Mel Gilden, author of *Surfing Samurai Robots*

"An engaging and unusual light fantasy . . .
There will be more adventures of Corwyn and Sebastian,
and I'll certainly read them."
Janice Eisen, *Aboriginal Science Fiction*

Other Avon Books by
Douglas W. Clark

ALCHEMY UNLIMITED

Rehearsal for a Renaissance

DOUGLAS W. CLARK

AVON BOOKS • NEW YORK

REHEARSAL FOR A RENAISSANCE is an original publication of Avon Books. This work has never before appeared in book form. This is a work of fiction, and while some portions of this novel deal with actual events and real people, it should in no way be construed as being factual.

AVON BOOKS
A division of
The Hearst Corporation
1350 Avenue of the Americas
New York, New York 10019

Copyright © 1992 by Douglas W. Clark
Cover illustration by Dean Morrissey
Published by arrangement with the author
Library of Congress Catalog Card Number: 91-93019
ISBN: 0-380-76310-9

First AvoNova Printing: March 1992

AVONOVA TRADEMARK REG. U.S. PAT. OFF. AND IN OTHER COUNTRIES, MARCA REGISTRADA, HECHO EN U.S.A.

Printed in the U.S.A.

RA 10 9 8 7 6 5 4 3 2 1

This book is dedicated to the ghosts of two writers:
William Shakespeare and Geoffrey Chaucer.
I set out to spoof your words, only to come away
enchanted.
For that, I am deeply grateful.

ACKNOWLEDGMENTS

Among those who contributed to the creation of this book, I particularly want to thank the following: my wife, Sharon—friend, companion, and inspiration on the greatest of journeys; Nancy V. Berberick, writer and fellow spirit, for her enthusiasm from the beginning; George Anderson, Melvin Eisenstadt, V.A.L. Lewis, and Doris Stremel for their patience through endless rewrites; Prof. Patrick J. Gallacher, a convivial host on a Chaucerian pilgrimage who allowed me to join his merry company; my editor, Chris Miller, whose suggestions have always improved my writing; my agent, Maria Carvainis, for her invaluable help in the business of writing; Bob Julyan, Karen McCue, Mary Rosenblum, and Neal Singer for critiquing various portions of the manuscript; the Southwest Writers Workshop for its continuing help to struggling writers; the University of New Mexico General Libraries; and finally, special thanks to Cynthia Goldblatt, Patty Sheehan, and Will Parker, among others, for encouraging me to trust that inner voice which is my surest guide to truth and beauty.

PROLOGUE:

The Summer's Tail

"LET AN ERA OF CHANGE BEGIN!"

The merchant representing the council of guilds shouted the words from the silk pavilion erected for this announcement, his voice ringing through the marketplace of the southern French town of Pomme de Terre. An exultant roar greeted him from the crowd. Echoes beat back upon the square from the upthrust peaks of the Pyrenees rising just beyond the town.

Sebastian turned to smile at the young woman next to him, ready for change. They would be formally betrothed in church in a few weeks, but he felt their engagement was official now, having told his master of their intentions moments earlier. And Gwen already looked the part of a bride; her clothing—though common—bedecked with flowers made her appear a queen among peasants, a royal spectator at a sheep shearing.

Sebastian only wished his own appearance was half so grand. Born the son of a nobleman, he still hadn't accustomed himself to his reduced status. That was one change he would willingly do without. The rough commoner's clothing that was now his lot itched something terrible and looked even worse!

Still, this was a time of excitement, with the duchy

1

eager to participate in the new order rumored to be taking place in Italy.

On the stage in front of the pavilion, a score of hairy shepherds dressed in animal skins began prancing to the sounds of a hornpipe and tabor. Sebastian glanced at his master, Corwyn, the local alchemist. "It's a pastoral play," Corwyn whispered. "I think they're supposed to be satyrs."

Sebastian struggled to repress a snicker. The shepherds' antics were unlike any morality play he'd ever seen, and such plays defined the limits of what he knew about theater.

Apparently, this was the case for the rest of the crowd as well. Isolated chuckles grew to guffaws, spreading to envelope the throng. The shepherds on stage ceased their prancing, struck motionless with embarrassment.

Then the laughter of the crowd faded, leaving behind only silence as the significance of what was happening sank in. Members of the council of guilds, gaudy in their new, imported clothes, shifted awkwardly on the wooden platform inside the pavilion where they had been watching. A mournful wind sighed down from the Pyrenees. People glanced about, questioning what, if anything, had really changed. How tawdry and downright medieval the duchy's celebration suddenly seemed.

When it came right to it, who among them knew how to conduct a proper renaissance? Sebastian wondered, using the term Corwyn had taught him for the changes being adopted from Italy.

"There goes the fifteenth century," a crone at the edge of the square muttered loudly enough for all to hear. "*Bon dieu!* What have we done?"

"Opened the door to every craze and passing trend the Italians come up with," a man's voice called. "And it's all that alchemist's fault."

Faces turned to glare at the small, rotund man next to Sebastian. Corwyn squirmed in his heavy robes.

For years, the former duke had barred the duchy from participating in the new European order. But when an untimely demonic possession turned the duke into a fugitive of the Inquisition, the duchy had found itself freed from its feudal past. The council of guilds pressed for greater autonomy under the duchess, and everyone had believed the duchy would immediately emerge to lead other nations in social change.

As if the duchy could be transmuted into a nobler social form merely because people decided they wanted it, Sebastian thought, eager to defend his master.

Across the square, the crone nodded to the man who had spoken. "We're acting like half-wits, probably on account of one of the alchemist's infernal elixirs. Something he put in the water, I'll wager. As if what's happening in Italy has anything to do with us!"

Corwyn edged backward through the crowd, trying to slip away unnoticed. Sebastian and Gwen followed him—as did every eye in the crowd. How eager people were to accuse the alchemist of administering an elixir of discontent to the duchy, Sebastian thought, when what they really wanted was to forego the lingering unease of gradual change. They wanted to transform the duchy with one quick potion.

Corwyn's only fault had been in linking himself to the Renaissance by predicting its coming.

"Well, summer's almost over," the crone went on, squinting up at mountain peaks that soon would be frosted with snow. "Maybe this Renaissance foolishness will sound better in the spring."

Sebastian hoped it would be a quiet winter in Italy. By the time April washed away dreary March and quickened the flow of life in plant and animal veins here in the duchy once again, maybe people would have forgotten this Renaissance obsession.

Otherwise, he suspected that—whatever happened—his master would be the one they blamed.

ACT 1:

A Midwinter Night's Scheme

IN A SHALLOW NICHE IN THE OUTER WALL OF THE DE'
Medici palace, twelve-year-old Niccolò Machiavelli
shivered and hugged his knobby knees to his chin. He
peered through a hole he had worried in the closely woven
fibers of one of the Flemish tapestries, gazing longingly
out at the two earthenware *scaldini* Maddalena had
brought into the room earlier. Niccolò wished the heat
from their coals would penetrate the heavy tapestry and
warm the frigid air close to the plaster. Still, he ignored
his discomfort as best he could and concentrated on the
man occupying the counting room on the other side of
the tapestry.

As he thought about the joke he had prepared for that
man, it was all Niccolò could do not to giggle.

Across the room, Cosimo de' Medici, head of the most
powerful banking family in Europe and uncrowned prince
of Florence, sat at his desk and cleared his throat in the
unconscious way he had that showed he was puzzled.
He brushed back thinning white hair with one hand while
tracking figures in a ledger with the other.

The light from a candle on the desk threw the heavy,
peasantlike features of Cosimo's face into bold relief.
There was little about the man, from his medium stature

4

to his mild, self-effacing temperament, that revealed the true extent of his authority. Even the long cloak he habitually wore was nothing more than the *lucco* of the average Florentine citizen. But Niccolò wasn't deceived by the lack of ostentation, for he had on several occasions witnessed firsthand (albeit discreetly concealed) as Cosimo wielded his indirect but very effective political influence. Hiding here was Niccolò's way of being close to that man and of sharing in the furtive, convoluted stratagems by which he exercised power.

Besides, crouching in the freezing, dusty niche playing games with an unsuspecting Cosimo enabled Niccolò to elude the old de' Medici's grandson, Lorenzo.

Niccolò wished that Lorenzo had inherited more of his grandfather's character. Lorenzo was older and larger than the slightly built Niccolò and dominated him mercilessly. Lately, Lorenzo had begun forcing Niccolò to call him *Il Magnifico* in the hope that this name for himself would catch on among the citizens of Florence. Apparently the ploy had worked, for earlier that day while crossing the Ponte Vecchio, Niccolò had overheard two men in conversation refer to ''Lorenzo the Magnificent.'' The men had been startled by Niccolò's sudden outburst of laughter. He only put up with Lorenzo's swaggering and bullying because the relationship gave him access to the de' Medici palace.

In the counting room, Cosimo snorted and shook his head, his finger jumping back to the top of the page to retrace its progress. Niccolò snickered into his hand, almost sneezing as he inhaled the brick dust that clung to his skin. He knew what baffled Cosimo, for Niccolò had been making subtle alterations in the ledger for weeks in an effort to attract the old man's attention. Tonight Cosimo had finally chosen the falsified ledger to review from among numerous account books kept by his clerics, and had discovered the baited figures Niccolò had left dangling for him. When he succeeded in piecing together the puzzle, he would find a series of errors (all seemingly entered in the hand of a mean-spirited cleric on Cosimo's staff) that made a small venture appear to be losing money instead of earning it.

Cosimo frowned at the ledger and cleared his throat again. The coarse sound belied the greatness of the man, Niccolò thought, as if any hawking commoner could rule the de' Medici merchant empire in his place. Idly, Cosimo picked up an onion from the side of his desk and hefted it a few times before biting into it, eating it raw like an apple. Niccolò, who had left the onion as a gift, smiled. He had taken to eating onions this way himself lately in an effort to be more like Cosimo.

As he munched the onion, the old man groaned and shifted in his seat. Numerous ills afflicted him this late in life, especially gout. Niccolò, watching from his hiding place, passed a hand lightly over the back of the tapestry hanging dark and obscure before him, longing instead to smooth away the lines of pain from the face of this unassuming patriarch of the city.

Suddenly, Cosimo grunted. His hand paused halfway to his mouth, then returned the onion to the desk. He leaned closer to squint at the ledger, turning it to better catch the candlelight. Niccolò watched eagerly as Cosimo studied the columns of figures. The old man picked up a quill, dabbed it in a pot of ink, and began making notations in the margin of the page.

It wouldn't be long before he discovered the surprise profit buried in those figures, Niccolò thought. Excitement rose in him.

The noise of a door opening startled Niccolò, and he bumped the tapestry. Instinctively, he reached both hands to quell the ripple that flowed across the surface of the cloth, fearful that the motion might betray his presence. Cosimo lifted his dark eyes from his work, but his attention was focused on the intruder approaching the desk. If Cosimo had noticed the faint rustle of the tapestry, he must have accepted it as the result of air currents swirling through the room.

Cosimo nodded tersely to the stranger, evidently having expected him. Yet Niccolò saw a look that went beyond mere recognition flicker across Cosimo's face. It was loathing, he thought, and something more. He struggled to identify what had been only a fleeting impression. But the look had vanished as quickly as it had appeared, and Cosimo's face resumed its accustomed stamp of calm self-possession.

The stranger bowed in front of Cosimo's desk and waited, his back to Niccolò. He was a well-proportioned man of medium height and with thick black hair. Snow glistened on his woolen cloak. He must have traveled through the mountains, riding straight to the de' Medici palace after the rigors of the road. Yet he was graceful, almost languid, as he brushed icy clumps from his fur collar and shook the snow off his red velvet cap. His movements barely jostled the heavy gold necklace that hung around his shoulders outside the cloak. To Niccolò, the cut of the man's clothes suggested that he was foreign, probably a person of importance. He must hold considerable rank to be granted an audience with Cosimo at this time of night. Even ambassadors and dignitaries waited for daylight.

Niccolò frowned at the stranger. He didn't care how important the man was, he resented this intrusion into what he considered his private time with Cosimo. Now the conclusion of their game would have to wait.

Cosimo ignored the man while he finished working a sum on an abacus and jotted the result in the ledger. But Niccolò wasn't fooled by Cosimo's air of indifference; his practiced eye noted the way Cosimo jabbed at the beads of the abacus and the way he crossed out the ledger entry twice before writing it to his satisfaction.

If the stranger was aware of the slight he endured at being forced to wait, his stance gave no indication of it. He stood casually, his manner polite though perhaps a trifle bored, giving the impression of a man who has looked at life and found it wanting.

Cosimo blotted the ink dry and pushed the ledger aside, then turned his attention to the stranger. "You're more morose than any man I've ever encountered, *signore*," he said as he studied the stranger. "One would think your wits were afflicted by risking so many ventures on the sea."

"Merchant ventures aren't what make me melancholy, *signore*," the stranger said, in a dialect Niccolò recognized as Venetian.

Cosimo's eyebrows rose. "No? I'd thought one such as you could scarcely blow on your broth to cool it without thinking of storms that might blow your ships to their graves." Cosimo's words were edged with a sarcasm Niccolò didn't understand. "Are you so successful a merchant that you can watch the sand falling in an hourglass without remembering sandy shoals that would clutch your vessels and hold them fast?" He chuckled without humor, startling Niccolò with this rare display of hostility. "Can you look upon the stone edifice of a church without seeing rocks to crush a ship's hull and spill your precious cargo on the waves?"

"Unlike my fellow countrymen, my tranquility isn't entrusted to ships' hulls or the vagaries of the sea," the stranger said. "As you well know, *signore*."

"Fellow countrymen, indeed!" Cosimo scoffed. "Even Cain and Judas were more likely to find men who would claim them as kin than you." He smirked. *"Bene.* If it's not business, then perhaps you're in love, and that's what makes you sad."

The stranger stared at Cosimo without answering.

"Quale? Not in love, either?" Cosimo feigned surprise. "Then whatever could it be that makes you thus?"

"In truth, you know why I'm so sad, and it wearies me," the stranger said.

Cosimo shifted, suddenly uncomfortable, though Niccolò thought it could have been from gout. "I'd do as well to try and make the devil laugh," the old man muttered. "Well, go ahead, then, persevere with your sad looks. If you were a man, as a man you are in show . . ."

"Come?" Suddenly the stranger's voice was taunting. "Don't you know me for a man—a gentleman—by these

fine Venetian garments I wear?'' He flung open his cloak, revealing a red velvet doublet and parti-colored tights.

"These days, two yards of red cloth are deemed sufficient to make a gentleman. You're counterfeit, a puppet.''

"A puppet? Ah, so that's the way it goes. *Sì, signore,* I'm a puppet for my master, as he is for you. But tell me then, who plays your strings?''

Niccolò, whose allegiance went automatically to Cosimo even though he didn't understand the tension between the two men, gasped at the magnitude of the stranger's offense. He resolved to slip from his hiding place if he could and avenge the old de' Medici by pissing in the stranger's saddlebags.

"You'd do well to speak with more respect for your master,'' Cosimo said. "To you, your master should be as a god, one that composed your features. *Sì,* and one to whom you're but a form in wax to be imprinted, within his power to leave as you are or disfigure.'' Cosimo stopped and cocked his head questioningly at the stranger. "Is something wrong with your face that causes you to wrinkle it so?''

The stranger sniffed the air. *"Mi scusi.* There's a smell of onions and garlic in here, and I have no stomach for them.''

"Are you implying that my exhalations are anything less than pleasant?'' Cosimo asked, his voice low.

"I'm saying only that the smell in this room hasn't come from me.''

Cosimo spread his hands, palms up, in an expansive gesture. "Then it might have come from anywhere in Florence, *signore,* and drifted here, for we hold the fragrance of onions and garlic to be but sweet odors breathing on the wind.'' He retrieved the onion from his desk and took a large bite, chewing with an open mouth.

Niccolò also opened his mouth and breathed out heavily several times, hoping to add to the stranger's discomfort with any traces of onion or garlic lingering on his own breath.

"Odious on the wind, these smells are, *veramente*," the stranger said, fanning the air, "and perhaps not breathed, but broken. Anyone breaking such an ill wind should be banished."

Niccolò's eyes grew wide as he listened to the man talk about breaking wind. Then his eyes narrowed. How dare this stranger speak to Cosimo so insultingly! Rather than pissing in the man's saddlebags, he decided to strew them with minced garlic and onions.

Cosimo glowered at the man. "You deliberately mistake my meaning in order to bait me."

"I seek only to show you I can give as good as I get," the stranger said, bowing again. He seated himself in the ornate chair across the desk from Cosimo, ignoring the older man's glare.

"Well have you proven it," Cosimo grumbled. "And so to the purpose of your journey. I want you on your way before you're recognized. Why have you come? What word do you bring from Venice?"

"My master runs short of money, and I have come for more."

There was a long silence as Niccolò and the stranger waited for Cosimo to respond. At last, the stranger asked, "Why do you just sit there, *signore*, without a word and your eyes closed?"

"I'm an old man," Cosimo replied. "Soon my eyes will be closed and I will remain still for all eternity. I practice now, that I might accustom myself to it."

There was another pause, then the stranger spoke again. "My master warned me that you would begrudge us what we need."

"Need?" Cosimo slammed his fists on the desk so vehemently that Niccolò jumped back from the tapestry, hitting his head against the wall of the niche. "I, begrudge you what you need? *Signore*, I think you forget yourself and to whom you speak."

"Well do I know to whom I speak," the stranger said. "Cosimo de' Medici, the man who would betray his city's ally and league himself with her greatest enemy."

Cosimo hushed the man anxiously, his eyes darting about the room. "Are you mad, *signore?* Think what you say," he demanded, and Niccolò, sensing Cosimo's fury at the charge, felt his own anger rise on Cosimo's behalf. Behind the tapestry, he clenched his fist and scowled at the stranger.

"If I'm mad," the stranger replied evenly, "wouldn't I be the least likely to recognize my state?" He waved a hand to dismiss the topic as if it were a trifling. "Besides, even were I mad, in your place I wouldn't be such a fool as to stand against my native city."

Cosimo stared hard at the man, furious, Niccolò thought, at his inability to curb the stranger's tongue. "I'd never stand against Florence."

"Ah? Then the council knows what you plan and approves of it?"

"The council does what I tell it to," Cosimo snapped.

"How convenient," the stranger said. "I was under the delusion that Florence was a republic. But I wonder— would the council approve of you entering into a secret agreement with Filippo Maria Visconti to destroy Venice?"

Niccolò was shocked by this outrage. Cosimo de' Medici conspire with the Duke of Milan, the most hated of all foreign sovereigns? Why, everyone in Florence feared Visconti's efforts to subdue Tuscany, and none more than the de' Medici. How could this man utter such lies? Besides, what reason could Cosimo possibly have for wanting to destroy Venice, the city that had allied itself with Florence against Milan? The man must be mad indeed to suggest such a thing. Cosimo should have him killed where he sat.

Cosimo clenched his big hands on the desk before him and swung his head ponderously from side to side, searching for a way to end the man's questioning or perhaps for a means of escape. "You go too far, *signore.*" Niccolò strained to hear, for Cosimo spoke the words very softly. "If I appear to be in league with Visconti, it's only to appease him for a time while I use his aid. What my fellow citizens fail to realize is that once Venice began her *terra ferma* policy of conquering neighboring states along the mainland to secure herself from land attack, she forever altered her destiny. *Terra ferma* will inevitably encroach upon Venetian thinking until her eyes are turned from the sea to gaze hungrily upon the whole of Italy, and Venice will become an even greater threat to Florence than Milan has ever posed. So I enlist the support of one devil to help cast out a greater one. Once we have disposed of Venice''—he spread his empty hands upon the air—''then I'll deal with Visconti. The pope and the King of Naples will be only too eager to come to our rescue and help rid Italy of a man so evil he would erase an entire city from the earth.''

''Thereby leaving everything from Liguria to the Veneto open to Florentine conquest,'' the stranger concluded.

Cosimo nodded. ''Eventually, all of Italy will be ruled by Florence, as well as the rich markets of the Levant. So you see, *signore*, I do this not to oppose my city, but to further her glory.''

Niccolò wiped his forehead with a trembling hand, surprised to find himself sweating despite the cold. Perhaps a fever was affecting his senses. Surely Cosimo couldn't have spoken the words Niccolò thought he had just heard the great man utter. He shivered harder.

The stranger's eyes wandered over the simple, understated elegance of the room. ''You frighten me, *signore*, for you display none of the extravagance expected from one in your position. Even your palace lacks the lavishness that adorns the least of Venice's structures. Could it be that you actually believe your own words?''

Cosimo frowned. ''What I believe is none of your concern. You have only to see that Venice is destroyed as planned.''

Niccolò's stomach churned at this admission of guilt. So the stranger's accusation was true! Cosimo must have reasons for acting as he did, the boy thought frantically, trying to convince himself. But what reason could justify such treachery?

"And so we return to the purpose of my visit," the stranger said, nodding to Cosimo as if conceding a point. "My master needs more money to proceed."

Cosimo rested his elbows on the desk. "You tell Hydro Phobius he'll not get another florin until the job is finished." The peculiarity of the name caught Niccolò's dazed attention. "This effort has already cost far more than we agreed," Cosimo went on, "and I'll not risk having my entire fortune go the way of Venice."

"Thus speaks the man who so loves the florin that he has it stamped with his own likeness," the stranger said. "Then how are we to continue? We need more equipment if everything is to be ready on time."

"Don't try to threaten me with talk of missing the deadline," Cosimo said coldly. "Venice must be destroyed by Ascension Day if the mercenaries I've hired are to finish a war against Milan before the summer's out. And I'll not pay their wages to keep them in my service a second year."

"We can do it by Easter," the stranger said evenly, "if we get the equipment we need."

Cosimo grunted. "I sometimes think your master is trying to sink Venice through sheer weight alone, so many of his infernal machines does he import."

The stranger shrugged. *"Tuttavia, signore,* the cost of this masquerade is high. There are accounts coming due, leases to be paid. Influential men must be encouraged to look the other way."

"Use your wits," Cosimo said. "That is, if you were given any when you were made. Doesn't Venice, the richest city in the world, have enough ducats of its own to provide you with what you need?" He waved off the stranger's protest before the words could leave his mouth. "Borrow the money or steal it. Accept it as gifts from wealthy mistresses if you must. These men whose influence must be purchased surely have wives and daughters hungry for affection; let them reward you for curing them of neglect.''

"Would you have us become gigolos?" The stranger sounded taken aback.

It was Cosimo's turn to shrug. "Love, like war, has no law but its own. Your master knows the truth of this. Indeed, as he practices them, love and war are the same." He leaned across the desk to jab a blunt finger in the air. "You can even go into legitimate business if you will and learn what it really means to wait anxiously for the return of a merchant ship. I don't care how you and your master do it, *signore,* so long as the job gets done and at no more expense to me. Ascension Day—no later! Then your master will get paid for his portion of the work." He sat back abruptly in his chair and drew the ledger to him again, signaling an end to the audience.

For a moment, the stranger didn't move. "Sickness is catching," he said at last bitterly. "Would that wealth were so as well—yours would I catch. Teach me how you multiply gold and with what art you attract the coins from your neighbor's purse."

Suddenly the stranger stood, swirling his cloak around him. The drama of the effect was marred, however, when his arm collided with the heavily carved chair in which he'd sat, toppling it to the floor. The stranger cried out and grabbed his arm, revealing a gash that rent his sleeve from elbow to wrist and cut deeply into his flesh. Niccolò's heart tightened in anticipation of the blood that would spill from the wound. But as he watched, no blood flowed, and Cosimo's face again twisted with the expression Niccolò had observed when the stranger first entered the room. It was terror that he had seen, Niccolò realized now, and this time it writhed across Cosimo's features unchecked. As Niccolò looked again at the wound, he understood the old de' Medici's feelings, for horror gripped his own belly with a chill as cold as wind blowing down from the frozen peaks of the Apennines.

Where the stranger had been cut, no blood welled forth, no flesh or bone lay exposed to view—only the grey, formless clay from which his arm was molded. The stranger wasn't a man at all, Niccolò realized as he clamped a hand over his mouth to stifle his moan of terror, but a simulacrum, a creature who possessed the semblance of life through the dark workings of magic.

In order to carry out his diabolical scheme, Cosimo de' Medici had apparently leagued himself with a far worse foe than Filippo Maria Visconti, for the creature before him now could be none other than one of the very fiends of hell.

ACT 2:

Much Adieu About Nothing

SEBASTIAN SQUINTED UP AT THE SAW-TOOTHED, SNOWY peaks of the French Pyrenees that towered over the southern outskirts of Pomme de Terre, gleaming impossibly white in the sun. The sharp crack of shifting snow and ice heralded an early thaw, and muted thunder rolled out of the mountains in the wake of an occasional avalanche.

With this promise of spring penetrating even the gloom of Lent, Sebastian strode eagerly toward the marketplace in the center of town.

Gwen, the tavern keeper's daughter to whom he was betrothed, kept pace at his elbow. Lately she'd been hovering closer than usual whenever they left the tavern, where Sebastian rented a room. He was beginning to suspect that she was trying to steer him clear of mishap.

As if he couldn't steer himself.

The shock of something cold engulfing one foot stopped him. He looked down to find himself standing in an ice-rimmed puddle, dirty water filling his shoe.

Gwen grimaced, then returned to an earlier conversation. "I'm sorry about the fuss Mama made over the goose grease this morning."

Sebastian gave a rueful smile and shook his leg free.

Neither a wet foot nor goose grease would spoil his mood today. He resumed walking, his shoe squishing at every step and leaving damp prints along the cobblestones like the trail of a one-legged man out for a stroll.

A warm breeze whispered against his skin, sharing lusty secrets. He drank in the raw, earthy smell of plowed fields beyond the walls of Pomme de Terre, an odor redolent of new beginnings. That's what he and Gwen needed, Sebastian thought—a new beginning, free from the annoyances of the winter past.

"You know my parents can't afford such luxuries," Gwen went on, still dragging the goose grease incident after him. She spoke as if correcting a stubborn child. "They have to save the best of everything for any nobles or rich merchants who come to the tavern."

Sebastian walked faster, the alternating *tap-splat, tap-splat* rhythm of his footsteps sounding loud in the narrow street. Gwen continued to lecture despite the pace. "And when Mama saw you using the grease on your bread and eating it yourself . . ."

The subject might have burdened her, but it didn't slow her down.

Some of the brightness had gone out of the air, like haze obscuring the sun. Sebastian glanced up at the sky, then remembered to keep his eyes on the street. Perhaps the change in light was merely caused by the way the street had wound deeper between the buildings, their drab upper stories leaning heavily into one another above the cobblestones like tired old men bowed down by the centuries.

"I can't help it," Sebastian said, infected by weariness. "Sometimes I forget how commoners are supposed to behave. At least this time I didn't eat your mother's wheat bread. I'm so tired of black rye and barley loaves I could choke."

When Gwen's mother had discovered him that morning in her kitchen with goose grease smeared over a chunk of coarse, dark peasant bread, she had taken it like a mortal injury. At first Sebastian had assumed she was upset with him for eating fowl during Lent. But his apologies had only angered her more until he finally realized her concern was that he would consume such a delicacy himself in any case.

Since arriving in Pomme de Terre the year before to become the alchemist's apprentice, Sebastian's life had been fraught with petty mistakes. But it was more than this that separated him from his fellow citizens, Sebastian told himself. It was also their unyielding provincialism, always holding themselves aloof from anyone whose origins stemmed from outside this narrow mountain valley. It didn't matter that when Sebastian's grandfather came to Gardenia under Edward the Black Prince toward the end of the fourteenth century, the duchy, like much of southern France, was an English fief. Nor did it matter that Sebastian's father later switched allegiance so his family could stay in Gardenia when the duchy fell to France during the decades of war between the two countries. And now that Gardenia, along with several neighboring fiefs, had declared independence from both England and France, Sebastian was regarded with hostility and suspicion still, for he remained the grandson of a foreigner, and therefore a harbinger of change. People in the duchy distrusted change even as they longed to participate in the new order that was rumored to be sweeping through Europe from Italy.

Besides, Sebastian's father and grandfather had maintained Anglo-Saxon traditions within the family, leaving Sebastian poorly versed in the French language and customs.

He hunched his shoulders against a sudden chill and threaded a path between half-thawed piles of winter garbage. "Alas, poor fowl," he murmured, unsure whether he meant the goose that had provided the grease for his bread or himself.

Ahead, an old man with a dirty beard and matted hair felt his way around the corner of a building. His woolen smock was ragged and filthy, the coarse *tibialis* wrapping his legs more rents and holes than cloth. He cocked his head at their approach, staring with sightless eyes.

Sebastian grimaced. One good thump on the man's clothes would send fleas and vermin jumping. Instead of skirting him, however, Sebastian pressed a coin in the beggar's hand, thinking a kind act might erase the annoyance he had sensed from Gwen all morning.

"Ah, *le damoiseau anglais*," the beggar said, curling his fingers around the coin. "Walked into a puddle, have you?"

Sebastian's eyes widened. "How'd you know I stepped in a puddle? And how'd you know it was me?"

The man cackled. *"Tiens, monsieur!* Only a nobleman—or a former one—walks with so arrogant a stride. And who but you would do so with one shoe sopping wet? I heard it slosh. So either you stepped in a puddle or you allowed a dog to cock its leg on your foot. Either way, you had to be the lordling, *Monsieur Anglais.*"

"I am not a lordling."

"You are the son of a lord."

"A former lord," Sebastian snapped, feeling the shame of his family's disgrace.

The man shrugged. "Whatever. And now you are apprenticed to the alchemist, the one the bishop calls the king of fools." He made a sign to ward off evil. "That makes you *un damoiseau*—a lordling, *Monsieur Anglais.* A prince of fools." The beggar laughed, his mouth gaping to reveal blackened and missing teeth.

Sebastian started to retort, then leaned forward to hear what the blind man was mumbling. "What did you say?"

Something cold and wet hit Sebastian in the back of the neck. He jerked upright with a gasp. Clumps of slush spilled through the collarless opening of his tunic-like gonel and down his back. *"Bon dieu!"* he cried, pulling at the garment where it bloused over his belt in back.

"As I was saying, only a fool stands under snowy

eaves on a sunny day.'' The beggar laughed. ''But I guess you know that now, eh, *Monsieur Anglais?*''

Sebastian lifted his head haughtily, then realized the gesture was lost on the blind man. ''Don't call me that. It's not my name.''

''It is if you answer to it,'' the man replied, chortling so hard he almost lost his grip on the building which held him erect.

Sebastian stomped away, too furious to think of a response. But as he approached the corner of another building, he thought of the beggar's comment about his walk and shifted abruptly to what he hoped was a less arrogant stride. He had to learn to act like a commoner, he reminded himself. At least he could begin to do that now, having finally laid his father's ghost to rest, with its relentless criticism of him whenever he had failed to act like a proper nobleman's son.

Gwen, hurrying to catch up with him, stepped on Sebastian's heel and made him stumble. He started to grumble at her over his shoulder when something rounded the corner, knocking him aside. Sebastian lurched into one of the piles of refuse lining the street and struggled to remain upright amid the treacherous footing. A huge sow, one of innumerable pigs allowed to scavenge in the streets, lumbered away toward a nearby alley.

Sebastian gave the retreating beast a savage bow. ''May we meet again after Lent, madam pig,'' he yelled, drawing his short sword. ''Preferably at dinner where I can attend you with platter and knife.''

He thought he heard Gwen chuckle, but she was only clucking her tongue as she stared at his feet. Sebastian looked down to discover his dry foot ankle deep in filth.

''*J'ai marché dans de la mer,*'' he cried in disbelief.

Gwen looked up at him and pursed her lips. ''You've stepped in the sea?'' She shook her head, her nose wrinkled. ''That's not what you stepped in. You mean *merde*, not *mer*. You didn't say it right.''

He eased himself from the refuse and started toward the marketplace again, his left foot slippery on the cobblestones, his right still oozing water at every step. He shivered and drew his gonel tighter around him, the back of the chemise underneath clinging cold and wet from the slush.

"*Alors!* At least you knew what I meant," he growled.

"I usually do. It's just that nobody else understands."

"And as for the goose grease," he went on, "I promised your mother I'd never use it again."

"I know. But, Sebastian, last week it was white bread, this week goose grease. What next? You don't make the same mistakes twice—you come up with new ones."

"I can't change overnight."

"But it's been almost ten months since you left the abbey and came to Pomme de Terre."

He winced at the mention of the abbey, where he had tried unsuccessfully to make a life for himself as a cleric. "*Sacré coeur!* Are you keeping score of my faults?"

"I'm only trying to help."

"I'm not a child, Gwen, stumbling at every step."

She avoided looking at his shoes, with their *squish-splat, squish-splat*.

A pair of urchins burst into the street ahead and stopped, elbowing each other and snickering as they pointed at Sebastian's feet. "*Alors!* It's the alchemist's apprentice, *le damoiseau anglais*," one boy whispered to the other.

The second boy eyed Sebastian suspiciously. "I don't believe he was really a nobleman, any more than I believe in the changes everyone talks about from Italy. It's all a fake, invented by his master."

Both boys crossed themselves at the mention of the alchemist.

"*Je les émeraudes*," Sebastian swore, taking a step toward them. The urchins laughed and ran away. Sebastian lifted his chin. Damn Corwyn anyway. Why couldn't he be like other alchemists, seeking to turn lead and mercury into silver and gold? That would at least be socially acceptable. Instead, Corwyn sought to purify the elements of the environment, concentrating on restoring them to their pristine, natural state whenever they became polluted or corrupt. And as if that wasn't enough, he had to specialize in a single element: water. No wonder the people of Pomme de Terre distrusted him!

In the weeks since the bishop had accused Corwyn of being in league with fiends, the old alchemist had disappeared frequently into the mountains with his lifelong assistant, leaving Sebastian to care for the shop. The people of Pomme de Terre, meanwhile, had grudgingly entered Lent, sullen over the restrictions of the season. That Lent fell so late this year only intensified their loss, for an early spring made abstinence all the harder to bear. Corwyn provided an easy focus for their resentment.

But today was a beautiful spring morning, Sebastian reminded himself firmly, and he would let nothing erode his spirits. After a while, he smiled. The encounters of the morning *had* been rather funny—in a peculiar, peasantlike way.

Gwen tugged on his arm. "The word is *emmerde*, not *émeraudes*," she said.

"What?"

"*Emmerde*. That's what you meant to say when you cursed those boys. It has to do with what the pig made you step in." She glanced at his foot, then looked quickly away. "You said something about emeralds instead. I thought you should know. Also, it wasn't a nice thing to say."

"*Sang dieu!* There you go again, pointing out my flaws."

"I'm just trying to—"

"I know, you're only trying to help."

The martyred look on Gwen's face made Sebastian feel as low as the *merde* on his shoe. She really did mean well, he reminded himself. He slouched along, his shoes splatting and slipping underfoot.

Abruptly, the street opened onto the marketplace. Three sides of the square were bordered by buildings, including the church which rose above the rest of the town. The fourth side of the square, opposite Gwen and Sebastian, was bounded by the River Ale. Further upriver stood the duke's castle, just visible beyond the buildings of Pomme de Terre, its grey menace dwarfed by the Pyrenees. The sight of the castle brought a pang of loss to Sebastian. Like *le Château d'Oignon*, the manor that had once belonged to his family, the duke's castle was a reminder of the birthright he now would never inherit.

Ignoring the averted glances of people who recognized him as the alchemist's apprentice, and the occasional snickers when some of them noted the condition of his shoes, Sebastian led Gwen past stalls selling goods ranging from ropes and fleeces to baskets and pottery. In one cluster of stalls, piglets squealed as they were thrust by their ears and tails into wooden pokes. Nearby, horses, mules, and sheep snorted and stamped and bleated with impatience. Through it all milled the people of Pomme de Terre, their expressions sullen, dressed in drab, homespun woolens. Few among them could afford imported linen or cotton garments or the even more costly silks.

Many stalls remained empty, particularly the butchers', for meat couldn't be sold again until after Lent. Fresh produce was also lacking. The liturgical calendar and the timing of the seasons had conspired so that only the solemn, the sober, and the sanctified could be purchased in Christendom today. Sebastian nodded to a pair of fur-clad noble matrons who were perusing hair shirts, flails, and bone relics at one of the stalls. Even nobles were reduced to seeking solace in the remains of dead saints.

The women lifted their wimpled heads in disdain. "The alchemist's apprentice," one whispered to the other. "They say his master is behind the peasants' demands to adopt the new ways from Italy." She crossed herself and nodded at Gwen. "Poor girl's family must be desperate to allow their marriage."

The second woman smiled condescendingly. "God be with you, child," she said to Gwen.

Sebastian scowled and hoped that, come summer, the two matrons would swelter in the furs they would wear even then to mark their noble status.

He and Gwen went directly to the fishmonger's stall so Gwen could shop for the tavern. The stall was filled with tubs of dried and salted fish—sardines and tunny from the Mediterranean, herring from the Baltic and North seas, and cod from the Atlantic coast—all poorly preserved and turning foul this long after the fall fishing season. Yet the fishmonger did a brisk business despite his decaying goods. During the forty days of Lent, fish was a necessity regardless how bad it became, and people flocked to the stall in hopes of getting the less rotten portions before their neighbors. Near the stall, customers held their noses against the stench. Indeed, the laws of Pomme de Terre, like those of other towns, required that the water in which the fish were soaked prior to cooking be thrown into the gutters only at night due to its smell.

Gwen surveyed the stall with dismay. "It's enough to make a good Christian despise Lent." She crossed herself hastily and approached the tubs.

Sebastian hung back. As an alchemist's apprentice, he was used to inhaling offensive fumes, but that seemed no reason to get too near the spoiling fish. Instead, he watched a peddlar, a latecomer to the market, unpack the deep baskets that hung from either side of his donkey. From the man's costume and the bright sash at his waist instead of the customary bit of rope, Sebastian judged him to be a Catalan from the eastern end of the Pyrenees. More interesting than the man's clothes, however, were the brightly colored caps he was stacking on a crude shelf across the front of an empty stall.

Intrigued, Sebastian edged through the throng for a closer look at the peddlar's silk, velvet, and satin wares.

They were unusually shaped—some tall and grand, others wide and floppy—and many sported bits of ribbon or soft strips of painted leather or feathers plucked from exotic birds. Sebastian sucked in his breath at the sight. Hesitantly, he reached for a peacock-blue velvet cap with dark blue leather trim.

Another hand grabbed the cap first. Sebastian turned to see the mayor's son, Pepin de Chien, a thick-bodied youth with a mind to match. Pepin made much of his father's position by wearing a nobleman's fur trim and, equally daring, hose with red stripes crisscrossing the gray woolen material. Sebastian rolled his eyes with disdain. Pepin was the only person in town who did more damage to the French tongue than Sebastian, but because of his father, Pepin was allowed to murder his own language with impunity.

Pepin rolled the cap between grubby fingers, then dropped it back onto the shelf. "Now here is a thing that discerns me nearly," he said, flicking the cap with a finger. He turned to one of his lackeys, the son of a councilman. "It is an effusive deed, don't you think, Ver, and a front to the church to sell anything so colorful during Lent."

Ver nodded. *"Oui*, Pepin, very offens—uh, effusive."

Sebastian gritted his teeth, finding Pepin's speech more "effusive" than the peddlar's deed.

The peddlar inspected the cap for smudges. "I planned to bring them for carnival, but was detained by a storm."

"Oh, a sad tale, *monsieur*." Pepin grinned. "But I think perhaps my father, the mayor, would want the city guards to comprehend you as an auspicious person."

"Comprehend, *monsieur?*" The peddler looked confused. "I'm afraid I don't comprehend. They are only caps."

"Oh, *oui, certainement*," Pepin agreed. "Only caps. But what kind of caps? my father would ask. And I, a doubtful son, would have to tell him." He poked at a stack, toppling it.

The peddlar scurried to retrieve his wares from the ground, accompanied by laughter from the crowd that was gathering. When he stood up again, his face was red. "I assure you, these caps are made in the best Italian fashion."

The laughter stopped. Sebastian held his breath.

"You mean these styles are from Italy?" Pepin growled.

The peddlar nodded vigorously. "The finest Italian merchants and noblemen are wearing just such caps as these."

Gwen edged in beside Sebastian, the crowd parting to let her pass with her basket of fish. "What's going on?" she whispered. Sebastian shook his head, his attention on the peddlar and Pepin.

"Tiens!" Pepin scoffed. "So much for the fabled new order from Italy. We finally free ourselves from the old duke and can precipitate in the changes we've heard about, and this is what we get—caps!"

Angry murmurs sounded from the throng. "Throw the peddlar in the stocks," Ver shouted. The cry was quickly taken up, and the crowd surged forward.

Pepin de Chien raised his hands. "Wait! That alchemist's behind this. Probably beleaguered himself to this peddlar, hoping to profit from our ignorance. I say a public lashing and time in the stocks would serve him right, as well."

"Alors! He's a sorcerer," someone cried. "The bishop said so himself."

"Come on," Gwen hissed. "We've got to warn Corwyn."

Sebastian's frustration suddenly became too much. He picked up the blue cap that had caught his eye. "How much?"

The peddlar had been cowering, eyes wide, but his demeanor changed abruptly. "For you, *monsieur*, only three crowns."

Sebastian hesitated. Even under the threat of the stocks, the wily old peddlar was exacting a high price.

"What are you trying to be, *damoiseau?*" Pepin demanded. "An Italian fop?" He took a few mincing steps, prompting more laughter.

Sebastian's anger decided him. He opened his purse and counted out carefully hoarded coins.

"*Alors!* You already had presentiments to nobility," Pepin said. "Tell us, *anglais*, is this what you wore on your father's manor? No wonder he died in disgrace."

Fury blinded Sebastian. His hand dropped to his sword. Before he could draw it, however, Gwen dragged him from the stall. Sebastian snatched up the cap and allowed himself to be pulled away. Voices grumbled on every side.

Pepin followed them. "*Non,* don't lay your hand on your sword," he called out. "Do you think you're still a nobleman to be wearing a nobleman's blade? That's not really a sword, *anglais*. It's only an overgrown dagger."

Pepin swaggered to show his lack of fear, but Sebastian saw his eyes shift uneasily.

"*Allons!* Sebastian, let's go back to the tavern," Gwen whispered as they reached the edge of the crowd. She glanced at the cap in his hand. "And get rid of that thing before it causes any more trouble."

Instead, he placed the cap on his head, tipping it forward rakishly while staring at Pepin. "If you have enough wit to keep yourself warm, let it show the difference between you and a horse," he said, "for in truth, it's all the wealth you have."

"And what wealth do you have, apprentice, that extinguishes you from an ass?"

"'Extinguishes,' Pepin? You can't even speak your own language." Steel sang as Sebastian drew the sword from its scabbard. "What I have is the blade you disparage—my father's sword." He grinned. "Let's see if it can extinguish such an ass as you, for by this sword, Pepin, I declare you a fool."

"Don't swear by it or you'll eat it," Pepin warned, backing up.

"I will swear by it that you're a fool, and I'll make him eat it that says you're not."

"Damn you to everlasting redemption!" Pepin's eyes darted to either side. "I'll have you opinioned for that. When my father's been reformed of this—"

Gwen's shriek cut him off. Sebastian spun and saw Ver and two other youths sneaking between the stalls toward his back. Then Pepin slammed into him, hurling him into the fishmonger's stall. Old, dry wood splintered as Sebastian fell through the structure. Tubs of foul water tumbled after him, drenching him and sending dead fish skittering over the cobblestones. People covered their mouths and noses and scurried away from the stench.

Sebastian gagged and tried to stand, but his feet slipped in a mass of fish, spilling him back onto the ground. Rough laughter filled the market, with Pepin's the loudest. The fishmonger roared in fury. Through a blur of brine, Sebastian saw Gwen attack Pepin with the fish she had purchased, beating him about the head and shoulders with a side of cod.

Suddenly, a scream rose above the noise. *"Bon dieu!* The river—it's turning colors. The alchemist has bewitched the water!"

Oh, Corwyn, Sebastian thought as he struggled to keep from retching, what have you done? He stood, wavering slightly.

At the bank of the river, onlookers moaned and wailed and fell to their knees. Gwen dropped the cod she had used as a weapon, allowing Pepin to escape, and started toward the river with the rest of the crowd. Sebastian caught her by the arm. She turned, confusion written on her face. "Sebastian, what's happening?" Then the stench hit her and she twisted away. "Oh," she said, one hand covering her nose and mouth, "you smell awful."

Sebastian shrugged, trying to pass it off. *"Allons!* We've got to warn Corwyn."

"That's what I said, but you didn't listen."

"That was before he started fooling with the river." Sebastian indicated the bank where people from the market were joining the hysteria.

"Sebastian, you don't think he's really enchanted the water, do you?"

"Not enchanted it, not if I know Corwyn. There's sure to be some rational, logical explanation. But if the townspeople catch him, he won't have a chance to explain."

Sebastian retrieved his sword and saw the blue cap lying unscathed nearby. He eyed his hand, slippery with salt and slime, then looked to Gwen for help. She grimaced as she picked up the cap, handling it as if it were to blame for what had happened.

Sebastian started toward the street away from the market, but Gwen hurried around him to lead the way. *"Pardon,"* she called over her shoulder, "but I've got to be upwind."

Frowning, Sebastian followed.

They had gone almost as far as the tavern when they met two individuals hurrying in the opposite direction. Corwyn, a short, heavyset man with a white beard and the black robe and conical hat of an alchemist, led the way, looking worried. Behind him came the skinny figure of Oliver, his assistant, picking his way delicately between the puddles and piles of rubbish, his features hidden by the oversized monk's robe and cowl draped over him.

"Sebastian," the alchemist cried, "what happened? You look a fright." Without waiting for a reply, he turned to Gwen. "What a pretty cap. Very becoming on you, *ma chère,* I'm sure." Suddenly his face contorted and he staggered back. "What's that smell?"

"I had words with someone," Sebastian mumbled. "And the cap is mine."

Corwyn studied the cap at a safe distance from Sebastian, lifting his eyebrows. "Yours, eh?" He shook his head. "What kind of trouble have you gotten into this time? It smells like you accused the fishmonger of cheating Gwen." He waved off Sebastian's spluttered protests. "Never mind. It's just as well you're back. I had a little accident upriver, and you know how touchy people can be over the slightest things."

"That's what we came to warn you about," Sebastian said testily. "What did you do to the river? The townspeople are outraged."

"*Oui*," Gwen added. "The bishop already had people believing you're the devil's twin. Now they think you've bewitched the water."

"Bewitched!" Corwyn glanced from Gwen to Sebastian. "It was just a harmless little mistake. A multicolored one, I must admit—quite stunning, actually. But perfectly rational. Don't people know I work with natural phenomena that have nothing to do with magic?" He paused to look at his diminutive companion, who was stirring a puddle with a stick. "Oliver, adjust your robe. Your tufts are showing."

Oliver straightened the garment over his spindly form, briefly revealing the straw base of a broom where legs would have been on a human.

"Master, you were on every tongue this morning even before you terrified everyone by playing games with the river," Sebastian said. "And none of what was being said about you was good."

"I wasn't playing games," Corwyn snapped, his thick eyebrows drawing together.

"Nevertheless, Corwyn, at the moment you lack support among either the townspeople or the nobles," Gwen said, taking the alchemist's arm. "You've been associated with the changes from Italy, which have everyone unhappy."

"What? Nonsense! I'm an alchemist. I don't have anything to do with the Renaissance."

"The Renaissance!" Gwen snorted. "Corwyn, those who look forward to it blame you because it hasn't arrived, and those who want the duchy to remain unchanged hold you responsible for anything new that occurs. Either way, people are upset with you and Sebastian.''

''*Oui,* and I haven't done anything,'' Sebastian muttered.

Corwyn glowered at him, then turned back to Gwen. ''What do you suggest, *ma chère?*''

''You and Sebastian should go someplace safe for a while. Maybe the monastery of St. Mathurin. Just until Pomme de Terre settles down again.'' She frowned. ''Although the way things are going, that may not be until after Lent.''

''But why should I abandon my research just because people mistakenly connect me with the Renaissance? It doesn't have anything to do with alchemy. In fact, the whole thing is vastly overrated; I only give it a hundred years—two hundred at most.'' Corwyn paused. ''Though people do seem to set great store by it.'' He shook his head, obviously puzzled by the unaccountability of taste.

''The people of Pomme de Terre are expecting some kind of alchemical transmutation from us,'' Sebastian grumbled. ''They think we can change conditions in the duchy overnight.''

Corwyn stared at him with a stunned expression. ''What did you say?''

''I just meant that's how other people see it,'' Sebastian said, uncomfortable with the intensity of Corwyn's gaze. ''I didn't mean anything by it personally.''

Corwyn fanned the air with his hands. ''No, no, you said people expect an alchemical transmutation.'' He frowned and worried his mustache. ''But if the Renaissance actually *is* a kind of transmutation, what philosopher's stone makes it happen?''

''Huh?'' Sebastian looked at Gwen and saw his perplexity mirrored in her face.

''Gwen, *ma chère,* perhaps you're right,'' Corwyn went on. ''Except that if things here are as bad as you say, you'd better come with us. People will link you with me through Sebastian." He slapped his hands together as if something had been decided and started back up the street the way he'd come. "Well, come along, you two. Don't dawdle."

"So we're going to the monastery of St. Mathurin after all?" Sebastian hurried after his master, then glared at Gwen as she pushed past to get upwind again.

"St. Mathurin?" Corwyn glanced over his shoulder. "Heavens, no! We're going to Italy."

"What?" "Italy!" Gwen and Sebastian responded at once.

Corwyn waved them to silence. *"Tiens!* It's obvious," he said, and Sebastian groaned. The old alchemist's loftiest flights of fancy began with that phrase. "The people of Gardenia haven't any idea what the Renaissance is about. The old duke kept the duchy ignorant of anything other than medieval feudalism. Now it's up to us to dispel that ignorance with the light of a newer, better way."

"But Corwyn, what about your research?" Sebastian objected. "And why us? Why not someone closer to the duchess? Or better yet, someone from the merchant guilds that were so eager to bring this change to Gardenia in the first place?"

"Research!" Corwyn scoffed. "What more important research could there be than this, as you yourself so aptly pointed out only minutes ago?"

Sebastian hesitated, trying to recall exactly what he'd said. Somehow, he didn't think he had suggested this. Then Corwyn stopped in front of the Reluctant Virgin, the tavern owned by Gwen's parents, and Sebastian remembered how enthusiastic he had been when he'd started from here earlier. He shivered in the thin sunlight, the breeze bringing a chill to his brine-soaked clothes.

"Non, like it or not," Corwyn went on, "we won't have any peace until this Renaissance matter is settled and the duchy of Gardenia is securely launched into

the coming age. We might as well take advantage of the situation. You said it yourself, the Renaissance is just another alchemical transmutation. We're the obvious choice to discover how to bring about the duchy's own renaissance. We'll be heroes, well rewarded for our effort. Besides, it's been a hard winter and all three of us''—he stopped to frown at the broom, Oliver, who was catching drips from the icicles on the tavern's eaves—''all four of us, that is, could use a holiday.''

A holiday, Sebastian thought. That's what he'd hoped to find in the marketplace less than an hour before—a brief holiday.

''I suppose you're right,'' Gwen said, her mouth pursed in doubt. ''How soon do we leave?''

''Oh, we have plenty of time,'' Corwyn said as he opened the tavern door. ''At least enough for you to bid your parents good-bye, I think.'' He glanced back toward the marketplace. ''If you make it quick.''

ACT 3:

Love's Labors Lent

AFTER HASTILY DEPARTING FROM POMME DE TERRE, THE four companions trudged along narrow, stony lanes lined with hawthorn hedgerows, their path a long arc down from the valleys of the Pyrenees, then east toward the Mediterranean.

Near sunset on the second day, Gwen straggled to the top of a small hill after Corwyn and Sebastian, gaping as Carcassonne rose to meet her from the other side. Four dozen round and square towers punctuated the double curtain of its crenelated walls. Steep, blue slate roofs capped most of the towers, and the waning light tinted the grey stone walls yellow and pink. Carcassonne looked too insubstantial to be real, a fairy city spun of clouds and dreams.

Gwen didn't trust the illusion any more than she did the reality; whatever its appearance, Carcassonne was a fortress built to intimidate vanquished Languedoc.

Corwyn and Sebastian were searching for Oliver, who had run on ahead and now was nowhere to be seen. Too exhausted to help, Gwen looked across the rich, burgeoning landscape stretching away on every side and felt again the dizzying openness that had terrified her since they'd left the Pyrenees. To the south, the distant moun-

tains marched across the land in an unbroken chain, beck-
oning her. She longed for Pomme de Terre, wanting to
drop to the ground and dig her fingers into the dirt like
roots to anchor her for fear of flying off the naked face
of the earth.

"Ah, there you are, Oliver," Corwyn crowed, breaking into Gwen's thoughts. "Come here."

The broom skulked over to Corwyn from behind a
walnut tree, its brushy base parting into two tufts like
stubby legs that rustled when it walked. On each side
hung a branchlike arm, one of which dragged the monk's
habit in the dirt. The stick that formed the broom's head
and trunk tipped forward, directing its attention to its
feet rather than to the alchemist.

"Look at me," Corwyn said.

The broom straightened slowly.

"Don't you know how dangerous it is for you to be
seen?"

The broom hesitated before bobbing its wooden handle
up and down.

"Then put your robe back on and don't take it off
again."

Oliver nodded again and thrust both arms into the
garment, becoming entangled in his eagerness.

Corwyn sighed. *"Allons!* Let me help." He extricated
his assistant from the robe and began dressing him correctly.

When Oliver once more looked like a small, emaciated
monk with oversized clothes, they resumed their trek,
anxious to reach Carcassonne before nightfall.

Here in the warmer lowlands, the air hung heavy with
the smells of spring, from fragrant reseda, roses, and
honeysuckle, to rank manure fertilizing the fields. Occasionally, a lingering smell of spoiled fish from Sebastian intruded on the air, but that odor had been
considerably reduced at a hot mineral spring the first
evening.

Gwen glanced at Sebastian. Tall and angular with a
northerner's ruddy complexion and straight, blond hair,

he made her feel lacking in comeliness by comparison.
If only he'd get rid of that ridiculous cap, rising like a
blue cloth muffin on his head, he'd be quite handsome
again now that he was clean.

She sighed, wanting to stop at a lichen-covered cross
that stood beside the road. It would be one among dozens
of shrines and sacred sites at which she had prayed along
the way, seeking help with regard to Sebastian and this
journey. Sebastian's inability to fit into her life in Pomme
de Terre dismayed her almost as much as did the prospects of traveling to Italy. So far, however, her pleas
had gone unanswered.

"Once we reach Italy, we'll start at Genoa and work
our way down to Florence, Rome, and Naples, then up
the Adriatic coast to Venice," Corwyn said suddenly,
overriding the rhythmic voice of a cuckoo from a nearby
thicket. "Venice will be the culmination of our journey."

"Why?" Gwen asked. "What's so important about
Venice?"

"What's so important about Venice?" Corwyn repeated, lifting his bushy eyebrows in disbelief. "Dear
child, it's the Pearl of the Adriatic, the penultimate Renaissance city." He flung his arms wide. "Ah, fair Venice, I speak of thee as the traveler does: *Venetia, Venetia,
chi non te vede, non te pretia.*"

"What does that mean?" Gwen whispered to Sebastian.

"I don't know," he answered, leaning close to her.
"He's only partial to Venice because it's built on water."

"Not so," Corwyn countered. "It's built on a hundred
or more separate islands, not on the water itself. However, its proximity to water does lend it a special significance to me, regardless of its current worldly
importance. But tell me, Sebastian, can't you translate
what I said from your knowledge of Latin?"

Sebastian blushed. "I don't know much Latin."

"How can that be?" Corwyn said. "Weren't you required to speak it at the Abbaye de Sainte-Tomate?"

"*Oui,*" Sebastian mumbled. "That, or remain silent.

As a result, I didn't say much while I was there. It was one of the problems I had with monastic life.''

"Ah.''

"*Tiens!* Master, you know I'm not good at languages.''

"I suppose that means Italian won't come easily, either.'' Corwyn sighed. "I had hoped you'd be better at it than you are at French.''

Sebastian's color deepened.

"Corwyn, what did it mean, what you said about Venice?'' Gwen asked, turning the conversation from Sebastian's faults.

"Oh, it was archaic Italian for 'Venice, Venice, he who has not seen thee cannot value thee,' a sentiment with which I heartily agree.'' He was silent a moment, then added, "Well, we shall all need instruction in Italian before we get there, but at the moment that problem is secondary.''

"To what?'' Sebastian asked.

"Money. We left Pomme de Terre in such a hurry, we didn't bring any. Lack of funds will become a problem long before speaking Italian will.''

Oliver cocked his stick head at this, pausing for a moment before going back to chasing butterflies.

The four companions emerged from a stand of sycamores onto the road from Toulouse and made their way with other travelers into the lesser walled town of Ville Basse across the river from Carcassonne. Corwyn led them over the bridge which spanned the Aude to the fortress on the opposite side, then up a steep, cobbled street to Carcassonne's main western gate. As they climbed, the stronghold loomed ever larger around them. No longer ethereal, it blotted out the night sky with a dark, ominous presence. They mounted a short stairway, and Corwyn ushered them into the first of what was actually a series of small, guarded portals leading through the twin walls and into the city.

Gwen felt reduced to insignificance. "So much stone,'' she wailed in a tiny voice.

"It's only a castle," Sebastian whispered. "Pretend these are the walls of a mountain valley."

But his words failed to console her, for Carcassonne had devoured them whole like a great stone leviathan gulping four Jonahs into its cavernous belly.

In the great hall of the castle, where trestle tables had been set up for travelers and beggars who sought food and lodging, Sebastian found it odd that there were no nobles or merchants present. The only exception was a scarred old knight with his squire and yeoman. Perhaps those who could shunned the fruits of Carcassonne's stunted bounty. Certainly little remained of that gracious Court of Love for which the castle had once been famous. The rushes strewn about the floor of the hall were filthy and rustled with vermin. Scarred murals covered the walls, but no tapestries or hangings softened the plastered hardness or warmed the chill of the gloomy, barren room. All hints of taste and affluence had long ago been removed or stolen, and the hall echoed with plundered austerity.

Once ruled by counts, the city now was administered by a seneschal, and whatever lowly friar the pope appointed to head the Inquisition in Carcassonne held more real power there than the seneschal and the local bishop combined.

The plight of Carcassonne called to something that ached in Sebastian's soul, an emptiness so vast he questioned whether anything could ever fill it. He saw a kinship between the city's decline and his own family's fate, with his father's bankruptcy and loss of title. To wealth and pomp, Sebastian and the city both were dead, Carcassonne living only on remembrance, he on alchemical philosophy.

A more practical concern suddenly occurred to him, cutting short his self-indulgence. He should avoid mentioning his ancestry while in Carcassonne, he realized. His grandfather had helped Edward the Black Prince pillage Languedoc, and there might still be some here who remembered that time and would hold his heritage against him.

Sebastian had only dim memories of his grandfather as a grizzled tyrant who still terrorized the household with his toothless roars. For the first time, Sebastian wondered what it had been like for his own father, growing up in a foreign land under the shadow of that indomitable warrior.

Corwyn intruded on Sebastian's thoughts. "These two scholars are studying works of ancient learning as they journey on a pilgrimage from Canterbury to the Holy Land," he said from across the table, indicating a rolypoly friar and a thin, impoverished-looking clerk on the bench beside him. The alchemist's face glowed with excitement. "They say they have copies of some Greek texts I haven't seen in a long, long time."

The friar, who had been leering at Gwen, dismissed Corwyn's words with a wave. "No, no, you've never seen these works before. They've been forgotten since antiquity and only recently rediscovered."

"Oh, but if they are what you claim, then I studied them as a young man," Corwyn said. "It will be good to read them again."

The friar frowned. "How can you have studied texts that were lost for centuries?"

"That was long ago, *monsieur*," Corwyn said with a sad, knowing smile. "Long ago, indeed. Much has happened to the world's knowledge since then."

"Long ago?" the friar repeated. "How long?" He turned to Sebastian. "How old is he?"

"Old," Sebastian answered.

"Ah, Alexandria," Corwyn mused, talking to the ceiling beams. "How I miss the wonders of that fair city of my youth."

"Very old," Sebastian added.

"But then her magnificent library was sacked and her flame of learning extinguished." Corwyn's voice faded into silence.

"Very, very old," Sebastian whispered. He looked at

the startled reaction on the friar's face. "If you believe him, that is," he amended quickly, not wanting to seem gullible.

The friar stared at the alchemist.

"*Alors!* How time slips away." Corwyn slapped his thighs and looked around the hall. "Maybe this Renaissance business isn't such a bad idea after all. I wonder what's holding up dinner."

The friar turned to the clerk sitting on the other side of him, his gaze flicking back now and again to Corwyn. Sebastian wished his master wouldn't drop these unorthodox pronouncements quite so casually; the details of his life had a tendency to disturb normal people.

An elbow from a broad, fierce-looking miller on Sebastian's left almost knocked him from the bench. The man, another one of the pilgrims, was stowing a set of bagpipes under his seat. "Have you heard what they're saying about the inquisitioner here in Carcassonne?" he asked in badly accented French.

Sebastian shook his head, fascinated by the man's thick red beard and the bristly hairs that protruded from a wart on his nose.

"He suspects himself of possibly having once harbored a heretical thought," the miller explained. "So zealous is he in carrying out his responsibilities that he is personally overseeing his own torture and questioning, determined to ferret out the truth. But he's finding himself as obstinate a victim as he is an inquisitioner, and they say it may be many months yet before he either breaks himself into confessing his guilt or proves his innocence to his own satisfaction. Meanwhile, the Inquisition is at a standstill here in Carcassonne." The miller's expression was guarded while he relayed this tale, for it was always wise to be cautious when discussing the Inquisition. He brightened when a pair of servants entered the hall. "Ah, dinner at last."

Sebastian turned away, as eager to eat as he was to be free of the miller's gossip. What the man claimed was ridiculous, though Sebastian wasn't about to say so out loud; the miller looked strong enough to out-wrestle any man in the room. Then his stomach churned as two withered herrings were plunked before him on a stale slab of coarse, grey alms bread. A scullion slopped sour wine from a pitcher into a large crockery mug and diluted it with water before placing it on the table, where it would be shared among the diners.

Sebastian glowered at the boy, too revolted to eat despite his hunger. After the incident in the market at Pomme de Terre, he doubted he could ever choke down another bite of fish.

The scullion sneered back at Sebastian and sauntered from the room. Sebastian looked to his companions, but Corwyn was engrossed in conversation across the table with the friar and the clerk. Oliver, intent on some purpose of his own, had followed the scullion out of the hall. Further down the table from Sebastian, Gwen was smiling for the first time since they'd left Gardenia while she listened to the tales being told by some of the pilgrims.

"Oh, *monsieur*," she said as a carpenter paused for dramatic effect near the conclusion of his story, "you mean to tell us the young bride really thought it was a sausage her husband offered?"

"Mais oui! After all, he was the village butcher and, it being their wedding night, she had never before actually seen what he was presenting," the carpenter replied. He spoke to Gwen, but his eyes were on a butcher from the group, who turned red with embarrassment.

"What happened then?" Gwen asked.

"She had the marriage annulled, of course. Her husband's fear of her teeth proved so great ever afterward that, even when he healed, he never came near her with a fully stuffed sausage again!"

This was greeted with hoots of laughter, which Gwen cautiously joined. Sebastian was glad to see her beginning to enjoy herself again, although others in the hall glowered in their direction.

Gwen bowed her head to avoid the scattered scowls

of disapproval. She looked ill at ease inside this castle which Sebastian found so comforting, her hands clasped primly in front of the loose mantle she wore over her homespun *gunna* and kirtle. The wool of the mantle was caught up at the waist by a woven leather girdle that hinted at rather than revealed her figure underneath. With her head down, she might almost have been trying to hide the beauty of her face, with her fair skin and coppery freckles dotting her nose and cheeks, Sebastian thought. He couldn't even see the auburn richness of her hair except where her coiled braids impressed their shapes against the white linen of her mother's scarf.

The other revelers ignored the attempted censure by their fellow travelers. When the laughter subsided, the butcher began a tale about a carpenter who most awkwardly lamed himself in an accident with a chisel. Unwilling to confess the nature of his injury, the carpenter used his craft to fashion a substitute for what he'd lost and thereby fooled his wife at night. To his dismay, however, his wife began to brag about his prowess to her friends, and soon every woman in town was anxious to seduce this man whose organ never tired, but remained always upright as if it was made of wood.

"And did he do it?" Gwen asked, making Sebastian smile at her growing confidence, so much more like the Gwen he knew. "Did he satisfy them all?"

The butcher shook his head. "With so many women, he knew his secret would eventually be discovered, so he took a vow of celibacy instead and joined a monastery. To this day, the women of that town remain in mourning. Not one of them will permit a man to touch her unless he first proves himself as immune to fatigue as the carpenter. And woe to any man who tries to undertake what none can hope to accomplish!"

The group guffawed, several pilgrims pounding the table in their enthusiasm. Gwen joined in until tears streamed from her eyes.

Sebastian also laughed, though not so heartily. He envied Gwen's ready familiarity with others of her class.

Sebastian had struggled for most of the past year to imitate this, without any notable success, and he felt drained by the prospect of continuing to force himself into a pattern he couldn't fit.

Unable to face either food or company, he left the table and wandered from the great hall, thinking perhaps he should check on Oliver. But what he really wanted was to be alone in this castle that reminded him of all his family had lost.

Ahead, a small monk appeared briefly, crossing the corridor, his demeanor pious and humble. Sebastian recognized the monk immediately as Oliver. He hurried to where the broom had been, but couldn't be sure which of several doors Oliver had entered.

He was on the verge of trying one when someone opened it from the other side. The scullion who had served the wine in the hall pushed through, preceded by an enormous covered platter. The boy scowled when he saw Sebastian and considered what to do while steadying the platter.

"I thought I saw a friend—" Sebastian began.

The platter tipped, cutting Sebastian off as the scullion scrambled for control. *"Attendez!"* he snapped, heading down the passageway.

Sebastian frowned, reluctant to attend anyone so presumptuous. Then he caught the aroma of pepper sauce emanating from the dish. Mouth watering, he started after the boy just as the youth disappeared, dish and all, through another door. Sebastian ran to catch up for fear of losing that delicious smell the way he had lost Oliver. He bolted through the doorway after the scullion—

And froze.

A feast greeted him in a room where nobles and richly dressed merchants sat around a long table. Sebastian tried to absorb the details of the scene, from the fur-trimmed *pelisses* and the silk and satin bliauts of the guests to the white expanse of the linen tablecloth; from the odors of boiled and roasted meats and fowls piled on giant serving platters to the spicy smells of sauces and gravies redolent with pepper, clove, nutmeg, and ginger. A baked goose, masquerading in the plumage of a swan, reigned over the feast from a nest of greens, surrounded by jellies and sweets.

At the far end of the table, perched on an ornate carved chair with a silk canopy, sat the bishop in his vestments and miter. At the end nearer Sebastian, in a chair slightly less elaborate than the bishop's, sat a man Sebastian assumed must be the seneschal, though his apparel was more like a count's than an administrator's.

The bishop and the seneschal were being served wine from gold goblets, while their guests made do by sharing goblets of silver. Suddenly, the seneschal grabbed a serving wench and pulled her to him, spilling his wine and distracting any attention Sebastian's arrival might have received.

"Ah, Jaquenetta," he said loudly enough for everyone to hear. *"Bon dieu,* you're fair! Shall I command your love and profane my lips on every part of you?"

"Monsieur, wine gives you more tongue than marrow," the wench replied, making a show of resisting his advances. "It lends you speech for what it might not let you accomplish."

"Tongue, is it?" the seneschal cried with glee, sloshing more wine on himself. "Well learned is that tongue that well can service, and mine can service well. You shall have it all, lips and tongue and more, so that it pleases you to the marrow." He stumbled to his feet, keeping an arm around her waist for support. "Come, Jaquenetta, have with me, *ma chère,"* he said, allowing her to half guide, half carry him from the room.

Sebastian stood, mouth agape. Apparently, what the miller had said about the inquisitioner was true, and the upper class of Carcassonne was taking advantage of the lapse in papal authority.

The guests and servants ignored the interchange between the serving wench and the seneschal. "Fowl is, as everyone knows, descended from *piscis,* or fish," the bishop admonished a bald, well-dressed monk who was carving the counterfeit swan with a vengeance, "and can therefore be consumed in good conscience during Lent. But why then should this venison be proscribed, when neither can it truly be considered flesh?" He stabbed a haunch from the nearest serving platter and held it dripping over the table. "That deer was, as you know, *sanguis*, in blood; that is to say, ripe as an apple which hangs like a jewel in the ear of *caelo*, the sky, the welkin, the heaven; and then falls like that same mature red fruit on the face of *terra*, the soil, the land, the earth. *Ergo*, we eat no flesh in partaking of it, *monsieur*, but only another form of that apple which *le bon dieu* provides."

"I'll drink to that, your grace," the monk mumbled around a mouthful of food. He drained the nearest goblet and bent to wipe his mouth on the hem of someone else's bliaut.

Just then the scullion Sebastian had followed returned with his now-empty platter and discovered Sebastian standing inside the door. "You!" the boy hissed. His scowl deepened. "I told you to wait where you were until I came to take you back to the others in the great hall."

Sebastian shook his head, dazed by all that was happening. "You said to attend you—"

The scullion rolled his eyes and Sebastian realized he had misunderstood yet another French expression. "*Stupide anglais*," the boy muttered.

Sebastian tensed, but before he could vent his indignation, a noble servitor stepped up and peered with disdain at Sebastian's rustic gonel and crude, cross-bound breeches. "*Qui es-tu?*" he demanded, his hand dropping to the hilt of his sword. "What are you doing here?"

Sebastian's hand automatically responded in kind. The cool touch of his father's sword felt reassuring under his fingers, though his mouth was dry and his heart hammered. Still, he held the man's stare with all the insolence of his upbringing. "How dare you speak so to me!"

The servitor hesitated, his eyes on Sebastian's sword. Then his attention shifted to the cap Sebastian wore, and

some unspoken question seemed answered. The tension
in his manner eased and he nodded slightly. *"Pardon,
monsieur.* I believe I have made a mistake. Have you
just arrived here from Italy?''

"No, I'm on my way there," Sebastian replied, startled by the man's sudden deference. His own manner
remained hostile and aloof out of long habit. "Why do
you ask?"

"Ah, then you must be the English knight who is
accompanying the pilgrims from Canterbury," the man
said. "I understood that you had declined our invitation
tonight due to a strict observance of Lent." He indicated
Sebastian's cap. "Your hatmaker is well versed in the
latest Italian styles, *monsieur,* a fact which finally alerted
me to your identity. I regret that I mistook you at first
for a mere villein and thought to upbraid you for your
impudence, so much out of keeping did the rest of your
traveling clothes seem from your station. Please forgive
my error and join us at table.''

The scullion raised his eyebrows at Sebastian, averting
his head so the servitor couldn't see. To Sebastian's
relief, the boy left the room without giving him away.

Numbly, Sebastian allowed himself to be seated between four Muscovite nobles in outlandish costumes and
a jewel-bedecked lady whose looks had begun to fade,
the blush of youth in her cheeks now replaced by the
rouge which the church was so fond of denouncing. The
woman studied Sebastian while her husband flirted with
a younger woman across the table.

Sebastian let out a slow breath as he realized how
close he stood to punishment or even death. If he were
caught, torture and disfigurement were the least he could
expect.

But he hadn't been caught. Instead, he was being mistaken for a fellow nobleman simply because of his sword
and cap and imperious bearing.

The aging beauty next to him gave him a wink and
ran her finger around the rim of a goblet. "Are you also
gifted with a clever tongue, *monsieur,* such as our host,

the seneschal, claims to possess?'' she asked in a husky whisper.

Sebastian's lip curled cynically and he reached for the goblet, wrapping his fingers around hers. He knew she would never have spoken to him had she been aware of his true station. An adventuress she might be, but she was also a lady, neither so daring nor so foolish as to encourage a lover from a lower class. Her prestige would result from seducing younger men at her own level or higher.

''Not merely clever, milady,'' he answered after draining the goblet. ''It's said that I possess''—he reached into his memory for the right phrase—''*la langue de dieu,* the tongue of god.''

She gasped and Sebastian let go of her hand, content to abandon her to her imagination. All he really wanted was to pretend to be a nobleman again for the evening, enjoying good food and lots of wine. He knew this was cheating on his vow to forego the wealth and pomp of the world, but so be it. It was only to himself that he would be foresworn. Besides, the frosts, fasts, hard lodging, and thin clothes he'd endured as a lowly apprentice would be his lot again after tonight.

His only real regret was that Gwen and Corwyn weren't there to enjoy his brief resumption of nobility with him.

Oliver, cheered on by the shouts of his newfound companions, shifted the two white cubes in his stick fingers, feeling the subtle variations that determined how the cubes would roll when thrown. The game was exceedingly easy, consisting of little more than making sure the right patterns of dots showed when the dice stopped. Yet despite its lack of difficulty, most of the players got excited every time Oliver won, jumping up and down and yelling as if he'd done something remarkable. Best of all, they rewarded him for playing, giving him little stacks of the gold and silver disks Corwyn set such store by.

Oliver had encountered the game while exploring the castle, stumbling into the partially darkened room before he realized it was occupied. He had started to duck out again, but stopped when a yellow-haired, beardless man with bright eyes extended the dice toward him and invited him to join the game. At the time, the yellow-haired man was the only one smiling. Since then, most of the money Oliver had won had come from him, and now it was the others who were smiling. They treated Oliver like some kind of hero.

Oliver was delighted to find such enthusiastic playmates, and he resolved to keep them happy as long as he could. The only problem lay in concealing his true form, although the deep shadows of the room and the draping folds of his robes helped prevent his discovery. Then, too, the other players were drinking something that seemed to affect their eyesight.

Before daybreak, however, Oliver would have to leave so he could retrace his steps through the castle. He had noted several incidentals here and there in his wanderings that he thought would bring Corwyn pleasure come morning.

All in all, Oliver had never been able to bring so much joy to so many people in one night before. It was certainly an event to remember.

ACT 4:

Lent's Labors Loaned

WHILE SEBASTIAN AND OLIVER PLAYED IN CARCAS-
sonne—Sebastian at his masquerade and Oliver at dice—
170 leagues to the east in Venice, Antonio Nessuno paced
the tiny quay at the end of a dark *calle*, or side street,
and waited, cursing the necessity which forced him to
appear as something he was not. The cool, sea-damp air
of La Serenissima, the most serene of cities, caressed
his skin but could not ease his restlessness.

Nor could it silence the song of enchantment that
hummed relentlessly in his head, urging him to return to
its source. Bad enough that he had to live with that
malignant source every day, Antonio thought; he wished
he didn't have to endure its song throughout the city as
well.

Beyond the quay, pale moonlight reflected off ripples
in the narrow canal, deepening the shadows cast by the
backs of the tall marble-faced buildings lining the canal
and street. Those shadows engulfed Antonio and he
strode the walkway in darkness, his worn riding boots
making scarcely a sound against the paving bricks, his
grey, travel-stained cloak shrouding the scarlet finery of
his clothes.

Brave conqueror, he derided himself, to have so easily

won the struggle over a woman's affections. But he had sworn to tell Jessica the truth tonight, even if it meant she would never see him again.

He stopped at the stealthy sound of footsteps approaching along the *calle*. "Who's there?" he whispered.

The footsteps ceased. "Antonio, is that you?" came Jessica's response, husky with forced confidence. "Tell me for certain, though I'll swear I know your voice."

Antonio let out his breath, relieved that it wasn't another of the unwelcome visitors who'd been wandering through Venice to arrive at his palace. He lifted the veiled lantern he carried and parted the cover so she could see the light spill across his face.

Her footsteps resumed, quicker now, and Jessica materialized from the shadows. He turned the lantern to better see her. Dark haired and dark eyed, she was so lovely the sight of her caught at his breath. Even her efforts to make herself inconspicuous for their tryst held a charming simplicity that only endeared her to him further, for her sea-green gown of embroidered moiré and her brocaded velvet petticoat were muddied at the hems from stealing through streets flooded by the recent high tides. A kerchief obscured her face, and a plain black shawl partially concealed her jeweled necklace and the silk voile ruffles and sleeves of her gown.

Also hidden by the shawl was the saffron circle which marked her, the emblem all Jews were required to wear at their breasts. Antonio noted how she clenched the shawl to cover the circle and wondered wryly which of them had more reason to fear being seen with the other tonight.

She hurried into his arms. "Oh, Antonio, I was afraid you wouldn't really come."

"Can you still doubt me, Jessica?" he asked, even as his heart ached at knowing how well-founded were her fears. He held her close, crushing her against his chest in an effort to quell his guilt and silence the song filling his head.

"It's not just you," she whispered into his cloak. "The whole city trembles with fear and rumors of late. First the floods and earthquakes started, and now they say the dead are rising to roam the streets. Two days ago, a score of Christians witnessed the bones of St. Mark assemble themselves in his crypt during Mass and walk unassisted from the basilica bearing his name."

Antonio shuddered, though not for the reason Jessica might think. He knew the dead (among other things) indeed walked the streets, and he knew where they were going. He was also aware that many of them were having difficulty keeping their parts intact along the way. They tended to shed loose pieces of themselves as they shambled toward their common destination, and in fact, that was how the Venetian patriarch and his underlings had recovered the relics of St. Mark in time for the annual processional in his honor next month. They'd followed his trail of cast-off bones and had finally discovered the bulk of the martyr's skeleton sprawled in an alley with a pair of drunken sailors, sharing their jug of cheap wine and winning their money at dice. Since then, the church officials had succeeded at keeping St. Mark's relics in the basilica only by chaining up his crypt.

Fortunately, the patriarch had been so relieved at finding the relics that he never thought to examine the dead saint's path, for like others of his kind, St. Mark had been on a direct course to a particular palace near the Rialto on the Grand Canal—the same palace that was the source of the wordless song luring Antonio even now.

He refrained from telling Jessica any of this, simply holding her instead until her trembling ceased and his own sense of guilt subsided.

Behind them, the wavelets on the canal lapped against the hull of the gondola tied to the mooring poles of the quay. Gradually, Antonio relaxed his embrace and led Jessica to the craft. The two gondoliers who had been lounging discreetly on the deck sprang up again, one fore and one aft, as Antonio returned. They wore matching Turkish-style outfits with balloon trousers and short, tight jackets that buttoned from navel to neck, as well as the tight-fitting round caps embroidered with silver stitching to indicate their employer.

Antonio handed Jessica into the craft and guided her to a seat of satin cushions inside the *felze,* the tentlike cabin draped in bright velvet and brocade. A Persian rug covered the floor and several small gold sculptures ornamented the bulwarks. Highly carved woodwork adorned the vessel everywhere, and at the gondola's prow, the *ferro,* a decorative iron counterweight shaped like a halberd, gleamed with gold leaf.

Antonio gave orders to the gondolier at the rear of the craft, then sat beside Jessica. The gondola glided away from the quay and into the center of the narrow canal. Water hissed softly around the hull. The muted splash of the oars dipping rhythmically into the canal had a lulling, hypnotic quality. Through the opening of the *felze,* the heavens glowed luminous with the golden patina of moonlight shining on high, thin haze. From across the water, the reedy, nasal notes of a crumhorn mingled with the sonorous tones of a viol as music drifted through the night. Jessica settled into the cushions and nestled against Antonio.

"Such a night," she murmured. *"Molto bene.* On such a night, the stillness and the moonlight become touches of silent harmony to the music in our ears."

Antonio concentrated on her words with difficulty, distracted by that other, supernatural music Jessica couldn't hear. It formed a bizarre counterpoint to the earthly melody floating across the water, and Antonio gritted his teeth as he fought against it, determined to exercise some scrap of free will over his life.

Jessica let her head rest in the crook of Antonio's arm and tipped her face up toward the sky beyond the rich hangings of the gondola. "They say even the smallest orbs sing as they move along their paths, and it's only our bodies of clay that prevent us from hearing their angelic harmony."

Antonio stiffened. "What do you mean, bodies of clay?" he demanded.

She turned to him, and he could just make out the puzzlement on her face. "Only that such music is for immortal ears, not ones like ours that will decay. What did you think I meant?"

"Niente," he said with a shake of his head, pretending it didn't matter. But her talk about bodies of clay haunted him like the air emanating from a putrid backwater, fouling the beauty of the night.

Besides, he added to himself, he didn't want to hear the celestial harmony Jessica had spoken of; a third source of musical distraction might be more than he could bear.

Jessica pulled back to peer into his eyes. In the dim light, he could see the worry on her face. "You don't look well, Antonio," she said. "You dwell too much upon the world."

"The world!" He snorted derisively. "The world is but a dumb show, Jessica, where we each must mime our part." He shrugged and added, "Mine is a sad one."

She shook her head. "You are much changed of late."

"Perhaps. This sadness makes such a want-wit of me, that I scarcely know myself."

They glided on in awkward silence, the romantic mood dispelled. To relieve the strain and ease into a subject he had struggled with for weeks, Antonio borrowed a phrase Jessica had used earlier. "On such a night," he began casually, as if his words weren't in earnest, "Jessica might steal away from her wealthy father and run with me from Venice as far as Belmont."

Jessica laughed. "That would be an unthrifty love, to leave my father's wealth and become your mistress. You forget, Antonio, I know something of what you're really worth."

He tensed again, then slowly exhaled as he realized she was speaking only of financial worth—not the uncertain value of his soul, if he even had one. *"Signorina dolce,* you have given me life and living," he said.

"Allow me to give you as much in return." He leaned close and whispered into the dark cascade of her hair. "Surely you know how I love you."

She turned from him and watched the backs of the buildings slide by as the gondola sailed through the continual darkness of side canals, veering away each time it approached one of the innumerable well-lit palaces of Venice or the heavily trafficked Grand Canal. Antonio too watched the walkways furtively as they passed, hoping he wouldn't spot another incipient houseguest lumbering toward his palace, smelling fishy from the canals and looking even more disheveled than when it had started its trek.

Although the bones of St. Mark had failed to reach their objective, many others among the previously living had succeeded, often after encountering numerous canals on the way. They would reach the edge of a canal unaware that they couldn't just walk across, and then would become thoroughly waterlogged while blundering around beneath the surface, sometimes for days, until they found a way out. This rendered their remains even less appealing than they'd been before their immersion, especially those of them who still had remnants of their former selves left clinging to their bones.

The creatures of magic that heeded the siren's call were little better. Ghastly products of reckless imaginations, most of them, they were an unruly lot who quarreled among themselves and displayed an astonishing lack of manners by gnawing on the misplaced parts the dead left lying around. Antonio found them all—artificial and nonliving alike—to be thoroughly repulsive unwanted guests with whom he was tired of sharing his quarters.

"You claim to love me," Jessica said at last, breaking in on the song in his head, "yet you're afraid to have it said that in a gondola were seen together Antonio and his amorous Jessica."

"You know we must be discreet and avoid the eyes

of the world,'' he said, uncomfortably aware how vulnerable he was before the world's gaze.

Jessica's shawl had fallen open, and her fingers traced the saffron circle on her gown. "Then is no one to know but you, Antonio, whether I am yours?'' she asked in a small, sad voice.

"Heaven and your thoughts are witness that you are,'' he answered.

She stared at the ripples on the water where the reflected opalescence of the night sky shattered into a thousand fragments of light. "On such a night,'' she murmured, picking up the refrain again, "did Antonio swear he loved me well, stealing my soul with many vows of faith, and never a true one.''

The accusation stung, and Antonio wanted to protest or pull away. Instead, he took her in his arms and kissed her. "On such a night did pretty Jessica, like a little shrew, slander her love,'' he said, speaking lightly, "yet he forgave her.''

Jessica chuckled a little, sounding polite. But when she spoke, there was no humor in her voice. "You don't have to pretend, Antonio. I know you only came to me because you needed money to pay the interest on the loan from my father. I also know I wasn't the first Venetian woman you approached. But it's all right, I love you anyway.'' She laughed again, and this time it was a sound wrought with pain. "I tried not to love you, but couldn't help myself.''

Antonio held her again, feeling her tremble with tiny, dry sobs that struggled in vain to rise past her throat. He wanted desperately to reassure her, but nothing he could say seemed adequate after the lies he had told. His life was an empty web of deception, and he had snared himself in his own trap, for now that he had come to love her she would never believe him again.

Jessica turned suddenly. "I overheard my father talking to Tubal today. He said the word on the Rialto was that Tunisian pirates had captured a galley bound for

Venice. He was gloating. Oh, Antonio, was your cargo on that ship?''

Antonio hesitated, wanting to tell yet another lie to protect her. But this time he couldn't. *"Sì.* Tomorrow I must leave Venice for a few weeks and arrange another cargo to replace the one I lost.''

"Must you? I'm frightened by all that's happening. It's like something called down by Moses to punish Egypt.''

" 'For I am a jealous god,' '' Antonio murmured to himself, wishing the wretched siren call in his head would stop.

Jessica shivered and nodded. "Father says these things are signs from Jehovah of the wrath to be visited on all Christians for your long persecution of our race.''

Jehovah wasn't the god Antonio had been referring to, and he wanted to warn her that the wrath to be visited on Venice would affect Jews and Christians alike. But he didn't dare tell her after all, despite his vows, for it would reveal the truth about himself and expose the shame that inhabited the core of his being. He almost wished his master, Hydro Phobius, had never had him made.

"Beware of loving me, Jessica,'' he said with a catch in his voice. "The devil can quote scripture for his purpose, and an evil soul, producing holy witness, is like a villain with a smiling cheek—an apple good on the outside but rotten at the heart. You don't know who or what I really am inside.''

"That you are Antonio is certain, and you are my love indeed, for whom do I love so much?''

From the cathedral clock tower on the piazza came the sounds of the two bronze Moors tolling out the hour. These were quickly joined by innumerable other clocks throughout the city, each with its own distinctive bells.

Antonio felt the clocks hurrying him toward a fate he wished to avoid. "Marry me,'' he blurted, still hoping he might escape, "and come away from Venice.''

Jessica laughed and drew back. "What, now? Why are you so impetuous?"

"*Adesso*," he insisted, "at this minute of this hour, grant me your hand."

"It's the last minute of a late hour—a time, I think, too short to make a world-without-end bargain in," she said.

"You're making light of me. You think I'm jesting."

"I've only taken your words, spoken without seriousness, in the vein you uttered them. Antonio, first you invite me to run away with you to Belmont, then you warn me away from you altogether, and now you want to marry me." She spoke with a smile, but he heard the effort in her voice. "How am I to know what to believe?"

"Believe that I love you, no matter what," he said.

"If you would truly marry me," she said after a while, "then bear this trial: wait twelve months, from this year to the next; if your love hasn't expired in that time, and this offer made in the heat of blood remains unchanged, then will I be yours."

"Twelve months!" Antonio groaned. "You don't know what will befall before then." He was silent a moment, gathering the strength to resist a little longer the seductive song that wore at his volition. His eyes stared fixedly at the water as if he might see some graveyard inhabitant groping around on the bottom of the canal, looking for a way to climb out.

Suddenly he turned. "Jessica," he whispered urgently, "listen to me. You must leave Venice, if not with me then with your father. Convince him to take you away, at least till after Ascension Day."

"*Come mai?* Why should I leave?"

"I'm afraid for you," he said, glad to be able to tell her the truth for once. "Have your father flee with you to the mainland. There's evil here in Venice."

Her face loomed close, her eyes holding his. "Antonio, what do you know about it? *Per favore*, tell me."

"Nothing." He turned away, unwilling for her to see him. "I . . . I don't know anything. Just the rumors every-

one hears. It's in the air; something feels very wrong."
He glanced back over his shoulder at her.

She shivered and pulled her shawl tighter, peering into
the surrounding darkness. "Yes, I feel it too."

"Then you'll go?" he asked.

"No." She turned back to him. "You know my father
would never agree to leave his business interests without
reason, especially with your note coming due after Pass-
over. The money I gave you may go to him, Antonio,
but it only pays the interest on your loan, not the principal. What can I tell him that would make him go?"

"Tell him how frightened you are. Tell him anything,
but convince him to leave."

She neither answered nor returned his searching gaze.

"Then marrying me and abandoning your father to his
fate is your only hope," he cried bitterly. "Leave your
father and let me save you!"

"Hope! And what hope is that?" she demanded, turning on him. "A kind of bastard hope, indeed, if it would
have me deny I am a daughter of his blood. Shall I be
saved by a husband, because marriage to him makes me
a Christian? Do you think to turn my back on my faith
by converting me to Christianity as your loving wife?
No, Antonio. I will not commit so heinous a sin as to
be ashamed of being my father's child."

"That wasn't what I meant by saving you." Antonio
sighed, then added in an angry mutter, "As if marrying
me would make anyone truly Christian or save an errant
soul."

For a moment she didn't answer. "Is it the note that
makes you like this?" she finally asked, her voice almost
too weary to be heard. "Because if it is, I'll get more
money for you somehow. I'll take it from his money box
when he's not at home so you can pay him back your
loan."

"No." Antonio tightened his jaw against the hard
necessity that had already driven him to accept her clothing money. He couldn't let her steal for him too.

"You know I'll do whatever you need."

"No," he said again, his voice harsher this time.

"Then what will you do?" she asked quietly. "He'll ruin you if you default on your loan."

Antonio shrugged, not knowing whether she could see the gesture in the moonlight. *"Non importa."*

"Antonio, he hates you. I don't think it's just because you're a Christian—"

Antonio shook his head. "I gave him reason, back when I first arrived—before I understood. It's something I now regret."

Jessica hesitated. "Whatever happened may not be the only cause. Oh, Antonio, I think he's beginning to suspect about us."

"What? Have you said anything to him, even by accident?"

"I don't think so."

"Maybe you've been followed."

"No, of course not."

"Then it's probably nothing." He grinned humorlessly. "Just guilt."

"And is that what troubles you, Antonio, or is it something else?"

He flinched. "I can't tell you, Jessica. Maybe someday."

She buried her head in the folds of his cloak. "There's so little I know about you, yet I love you more than I can say."

"And I love you, Jessica," he said, knowing it was so. Despite all his oaths to give her up if necessary, he had only perjured himself by making them, proving himself false by being true. How he hated this deceit! But that was all the more reason why he must be careful. Love for her threatened to transform him, to refashion his will until it ran counter to his creator's intent. He stroked her hair and wished love didn't hurt so much or involve such risk to them both.

"Don't leave Venice tomorrow," she begged.

Her voice rose muffled through the thick cloth of his cloak, the sounds as frail and indistinct as the mist that had begun to drift in from the lagoon, groping in tendrils at their feet. It was as if the outer world was mirroring Antonio's internal state, for soon nothing would have substance for him beyond the compelling, supernatural song in his head.

"I must leave," he said, meaning both Jessica within the hour and Venice by morning. He had to hurry if everything was to be ready before Ascension Day, as his master had ordered. "But I'll come back."

"Will you, Antonio?"

"Do you think I'd ever lie to you?"

But when she shook her head silently against his chest, he could only despise himself all the more for continuing to betray her trust.

ACT 5:

The Pardoner's Tale

SEBASTIAN WOKE WITH A START, CERTAIN THAT SOME-
one was stomping on his head with hobnailed boots.
Bagpipes skirled in the inner courtyard just beyond the
great hall, then receded to the accompaniment of creaking
harnesses and clopping hooves. Distant thunder underscored the din. Sebastian held his head to keep it from
falling off. Groaning, he sat up, promptly wishing he
hadn't. He peeled his eyelids open and found Gwen staring at him. There was no pity in her gaze. Guiltily,
Sebastian remembered she had been waiting up when
Oliver had led him, stumbling and singing bawdy tavern
songs, back to the hall from the clandestine feast around
dawn.

With a grimace, Sebastian shoved the memory aside
and looked around. The pilgrims were gone from the
hall, probably driven from it by the miller's bagpipes as
he played them out of town. Sebastian wished the miller
a speedy trip to someplace more suitable than the Holy
Land.

Corwyn and Oliver were nowhere to be seen. Before
Sebastian could ask Gwen about them, however, Corwyn
bounded in. He shook rain from his robes and rubbed
his hands. "Good news," he said. "I've arranged for

horses to take us to Narbonne. We'll leave when the weather clears.''

Sebastian winced. "Must you yell?"

"Eh?" Corwyn peered closely at his apprentice, then stepped back, fanning the air. "Whew! What happened last night? You smell like the dregs of a wine barrel."

"Pardon," Sebastian said, glancing at Gwen. He tried to meet her eyes, but she wouldn't look at him. "I was led astray by fallen companions. Believe me, I'm repentant this morning."

"Well, I'll wager you put up a fight before giving in," Corwyn said dryly. *"Tiens!* First fish, now wine. What will you stink of next?"

Sebastian opened his mouth to object, but Gwen took the alchemist by the arm, drawing him away. "Did you say something about horses? Corwyn, I'll walk; you two ride. I can keep up, really I can."

Corwyn looked at her in surprise. "Don't you know how, *ma chère?"*

Gwen bit her lip and shook her head.

"Well," the alchemist said doubtfully, "I don't suppose we have to ride. After all, we're not in any hurry, though the horses are waiting in the courtyard."

"Arrêtez!" Sebastian interrupted. He flinched and dropped his voice to a whisper. "Where did you get money for horses?" Then he remembered something from the previous evening. "Oliver."

Corwyn nodded and pulled a purse from his robes. "Seems he heard me talking about our lack of money yesterday and decided to help. He gave me this a little while ago. I wondered how he came by it, but thought it impolite to ask."

"I know how he came by it," Sebastian growled. "He won it gaming last night with the same companions who led me to drink."

"Sebastian!" Gwen exclaimed. "Gaming as well as drinking—and during Lent!"

"I was drinking; Oliver was gaming." Sebastian was glad he hadn't told her about the feast. "Master, that creature of yours has the devil's own way with dice—a fact which one of the churchmen present looked upon with particular disfavor since he was the one doing the losing. It's just as well those pilgrims have gone.''

Corwyn hefted the pouch, making the coins clink. ''Hmmm, then it's too late to return the money. Besides, I spent most of it. But I must warn Oliver not to gamble in the future, at least not with clerics. Too bad—he was so pleased to have found a way to help. Ah, here he comes now.''

The broom waddled toward them shyly from the doorway, his monk's habit bulging as if he had become suddenly plump. Corwyn's brows furrowed. ''What have you been up to?''

Oliver reached into his robes, withdrew a loaf of bread, and set it on the table. He followed this with another loaf, two flasks of wine, a roast hen, and a meat pie.

''Uh oh,'' Corwyn muttered. ''I think we're in trouble.''

Gwen looked at the alchemist. ''What do you mean? Where did he get all this?''

Sebastian didn't care where Oliver had acquired this sudden wealth—his stomach revolted at the sight of food and he only wished the broom would put it back.

Oliver continued piling items on the table with puppylike enthusiasm. He produced a cheese and several ''duke's rolls''—small loaves of fine white bread shaped like Sebastian's cap—followed by silver table knives, the gold goblets the bishop and the seneschal had used at the feast, and a pair of candlesticks.

Corwyn stroked his beard and nodded. ''We're in a lot of trouble.'' His head jerked up at the sound of approaching steps. Sebastian jumped to his feet, then waited for the room to steady.

The scullion from the previous night entered the hall and frowned at Sebastian. ''Oh, it's you again. I thought everyone was gone.'' Suddenly he noticed Oliver, frozen in the act of withdrawing a stack of parchment sheets from his robes. The boy's eyes widened as his gaze swept the goods on the table.

Corwyn stepped between the scullion and Oliver. "I realize how this must seem, but if you'll just let me explain—"

"Thieves!" the scullion shrieked, bolting from the hall. His voice echoed eerily in the corridor outside. "Villains! Murderers! Call the guards!"

Corwyn turned to Gwen. "I'm sorry, *ma chère*, but you'll have to ride after all." He grabbed Oliver, who had stuffed the parchment sheets back in his robes and was gathering up the pile on the table. "Come on. We're heading for Narbonne right now." He dragged Oliver away, with the broom still struggling to recapture his loot, and led Sebastian and Gwen at a run to the courtyard where three swaybacked nags waited in a slight drizzle. One of the horses carried a sidesaddle. Sebastian boosted Gwen up, then left her to arrange her legs while he clambered onto his own mount. Oliver clung to Corwyn's back while the alchemist swung into the saddle of a dappled grey hackney.

"Quickly," Corwyn cried, "before word reaches the gate." He kicked his heels into his horse's flanks, jolting the animal from its doze. It rolled its eyes, then lumbered into the narrow passageway leading from the castle.

"Wait!" Gwen wailed as her mount jerked to a trot behind Corwyn's. She thrashed about in an effort to get properly seated in the unfamiliar saddle, succeeding only in losing the reins.

"Can't wait, child," Corwyn called over his shoulder while urging his nag to greater speed. "Time to go."

Stone walls flung back the clatter of hooves on cobblestones in a deafening cascade. Sebastian, bringing up the rear, watched helplessly as each jounce of Gwen's mount threatened to dislodge her. They cleared the barbican and crossed the city's main square, dodging the communal well in the center. Gwen leaned over her horse's withers in a desperate grab for its neck, missed, and ended up sprawled on her stomach across its back.

Her legs dangled over one side of the horse, her head and arms over the other. "Corwyn!"

Sebastian started to rein in. Corwyn looked back, but didn't stop. "I'm sorry, Gwen," he called. "Hang on. Sebastian, keep up."

Sebastian kicked his horse again in disbelief, wishing there were something he could do to help Gwen.

They hurtled down the narrow street that was one of the thoroughfares into Carcassonne, wreaking havoc with their passing. Carts overturned as tradesmen veered aside. Women spilled baskets of goods in the mud. Children chased after the horses, shouting with excitement. Chickens squawked and burst into flight. Corwyn's tall, pointed hat flew off in the wind and flapped back against Oliver, tied to Corwyn's neck by a cord. Gwen's hair— not yet braided for the morning—flounced wildly on one side of her horse while the skirts of her *gunna* and kirtle billowed up on the other, much to the delight of several older boys. Sebastian grabbed his cap to keep from losing it and swore at every jarring step.

Finally, the four companions burst through Porte Narbonnaise, the main gate to the east, and into open countryside, leaving a trail of screams, threats, squeals, and curses to mark their path through the city. Still Corwyn kept up the pace, prodding his horse like a madman. They pounded along the muddy track as it wound over low hills and through occasional clusters of trees. Sebastian glanced back for a last look at Carcassonne and was surprised by how small it appeared in the grey, overcast light of day—so diminished from the imposing presence of the previous evening. For some reason, this made him sad, and he didn't turn around again.

They overtook the pilgrims on the far side of a cypress copse. At last Corwyn drew up, horse and rider sweating profusely. Sebastian grabbed Gwen's reins and slowed her horse, his own mount too winded to run any farther. Foam flecked the creature's bridle and lathered its coat, making the horse look piebald. Sebastian helped Gwen sit up, dismayed by her ashen appearance. Ignoring the pilgrims who milled around them, he turned on Corwyn. The alchemist was adjusting his worn, black cassock which had been thrown into disarray by the ride, exposing the white gown he wore underneath.

"Look what you've done," Sebastian snapped. He waved at Gwen. "She could have been killed."

"Would you rather we'd stopped and been caught?" Corwyn asked softly.

"That's another thing," Sebastian went on, his anger rising. "We're always at risk of being caught for one reason or another. We skulk around, living among cutthroats and thieves in the most miserable part of town, only to wind up running for our lives ahead of some mob. Well, I'm tired of it!"

"Sebastian, now isn't the time," Corwyn cautioned. "Could we wait to discuss this?"

"Alors! People claim alchemists are frauds—and for good reason. You go off with your tricks to raise money for your work, leaving me with the retorts and alembics and caustic powders, carrying out endless calcinations, fermentations, and sublimations until all hours of the day and night, blowing on laboratory fires until my face is blackened with ash and heat. And all for what? Our work always comes to naught!"

"Sebastian," Corwyn hissed, "you're talking about things you shouldn't discuss in front of strangers." He tipped his head to indicate the pilgrims, who were pressing in to hear.

"Don't let your master frighten you," said the pilgrim leader. "Tell on, and never mind his threats."

Sebastian opened his mouth to respond, then closed it in embarrassment. He had been unaware of their presence, so angry was he with Corwyn.

For a moment, nobody spoke. "God save this merry company," Corwyn exclaimed brightly at last, slapping his thighs. "We've ridden hard to catch up in hopes of joining you as far as Narbonne."

His words fell into an answering silence like stones tumbled down a dry well.

"That's true," Sebastian added, following Corwyn's lead. "I saw you ride out of the courtyard. Knowing how eager my master was to accompany you, I warned him you were leaving. He loves a pleasant conversation."

"Hrrmphhh," the leader of the pilgrims muttered, looking doubtful. "Your lord is wise to want to join us then. But can he tell a good tale to enliven the journey? We need fresh entertainment."

"Who, sire? My lord?" Sebastian answered. *"Oui, oui,* he can tell a tale more than well enough, trust me." He was about to stop when he noticed questioning frowns from several high-ranking pilgrims who had been at the feast the night before. A pardoner there was in particular who glared at him with fierce, wide eyes. Obviously, Sebastian's fellow revelers wondered how he could be a nobleman by night, and a mere apprentice the following day.

"Why, if you knew my master as well as I," Sebastian went on, seeking to raise Corwyn's status and thereby his own, "you'd be in awe at the wonders he's capable of working. He has taken on many great enterprises which I wager would be impossible for anyone else, unless they learned how to do them from him. In short, I assure you, he's a most remarkable man."

"Sebastian, this is unnecessary," Corwyn said. "Hold your peace and say nothing more."

"You hold yours," the leader warned Corwyn. He turned to Sebastian, his tone mocking. "Tell on, I pray you, good sir. What sort of man is your master then? Is he a cleric? A canon?"

"Non, he's greater than any cleric or canon," Sebastian said heatedly, flushing at the chuckle that spread through the pilgrims. He shook off a restraining arm from Corwyn. "He's been studying his craft for eleven hundred years. I tell you, he knows such subtleties that, if he wanted to—and with help from me—he could turn this path into gold all the way to Narbonne."

"Benedicite!" the leader exclaimed. "Gold from an

eleven-hundred-year-old man, eh? That certainly is a marvel—especially when so ancient and powerful a person wears dirty, tattered clothes. Tell me, why does your master dress so poorly if he can do all you say?''

Desperately, Sebastian sought an answer. *"Tiens!* We must hide what we are, for men would kill us for our secrets!'' The laughter increased. Corwyn shook his head and withdrew to where Gwen waited at the edge of the throng, leaving Sebastian to his fate. ''Actually, we don't bother with the gold of traditional alchemy,'' Sebastian went on, suddenly aware of predatory looks from some of the pilgrims. ''We're aquatic alchemists, specializing in the single most noble element. Forsooth, as I'll tell you, my master and I can transmute any stream, regardless how foul or polluted, into pristine water.''

The pilgrims fell silent, regarding Sebastian with hesitant awe. The mood shattered, however, when Sebastian's horse chose that moment to relieve itself, sending a hissing stream of urine to splatter in the mud. ''Transmute that,'' someone called out as the pilgrims howled with laughter.

Their leader chortled and clapped Sebastian on the shoulder. ''A worthy tale, lad. Aquatic alchemists, indeed! Between your storytelling and her riding''—he pointed to Gwen—''you'll certainly ease the tedium of our journey. By all means, join us.'' Still laughing, he wheeled his horse and resumed his position at the head of the company.

Several pilgrims congratulated Sebastian on the inventiveness of his story as the group fell into place to resume the ride. Sebastian suffered their compliments with ill grace and rejoined Corwyn. The old alchemist also seemed subdued by the jests at his expense. He even neglected to upbraid Sebastian. ''They laugh now,'' he muttered loudly enough for Sebastian to overhear, ''but let them lack fresh water for a day and they'd be glad enough to have an aquatic alchemist in their midst.''

Some people, including Gwen, had dismounted during the lull. Now they returned to their saddles to resume their ride along the acacia-lined avenue—except for Gwen, who stood by her horse chewing her lip and eyeing the beast fearfully.

A woman Sebastian remembered from the night before as a five-time widow from Bath drew up beside her. "Don't worry, dear. It's not as difficult as it seems," she said. The woman was arranging her numerous kerchiefs and scarves with the air of someone in the market for another husband. "Unlike men, horses are easier to mount and usually worth the ride."

"Dame Alice, I don't know which you defame more, man or beast," said the corpulent friar from the night before. "Perhaps you confuse one with the other." He turned to Gwen. "A woman mounts a horse by sitting in the saddle, though she never rides the animal astride. When she's with a man, however, it is properly he who rides by occupying her saddle, and it is she upon whom he's mounted even when her legs hug his sides." He winked. "If you would learn, child, gladly would I teach."

"Hubert, you deliberately misspeak another man's words." Alice gave the friar a playful shove that nearly unhorsed him as she pointed to the thin, serious-looking clerk off to one side. "When the clerk offers to teach others what he's learned, he means it in all innocence. You just leave this girl's saddle alone."

Corwyn cleared his throat. "Enough of this. Gwen, mount up." His face reddened. "I mean, let's go." He dug his heels into his horse's flanks, spurred by Hubert the friar's snickers. Suddenly Corwyn jerked back on the reins and whispered to Oliver, who reached into his robes and withdrew the manuscripts he had started to produce earlier at the castle. "Speaking of learning," Corwyn said, handing the parchment sheets to the friar, "I believe these belong to you and the clerk. We found them in the great hall as we were preparing to leave."

Hubert the friar's expression turned suspicious. "How convenient that you happened to find them so soon after our departure. We hadn't even discovered they were missing. Perhaps these translations are more important than you led us to believe—and more valuable.''

"I already told you," Corwyn said, sounding exasperated, "these texts are poor descendants from the original Greek. They were badly translated into Arabic centuries ago, then translated into Latin before reaching you. They're worthless.'' He scowled at Oliver.

"How would you know about the original texts?'' Hubert the friar snorted and held up a hand to fend off Corwyn's answer. "Oh, I forgot. You're eleven hundred years old.'' He glanced at Sebastian and snickered. "That makes you an expert on ancient learning.'' His snickering crescendoed into peals of laughter.

Corwyn prodded his horse, his face grim. Sebastian felt his own face grow hot, knowing he had spoken too freely. He vowed to make up to Corwyn for his mistake.

After a while, the drizzle stopped and the clouds thinned. Soon the pilgrim company, including the four newcomers, was riding across a landscape that flattened out as it approached the sea. Vegetation grew arid and sparse, allowing the bones of the earth to show through.

As they traveled, the pilgrims spread out according to rank. The nobles, and those wealthy enough to aspire to that status, rode at the head. To Sebastian's dismay, Corwyn and Gwen gravitated to the rear of the company among the commoners and lesser clerics. Oliver clung to Corwyn as if the alchemist might disappear. Gwen, perched uncomfortably on her horse, rode between Corwyn and the widow Alice, who seemed to have taken the younger woman under her protection. Dame Alice was explaining how she had gained control over each of her husbands. Hubert the friar hovered close by, a fly drawn to marzipan.

Sebastian pulled as far ahead as he dared, while the pardoner glowered at him from the rear of the company. The pardoner had long, straight hair, yellow as wax, that hung over his shoulders in lank strands, and his chin lacked any trace of a beard. Sebastian wondered if he might be a eunuch or even a woman. The pardoner took a swig from a skin that hung from his saddle, then suddenly rose in his stirrups and stretched his scrawny neck. "O gluttony," he cried in the high, thin voice of a goat, pointing at Sebastian and drawing the attention of the other travelers. "O cursed cause of mankind's fall, the origin of our damnation."

Sebastian adjusted his cap and sat straighter in the saddle, adopting the haughty reserve he had projected at the feast. But it was insufficient against the pardoner's venom.

"O drunken man, falling down like a stuck pig, your senses lost and your breath soured by wine."

Sebastian flushed and dropped back beside his companions, followed by the staring eyes of the pilgrims. "What's this all about?" Corwyn whispered while the pardoner launched into a bitter sermon against the sins of appetite.

"I was given a seat at the feast last night after he was denied one," Sebastian answered, careful not to breathe his wine-soured breath on his master. "I think he holds it against me."

Gwen's eyes widened. "What feast?"

"And thou, O gambler," the pardoner screeched, pointing at Oliver and saving Sebastian from having to answer. "Thy gambling is the mother of lies and contrary to all honor."

Corwyn's brows knitted in thought. He leaned closer to Sebastian, jerking his head at the pardoner. "By any chance, is he—?"

Sebastian nodded and patted his horse. "We're riding on what he lost to Oliver."

"God's bones!" Corwyn responded angrily. His words came out loud in a sudden stillness as the pardoner paused to take another swig from his skin.

The pardoner wiped his mouth and turned exultantly on Corwyn. "Behold, the alchemist, leader of these miscreants, cursed by his own swearing. Repent, O blasphemer, from turning substance into accident through thy wicked arts." He swayed on his horse, apparently enraptured by the force of his words. A hiccup startled him, and he scowled over his audience as if daring anyone to challenge him.

"Why, he's been drinking!" Gwen gasped.

"The waters of Lourdes," Dame Alice said, indicating the skin hanging from the pardoner's saddle. "Those waters must be very potent indeed, for they miraculously replenish themselves at every tavern we pass. And so strongly does the spirit flow in them that when he drinks, he's quickly overtaken and moved to speak in tongues." She wrinkled her nose and added dryly, "He also falls off his horse."

The pardoner's feverish gaze settled on Gwen. "And thou, O lecherous woman, approach with bowed head and an offering of silver, for my holy pardons from Rome can save thee. In return for your penance of rings or jewels placed in my hand, I'll enter your name in my roll—"

"By the cross of St. Eleyne!" interrupted the pilgrim leader. "Be still or I'll take your two jewels in my hand and cut them off so you won't have to carry them any longer. You can keep them in one of your reliquaries. I'd rather be damned than listen to you."

The pardoner spluttered and swayed in his saddle, too furious to speak. He grabbed the skin and drank.

The leader turned to Corwyn. "What manner of man are you? You stare at the ground, as abstracted as if searching for a hare among the daisies, yet you arouse such spirited reactions from others. You're not even of sufficient stature to be imposing—though perhaps that lack is offset by your girth. The rest of you, let this man approach. Now, sir, you know how we entertain ourselves on our journey. Give us a merry tale, and quickly."

"I don't know any tales, except for a rhyme of chivalry I learned years ago," Corwyn muttered, coming forward.

"That should be good." The leader winked at the other pilgrims over Corwyn's head. "Now we'll hear something refined, I think, from a man knowledgeable in the ways of alchemy.''

While Corwyn gathered his thoughts, Sebastian tilted his cap rakishly and straightened his gonel. Catching Gwen's eye, he led her to the head of the company with Corwyn. The knight he had seen in the great hall was there with his squire and yeoman, as well as a prioress named Eglantine and her entourage. Madam Eglantine looked Sebastian and Gwen over and sniffed, then returned her attention to a whippet on her lap. One of the servants had stepped on the dog's paw at the feast, and Madam Eglantine, distraught over the accident, had carried the dog ever since. A well-dressed monk who had also been at the feast glanced at Sebastian and Gwen disdainfully. The knight stared straight ahead, refusing to acknowledge them.

''There once was a knight named Sir Topaz,'' Corwyn began, ''who wore more rings than the pope has. The maidens all pined for him, and waited supine for him, but he had no more sense than a stone has.''

Inwardly, Sebastian cringed at his master's doggerel. Outwardly, he drew himself erect, pretending he was a valiant knight like the ones in the popular romances, known to the world only by an appellation of great worth such as Sir Onyx or Sir Beryl. But each time he lifted his chin with noble arrogance, imagining the deeds that would win him renown, one of the pilgrims would look at him with a knowing smirk and spoil his daydream, twisting it into a parody of valor. Then Sebastian would slump in his saddle like a marionette with severed strings.

At the rear of the company, the pardoner and a florid summoner with scabby brows and boils were passing the waters of Lourdes between them. They launched into an impromptu duet of ''Come hither, love, to me,'' the summoner singing bass while the pardoner accompanied him in falsetto.

''It befell upon a day,'' Corwyn went on in a louder voice, ''as he dreamed that he lay, with the Elf Queen who—''

"For God's dignity, no more of this!" interrupted the pilgrim leader. "The devil take your illiterate rhyme. It makes my ears ache."

Corwyn scowled. "Why won't you let me finish? It's the best rhyme I know."

"I can best answer that in kind," the leader growled. He sat up, aping the manner of a schoolboy reciting a lesson. "Speaking plainly, and in a word, your lousy rhyme's not worth a tur—"

"By St. Ronyon," shouted the pardoner, cutting the leader off and sliding to one side of his saddle, "I'll tell a tale!"

This led to consternation among the gentles at the head of the company. "No, don't let him tell us another of his ribald stories," said Madam Eglantine. She turned to the pardoner. "Tell us something moral, that we may learn from it, and then we'll listen."

"A moral tale," the pardoner replied with a sly smile. "Very well, give me a moment while I think of something decent." He sucked on the water skin until the vessel's sides collapsed, then wiped his mouth. "There are many tales I could tell of young girls I've helped along the road to motherhood, then compensated afterward with pardons for their licentiousness." He grinned, and Sebastian wondered if the pardoner was trying to bolster his masculinity. "Instead, however, I offer a tale which testifies to the fate of an even greater fool than this Sir Topaz. A Venetian glassmaker, he was, and a master of his craft, until avarice mastered him and left him in need of my wares."

Sebastian, intrigued despite himself, dropped back a pace to better hear the pardoner over Corwyn's grumbles.

"*Radix malorum est Cupiditas,*" the pardoner went on. "'The love of money is the root of all evil.' So good at his craft was this artisan that he rediscovered how to make colorless glass, a skill lost since Roman times. When coated with a tartar of mercury and tin, this glass made mirrors superior to any burnished metal."

The prioress sighed and fingered the small, oval silver

mirror that hung from a cord at her waist. Most mirrors were dull and cloudy, distorting the reflections they cast, yet so powerfully did they grip the imagination of society that even a poor mirror was virtually priceless. As a result, Sebastian's fellow travelers gave the pardoner their rapt attention, and even Corwyn stopped grumbling to listen.

The pardoner nodded, acknowledging his audience's interest. "A worthy achievement, but for the glassmaker it was not enough. Out of greed, he entered into a secret pact. A stranger wanted a large sphere blown from the new colorless glass, and the outside of the sphere coated with tartar. The glass would be transformed into a mirror—a spherical mirror that reflected only on the inside, turning images back upon themselves within it, unseen by the world outside."

There were doubtful frowns at this, with the most pronounced coming from Corwyn. Sebastian wondered how much—if any—of the story to believe. It sounded impossible, yet the details seemed too bizarre to have been invented.

The pardoner laughed, wobbling in his saddle. "Yes, it is difficult to know which was the greater fool, the glassmaker or the stranger. After a time, the glassmaker began to suspect the stranger was really a fiend, and that the mirrored sphere was to be used for some hellish purpose. Yet he finished his task and was paid, whereupon the stranger took his sphere and left, never to be heard from again.

"Soon, however, another incident reinforced the glassmaker's belief that he had participated in some unholy deed. A wealthy heiress, La Bella Donna, who lives on the mainland near Venice, saw the glassmaker and fell in love with him. La Bella Donna told the glassmaker that he could win her hand, and thus her wealth, in marriage if he chose correctly which of three small caskets held her portrait. The penalty for choosing incorrectly required an unlucky suitor to go into exile, never to return to Venice and never again to seek a woman's hand in marriage.''

"Surely the glassmaker wasn't fool enough to submit to such a test,'' interrupted the widow Alice.

"Ah, but he was,'' the pardoner said. "Too often, such is the penalty for love.'' He leered at Alice drunkenly and took another swig from the skin before continuing. "Naturally, the glassmaker was reluctant at first, for the Venetian senate deals harshly with artisans who attempt to leave the city. Venice is determined to keep its glassmaking skills to itself. But La Bella Donna urged him, promising to help him make the correct choice. At last he agreed. He chose the casket La Bella Donna indicated, and when it turned out not to hold her portrait after all, he took it as a sign from God that his soul was forfeit. He fled Venice, as required by his agreement, and lived by his wits, fearing pursuit. Shortly after he came to me, believing it was too late to save himself in this world but hoping my pardons could redeem his soul in the next, Venetian agents caught up with him. They left his body in the street as a warning to other artisans who might think of escaping Venice. So his avarice led to his untimely end.''

"Was it his avarice that killed him or yours?'' the pilgrim leader demanded. "I hope the Venetian agents paid you well for telling them how to find their victim.''

The pardoner rose in fury in his stirrups, only to topple from his horse. The leader waited to see if he would rise, but the pardoner lay in a stupor in the mud. "It's hard to say which was worse''—the leader sighed—"the pardoner's lies or the alchemist's rhyme.'' He nodded to Sebastian. "You there, villein. Get him back on his horse.''

Sebastian shot a glance at his master as he dismounted. Corwyn looked too distracted to countermand the pilgrim leader's order. "What purpose could a mirrored sphere possibly serve?'' the old alchemist asked when he noticed Sebastian watching.

Sebastian shook his head unhappily. He had decided

there wasn't any truth in the pardoner's tale, and so was unconcerned about its technical aspects. Yet the tale refused to be dismissed entirely. As he and a couple of other commoners lifted the pardoner to his horse, Sebastian kept thinking about the images a mirror reflects. It occurred to him that those images are limited to what the mirror is allowed to see.

He had to admit that he and Gwen and Corwyn were a scruffy-looking lot, and therefore were treated like commoners or peasants. But what if they changed the images they reflected? It was a dangerous, heretical thought . . . but it wouldn't go away. After all, Sebastian reminded himself, he had been mistaken for a nobleman at the feast the night before. As strangers, the three of them—four, if he counted Oliver—could travel to Italy as princes if they wished, and other nobles, unaware of their disguise, would accept them without question. All they had to do was change the way they dressed and act accordingly. How difficult could it be?

Sebastian was particularly determined not to let the Italians humiliate Gwen for her humble origins. Transmuting her outward appearance and revealing her true, inner nobility would save her from that. In addition, it would also prove Sebastian's skills to Corwyn in this strange, new form of alchemy, even as Corwyn sought to work the same transformation on a larger scale within Gardenian society.

Sebastian scarcely noticed the rest of the journey to Narbonne, so excited by his plans did he become.

ACT 6:

As He Likes It

As a girl, Gwen had often fantasized about being suddenly turned into a princess. Now, faced with a parody of that dream, all she could do was shuffle awkwardly while Sebastian stared at her, his face wrinkled in thought, clucking his tongue. She felt self-conscious in the floor-length, variegated bliaut he had selected for her, its enormous sleeves loosely knotted to keep them from trailing on the ground. Even more clumsy was her elaborate hennin—a brightly colored conical hat several feet long and tipped with a silk streamer. The cone projected so far up and back from her head that Gwen had to be careful not to dislodge it when she moved.

Sebastian pulled the bodice of her bliaut up so it bloused over the belt at her waist, then studied the result, pursing his lips.

The seamstress, a tall, cadaverous Narbonnaise with the face of a vulture, continued tightening the laces that ran from underarm to waist on each side of the bliaut. The bodice drew snug, accentuating Gwen's bust. With a sniff, the seamstress tugged on the skirt of the bliaut, pulling the bloused folds of the garment back through the belt to set off Gwen's waist.

Gwen squirmed and gazed forlornly at her old clothes.

Practical, bulky garments in drab, familiar colors, they lay heaped in a corner of the tiny shop, cast aside for the expensive silks, satins, velvets, damasks, and brocades spilling from racks along the walls.

Frowning, Sebastian pulled the bodice of Gwen's bliaut out over her belt again. Gwen frowned back at him, matching his expression, but he didn't appear to notice. Trying on their new outfits for final fitting had immersed him in a type of behavior that was alien to her—the manner of the nobility. When he looked at her that way, he seemed to see not her as she really was, but as some vision of what he wanted her to become, and it frightened her.

Sebastian's own outfit, almost as lavish as Gwen's, consisted of a tunic and surcoat of brilliant motley; particolored hose; crackowes whose upturned, pointed toes extended so far beyond his feet that they had to be held up by fine gold chains attached to his heavy hose; and of course the jaunty blue cap he had purchased in Pomme de Terre.

"Stand still," he told Gwen. He held a bolt of burgundy satin up to her shoulders and nodded. *"Très bien!* A costume fit for a noblewoman!"

Gwen blushed. She wasn't a noblewoman. It wasn't befitting for her to dress like one. Yet she reached out hesitantly to stroke the material.

The seamstress peered down her beak at Sebastian. "Now that *monsieur* has seen the actual cloth against the *mademoiselle*'s skin, perhaps *monsieur* would be willing after all to consider a different fabric and color."

Gwen snatched back her hand. She might be as elegantly attired as a duchess, but she was too plain to wear such rich clothes without being given away. She glanced with dismay at a small shop mirror. As the seamstress had warned three days earlier when they'd selected materials, the royal blues and purples, the magentas, and the emerald greens Sebastian had chosen for Gwen clashed with the red in her hair and overwhelmed her skin's fragile natural cast, turning her complexion sallow.

Her freckles, which she'd always hated, stood out like stains against her pallor. With a perverse kind of alchemy, her low-born features transformed luxurious satin into something gaudy and brittle. Gwen knew she would never resemble the fair-haired, unblemished northern maidens the troubadours sang about. She could never pass for a noblewoman.

"Burgundy is—" Sebastian began, irritation in his voice.

"Yes, yes, I know," the seamstress interrupted. "'Burgundy is a noble hue.' You've said that about every color you've chosen."

"Mais oui! I want our costumes to look regal, my lady's most especially." Sebastian lifted his chin. "The Italians must have no doubt about our status."

"Oh, don't worry about that, *monsieur,"* the seamstress muttered, sizing him up like carrion. "All of Italy will know of your royal status as soon as they see the queen of the Gypsies and her jester."

Sebastian glared at the woman until she flung up her hands in defeat. "Very well. If *monsieur* wants to dress the *mademoiselle* up like a Romany tart at a heathen revel, what business is it of mine? No one need know I stitched her clothes. But the mantle, *monsieur*—please, not burgundy, not satin, not with the *mademoiselle*'s complexion. They make her look too . . ." The seamstress waved her arms as if she might take flight in her effort to find the right expression. "Too *blah!"*

Gwen studied her hands, disheartened by the seamstress's words. Was her complexion so unsightly? Maybe she should wear gloves to hide her hands. They were chapped and raw from work and weather—a peasant's hands or a housewife's, not the hands of a gentlewoman, protected by leather.

The seamstress indicated the mirror Gwen had looked in earlier, her attention still on Sebastian. "Perhaps we should ask the *mademoiselle*'s opinion," she suggested haughtily.

Gwen peeked into the mirror again, only to find her

reflection unchanged. Her face still looked wan and blemished with freckles; the red of her hair still formed an unruly contrast to her clothes. She touched her face, wishing she could conceal her features.

The seamstress squinted at Gwen with a disapproving grimace. *"Mademoiselle,* know yourself," she reprimanded sharply, retrieving the mirror. "It's not the glass, but *monsieur*'s fabrics and colors that slander you. They prevent you from seeing yourself properly, for all that your features are reflected in the mirror." Her expression became perplexed. "And you a noblewoman? You lack a noblewoman's arrogance."

"Do I?" Gwen asked lightly, fearing she had already been discovered. This charade meant so much to Sebastian. She blushed again. "Then I confess it, this modesty is counterfeit."

The seamstress shook her head. "It's not the modesty that's counterfeit. The flush of your complexion testifies to the truth of that."

Gwen grew irritated at the continued emphasis on her complexion. "Counterfeit, I assure you."

"Well, something about this is. Take heart then, and counterfeit a noblewoman. But remember, what are good manners in the country are as ridiculous at court as the behavior of court is mockable in the country." She turned to Sebastian and added sourly, "Which returns me to the motley-minded *monsieur,* who'll probably swear he's been a courtier."

"If any man—or woman—doubts that I am, let him put me to the test," Sebastian answered, resting his hand on the hilt of his sword. "I'm no villein. I'm the younger son of the lord of d'Oignon. He was my father, and that person is thrice a villein who says such a man begot villeins."

Poor Sebastian, Gwen thought, still trying to live up to the memory of his father—and not even aware that the memory continued to haunt him.

"God help us," the seamstress said. "It's such fools as this that fill the world with ill-favored children." To

Sebastian she added, *"Monsieur,* in your case, I'm sure you were raised as a nobleman. An English one. One who dances well, flatters the ladies, undoes honest tailors, and pursues incessant quarrels." She eyed his short sword. "Though perhaps without ever fighting one." Sebastian gurgled incoherently as the seamstress continued. "Now, what about the mantle? A soft velvet in pumpkin or rust would be perfect for the *mademoiselle."*

"Pumpkin or rust!" Sebastian scoffed. "Peasant colors! The mantle is to be of burgundy satin."

The *mademoiselle*—they spoke about her as if she weren't there, Gwen thought. She eyed her old clothes with new insight. Little wonder that the muted earth tones of the coarse, homespun materials looked fitting against her skin. They, too, must be peasant fabrics and peasant colors. The realization made her long for the comfortable familiarity of her old life in Pomme de Terre.

But Sebastian hadn't been comfortable in Pomme de Terre, she reminded herself, despite her efforts to make him so.

The seamstress drew herself up with the injured dignity of a scavenger driven from its meal. *"Oui, monsieur.* I'm sure you know best. After all, I'm but a lowly, ignorant seamstress, even if I have sewn costumes for noblewomen these many years. I'm sure *monsieur* has seen more of the world than I, despite the fact that he apparently comes from the remotest reaches of Christendom where people dress like savages. Undoubtedly *monsieur* is also more current in the world's fashions than I, especially among the Italian gentry whom many of the ladies I serve often visit."

"Sebastian—" Gwen said hesitantly, looking again at her hands.

"What?" he snapped.

She'd been thinking about the difficulties he'd had in Pomme de Terre and how hard she'd tried to help him. Now they would be entering his world, traveling among the nobles of Italy. It was only right that she trust his instruction. "Nothing," she said. She hid her hands in

the folds of the bliaut and turned to the seamstress.
"We'll do as my lord likes. Please see to it."

"*Oui, mademoiselle.*" The seamstress looked at Sebastian and shook her head, mumbling to herself. She
took the satin and began measuring.

Just then Corwyn trudged into the shop, followed
closely by Oliver, crowding a space already full before
they entered. "The pilgrims are finally on their way to
Montpellier," the alchemist announced, sounding relieved. "They're meeting a boat there that'll take them
to Italy and on to the Holy Land. Frankly, I couldn't
have stood another day of Hubert the friar and that clerk,
whatever his name was. Let ignorant men get their hands
on a few badly translated manuscript fragments and they
think they're experts on ancient learning." Corwyn
paused to slap Oliver's hand as the broom attempted to
sneak a pair of needles and a spool of thread into his
robe. "Wait till those two get to Italy and discover what
real learning is. Wait till they experience a new Alexandria, reborn from the ashes of the old!"

"Did you go with them to the cloister at Beziers?"
Sebastian asked.

"Yes, but the manuscripts there aren't any better. I'm
beginning to think that the restoration of classical knowledge is the philosopher's stone responsible for the Renaissance. It isn't a new order that's being created, but
the re-emergence of an older one, forgotten now by all
but me. However, France is still a cultural backwater,
as yet unredeemed by the changes taking place in Italy."

"Travelers!" the seamstress scoffed, turning predatory eyes on Corwyn. "You wear strange suits and decry
your native country. By my faith, I'll wager you've sold
your own lands to see those of other men. Then, having
seen much, you'll have nothing."

"We'll have gained experience," Corwyn said know-
ingly.

"Experience that'll make you miserable. I'd rather
have a motley fool"—she pointed at Sebastian—"to

make me merry by railing against fortune than experience to make me unhappy. And to travel for it, too!''

The seamstress looked smug, and Gwen had the feeling she was disappointed when Corwyn proved too busy examining Gwen's clothes to take up her challenge.

"Well, what do you think?" Sebastian asked his master.

"What do I think of what?"

"Our costumes, of course."

"Hmmmm." Corwyn stroked his beard and eyed Sebastian and Gwen from all sides, his face impassive. "They're certainly . . . colorful."

Sebastian's face dropped. "You don't like them."

"I didn't say that. It's just—" He broke off and peered more closely at Gwen. "Are you all right, *ma chère?* You look washed out."

Gwen considered what to answer. When Sebastian had first proposed his plan for masquerading as nobles while in Italy, she'd expected Corwyn to denounce it. Instead, the alchemist had agreed, seemingly too distracted by his own worries to argue with Sebastian.

Gwen opened her mouth to say as much, then hesitated when she saw how anxiously Corwyn was watching her. She couldn't bring herself to tell him the plan was hopeless. She nodded instead. "I'm all right . . . I suppose."

Corwyn chuckled. "Wait till we get to Italy. You'll feel better there."

But Gwen remained unconvinced, not wanting to go anywhere except home to the Pyrenees.

Just then, Corwyn saw his new robe lying to one side. He grabbed it eagerly and held it up. It was a simple design—fur-lined, velvet, and purple (royal purple, of course, at Sebastian's insistence, though Gwen noticed how stunning it looked against Corwyn's white hair and pale, blue-veined skin). The alchemist ran his hands over the rich folds. "Clothing really hasn't changed much since ancient times." He sighed. "In an age when worthless manuscripts are hailed as the culmination of classical minds, it's reassuring to know that even modern fashions really only wrap or drape the body, then bind the cloth in place with ties or pins. So it was also in my youth. Clothing is such a simple craft.''

The seamstress snorted, peering at her work as if she found something distasteful in it. Sebastian smirked. ''Perhaps we should leave her alone to pursue her simple craft,'' he said to Corwyn, indicating the seamstress. ''We can send Oliver for our clothes when they're finished.''

''Ah, yes, the further services of Oliver.'' Corwyn chuckled. ''It'll be good to travel in proper style, thanks to the skills of our good companion, Oliver.'' He nudged Sebastian and they both grinned like two boys with a secret. Oliver, who had remained near the door since being rebuked by Corwyn, advanced closer, eager to join in their mirth without understanding its cause.

Gwen excused herself and ducked behind a screen to change her clothes. Although Corwyn had ordered Oliver to limit himself to gambling rather than outright theft, Gwen still considered this a questionable use of the broom's innocence—especially during Lent.

Soon Gwen was once more clad in the rough, scratchy familiarity of her *gunna* and kirtle. She emerged to find Sebastian in his own clothes again as well, and Corwyn had laid his new robe aside. Gwen started toward the door, then paused. She unclasped a small, silver pin given to her by Hubert the friar and dropped it in the seamstress's lap. The seamstress didn't respond until Gwen reached the threshold. Suddenly, her voice rang out.

''Farewell, *mademoiselle* traveler. Despite the prevailing custom in Italy, you needn't bother to affect a lisp there so the courtiers can flatter you by swearing they find it pleasing. Nor do you need to disparage your native land to win their approval. I'll tell you as a friend, in your ear, that though you're perhaps forest born, you've been well tutored. Your uncle''—she indicated Corwyn—''must be a great magician, for he has invested you with the rudiments of true nobility. You may chide

God for your countenance, but I doubt not you'll soon be sailing the canals of Venice in the gondola of a nobleman.''

Gwen stepped into glaring sunlight, puzzled by the woman's words.

"Just because we told her Corwyn is your uncle," Sebastian groused when they were outside the shop, "I don't see why she assumes he's responsible for your instruction. After all, I'm the one—bear yourself more seemly, Gwen—who's teaching you how to act like a noblewoman.''

Gwen bit back a retort and lowered her head in the attitude of exaggerated modesty he had demonstrated for her earlier.

Around them bustled the shabby, cluttered, noisy little town of Narbonne, insignificant except as a minor center of the wine trade. Heat and dust filled its crooked, narrow lanes, relieved only by the fragrance of mimosas, carnations, and roses blossoming everywhere. Ahead of them, the new cathedral, still under construction, rose above the town. Gwen had sought its cool interior soon after her arrival, praying for an answer to the dilemma raised by Sebastian's proposed masquerade. Still she had received no answer, and she couldn't help wondering if the saints were too busy to be bothered with a commoner during Lent.

Gwen's gaze slid away from the cathedral, irked with the forces of both heaven and earth.

"I've arranged for a merchant ship to carry us to Genoa," Corwyn said, interrupting her thoughts. "I just hope I don't get seasick this time. It's been known to bother me, and travel by water is still uncertain this early in the year. But the vessel will make frequent stops along the way, giving us time to learn Italian. Besides, I thought it best to travel inconspicuously since we'll be leaving France as commoners and arriving in Italy as nobles." He frowned. "Sebastian, this plan of yours had better work. Somehow we failed to impress that seamstress."

"N'importe!" Sebastian said airily, dismissing the

seamstress with a wave. "I was raised as a gentleman from birth, though lately my keeping has more closely resembled the stalling of an ox." He paused, his expression somber. "For the past year, I've trained as a peasant, hiding all noble qualities. Now the spirit of my father rises against this servitude, and I'll no longer endure it."

Unexpectedly, he turned to Gwen and smiled, then reached for her hand. She felt his fingers encircle hers, gentle as a promise, telling her with a touch how much this venture meant to him and how much he wanted to share it with her. She smiled back, letting go of reservation, trusting his unspoken pledge.

"Is it so disagreeable then, being my apprentice?" Corwyn asked, sounding miffed.

"Truly, master, in itself, life in Pomme de Terre with you is good enough, for the most part," Sebastian hurried to explain. "It's only in being so rustic that I find it lacking. I think even you'd have to agree with that. Of course, learning from you is always rewarding, regardless of the conditions. But it also tends to be somewhat tedious on occasion, merely for being so far from the opportunities of court." He frowned, apparently befuddled by the effort to both justify and placate. Gwen smiled to herself and squeezed his hand. "It's just so solitary, you see," he went on. "And even that wouldn't be so bad, except for being isolated all the time." He faltered again, then let go of Gwen to wave his hands. *"Sang dieu!* I only want us to treat Italy as an opportunity, not as banishment."

"Tiens!" Corwyn sniffed. "Just be careful. I don't want anyone to get hurt. And watch your language!" He glanced at Gwen, then looked away when he found her watching.

This disheartened Gwen all over again, for she was certain they were trading the remoteness of Gardenia, with its trees and stones, for the painted pomp and flattery of Italian courts. But worse was the thought that perhaps Corwyn, too, recognized her inability to carry off her role once they arrived.

Off to one side, a shallow harbor cut through a salt marsh separating the town from the sea. Corwyn had said the harbor was silting up and Narbonne would eventually be stranded, though for now women still washed clothes at the water's edge by beating them against the rocks. Gwen watched the women, their motions as relentless as the tides. The sight of their crude, peasant clothing encrusted with brine made her skin itch. Despite herself, she found herself longing for the pampered softness of her new clothes.

The seamstress's parting words returned to her, lending weight to a half-formed decision. If Sebastian was determined to conduct this charade, so be it. Even though she knew her efforts were doomed to failure, she would do her best to mold herself to whatever he wanted her to be. At least she could dress well while it lasted.

Maybe she would finally taste the goose grease previously reserved for others.

At that moment in Genoa, the Venetian merchant Antonio Nessuno was meeting with the captain of a Genoese galley in a waterfront wineshop.

"This cargo, *signore*," the captain said, leaning forward until his breath blew hot in Antonio's face, carrying the smell of cheap wine and onions. "Just what is it you wish me to carry to Venice in such secrecy?"

"No questions," Antonio repeated, shaking his head. "That has to be part of the agreement."

The captain shrugged and grinned. "*Bene*. Pay me adequately and I'll ask no questions." His grin broadened. "After all, I can always find out what the cargo is once it's aboard the *Magdalen*."

Antonio started to stand up, but the captain grabbed him with a massive hand, forcing him to remain at the table. "Ho, *signore*, can't you take a joke?" He clapped Antonio on the shoulder.

Antonio righted himself, scowling. "If you won't abide by our deal—"

"*Benissimo*." The captain laughed. "I don't need to

know what your cargo is, only what it weighs and how much space it occupies."

Antonio pushed a parchment sheet across the table. "Here are the figures."

The captain squinted at the sheet and whistled. "That is a hefty cargo, *signore*."

"Can you do it?" Antonio asked, leaning forward anxiously.

"Oh, *sì, sì*," the captain replied. "For the right price, I can do anything."

"Good. You'll pick up the cargo from the Ottoman Turks as soon as possible and take it directly to Venice." He narrowed his eyes. "I'm entrusting this venture to the hull of a single ship, gambling my entire estate on the fortune of the present task. See that you don't engage to carry any other cargo or passengers on this trip. Is that understood?"

"Sì capisce, signore. Whatever you say." The captain smiled beatifically, revealing gaps in his blackened teeth.

"When you get to Venice, your ship's log and cargo manifest must show you've come from Spain with a load of wine. The Venetian port officials must not suspect you're from Genoa, do you understand?"

The captain's smile twisted into a sneer. "I'm no fool, *signore*. The Venetians know how much we hate them for our defeat at Chioggia in my father's day. They would be very suspicious of any Genoese ship that arrived in their lagoon. But if this cargo will help Genoa avenge herself against Venice, I would deliver it to the archfiend himself, and then lie to the Holy Father in Rome about what I had done."

"Good. It's settled, then." Antonio started to rise.

The captain's hand on his arm stopped him. "Ah, but dealing with the Turks and sailing into Venice—these measures could cost me, *signore*. I must be paid enough to offset the danger."

"I thought you were anxious to avenge yourself on Venice."

"I am, of course," the captain said, and rubbed his hands. "But even vengeance can be pursued at a profit."

Antonio hesitated. "Five thousand ducats."

The captain shook his head.

"Ten thousand."

Again the captain shook his head. "Thirty thousand."

"Thirty thousand!" Antonio shouted, forgetting himself. He half rose from his bench before realizing all eyes in the wineshop were on him. He sank back down. "What you ask is out of the question."

The captain shrugged and pushed the parchment sheet across the table to Antonio. "Then good luck, *signore*, finding a ship to do this."

Antonio toyed with the sheet. "You know all my fortunes will be at sea in your ship," he said. "I have neither money nor commodity on which to raise such a sum."

"Do you think me a fool?" the captain demanded, his eyes burning. "In my line, I can't afford to contract with a man whose secrets are unknown to me." Antonio flinched, but the captain continued as if he hadn't noticed. "You're heavily in debt to Shylock, and your debts there alone might have disabled your estate, were it not that you play the gigolo with his daughter to keep the Jew at bay." The captain grinned. "But I also know, *signore*, that you make quiet pilgrimages to Belmont, perhaps to drop your anchor in another potentially lucrative port. Could it be that your attentions have caused the wealthy heiress, La Bella Donna, to swell more than your business accounts?" The captain laughed as rage and revulsion struggled for control of Antonio's face. "In any case," the man went on, "I think you can raise the money, *signore*, from one lady or the other."

Antonio fought down an urge to gut the captain where he sat for speaking so vilely about his relationship with Jessica and for suggesting he was carrying on a romantic involvement with La Bella Donna. Slowly, he withdrew his hand from his dagger. At least his true association with La Bella Donna remained undiscovered. With luck, he could avenge himself on the captain for his remarks by postponing payment for the man's services until after Ascension Day, when all claims against Antonio would become worthless.

"Very well," he whispered hoarsely at last. "Thirty thousand ducats." He shoved the sheet back across the table and stabbed a finger in the air. "After delivery."

"Half in advance," the captain said, holding Antonio's stare. "As a pledge of good faith."

"Do you doubt my word?" Antonio hissed.

"When it comes to money, *signore*, my right hand doesn't trust my left." He laughed again. "But someone must count the coins and keep my accounts, so I'm forced to trust myself. You, however, I don't have to trust, so forgive me if I sound suspicious. Half the money in advance, with the rest on delivery before the cargo is unloaded."

Antonio thought furiously about where he might find another ship that could make the voyage on such short notice, knowing as he did so that the effort was futile. This had to be done in the strictest confidence, and making veiled inquiries about another ship would take time. Besides, most other ships had already sailed for the spring *muda*, one of the two main merchant shipping seasons. He was lucky to have found a ship that had been delayed by repairs.

Somehow, he would have to raise the money. He couldn't borrow it from Shylock, not with his current debts. Antonio had nothing left to offer as collateral . . . except perhaps his own flesh. But what value could there be in that?

Antonio grinned as he pictured Shylock's surprise should he ever discover the true nature of that flesh. Then an idea struck him. Maybe there was value to his flesh after all.

That Shylock despised him, he knew, and for good reason. It troubled Antonio to recall how he had often insulted the moneylender after arriving in Venice. Other merchants also did it; at the time it had seemed a way for Antonio to gain acceptance into Venetian society. And now, Jessica said that Shylock had begun to suspect the two of them, which could only add to the man's hate. Yet all of this might work to Antonio's advantage, even so. If the stakes were high enough—if Antonio offered himself as bait—Shylock might be induced to loan still more money to him in hopes that Antonio would default.

With a nod to the captain, Antonio called to the wine-shop owner for pen and ink and another sheet of parchment. He wrote a draft for the amount against a certain Milanese bank, postdating it to allow time for the necessary arrangements, then passed the draft to the captain and stood up.

"Tell me one thing, *signore*," the captain asked as Antonio turned to leave. "This cargo, whatever it is—will Venice come to regret its arrival?"

Antonio thought of the fragile sea floor underneath Venice, and imagined the devastation that would accompany its collapse. The waters of the Adriatic would boil, swallowing the city. Even now, forces throughout the Venetian lagoon worked to prepare this fate. The cargo Antonio had negotiated would merely hasten the city's demise, controlling the precise date on which it sank.

"They will regret it as surely as if it were a gift from hell," he said, taking no satisfaction in his answer.

The captain nodded. "Then it's a good thing I do for you, *signore*, both for the benefit of my soul and the profit of my purse. And my father's spirit can rest in peace."

Antonio merely grunted. He himself had no father, but the foul spirit of his master, Hydro Phobius, chafed within him till he could scarcely endure it, and Antonio longed to revolt against this servitude, if only he knew a remedy. Instead, however, he must soon return to Venice and the sorcerous music infecting the city's air. His own actions, together with Jessica's refusal to escape to the mainland, exposed her to terrible danger, and Antonio found neither peace nor profit in anything he accomplished.

ACT 7:

A Comedy of Airs

A HUSH SETTLED OVER THE PIAZZA EMBRIACI IN GENOA as puffing clerics in their gaudiest vestments arrived from the nearby church of Santa Maria di Castello, carrying silk banners and a jewel-encrusted reliquary around the piazza on their way through the city. The crowd of on-lookers fell back to make room, forcing Corwyn to one side of the square and separating him from Oliver. Under his breath, Corwyn cursed the Genoese mania for pa-rades, which had tied up streets throughout the city while people celebrated Easter.

Too hemmed in to find Oliver and too short to watch the procession, Corwyn sought refuge in the Embriaci palace behind him. Although a stranger, he was now dressed like a nobleman, and a shiny gold ducat pur-chased his admittance, however begrudging, to the build-ing for which the piazza was named.

Hospitality, Corwyn had quickly learned, was just an-other commodity in this merchant republic, available for a price. He was certain this also held true for the banquets he and his companions had been attending. Even now, Sebastian and Gwen were preparing for another one, to be held that night at the Ducal Palace. Corwyn suspected the banquets carried their own price—so far, he simply hadn't been presented with the bill.

A valet in Embriaci livery led Corwyn through a servants' corridor to a back stairway, where the alchemist was turned over to another member of the household staff. From there, he was conducted by a series of stairs and escorts to the palace roof, a new attendant replacing the old at every landing, each willing to convey him further at a ducat apiece. By the time he reached the roof, Corwyn figured he had greased the palm of every servant and member of the Embriaci family. At this rate, he would soon need to find another dice game for Oliver—although if Oliver didn't start winning again, and soon, even that wouldn't help.

A breathtaking view awaited him on the roof. Beyond Genoa's bay, a purple-blue sea sparkled in sunlight, dotted with galleys and fishing boats. To the sides stretched thirty leagues of rugged Ligurian coastline. The sight of so much water brought a pang of regret to Corwyn at being separated from his aquatic studies. He longed to abandon his search for the key to the Renaissance, a quest which so far had yielded only frustration.

For some reason, looking at the sea made him think of the little glass balls some of the fishermen used as floats for their nets, and he recalled the pardoner's story of a huge, clear glass sphere turned into a mirror. Corwyn found the tale oddly disquieting. The pardoner hadn't mentioned the purpose of the sphere, which was technically impossible in any case. Perhaps that was what bothered Corwyn. The whole idea was so preposterous that he couldn't conceive of anyone making it up.

He shook off the memory and turned to consider the city itself. Genoa clung to a narrow strip of land at the base of steep, pine-covered mountains that threatened to tumble the city into the bay. Slate roofs stretched toward the mountains like undulating waves caught in stone. Spires and domes from a hundred churches rose above Genoa's lesser buildings, only to be overshadowed in turn by the three dozen fortified towers of the city's principal families. From these towers, including the Torre degli Embriaci on which Corwyn stood, the citizens of Genoa defended themselves from attack and, at least as frequently, launched assaults on neighboring families within the city.

A labyrinth of *caruggi,* or narrow streets, cut deep canyons through the city, each virtually swallowed up by the buildings rising on either side. Leaning over the edge of the Embriaci tower to peer into one of these crevices, Corwyn spotted the procession that had disrupted the Piazza Embriaci. Brightly colored banners and clothes flashed in occasional shafts of sunlight. Distant horns blared, and drums beat a lively tattoo. Women appeared on balconies to wave and strew flowers on the throng: roses, clematis, and wisteria, and blossoms of potted orange and lemon trees plucked from the hundreds of gardens dotting the city's housetops and balconies. Overhead, sunshine shimmered off Genoa's roofs and towers in heavenly benediction. It was as though God and man alike were smiling as the Genoese celebrated rebirth at every level—of the seasons, of the soul, of civilization.

Corwyn wasn't smiling. He felt isolated in a city of illusion, enchanted by shape shifters who toyed with his perceptions. Even clothing here ceased to be simple. All in all, this Renaissance quest was proving as elusive as the search for the philosopher's stone that would turn lead into gold.

When the piazza below had cleared, Corwyn descended and started on his way. At street level, he found Oliver prodding a corpse at the rear of an alley. The broom was trying to get the man to play with him. Corwyn sidestepped the body and noted the manner of death. To his relief, the man hadn't died of plague, but instead had been stabbed.

Corwyn hauled Oliver out of the alley and together they wandered through the narrow lanes. Overhead, lines of wash hung between the buildings to dry. Once in a while, Corwyn and Oliver passed beautifully carved portals marking the entrances to half-hidden palazzos or lamp-lit flower-bedecked shrines to the Virgin Mary.

At last they reached the building that housed the library for the University of Genoa. Corwyn led the way inside to a large room filled with books, each laid flat and crowded together on rows of low shelves. The air hung thick with the smells of leather and parchment, of fresh ink and ancient knowledge. Across the room, scholars copied everything from occasional verses to entire manuscripts. A few of the books they consulted appeared to have been printed with the new system of movable type recently introduced from Germany.

Corwyn's spirits soared in a rebirth of hope. The key to the Renaissance had to be within this room, where the learning of antiquity was housed. Rediscovery of that knowledge would be the first step toward cultural revival. Leaving Oliver at the door, Corwyn strode to the center of the floor.

A pair of identical, grave-looking men hurried toward him, vying with each other over who would be first to greet this potential new patron. Twins and rival scholars, the one in the lead explained when he reached Corwyn, both men even bore the same name, differentiated only by the fifteen-minute interval which had separated their births. Between them, they administered the library.

Corwyn told both men what he sought—the knowledge needed to unlock the riddle of the Renaissance, and with it the restoration of ancient civilization.

"You have come to the right place," responded the first man, introduced as Antipholus the Elder. "Here, we are bringing the dead to life." His words, fierce with pride, gave Corwyn shivers of anticipation as he imagined Alexandria restored to life.

"Thanks to us—and especially me—the splendor of antiquity lives again in Genoa," the elder Antipholus went on. He grabbed Corwyn by the elbow as Antipholus the Younger tried to edge around from the other side, then spun the alchemist toward one of the desks, treading on his brother's foot in the process. Antipholus the Younger yelped and grabbed his foot.

"But if you're interested in classical learning," Antipholus the Elder said, ignoring his twin, "then perhaps you are also a supporter of the arts. Allow me to introduce you to a project to which I have humbly dedicated the past eighteen months of my life." He half led, half dragged Corwyn across the room. Antipholus the Younger hobbled after them, mumbling angrily.

At his desk, Antipholus the Elder indicated a huge book. "Despite an inexcusable lack of financial support from the peasants who pass for noblemen in this city, I have produced a definitive study of the marginal comments inscribed on three pages of what may once have been a partial copy of Plato's *Republic*." He thumped the heavy book for emphasis.

Corwyn stared at the book with dismay. "But Plato hasn't really been forgotten, just ignored," he said. "What about other great minds of antiquity?"

Antipholus the Younger chortled at his twin's discomfiture. But Antipholus the Elder dismissed Corwyn's objection with a wave. "Other minds are as nothing compared to Plato's."

Next to Antipholus the Elder's book lay three sheets of ancient parchment, evidently the manuscript on which his commentary was based. Corwyn picked up the pages and examined them, his hopes writhing away like wisps of smoke. The Renaissance couldn't possibly be founded on knowledge as fallacious as this. The text appeared to have been copied by someone just learning Greek, possibly as part of an exercise. The letters wobbled so uncertainly Corwyn could scarcely read them. In the margins, a second hand had jotted a series of faded notes which bore no relation to the manuscript. The notes looked like declensions of irregular verbs or maybe an ancient shopping list. "You spent eighteen months on this?"

"On the margin notes, not the text," Antipholus the Elder explained. "Naturally, I had to discipline myself to the demands of working with less fundamental aspects of the manuscript before daring an even greater project.'' His voice grew grandiloquent. ''It's disgraceful how the significance of these notes went unrecognized prior to my work. Do you realize what effect my findings could have on the future of scholarship?''

''I'm afraid I do,'' Corwyn muttered, returning the parchment sheets to the desk. ''All too well.''

Antipholus the Elder flung out his arms expansively, smacking the younger Antipholus in the face. ''Next, I will undertake to translate all three pages of text in their entirety.''

Antipholus the Younger groaned and clutched his injured nose.

Corwyn thumbed through the elder Antipholus's book without interest. ''If it took eighteen months to prepare this study of the notes, it could take you years to translate three pages of actual text.''

Antipholus the Elder nodded. ''Provided, of course, that I find a patron noble enough to understand the importance of my work.'' He gazed meaningfully at Corwyn's expensive robes.

''Of course,'' Corwyn repeated dryly. ''Such an endeavor as this requires a wealthy dupe to support it.''

Antipholus the Elder scowled. Before he could respond, however, his brother pushed him aside. ''Ah, leave off, why don't you!'' the younger Antipholus cried. ''Can't you see the *signore* doesn't want to be bothered with your Platonistic drivel? Obviously, he's a well-bred, cultured gentleman, a true connoisseur of the liberal arts. One such as he can appreciate the natural superiority of so elevated a mind as Aristotle's.'' He leaned on his brother's desk to smile at Corwyn, the three parchment sheets crumpling under his hand. ''Perhaps you would care to see what strides I've made in advancing the study of Aristotle's *Poetics*?''

Uttering a shriek, Antipholus the Elder shoved his brother away from the desk and straightened the crumpled sheets. The parchment, brittle with age, disintegrated under his fingers.

Antipholus the Younger pulled Corwyn to another desk across the library and pointed to a leather-bound volume. "It has taken years of effort," he whispered, "but at last I have concluded that Aristotle's great study of tragedy was only half of his complete, original text on the subject of drama." He leaned closer to be heard over his twin's rising moans. "There was another half, which has long been missing."

With a cry of glee, Corwyn pounced on the book the younger Antipholus had indicated. "You mean you've found the volume that deals with comedy?"

Antipholus the Younger frowned. "How did you know there was a volume on comedy?"

Corwyn was too busy glancing through the book to answer. Across the room, Antipholus the Elder's wailing shifted to curses as he tried to restore the parchment sheets. "Why, this is only the portion on tragedy," Corwyn said to the younger Antipholus at last, not bothering to hide his disappointment.

Antipholus the Younger took the book from Corwyn, shaking his head as if the alchemist were obtuse. "Of course it is. I haven't found the other volume. I don't even know that it still exists. I've simply concluded that there once was such a work."

"But everyone knows that," Corwyn snapped.

"They do?" Antipholus the Younger looked crestfallen. "Who told them?" He glared suspiciously over at his brother.

"If you really want to do some meaningful scholarship—" Corwyn began.

A howl from Antipholus the Elder cut him short. "You blaspheming Aristotelian pig, you have destroyed a work of Plato's!" He lifted his hands and spread his fingers, letting fragments of parchment flutter to the floor. With a bellow, he grabbed the tome he had written and charged his twin. The younger Antipholus wrenched his own leather-bound volume from the desk and hurled it at his attacker. The book flew wide, and Antipholus the Elder began pummeling his brother with the Plato commentary.

"Wait!" Corwyn cried. The two brothers paused. "Where are the works of the great Ionian experimentalists and the researchers at the library of Alexandria? Where are books by the likes of Democritus, Aristarchus, Eratosthenes, and Archimedes? Don't you have anything by them?"

"Aristarchus?" the elder Antipholus repeated to his twin. "Eratosthenes? Who are they?"

Antipholus the Younger shrugged, his hands around his brother's throat. "He must be mad," he said, jerking his chin at Corwyn.

"And this is all his fault," Antipholus the Elder snarled.

The brothers exchanged glances, then rushed Corwyn with identical roars. A barrage of books from Oliver slowed them down just long enough for the alchemist to escape. On his way through the door, Corwyn snagged Oliver, who was throwing every book and manuscript he could grab. The broom resisted, enjoying this new-found game. When the alchemist finally maneuvered him outside, Oliver stood sulking, staring at the ground and kicking up swirls of dust from the cobblestones with his brushy base.

"How dare you throw books like that!" Corwyn raged, venting a wrath that did not properly include the broom. "If you're going to behave like that, I don't want you with me. Go back to the inn and wait for Gwen and Sebastian."

Slowly, Oliver shuffled away. He peeked over his shoulder once in a while in case Corwyn should relent.

"Go on," the alchemist ordered. He waited until the broom was out of sight, then sighed and resumed wandering.

Corwyn intended only to view some of the town, then return to the inn for a rest before the banquet he and Gwen and Sebastian were to attend that night. But his wanderings became a nightmare, haunted by ghostly memories and tainted by defeat. All around, new buildings cried out an ancient heritage, proclaiming their debt to classical architecture. Modern statuary, animated by Greek and Roman aesthetics, stared from their pedestals into that older world, bridging the thousand-year gulf during which freestanding sculpture had lain forgotten. Throughout the city, practitioners of every trade looked to long-dead authorities for inspiration, promising the return to classical civilization that Corwyn expected from the Renaissance. It should have been so simple, he thought, so obvious.

Yet each time, Corwyn was disappointed. For all its debt to the past, he discovered Genoa to be a living city— brash, arrogant, and self-possessed. Its forms echoed those of his youth without ever fully realizing them. Instead of resurrecting antiquity, Genoa transformed it, whispering to Corwyn of Alexandria, but with its real attention on the present and dreaming of even greater glory in the future.

Genoa wasn't going to tell him how to initiate a renaissance in Gardenia, he realized at last, for Genoa itself had failed to properly achieve this goal. Although the city boasted of its accomplishments, it betrayed its claim as a Renaissance city, and this duplicity grated on Corwyn. It was one thing, he thought as he hitched up his extravagant new robes, for him to masquerade as something he wasn't; but it was unforgivable for an entire city to do so.

Oliver tried to leave Corwyn with a show of nonchalance, but his feelings were hurt. In fact, this whole trip was proving tedious. Since they had left Pomme de Terre, Corwyn and Gwen and Sebastian had become increasingly preoccupied, and they never played with him. All Corwyn wanted him for these days was to win money at dice or cards. Oliver was tired of winning. The games weren't challenging anymore. He'd even taken to losing on purpose lately, throwing the games to strangers just to add a bit of excitement. But that only caused Corwyn to fret all the more.

So Oliver swished along the streets, avoiding the crowds as best he could. It was frightening being in a strange city all alone, especially for a creature who normally shunned strangers. Yet overriding even fear was his loneliness and the need for someone to play with. No one had time for him anymore.

At one of the secluded piazzas that dotted the city, Oliver came upon a man who seemed to have time to spare and, even if he didn't act eager to play, at least he put up with Oliver's hesitant advances. By standing on the wooden platform beneath the man, Oliver could just touch his feet and set him swinging in the cool, sea-damp air. Some of the passersby stared disapprovingly, but the broom ignored them, grateful to have found a playmate. But after a while Oliver tired of this when his newfound companion disregarded the broom's motions to switch places so Oliver could swing for a while. The man continued to dangle peacefully from his rope, turning slightly in the breeze. At last the broom gave up, leaving the man to his own devices.

Oliver sat on the edge of the scaffold and thought. After a while, an idea began to form. If Corwyn, Gwen, and Sebastian were too busy with their own game to play with him, then he would join their game instead. He wasn't sure what the point of their game was, but he knew it had something to do with fancy clothes and the extravagant way the three humans had been acting. Oliver too could do that. The banquet that evening offered the perfect opportunity to start.

Oliver bounded down the street, imagining his friends' surprise when they found him joining their game.

Sebastian, seated at a banquet table between the boiled capons and a bowl of sugared almonds, surveyed the main hall of Genoa's Ducal Palace. More spacious and better lit than the drab castle halls he was used to, the vast chamber had a parquet floor covered by colorful straw mats instead of rushes, imported tapestries adorning the walls, and numerous glazed, leaded windows. Gaily dressed court musicians played a sprightly air on viol, pipe, tabor, and mandolin, the melody wafting delicately through the room. Around the hall, gilt-covered children and slaves posed in elaborate set pieces from Greek and Roman mythology. One boy, suspended from a cable, swung like blind Cupid overhead, golden wings sprouting from the leather harness that held him, his drawn bow aimed at the diners around the banquet table. Only his shallow breathing belied the illusion of sculpture.

At the head of the table next to the host's right elbow sat a sad-faced monkey in blue and yellow silk livery, attached to a perch by a gold chain. The creature waited for table scraps from its master with an abject air, occasionally jangling its chain.

The monkey made Sebastian uncomfortable, and instead of watching it he studied the hall, for the room epitomized everything classical about the city. Sebastian hoped Corwyn was satisfied. After all, this was what they had come to Italy to find. Yet the alchemist had been subdued since their arrival, leading Sebastian to wonder whether he had somehow angered his master, and if that accounted for Corwyn's distracted state. Of course, tonight Corwyn was concerned about Oliver, who hadn't returned to the inn that afternoon. Maybe Corwyn simply hadn't noticed yet that they had discovered here in Genoa what they sought.

Sebastian, however, *had* noticed. He grunted with contentment and let his gaze drift over the long banquet table. It was laden with food ranging from turbot to peacock, from wild boar to hazel grouse, with fine breads, sausages, cheeses, and even a few vegetables for variety. The table itself was covered with a white linen tablecloth that extended to the floor. What Sebastian found most extraordinary, however, was that, instead of the customary trenchers of stale bread given to the diners to soak up juices and gravies, each guest had been given an individual platter, with silver utensils arranged on either side. Sebastian was familiar with the spoon and knife at his place, although in his experience guests usually brought their own. But the purpose of the little serving fork eluded him, as did the folded square of linen underneath. Finally, he realized the square of cloth must be to protect the more expensive tablecloth from spills, and he spread his cloth under his platter. He signaled across the table for Gwen to do the same, then helped himself to the food.

This banquet, hosted by the Count of Carmagnola, governor of Genoa under the Duke of Milan, was so much more refined, more elegant, more *civilized* than the gluttonous feast Sebastian had stumbled upon in Carcassonne, and being invited to the Ducal Palace represented a stroke of good fortune. Sebastian, Gwen, and Corwyn, seated next to the head of the table, were finally being treated in the manner they deserved.

Of course, Sebastian recognized the deception being carried out here—not the fraud he and his companions committed by appearing as nobles, but the more fundamental deceit of Genoese merchants masquerading as aristocrats. Wealth made a nobleman of anyone in this supposed republic. Yet pretense merely left the citizens hungry for true nobility, and they had received Sebastian and his companions eagerly. Very eagerly indeed, Sebastian thought, catching the gleam of candlelight from the gold chain around Gwen's neck. Delivered that afternoon, the chain had been sent from an anonymous Genoese merchant to "the assistant of Lord Corwyn, alchemist and scholar." Sebastian had given the gift in turn to Gwen, much to her delight. He smiled now as he saw her finger it unconsciously while she sat across from him, dressed in her variegated bliaut, listening to the gray-haired Count of Carmagnola on her left. If only Gwen didn't look so pallid, she would be the most beautiful woman in the room tonight. At least she was more animated than she'd been since the evening she'd spent with the low-class pilgrims in Carcassonne.

The count paused to feed the monkey from his plate, then encouraged Gwen to do the same. For all their pretensions, the Genoese were a gentle people, Sebastian decided, feeling pleasantly superior, and he thought perhaps he could even find it in his heart to stay and become a citizen.

Suddenly, he became aware that the woman on his left—a stunning Genoese in a muted gown that underscored a surprisingly fair complexion—had spoken. Sebastian turned. *"Scusatemi?"*

"Your cap," she repeated, one pale hand shaping circles in the air to facilitate her words. "It's very . . . *proprio."*

Sebastian hesitated, struggling with his dubious command of Italian. He reached up to the cap he had purchased in Pomme de Terre. He thought the word the woman had used meant "suitable" or "appropriate," and decided to take it at that. *"Grázie,"* he said, nodding. But he was left with an uncomfortable suspicion the word also could mean "peculiar."

"Non fa niente." She waved it away. "And the lady's hat?"

Sebastian glanced at the hennin he had chosen for Gwen in Narbonne, the long cone held precariously aloft as it jutted up and back from her head. "Ah," he said, pleased to have his taste in clothes recognized. "The lady's hat."

"Sì. I haven't seen anything like it for years. I think my mother had one when I was a girl." The woman frowned. "Or was it my grandmother?" She shrugged and brightened. "The three of you are so charming."

"Grázie," Sebastian said again, with diminished enthusiasm. But the woman had already turned to the gentleman on her left, the two of them chattering too rapidly for Sebastian to follow. Occasionally they smiled in the direction of Sebastian and his companions, lifting an eyebrow in an odd gesture Sebastian had noted before here in Genoa. For some reason, it made him feel self-conscious in his upturned crackowes and his form-fitting,

pied clothes. The Genoese wore short, broad shoes that
gave their feet a ducklike appearance, and the only other
person he'd seen in pied or motley had been a jester.
They wore subdued colors, like the gown of the woman
on his left, combining these in intricate patterns. Instead
of tailoring their clothes to the human body, moreover,
Genoese clothing redefined human shape. Women wore
great ballooning gowns that made them look swaybacked
and pregnant, topping these with bulbous hats from
which horns and coils protruded. The men, on the other
hand, wore padded doublets and jerkins that emphasized
their torsos, giving them a massive, formidable appearance. Then they ruined this effect by adopting big floppy
bonnets and a slashed styling to their clothes which Sebastian had at first taken as evidence of former sword
fights, with the cloth seemingly cut to pieces and the
linings coming out. Besides, the men's tight hose made
their legs look spindly beneath their bulky bodies. And
the exaggerated codpieces the men wore—at least, Sebastian hoped they were exaggerated!

Obviously, the latest fashions hadn't yet reached
Genoa from the rest of Italy.

Just then, the count's monkey uttered a shrill cry and
spat out something the count had fed it. The count chuckled and lifted his eyebrow in that expression which so
irritated Sebastian.

The cry startled Gwen and she jumped, smearing her
mouth with the goose grease she was eating. Looking
about for something to wipe her face, she leaned forward
and grabbed the tablecloth before Sebastian could stop
her. The woman on Sebastian's left clucked at Gwen and
shook her head. From her lap she retrieved the square
of cloth that had been at her place and touched it to her
lips with an elaborate gesture. Gwen's gaze dropped to
where her own cloth rested under her platter, and her
face reddened. She glared at Sebastian, who felt his face
go hot as well.

The tension was broken by the count's laughter as he
turned to Gwen, leaving Corwyn in mid sentence. "What

charming comments this little *francesa* is making on our social conceits, pointing out the foolishness of individual napkins when there is cloth enough for all on the table,'' the count said. He took the tablecloth from her hands. ''Allow me,'' he said, and used the hem to wipe the grease from her mouth.

A chuckle flowed along the length of the table, making Sebastian squirm. Something about their host's smile and the mirth he had precipitated seemed out of place. Gwen too looked uncomfortable as she thanked the count. As demurely as she could, she withdrew her napkin from under her platter and placed it in her lap. As for Corwyn, he looked more somber and withdrawn than ever.

Sebastian regretted having compromised Gwen, though it was an accident, and he resolved not to let it happen again. So when she picked up her fork, her expression perplexed, he glanced at their host before signaling to her. Her gaze was downturned as if to avoid further embarrassment and she didn't see him. Sebastian cleared his throat and huffed a few times—much to the amusement of the woman next to him—before catching Gwen's attention.

When she finally noticed him, he made an elaborate show of skewering an olive with his fork. The olive skittered across the plate, unscathed. Gwen frowned. Sebastian stabbed again. This time the olive jumped off the platter and rolled across the table, leaving a damp trail on the cloth. Sebastian grabbed the olive and dropped it back on his plate. He licked his fingers, painfully aware of the eyes of the woman next to him. Gwen shook her head firmly once, then refused to look his way again.

On Sebastian's right, Corwyn began pontificating to the count about Greek and Roman learning, his movements becoming animated as he warmed to his topic. Around the table, people leaned forward to listen. Yet Sebastian couldn't shake the feeling that amusement lay beneath their interest.

Abruptly, he realized Gwen was eating olives with her

fork while she listened to Corwyn. Instead of spearing them from the platter, however, she picked up each olive by hand and jabbed it onto the tines, then raised the fork to her mouth and delicately plucked off the olive with her teeth. She caught Sebastian watching and smiled with extravagant sweetness, then went back to listening to Corwyn.

Sebastian was glad to see some of Gwen's former spirit, but wished she'd picked a better time and place. "Gwen," he hissed, "for God's sake, this isn't a game—it's in earnest."

She ignored him, although he managed to attract the attention of several other guests. They stared first at Sebastian, then at Gwen as she transferred olives from fingers to fork to mouth.

The count again turned to her, apparently little captivated by Corwyn's words. "Is our *francesa* guest commenting upon our use of eating forks now?" he asked.

Gwen looked at him, startled in the act of transferring another olive to her fork.

"Perhaps you ridicule them because they're of Venetian origin, recently imported into Genoa?"

The man's tone held more of an edge than previously, and Sebastian noticed tension among the other guests at the mention of Venice.

"Perhaps you seek to show how much we, who consider ourselves heralds for the restoration of manners and good taste in an uncultured world, have to learn from those who are commonly deemed our social inferiors?"

Silence fell around the table. Gwen's fork clattered to her plate and she fiddled nervously with her hennin.

"But that's just the thing," Corwyn announced abruptly. "You're not really restoring the ways of the ancient world at all. That's what I've been trying to explain. Oh, you make a good start, I suppose, but you get everything muddled. You take something the ancients said or did and you try it for yourselves, only to bungle it. But I can help get you back on the proper course. I can advise you on how this rebirth of classical civilization should rightfully be done.''

A slow smile spread over their host's face. "Of course you can," he said, his honeyed voice almost masking his malice. "That's why we invited you and your companions here this evening. The Antipholus twins sent word of your great learning. Say on, I pray you, good lord, and tell us what we should be doing. We're all eager to hear what you have to say." He lifted an eyebrow and motioned to the assembled guests, who were whispering among themselves and grinning at the alchemist.

Sebastian scrunched lower in his seat, unease tingling in his spine. Corwyn, eyes downcast, played with his fork. Whatever was bothering him, Sebastian realized, ran deep—so deep the events of this room seemed scarcely to reach him.

Gwen also glanced furtively at the alchemist. At the same time, she reached for her goblet, knocking it over. Wine spread across the tablecloth—an expanding purple offense against the clean, white fabric of proper order. The count glared at the stain. "Get a serving wench to clean this up!" he ordered the servants hovering at the back of the room.

Gwen sprang to her feet at his command, using the front of her gown like an apron to sop up spilt wine. Her hennin, dislodged by the motion, toppled slowly, gathering momentum until it came to rest across the count's platter like a felled tree. "What are you doing?" the count demanded. He thrust the hennin aside, trailing the silk tippet through his food. "I called for a serving wench.''

Gwen faltered. Her face grew red and she dropped her eyes. "I . . . I . . . .''

Chortles flowed the length of the table. Sebastian leaped to Gwen's aid. "Where we come from, the nobility clean up their own spills," he lied, leaning across the table to soak up wine with his napkin.

"Strange custom," the count muttered, staring at the

wine-stained front of Gwen's gown. "I hope it isn't contagious."

Servants materialized, their expressions reproachful. Gwen, looking chagrined, plopped back into her chair. Sebastian returned to his own seat, aware of the disdain from the woman seated next to him. The music in the hall only partially disguised an undercurrent of suppressed laughter.

Genoa must be peopled by sorcerers and witches, Sebastian thought sourly, for things in this hall were not what they seemed.

Suddenly, a trumpet sounded outside the door, announcing a new arrival. The fanfare cut off in mid note. "*Ehi!* You can't go in there," someone cried.

The door burst open and a diminutive figure rushed in. The intruder was dressed in an outlandish houppelande—a high-necked, bag-sleeved velvet robe with stitched pleats, its broad shoulders drooping over the wearer's scrawny frame. A tall, rounded hat that pinched in at the middle, then broadened out again to form a wide brim sat low over the intruder's head, resting on the upturned collar of the houppelande and veiling the wearer's face. Ostrich feathers from the hat trailed on the ground.

The porter and another man rushed into the hall. The intruder ducked under the banquet table and crawled the length underneath, his progress marked by startled shrieks and curses from the guests as he groped his way in the dark. When he reached Corwyn, the intruder flung himself under the alchemist's robes. Corwyn leaned on the table, his head in his hands. "Oliver, what have you done?" he moaned.

"What has he done?" bellowed the man who had accompanied the porter. "I'll tell you what he's done. He's stolen a gold necklace from me, that's what. Had one of my shop boys deliver it to him this afternoon, and now he won't pay me for it. If you know this thief and value his life, you can settle what he owes."

"Is this true, Oliver?" Corwyn asked. "Did you steal this man's necklace?"

A calfskin-gloved hand reached up over the edge of the table and pointed to the gold chain around Gwen's neck. She clutched it with one hand and glared accusingly at Sebastian.

"I thought it was a gift to me," Sebastian protested.

The gold merchant pounced on the necklace with a cry of glee. Before he could take it from Gwen's neck, however, the count raised a hand. Tears of laughter were streaming down his face, and it was some time before he regained mastery over his voice. Indeed, the entire hall had erupted in laughter. Even the gilt Cupid broke his pose to smile. "How much," the count choked out at last, "for the necklace?"

"Two hundred ducats," the merchant replied.

The count frowned, then nodded to the porter. "Pay him." Under his breath, he muttered, "This jest has cost me considerable expense."

The merchant, looking satisfied, followed the porter out. The count lifted the tablecloth and peered underneath. "It's all right, they've gone," he said as if calling a child. "You can come out now." Hesitantly, Oliver emerged from beneath Corwyn's robes and stood beside the alchemist, where he began to preen his ruffled clothes. The count studied Oliver, one eyebrow lifting. "A curious little fellow," he said to Corwyn. "Yet a trusty fool, I'll wager, that often lightens your cares with merry jests." The count turned to his monkey, a sly smile sliding over his features. He hooked an eyebrow up again. "How well I know the value of such entertainment."

And Sebastian, watching the candlelight glint off two gold chains—one around the monkey's neck and one around Gwen's—knew that he, Oliver, Corwyn, and Gwen had been purchased for the count's amusement tonight as surely as any beast. That explained the curiously disdainful raising of the eyebrows Sebastian had noticed, as well as his own distaste for the monkey's captivity. It also explained the invitations he and his companions had received from the leading families of Genoa—bored by a long winter and the hardships of Lent, the Genoese had passed the foreigners from house to house like a troop of trained animals.

Bitterness rankled within Sebastian. Corwyn might be oblivious of this insult, locked away as he was in some personal crisis, but Sebastian wasn't, and he resolved that he and his friends would never be treated this way again.

ACT 8:

The Captain's Tale

SEBASTIAN FIDGETED AS HE SAT IN AN ALMOST EMPTY wineshop down by the harbor, alternating between remorse and indignation. He glanced up at Gwen and Corwyn, who had been staring into their wine cups in silence, and wondered guiltily whether they blamed him for their treatment at the governor's banquet last night. But then the memory of that evening caused Sebastian's anger to flare anew.

What buffoons these Genoese merchants were to behave so!

He sighed and began picking at the recollected bones of the event as if there might still be meat on them, trying again to determine how their masquerade could have been perfected.

"Time to move on," Corwyn said at last without looking up. "We've exhausted what little Genoa has to teach us."

"I don't know about exhausting Genoa," Sebastian groused, "but it has certainly exhausted me." He leaned closer to be heard over a drunken discussion between the two other occupants of the shop, who were seated at a nearby table. "What gripes me is having to sneak out of yet another town with our tails between our legs."

113

"Sebastian, let me remind you that the purpose of our visit is not simply so you can indulge yourself in fantasies of restoring your family's glory," Corwyn said.

Sebastian winced. So Corwyn did hold him responsible. As if what had happened was all Sebastian's fault!

"Our task is restoration on a grander scale," Corwyn went on. "This is the ultimate test of alchemy—the transmutation of an entire society. That's why we're here." He shrugged. "Genoa simply turns out to have little to offer."

Sebastian bristled at Corwyn's determined nonchalance. Besides, if what Corwyn sought could be viewed as an alchemical transformation, then so could Sebastian's goal of turning himself and his companions into nobles.

"Master, how can you say Genoa has little to offer? Open your eyes." Sebastian waved to indicate the city beyond the greasy wineshop. "Can't you see it?"

"What I see is a city that is financially and culturally bankrupt," Corwyn said. He glanced at the two men drinking nearby and dropped his voice. "I see a once vigorous and independent city-state which has fallen into decline, paralyzed by envy of its more successful neighbors, especially Venice." He stared pointedly at Sebastian. "You would do well to remember that lesson yourself."

"Huh?" Sebastian ignored Corwyn's concluding barb and whirled around as if he might catch a glimpse of the alchemist's vision—so different from his own—lurking in the shadows. All he saw was Oliver, hovering near the two strangers at the other table. "You see all that? Where?" He glanced at Gwen for support, but she was leaning back, eyes closed, strangely relaxed in this dismal setting.

Corwyn sighed. "Sebastian, when will you learn to see beneath appearances to the underlying reality? You've been so busy with your own masquerade that you failed to notice the even greater one being perpetrated around you."

Sebastian felt himself blush. His master had seemed no less eager to carry out their masquerade than he—and no less affected by their treatment last night. To hide his discomfort, he watched Oliver slink away from the neighboring table under the baleful glare of the two men. "What do you mean?" he asked.

"Did you know that every year, Genoese men sell themselves into slavery as oarsmen on the galleys in order to feed their families?" Corwyn asked.

"Yes, but only the poor do it." Sebastian paused when Gwen opened her eyes as if she might say something. She pressed her lips tight, and he went on. "The wealthy merchants here live like kings, and are even admitted to the nobility for a price."

"Ah, your venerated nobles again," Corwyn replied.

Sebastian tensed. Corwyn laid a hand on his shoulder, but he shook it off. "You wanted to be accepted as a nobleman here as much as I."

Corwyn shrugged, said nothing.

"We can still do it," Sebastian insisted. "I've been going over everything that happened and I can correct what went wrong." That was an overstatement, but he wasn't about to give Corwyn the satisfaction of backing down. Sebastian was determined to show that he too could perform notable feats of social alchemy. He so wanted both Gwen and Corwyn's approval. He turned to Gwen.

"What are you looking at me for?" she demanded, breaking the sulky silence she had maintained since the banquet. "Are you going to suggest it was my fault?"

"No, but—" Sebastian broke off, anger flaring at himself, the situation, his companions. In the midst of berating himself, he noticed that Oliver had shed his monk's robes in a darkened corner of the room. Sebastian decided he didn't care. What did it matter how much damage the broom did now if Corwyn and Gwen were going to give up anyway? Gwen would remain a commoner until she stopped seeing herself as one, and even if Sebastian could change that, Corwyn would remain so withdrawn that he wouldn't recognize what his apprentice accomplished.

This made Sebastian angry. He rounded on Corwyn. "I can pass her off as a noblewoman in the next town," he hissed. "A duchess." Immediately, he regretted his extravagance, but stuck out his chin and waited for Corwyn to respond.

Corwyn laughed, then sobered when Gwen stared at him with hurt eyes. "I'm sorry, *ma chère*," he told her. "I didn't mean to laugh at you. It's just that Sebastian's being preposterous." Gwen said nothing. Corwyn looked uncomfortable, then glowered at his apprentice.

"I just want Gwen to have the best in life," Sebastian told his master, pounding the table for emphasis. As he did, the depth of his passion startled him. "I want her to enjoy the same privileges as that Genoese lady next to me last night."

"Did you find her beautiful?" Gwen asked abruptly, a strange expression in her voice.

"Well, yes." Sebastian hesitated, then added, "Conceited and arrogant, of course, but attractive enough."

"I see. And what about her clothes? Was her attire appropriate?"

"I suppose her outfit was rather stunning." Sebastian wondered uneasily where this was leading.

Gwen nodded, as much to herself as to him. "Yes, I thought so too."

Sebastian waited for an explanation. "Why?" he asked at last. "What's this about?"

"Oh, nothing," Gwen said. "Except that she was dressed in colors of olive and mustard." She held his eyes. "Hardly noble colors—or so I've been told."

"What difference does that make?" Sebastian mumbled, feeling himself go hot again. He looked away, found Corwyn. "Anyway, what about my wager?"

"Gwen's not a lump of lead for you to practice on," Corwyn snapped.

At this, understanding dawned like some terrible sun

on Gwen's face. "Is that what I am?" she asked Sebastian. "An alchemical transformation?"

Sebastian squirmed. "It's not like that. I only wanted to save you from humiliation."

"Sebastian, this experiment of yours is getting out of hand," Corwyn said. "I'm putting a stop to it before someone gets hurt."

Dismay dragged at Sebastian's shoulders. If Corwyn stopped him, he'd have no way of protecting Gwen, nor would he have any way of proving himself worthy of his master's approval.

Gwen placed a hand on Corwyn's arm. "No, let him go ahead." She gave Sebastian an enigmatic look. "Perhaps it's time that, like the phoenix, I lent a hand in my own transformation."

Renewed optimism swept Sebastian at her words, though it was partially offset by her look, more resigned than eager. Well, she'd see in time that he was only trying to help her.

Corwyn grumbled, then went on more gently. "Sebastian, think what you're doing. The purses of Genoa's nobility are filled with little more than dreams of a bygone era. Why else would noble status be auctioned off to the merchant class? The poor sell themselves in order to survive, and the nobles sell their titles for the same end. Even the city does it, delivering itself into servitude whenever it must in an effort to recover its losses. For all its appearances of prosperity, Genoa is so destitute that it periodically enslaves itself to some foreign ruler to fend off economic collapse. As soon as the economy staggers back to its feet, the citizens revolt and form another independent republic, until the city's finances are once again depleted and the cycle starts all over. That's why Genoa is presently under the rule of Filippo Maria Visconti, despite how vehemently the Genoese hate the Duke of Milan, and why the former Genoese doge, Tommaso Fregoso, threatens to retake the city even now from his vantage point along the coast."

Sebastian sagged under Corwyn's hand. "I didn't realize,'' he whispered. A sudden thought struck him, and he wondered whether his grandfather had faced this much difficulty when he had traveled to France under the Black Prince, earning himself a new title and a holding of land with which to reestablish his family. Had he felt like an outsider in Gardenia? Even so, it was only more reason for Sebastian to push ahead. If his grandfather had succeeded, so could he.

Corwyn patted his shoulder. ''That's why we should move on to another city which better exemplifies the true potential inherent in the present Italian experience.''

''Huh?''

''The Renaissance,'' Corwyn explained, sounding testy. ''The emergence of a new Alexandria. Haven't you followed anything I've been saying?''

Rather than answer, Sebastian searched the room for Oliver, who seemed to have disappeared.

''But where should we go?'' Gwen asked, sounding wistful. ''Maybe it's time to return to Pomme de Terre.''

Corwyn snorted. ''Not until I've learned how to bring the duchy into the Renaissance. Even the bishop will have to admit that such a transformation is the work of an alchemical master.''

And not until I've transformed us all into nobles, accepted as equals by these pompous Italian peasants, Sebastian vowed silently.

''Perhaps we should go to Florence,'' Corwyn went on. ''Cosimo de' Medici is said to have a library there worth looking at.'' He snorted, then waited for an outburst from the other table to fade before continuing. ''Although after the library here in Genoa, it's hard to believe anyone in Italy would recognize true learning.''

The old alchemist lapsed into silence. Gwen sat back, her eyes closed again. Sebastian held his tongue, reluctant to intrude on their privacy. Besides, he had regrets of his own to consider, especially after that rash boast he had made about passing Gwen off as a duchess. A noblewoman was one thing, but a duchess! All he really wanted was for the three of them—four, counting

Oliver—to move in respectable society without criticism or censure.

Lacking anything better to do, he eavesdropped on the two men at the nearby table.

". . . borrows from the Jew, then beds the old man's daughter and charges her for it," a seaman was saying. "He uses the money he gets from her to repay the debt to her father, while he invests the original loan in expensive cargoes."

"Is she a pig, that she has to pay for her pleasure?" the second man, a cleric, asked.

"No, she's very beautiful."

"Then why does she pay him?" the cleric scoffed, his voice belligerent with wine. "You must take me for a fool, to think I'd believe such a tale." He struggled to rise.

"God's truth, cousin," the seaman protested. He restrained the cleric with a huge, weathered hand, his movements those of someone accustomed to authority. "You think I'm making a game of this, but I'm in earnest. I sent an agent to Venice to learn more about this merchant after agreeing to carry one of his cargoes."

Which meant the man must be a captain, Sebastian realized.

So far into their wine and so intent on their conversation were the two that they failed to notice when a broom, which had been standing in a corner of the shop, moved to rest against a chair next to their table. Sebastian saw, however, and stiffened. But anything he did might alert the strangers. He held still, his eyes on the knife the captain wore on a leather strap that crossed over one shoulder and hung down under the opposite arm.

The cleric shook his head ponderously. "Only a Venetian could devise such a scheme," he muttered, awe tempering the sound of his envy. "He pays off the loan from the Jew by working up a sweat in the bed of a beautiful woman, then keeps what he gets for his cargoes as profit."

"*Sì.*" The captain grinned. "Or he would have kept

it, if I hadn't found a way to divert the money to my own pocket.''

The cleric stared. The two were silent so long Sebastian was sure they would notice Oliver, who was cautiously relieving each man of his money pouch. Sebastian glanced quickly at Corwyn, then realized the alchemist couldn't see the broom behind him. But Corwyn looked as though he too were listening to the conversation.

When the cleric finally spoke, his voice emerged as a whisper Sebastian strained to hear. "How?"

"Non importa," the captain said, dismissing the question with a wave that almost bumped Oliver. "What is important, forsooth, as I'll tell, is that he's having to borrow from the Jew again in order to pay me to deliver his cargo. It's already loaded aboard the *Magdalen*—twelve huge bronze canisters, each the size of a tun of wine.'' He lowered his voice. "From the Ottoman Empire.'' The cleric's eyes widened. The captain nodded and went on. "I sailed as far as Rimini with them, then left the *Magdalen* and her cargo safely harbored while I came back to wait for payment. Once the merchant gets his new loan and deposits it into a certain bank in Milan, I'll be on a fast horse to Rimini to take his cargo the rest of the way to Venice.'' The captain elbowed his companion. "Apparently the Jew's daughter isn't the only woman this merchant beds for money. He also visits the villa of a wealthy heiress on the mainland. But it would take stamina to work off what that poor fool is having to borrow this time—he'll never keep it up in bed.'' The captain let a finger dangle limply to underscore his meaning, and both men roared with laughter.

Oliver, two leather bags dangling from a stick hand, inched away from the table.

"This cargo must be valuable,'' the cleric gasped. "But why are you helping a Venetian?''

The captain sobered. "Ah, here's where my tale offers sentence as well as solace. The cargo I carry will help put the 'Pearl of the Adriatic' where she belongs—at the bottom of the sea.''

The cleric's scowl spoke his disbelief.

"No, it's true," the captain assured him. "I don't know what the cargo is, but it's from the Turks"—he shrugged expressively—"and the entire business smacks of witchcraft. What's more, the merchant behind this scheme has contact with Cosimo de' Medici of Florence." When the cleric scowled more deeply, the captain held up a hand. "My agent followed him straight to Cosimo's palace after we concluded our deal. Apparently Cosimo refused him the money, however, because from there the merchant went directly to the Jew."

The cleric whistled softly, then leaned closer. Neither noticed the broom, which now leaned against the doorway to the kitchen. "Perhaps this could work to the advantage of Genoa before it's over."

The captain nodded and smiled. "Perhaps it could, cousin. Perhaps it could, indeed." He banged the table and called out to the owner for more wine, then dropped his hand to his side where his money pouch had hung. Suddenly he scowled at the cleric. "Cousin, if you think to jest with me, I warn you I take your game in earnest, too."

The cleric looked puzzled.

The captain held out his hand, palm up. "Return my money, cousin, or it'll go badly for you."

Still puzzled, the cleric reached for his own purse, then glared at the captain when he encountered only air. "I think perhaps it's you who owes me, cousin," he said, giving the last word a vicious emphasis.

The captain glanced over to where Sebastian and his companions were seated, eyeing the distance which separated the two tables. Apparently he decided it was too far for them to have committed the theft, for he turned back to the cleric.

"*Bastardo!*" he cried, and swung a fist drunkenly. The cleric blocked the blow, but toppled from his stool. Soon the two men were pummeling each other on the floor.

"*Va bene!*" the wineshop owner cried, emerging from

the kitchen. He hustled the two combatants out the door and into the street. Then he approached Sebastian, Gwen, and Corwyn. "Can I get you more wine?" he asked, sounding out of breath.

Sebastian discovered to his surprise that Oliver, in his monk's habit once again, had rejoined them and was slipping the contents of the stolen purses into Corwyn's money pouch, apparently still unobserved by Corwyn. The alchemist shook his head at the shop owner and reached into his pouch for a coin to pay for their wine. He stopped with his hand outstretched and frowned. The coin in his palm was gold. He withdrew a few more coins and stared at them, evidently surprised to find so much money remaining in a pouch he had thought almost empty. As he paid the shop owner, Corwyn looked happier than Sebastian had seen him in some time.

That done, however, the alchemist turned serious again. As the owner retreated to the kitchen, Corwyn stroked his beard. "I think maybe we'll go to Florence next," he said. He smacked his thighs with resolution. "Not that I believe a word of what those two thieves said, mind you. Nevertheless, checking out the library of Cosimo de' Medici would also allow us to inquire about this rumor at the same time." He gave one last, perplexed look around the shop in which gold had made itself magically appear and pushed himself to his feet.

"Might as well get started," he said.

"Thirty thousand ducats," Shylock said, stroking his beard and pacing the stone pavement of the *campo,* one of the tiny open squares that dotted Venice. "Well."

Antonio gritted his teeth. They had been over the terms of the proposed loan on a dozen different occasions, yet still the moneylender dragged the process out, refusing to give an answer. Antonio suspected Shylock enjoyed holding him in suspense, as though their relationship had taken on a personal dimension for the moneylender. Antonio tried to keep the annoyance from his response. *"Sì, signore,* for three weeks."

"For three weeks," Shylock said. "Well."

"For which, as I told you, I shall be bound by contract."

"Antonio bound." Shylock continued pacing, apparently oblivious of Antonio's irritation. "Well."

"Will you stake me?" Antonio demanded. "What's your answer?"

"Thirty thousand ducats for three weeks, and Antonio bound," Shylock mused.

Antonio stepped to block Shylock's path. "*Sì*. What's your answer to that?"

Shylock looked up from his thoughts. "Antonio is a good man." His words were matter of fact, yet his tone managed to call the statement into question.

Antonio clenched his fists, struggling against anger. If he didn't get the loan tonight, it would be too late; the cursed mercenary captain from Genoa wouldn't get paid in time to deliver his cargo of Turkish detonators to Venice by Ascension Day. Antonio had no choice but to play along with Shylock. "Have you heard any imputation to the contrary?"

Shylock started as if surprised by the question. "Ho, no. No, my meaning in saying you're a good man is to have you understand that I find you sufficient." A shadow passed over his face, belying his words, then vanished. "It's your means that are uncertain. The news on the Rialto is that one of your ships met with pirates recently. Perhaps you would be unable to repay so great a loan on time."

"Have I ever missed paying the interest on what I've already borrowed?" Antonio asked, ashamed of having accepted Jessica's clothing money to make those payments to her father.

This time Shylock's glare went unmasked, revealing a terrible fury. Antonio recalled Jessica's warning. Could it be that Shylock had indeed discovered what his daughter was doing with her clothing money? Or worse, that she was in love with Antonio? But, no—Jessica and Antonio had both been careful to avoid suspicion.

"Shylock, do you hear?" Antonio asked at last when the moneylender failed to respond.

The veil that guarded Shylock's thoughts closed again, and his face resumed smiling. Across the *campo*, light reflecting off the water in the canals played across the faces of the buildings in subtle, shifting patterns as insubstantial as his smile. "I'm debating my present store. I don't have thirty thousand ducats instantly at hand, but what of that? Tubal will furnish me. *Però dolce!* How many weeks do you desire it for?"

Antonio ground his teeth. "You know how much I need, and for how long."

"Oh, *davvero*, thirty thousand ducats."

"And for three weeks," Antonio snapped.

"I had forgot. Three weeks, you told me. Well, then, your bond and—let me see—thirty thousand ducats. It's a good round sum."

"Well, Shylock, shall I be beholden to you?"

"Three weeks from fifty-two—let me see the rate." The moneylender paused. "You're already beholden. Why should I now increase your debt by so much more, when you have yet to repay the principal you've previously borrowed?"

"Don't worry, I won't forfeit." Antonio kept his voice light to disguise the lie, yet the question inevitably brought up his worries about Jessica. It wasn't just that he depended on the money from her to pay the interest that stalled her father; their relationship held far more for Antonio now than that. What concerned him most was that she had failed to meet him three nights ago as planned, and she hadn't sent word to him since. Could she have discovered who—or what—he really was? Antonio's face flamed.

"Within these two weeks—that's a week before the bond expires—I expect a return of three times the value of the loan."

Shylock snorted, but any doubts he held remained unspoken. "Perhaps, *signore*. But what would it profit me should you forfeit? You have nothing more to offer as your bond.''

Antonio shrugged. "I would be friends with you. Lend me the money out of kindness.''

"You speak to me of friendship and kindness?'' Shylock answered, laughing without humor. *"Signore* Antonio, many times your fellow Christians have berated me about my moneys and my usury. Still, I've borne it with a patient shrug. You call me misbeliever, cutthroat dog, and spit on me, and all because I use that which is mine. Now it appears you need my help. You come to me and say, 'Shylock, I would have money'—you that spat on my beard and booted me as you would kick a strange cur over your threshold. What should I say to you? Should I not say, 'Has a dog money? Is it possible for a cur to loan thirty thousand ducats?' Or shall I bend low and, with a bondsman's whispered humbleness, say, *'Bello signore,* you spat on me last Wednesday and spurned me another time and called me dog and for these courtesies I'll lend you money'?''

"I never spat on you,'' Antonio said, taken aback. "I said things I now regret, yes, but never that.''

"No?'' Shylock's expression again reflected some inner intensity. "There are many ways of spitting on a man, *signore*—including through his daughter.'' Then he waved as if to dismiss the matter and seemed to calm himself. In the distance, muffled calls sounded as the crews of passing boats hailed one another. "But if it wasn't you, perhaps it was another.''

Antonio's stomach tightened, and he wondered again whether Shylock had discovered his relationship with Jessica. "If you won't lend the money as a kindness between friends, then do it in sport,'' he said, trying to redirect the discussion. "I offer myself as my bond.'' But his face burned at knowing he wasn't truly his own master. He drew a deep breath and plunged ahead, certain that Jessica would never forgive him should she discover how he was deceiving both her and her father. How could she, when Antonio couldn't forgive himself? "If it befalls that I don't repay you at the set day and place, then I'll forfeit a pound of my flesh, to be cut from whatever part of my body it pleases you,'' he said in a whisper.

"Bah! What good is that?" Shylock appeared indignant, yet his eyes betrayed interest. "A pound of man's flesh isn't as highly esteemed in the marketplace as mutton or beef or goat. Is this a game?"

"No, I assure you, I'm serious. If you'll lend this money, lend it not to a friend, but rather to your enemy. Then, if I forfeit, you may with an easier conscience exact the penalty.'' Antonio thrust out his hand. ''To buy your favor, I extend the very flesh of my body. If you'll accept my offer, so; and if not, *addio*.''

Shylock scowled at the proffered hand without taking it. "If you forfeit, that's not the part of your flesh I'll demand.''

Antonio's skin crawled. He shrugged to conceal his dismay. "My ship will arrive well before that time.''

"Then meet me at the notary's,'' Shylock snarled. "Have him set down the terms of this 'sport' of yours. I'll go and bag the ducats and meet you there presently.'' He turned and strode off.

Alone with a soft breeze that drifted in from the lagoon, Antonio stared at his hand. The flesh he had pledged to Shylock could never be collected, yet this knowledge gave him scant peace of mind. For of all the secrets Antonio guarded, the one he had just placed in jeopardy was the one he most dreaded to divulge.

ACT 9:

Thy Fair Lady

"BON DIEU!" SEBASTIAN EXCLAIMED SOFTLY, LEANING across his horse's withers toward the mount shared by Corwyn and Oliver. "I think I've done it. I really think I've done it."

He stared in admiration at Gwen, riding sidesaddle ahead of them through the streets of Florence on a fine white palfrey, a hooded goshawk tethered to one arm while a sleek greyhound loped along at her feet. Little silver bells and colored silk tassels jangled from the mare's saddle and bridle at every prancing step. Gwen sat the animal as regally as someone born to the blood.

Sebastian smiled, pleased with his handiwork. Then he frowned slightly. Gwen had insisted on choosing her own costume. The thick, rolled pleats of the voluminous houppelande she had selected billowed from her tightly belted waistline, and the olive and cinnamon colored velvet was trimmed with fox fur at the hem and at the cuffs of her long funnel sleeves. Atop her head perched a bulbous hat with hornlike coils on either side. A gold necklace studded with malachite hung at her breast.

This wasn't the apparel Sebastian would have chosen, but he had to admit it suited Gwen. She was a vision of loveliness and nobility.

He also knew what it cost her to maintain that image, poised on the awkward sidesaddle for the few Florentines who were around today to admire. Although she disguised her annoyance, Sebastian could read the slight, telltale set of her mouth, seen now in profile. Besides, she had told him how grotesque she felt, encumbered by the clothes and forced by the saddle to face the side, her legs bunched uselessly beneath her. It was ridiculous, she'd snapped, being put on display just so he could win a bet.

Sebastian assured himself that she would thank him for it once she had been accepted by the aristocracy. Meanwhile, at least her distaste wasn't obvious to others—except perhaps Corwyn. "You've done it, all right," the alchemist growled from his horse, seeming to mean something less than what Sebastian intended. "If you're lucky, maybe in time she'll forgive you."

Sebastian frowned, but refrained from asking what his master meant.

They reached the unusually deserted Ponte Vecchio, hurried by a breeze that sprang up, heavy with the scent of rain and carrying clouds from the Ligurian Sea some thirteen leagues to the west. Then the shops and houses lining the sides of the narrow bridge closed around them. From the rear of several of the two- and three-story structures came the bleating of animals awaiting slaughter, for butchers found the Arno River a convenient way of getting rid of wastes.

At the far end of the street, the buildings on either side of the bridge framed the square, crenelated tower of the Palazzo della Signoria beyond. The seat of Florentine government, the palazzo rose above the red tile roofs of the city, challenging the Cathedral of Santa Maria del Fiore, with Brunelleschi's half-built cupola and Giotto's campanile, for dominance of the sky. Only the Florentines would be so foolhardy as to flaunt their worldly might above even the sanctity of the church, Sebastian thought with a grim smile. As if merchant-princes constituted true nobility!

The Florentines were exceedingly proud of their architecture, as they were of all their accomplishments. Nevertheless, Sebastian thought the buildings of Florence were less grand than those of Genoa, although the cumulative effect was somehow greater. Perhaps that effect was due to the openness of Florence, and the way the city nestled in the Arno valley like a sunlit jewel in a sculpted basin.

Sebastian and Corwyn followed Gwen onto the Ponte Vecchio, their horses' hooves reverberating against the bridge. Not until they reached the center of the span, however, which was free of shops, could they see—and smell—the Arno. The stench made Sebastian gag. Gray, filth-laden water drifted beneath them, dispelling some of Florence's luster and revealing a flaw in the jewel. Sebastian held his nose and was about to hurry on when a disturbance at the far end of the bridge brought him to a stop. At the sound, the shopkeepers quickly shuttered their tiny stalls and the sparse crowd drew back from the middle of the street.

A man on foot raced by, his face contorted with urgency, pursued by a shouting throng, their swords drawn. The running feet thundered over the bridge. Sebastian scarcely had time to spur his horse between the mob and Gwen before they vanished down the street in the direction from which Sebastian and his companions had come. The palfrey shied and Gwen murmured to soothe it. After a while, shops began opening again as if nothing had happened. One of the butchers noticed Sebastian's puzzlement and shrugged. *"Umori,"* he said. Sebastian stared, bewildered. "Unrest between the factions," the butcher went on. He gestured as if trying to transcend the limits of language while Sebastian struggled to make sense of the man's Italian. Between the Tuscan dialect, with its vast store of idiomatic expressions, and the local habit of aspirating consonants, Sebastian was having even more trouble in Florence than he'd had in Genoa.

"Guelph against Ghibelline," the butcher explained, "the major arts against the minor, rich against poor,

Albizzi against de' Medici.'' He shrugged again. ''It's Florence. Every day, something happens. *Sfogarsi.* Someone dies, life goes on.'' He laughed good-naturedly. ''Last month, old Piero's stallion caught scent of a mare and galloped after her, overturning Piero's cart and dragging it clattering through the streets. From the noise, everyone thought there was an uprising. By the time Piero caught the horse, the *signori* had barricaded themselves in the palazzo and were preparing for civil war.'' He laughed again while his gaze measured Sebastian. ''Perhaps I could show you some fresh veal in my shop while I tell you more.''

Sebastian figured out what the man had said and shook his head. This was a strange city, he thought, one equally obsessed with art and violence.

He tried to catch Gwen's eye, but her saddle turned her away from him. Finally, Sebastian angled his horse back to Corwyn and Oliver, content to remain on the bridge until he was certain they wouldn't encounter more armed rabble at the far end.

The alchemist was staring at the river with a wistful expression. ''What do you see?'' Sebastian asked, peering over the side. The river looked unchanged. ''How disgusting!''

''Yes, isn't it,'' Corwyn replied. But his voice didn't sound disgusted. It sounded full of longing.

Sebastian looked sharply at his master. ''What's the matter?''

Corwyn paused to lower a fidgety Oliver to the ground, then sighed. ''Corrupted water is like an invitation, begging me to return to my proper studies. If the Florentine council would retain me, I could clean up the Arno. Instead, I'm off chasing after a way to transmute Gardenia into something it's not.''

Across the river, a muffled cheer rose from the town. Sebastian scowled. Evidently the horse race, which took place in the streets and which most of Florence was attending, had gotten under way. Sebastian had planned to be there with Gwen, for it was a perfect opportunity to be seen by the Florentine aristocracy. Instead, Corwyn had informed him that he and Gwen were needed to help examine the contents of Cosimo de' Medici's library.

"But I thought you said you'd discovered the philosopher's stone that makes the Renaissance work," Sebastian said with a touch of belligerence. "That's why we're off to see this library instead of watching the race with the rest of Florence. You told us you finally knew how it's done, and that all we had left to do was learn how to apply it to Gardenia."

"I did." Corwyn's shoulders slumped. "I do. It's knowledge, classical knowledge of the kind I grew up with in Alexandria. That's the key to the whole transformation. Everything else, from art to commerce"—he waved a hand at the city around them—"derives from that source."

"Then why don't we just copy whatever books we need and take them back to Gardenia? You could set up your own library, start a school for classical learning, and the Renaissance would follow."

"But that's just it." Corwyn sighed. "I can't find the right books." He waved for silence before Sebastian could speak. "Oh, I know that such knowledge must be behind the transformation we see taking place here in Italy, and I believe it would cause a similar change in Gardenia. But I can't find any examples of the Italians actually doing it right. Not completely. They come close many times, but in the end they inevitably veer off from true classical forms into something different. It's all because the texts they rely on for knowledge are deficient."

"So what do we do?" Sebastian demanded.

"Keep looking," Corwyn said, his voice heavy with resignation. "We have to find the source from which everything else derives here in Italy. When we find it, we'll also find the great works of classical learning."

Corwyn lifted Oliver up behind him again, frowned, and checked beneath the broom's robes for contraband. He pulled out a plucked hen, returned it to its rightful owner, then motioned for Gwen to lead on across the bridge.

As they approached the opposite bank, the cheering from the city reached a crescendo, then faded away as the horse race apparently ended. Sebastian felt glum as he rode in silence behind his master into the heart of mercantile Florence.

Eventually, they reached the Mercato Vecchio, center of trade since ancient times. Farmers' carts heaped with produce crowded the market. Laborers and slaves carried bales of wool and silk or barrels of grain and leather. Wine merchants called out the virtues of their casks, each shouting that his were the choicest. The houses of feather merchants, stationers, and candle makers overlooked the square, while around the perimeter stood the shops of drapers and second-hand clothes dealers. Filling the square itself were the booths and pushcarts of fishmongers, bakers, and fruit and vegetable dealers. The resulting smells—a blend of tallow and olive oil, of tanned leather and spices—turned Sebastian's stomach. He looked around for respite and saw the Palazzo de Tosinghi, an austere, fortresslike dwelling left over from older times, glaring down on him with a ferocity akin to his father's.

The insignificance Sebastian felt in the face of the palazzo threatened to unearth memories he had thought safely buried, and he resolved again to never let anyone make Gwen feel inferior. With that, he plunged into the teeming market after his companions, who were working their way toward the opposite side.

They were halfway across when crowds of singing, shouting revelers on their way back from the race flooded in from the side streets, multiplying the confusion. Several groups carried the banners of guilds or divisions of the city. Occasionally rival groups met and scattered fights broke out, resulting in broken bones and stabbings. But the pageant of Florentine life swirled around the fights unimpeded.

Most men still wore the traditional *lucco*, a dark,

ankle-length gown with long, wide sleeves and an attached hood. Some, however, preferred brighter, more daring styles—colorful capes and satin jackets, stockings adorned with silver lace, feathered velvet caps and turbans, and intricate jewelry. The women—their fair hair often dyed that way and their pale complexions obtained by bleaching and powdering the skin—displayed wardrobes more costly than the houses they lived in.

Sebastian managed to catch up with his friends just as a sudden shower sent everyone running for cover. Everyone except Gwen. *"Avanti!"* Sebastian yelled to her as he and Corwyn slid from their horses and squeezed under the awning of a nearby booth. "Get out of the rain."

But Gwen remained on her horse, looking as indifferent to his command as to the rain that wetted her, serene in her depiction of nobility. So convincing was she that it took Sebastian a moment to realize she probably was afraid to dismount in public, where any trace of clumsiness might dispel the impression she'd created of someone skilled in horsemanship.

A young bystander, his *lucco* made of fine linen and trimmed with fur to prevent anyone from underestimating his status, gave Sebastian a shove. *"Silenzio!* Is that any way to address a lady?"

Sebastian was too taken aback to respond. The youth swept off his bonnet and bowed to Gwen. *"Signorina,* may I offer my assistance?" With that, he ordered four of his comrades—all in their mid teens, Sebastian guessed—to grab the awning poles at the corners of the booth. The booth owner screeched in protest as the young men tore the poles loose and carried the awning to Gwen, where they held it over her and her horse. Corwyn, abruptly exposed to the rain, turned to Sebastian. "Yes, you certainly have done it this time," he grumbled.

"I don't understand," Sebastian snapped. "This wasn't supposed to happen. All I tried to do was raise her to a level equal to my own." He glanced quickly at his master. "To our level, that is—yours and mine. I wanted her to feel comfortable."

The young bystander next to Sebastian scowled fiercely. "You? On a level with her?" He jerked his head to indicate Gwen. "Don't be presumptuous—it'll cost you a beating."

"Is the lady's manservant being impertinent?" a second youth asked. "She's obviously a foreign noblewoman. Yet it sounded as if this fool was claiming to be her equal."

"She's what I've taught her to be," Sebastian said angrily. "And, yes, she is my equal."

"What'd he say?" the second youth asked, tugging on the sleeve of the first. "Why can't the English learn to speak? I can't understand his accent."

Steel sang as the first bystander drew his sword, ignoring his comrade's question. "Why, you miserable wretch," he hissed. He pushed his face into Sebastian's. "You're obviously nothing more than the lady's footman."

Sebastian opened his mouth to retort, his hand on the hilt of his own sword. The clanging of a nearby bell made him pause.

"That's the signal they use to start and close each market day," Corwyn whispered, pointing to a bell mounted on a tall marble column in the center of the square. "It also serves as a warning whenever a thief is loose in the market." He lifted his white eyebrows meaningfully. "This might be a good time to exercise restraint in the face of overwhelming experimental error. Shall we find our light-fingered friend and continue on our way?"

Sebastian searched the crowd for Oliver and finally spotted him leaving one of the stalls, walking more heavily than any broom had a right to. His hooded head was down as if in prayer, his hands clasped in front of him inside his draping sleeves. An army of beggars quickly surrounded the counterfeit monk, their wooden bowls out thrust as Oliver handed out stolen wealth like a gooseboy feeding his flock.

Sebastian winced and let his hand drop from his sword,

yet he also hoped Oliver would save some loot for his companions. They were running low on funds. "I merely said that it's upsetting to see the lady getting soaked like a common servant such as me," he muttered to the youth who stood glowering at him.

"What's that?" the second youth demanded. "His Italian's atrocious. I can't understand."

"He said something about the rain in *Spagna*, I think," the first youth replied, shaking his head. "Damned English can't speak without murdering the Italian tongue. It will forever condemn them to the gutter of humanity." He sheathed his sword and approached Gwen. "*Signorina*, I am Lorenzo de' Medici, also called *Il Magnifico*. I have organized a hunt for tomorrow and would be honored if you and your father"—he indicated Corwyn— "would join me."

Gwen hesitated, looking quickly to Sebastian. He groaned at discovering the youth belonged to the de' Medici family, whose library Corwyn would be using. With a slight motion to Gwen, he shook his head no.

"Well," Gwen told Lorenzo, "I don't know. It was a long journey, and—"

"*Signorina*," Lorenzo objected, "surely you wouldn't refuse me."

Sebastian shook his head at Gwen again, firmly. A trace of annoyance crossed her face. "You are very kind, *signore*, but—"

"I have never known a wellborn lady to turn down a hunt," Lorenzo said. Then, catching the direction of Gwen's gaze, he added, "You can even bring along your manservant, if you wish."

"He's not my servant," Gwen said. "He's my . . . my betrothed."

The Italian word—*fidanzato*—sounded awkward, though whether from unfamiliarity or something else, Sebastian couldn't tell.

Lorenzo shrugged. "Whatever," he said with an indolent smile. "He may come too, as if he were truly welcome."

While Lorenzo's attention was again fixed on Gwen, Sebastian shook his head emphatically. Gwen, observing him, tightened her mouth. "We should be glad to come," she said. "At least, I would."

With a smile, Lorenzo stooped to kiss her hand.

"Oh, look," Corwyn called out gaily, grabbing Sebastian as the latter surged forward to intervene. "The rain has stopped. Come Gwen, Sebastian. And there's Oliver. Now we can continue on our way." Firmly, he guided Sebastian toward the north side of the market. Gwen nodded to Lorenzo's companions who had sheltered her. They fell all over themselves sweeping off their bonnets and bowing as she rejoined Corwyn and Sebastian.

"Until tomorrow, *signorina*," Lorenzo said, bowing again as well. "We leave from the San Gallo gate at dawn."

When they were safely on their way once more, Corwyn let go of Sebastian. Sebastian fumed, wondering which bothered him more: his being taken for Gwen's servant, or her acceptance of Lorenzo's attention.

The next day, clear skies offered a break in the rainy weather, although by mid morning clouds were building again to the west. Gwen watched them form, sitting restlessly on her palfrey on a sunny, olive-covered hillside north of Florence. She didn't really want it to rain again, she told herself; she just wanted to be free of the stultifying role which had trapped her. She longed to race through the fields with an abandon available only to commoners.

A vagrant breeze rustled the cypress and olive leaves, calling her. The sweet smell of white orris blossoms beckoned from low stone walls that terraced the countryside. Somewhere nearby, a nightingale sang a haunting appeal. Even her horse, shying skittishly and pawing the damp, fertile ground, seemed eager to spirit her away. After they escaped, Gwen told herself, she and the mare could rest in the shade of a fig orchard next to an old church, its gleaming, sun-bleached brick walls and red roof tiles just visible beyond the vineyard to her right.

Instead, she sat with rigid, ladylike poise in the wretched sidesaddle, uncomfortably warm under heavy clothes and close questioning as she parried the efforts of other women on the hunt to learn more about her and her companions. She held her mount in check and kept her responses vague, pretending not to notice the difference between what was asked and what she answered.

Damn Sebastian, she thought—and immediately regretted it. He was only trying to help; she knew that. But he couldn't treat her like property, even if they were betrothed.

At least the hunt gave Gwen an excuse to escape the city for a while. These gentle hills could scarcely compare to the wilds of her native Pyrenees, but she welcomed any similarities. Besides, anything was better than remaining in Florence today, where she and Sebastian would have been expected to help Corwyn and Oliver continue examining Cosimo's library. She felt a touch of guilt at this, but was at a loss as to how to deal with the alchemist's strange dejection of the day before, after he had found in the library the very works he sought.

Dogs bayed in the near distance, recalling Gwen to the hunt. Beaters and kennel keepers combed a lightly wooded area halfway down the hill, doing the actual work while the noblemen sauntered along for the kill. The women remained on higher ground, ostensibly to admire the men or to hunt smaller game, though today they were occupied with gossip and with politely determined prying.

Gwen was fending off another question about her family when Sebastian rode up. He looked around anxiously at the women surrounding Gwen, apparently trying to gauge how much had been said, how much revealed. Gwen tightened.

"Good day, ladies," Sebastian said, tipping the ridiculous blue cap he still wore from Pomme de Terre. Except it didn't look so ridiculous anymore, Gwen realized. Her tastes had become accustomed to the flamboyance of Italian styles. At least he had exchanged his motley attire for the slashed styling popular here in Italy. She smiled— he had even started wearing a modest codpiece.

There were coy whispers and titters among the women at Sebastian's greeting. Harnesses creaked and jingled to the restless stamping of horses, the animals shifting as if at random to give their riders a better view of the new arrival. One young woman even made so bold as to try holding his eyes in a blatant attempt at flirting. With a pang, Gwen realized that wild animals weren't the only quarry being hunted this morning, for Sebastian—betrothed or not—was considered eligible game by these women.

Sebastian looked uncomfortably aware of their interest. Yet Gwen noticed that he also sat straighter in his saddle. "Might I have a word alone with you, *senilità?*" he asked. The other women snickered. Gwen considered telling him he'd used the wrong word again, and that she wasn't senile, but decided against it. She nodded and let him lead her a short distance away.

"You didn't say anything, did you?" he asked when they wouldn't be overheard. "You didn't let anything slip that might tell them who you—or we—really are?"

"Of course not," she snapped. "What do you take me for?" She looked at him sharply. "But maybe that's obvious."

His jaw dropped. "What on earth?" He edged his horse closer. "What's the matter, Gwen? Is anything wrong?"

"Nothing's wrong," Gwen hissed, seething. "With you. I've won your bet for you, haven't I? It's gotten you what you wanted—to be one of the aristocracy again, and able to brag of being betrothed to a noblewoman as well. That's enough for you. Never mind the cost to me—I don't matter, I suppose?"

"You've won my bet! You've carried off the masquerade! Why you presumptuous—how can you say that?

Look what you've become with my help! I've won the bet only by teaching you to carry this off and shown Corwyn that I too can perform feats of social alchemy.''

His words stung deeply. "You *don't* care," she said, shocking herself with the thought. "All you want is approval from Corwyn. I'm nothing to you—not even so much as that cap."

She spoke in Italian, calling it a *berretto* and pointing to the cap from Pomme de Terre.

"Of course I care," he said. "And the word is *baratro*, Gwen. A noblewoman should speak correctly."

For a moment she simply stared. "Poor Sebastian," she said at last. "Night and day he slaves to make me a proper lady. Doesn't rest, doesn't eat. So much effort required to turn me from a peasant into a noblewoman, just so he can prove he's an alchemist like his master. The only problem is, I speak the language better than he. A *baratro* is a gulf or chasm, Sebastian. Unless you're referring to the gap between your ears, the word you want is *berretto*, or cap."

He looked startled, his mouth forming the words soundlessly as he considered this. Then he smiled and reached out a hand to her, suddenly gentle. "Gwen, I know you're tired. You ache from that saddle, your nerves are raw. But think what you're trying to accomplish. You've set out to adopt the majesty of a noble lineage, the greatest possession a person can have. Nobility flows in the hearts of the greatest men and women, and that's what I'm helping you to acquire. And acquire it you will." He patted her arm. Gwen gritted her teeth against his touch. "Now, let's go back over there and try it again."

He led the way back to the cluster of women. Gwen could see them watching surreptitiously, whispering as she and Sebastian approached. For a moment, panic clutched her. What had they heard or seen? Then she cast this fear aside, recognizing it as Sebastian's, not her own.

"Remember," he said softly, dropping back to ride

abreast of her, "keep to two subjects: the weather and everybody's health. Don't let yourself go on about things in general. I'll help you along, *ma chère;* you'll be quite safe."

Without thinking, she swung to slap him, but he was on the opposite side of her horse and her aim was thrown off by the sidesaddle. She succeeded only in knocking the cap from his head. Sebastian gazed at her, clearly startled, then dismounted and picked it up. Neither of them looked at the nearby women, though Gwen could feel the women watching, their whispers like the hiss of snakes. In spite of herself, Gwen felt sorry for Sebastian, whose face burned red with humiliation.

Lorenzo rode up before Sebastian could remount, thundering close to the group before reining in hard. Dirt showered Sebastian. "I might have known I'd find you here, hunting with the women," Lorenzo said as Sebastian brushed himself off. "It's just as well, perhaps. You weren't missed among the men."

Sebastian's face turned darker and he swore, falling back on his native Anglo-Saxon tongue in his anger. He grabbed for his sword, but Lorenzo swung his horse's hindquarters lazily around and kept Sebastian too busy dodging the beast to draw his weapon.

"The first kill was very exciting, *signorina,*" Lorenzo said. "I'm sorry you missed it."

Gwen opened her mouth. Before she could respond, however, Sebastian eyed her pointedly and blurted out, "Will it rain, do you think?"

Lorenzo looked askance at Sebastian, his face torn between perplexity and irritation. Sebastian stared at the azure sky as if the prospect of rain really worried him.

Gwen knew Sebastian expected her to follow his conversational lead. She scowled instead, trying to remember what game the men were hunting. "Did you kill a boar?" she asked Lorenzo.

On the other side of Lorenzo's horse, Sebastian shook his head at her.

"A boar?" Lorenzo repeated, then grinned. "There are no boars near Florence."

"I mean a bear," Gwen said quickly. Maybe that was what the nobles always hunted in the stories she'd overheard in her parents' tavern.

Sebastian signaled more vehemently for her to quit this conversation.

Lorenzo's grin grew into a chuckle. "How funny, *signorina*. There are no bears here either."

"A hare, then," Gwen said in confusion. "Perhaps I used the wrong word. Was it a hare you killed?"

Sebastian threw up his hands in despair.

Lorenzo laughed outright. "Ah, *signorina*, now you're playing a game with me, are you not? It is you women who are hunting hares; we men are after bigger game. I killed a roebuck, a fine one, and I'd be very happy if you would take it. A lady enjoys the hunt ever so much more with something to show for the day's activities."

Belatedly, Gwen looked to Sebastian. He rolled his eyes and turned to remount his horse, ignoring her unstated question. Gwen studied the two men in anger. Each was intent on forcing her into a mold that would fit her supposed station. She felt suffocated.

Before either man could react, Gwen slid from her horse and uncinched the sidesaddle. She let the wretched contraption fall to the ground, then gripped the horse's mane and bridle and clambered onto the animal's back, using the saddle for a step stool. She heard gasps of shock and outrage from the other women as she swung her leg over to straddle the beast, hitching up her skirts in the process. Her bare legs clung to the animal's sides. Sebastian and Lorenzo stared. Gwen glared back at Lorenzo.

"Keep your kill," she said. "I'll either get my own, or find excitement enough in the hunt itself to be sufficiently rewarded. Now, shall we get on with it?"

Without waiting for an answer, she kicked her heels into the animal's flanks, spurring the mare into a jolting trot across the field toward the other men, where the real hunting was taking place. Behind her, Sebastian's plaintive wail of "Gwen!" was all but overshadowed by Lorenzo's triumphant cry, "Now there goes a lady with spirit!" She heard both horses gallop after her, but was too exhilarated by the chase and too scared of falling off to look back or stop.

One way or another, she was determined to have some fun on this trip—even if it meant acting like a peasant again.

ACT 10:

Cosimo, Prince of Florence

"WHEW!" SEBASTIAN WRINKLED HIS NOSE AS HE, Gwen, Corwyn, and Oliver waited in the courtyard of the de' Medici palace for an audience with Cosimo de' Medici. "Something's rotten in the city of Florence!"

Gwen shushed him. "Sebastian, you may have been raised in France, but your nose is decidedly English. That's onions and garlic you smell. Careful what you say—Lorenzo tells me Cosimo's partial to them."

"Oh, so it's Cosimo's offense that's rank, then," Sebastian grumbled, irritated with her for bringing up Lorenzo. "I should have known." He considered adding that, since Florence had abolished its noble class a hundred years earlier, this so-called de' Medici "prince" was nothing more than an overrated moneylender. Discretion fought with his usual nature, however, and for once emerged the victor.

Instead, he went back to worrying about his master. Whatever Corwyn had seen two days ago in Cosimo's library had left him downcast. Last evening, the alchemist even suggested they return to Pomme de Terre rather than continue their journey. But perhaps Corwyn's silence now was merely concern over their upcoming audience. Cosimo de' Medici's "invitation" that morning had made it clear that he wanted to see the four of them, immediately.

The old de' Medici must have heard from Lorenzo about Gwen's wild, bareback ride on the hunt yesterday, Sebastian thought. Cosimo probably intended to reprimand all of them for her behavior. Sebastian would defend Gwen, of course, even though she never should have stripped the saddle from her horse and ridden it astride. Now they were in danger of being found out. Cosimo could have them imprisoned, even executed.

In the shadowed gallery surrounding the courtyard, Corwyn lurched like an irresolute specter among the works of sculpture on display. Sebastian thought the classical themes portrayed by many of the statues should please his master, although the alchemist was so distracted he might not have noticed.

Gwen, silent now as well, wandered from the courtyard where Sebastian stood and into the gallery with Corwyn to inspect a life-size, nude bronze statue of David. It was a shockingly sensual piece, and Sebastian felt embarrassed by Gwen's interest. A half smile formed on her lips as she examined the sculpture's midsection, where, although male, it was of childlike proportions. Sebastian grimaced and ran a hand over the front of his breeches to check his padding. At least if the *David* was anything to judge by, the Italians needed as much help filling their codpieces as did Sebastian.

In the courtyard, Oliver darted about, chasing sunbeams and urging the others to play. Sebastian brushed the creature aside. Oliver shrugged and ran to Corwyn, who ignored the first few tugs on his sleeve. Finally, the alchemist barked at the broom to hold still. Oliver did as he was told, squirming and fidgeting at Corwyn's side like an unruly child. Sebastian frowned at the broom's lack of decorum, ignoring his own restlessness.

At length, a handsome, older woman appeared at one of the doors that opened onto the courtyard. From her Circassian features, it was evident she wasn't native Florentine, but rather the slave, Maddalena, whom Sebastian had heard about, purchased for Cosimo when he was a young man. Their illegitimate son, Carlo, was now rector of Prato and protonotary apostolic—further proof of Cosimo's power.

Maddalena told them to follow her. Though phrased as a request, her tone was clearly one of command. "Don't say anything," Sebastian whispered to Gwen as they trailed after Maddalena through the door. "I'll tell Cosimo you've been too much in the sun here in Italy and that the heat affected your senses. You're a woman; he'll understand."

Gwen gave him an enigmatic look. "Do you think to claim I'm frail, simply because I'm a woman?" Without waiting for an answer, she strode ahead.

Maddalena led them to a large corner room of the palace—the counting room, she said as she ushered them in, then closed the door, remaining outside. Sebastian, following behind Corwyn, discovered the chamber to be surprisingly spartan. A few Flemish tapestries adorned the walls, and an ornately carved desk and set of chairs occupied the far side of the room. The only other furnishings were bare stools and high tables for keeping the numerous ledgers. The heart of the de' Medici merchant empire possessed a lack of ostentation that was unsettling.

The stronger smell inside the room added to Sebastian's discomfort. Looking about, he saw a rough-hewn old man in simple garb sitting behind the carved desk, munching a raw onion. Sebastian decided the man must be Cosimo's chief clerk and, since Corwyn obviously wasn't up to handling matters today, approached him. "*Signore*," he said, allowing condescension into his voice to ensure that the man was aware of the difference between their stations, "if you would be so good as to summon your master, I would like to explain yesterday's misunderstanding." He fanned the air and scowled at the onion to signify his displeasure.

Corwyn cleared his throat. "Sebastian," he said

softly. Sebastian motioned behind his back that everything was under control.

"Be careful, Sebastian," Gwen hissed in his ear. "Our safest path here is caution."

Sebastian's scowl deepened. That was just the kind of misgiving that would trouble a woman.

The old man's eyes flicked over Sebastian, then settled on Gwen. He rose with the stiffness of someone troubled by gout, bowed deeply, and held out a chair beside the desk. With a nod, Gwen allowed herself to be seated. The old man indicated for Corwyn to take the remaining chair and reseated himself behind the desk. Taking up a knife, he sliced the onion and offered portions to Gwen and Corwyn. Gwen declined with a murmur; Corwyn politely nibbled a piece.

Sebastian coughed loudly, letting his impatience show. "The lady has been much distracted lately, mumbling to herself and behaving oddly." He looked at Gwen as he spoke, hoping she would follow his lead. "She needs rest, *signore*, so if you would summon your mast—"

"You are unwell, *signorina?*" the old man asked in a gravelly voice, cutting Sebastian off.

"I am fine," Gwen replied. *"Molte grazie."*

"Then welcome to Florence, although I feel I'm receiving my fair city's conqueror. Certainly you have made a conquest with your arrival. My grandson Lorenzo talks of nothing else. And yet what he can tell me amounts to little, for much about you remains a mystery."

Grandson! The room shifted alarmingly as Sebastian, still standing, realized who the old man was. And Sebastian had just insulted him!

So much for avoiding execution.

Suddenly, something about de' Medici—perhaps a similarity in the hands or in the frowning expression—struck Sebastian. It was as though Cosimo had assumed the form of Sebastian's father and had returned from the dead to chide him for failing to live up to his dread commands. "Ah, poor ghost!" Sebastian murmured, staggering back. "I'd thought you safely buried."

"Sebastian," Corwyn whispered, grabbing his apprentice by the elbow. "Are you all right?"

Gwen awarded Cosimo a disarming smile as if nothing unusual was happening. "Now I understand where Lorenzo comes by his charm," she said. "But what's so mysterious about me?" She spread her hands, palms up. "I'm an open book, *signore,* for all to read."

Sebastian trembled as he stared at Cosimo, knowing the figure he saw was only an image formed in his brain, yet stricken by the force of it. "Are you here to sharpen my purpose of restoring the family name?" he asked softly. "Or would you have me look to my poor mother, divided from her judgment? What duty have I forsaken this time, that you've come to remind me of? Speak!"

"Sebastian!" Corwyn hissed, shaking him. "Who're you talking to?"

"You may be a book," Cosimo grumbled to Gwen, his gaze darting from her to Sebastian, "and perhaps even one that is open, as if for all to read. But what language are you written in, I wonder? Not Italian, for though you speak the tongue well, your accent places your nativity elsewhere. France, I think."

Sebastian shook his head to dispel the illusion. Once framed, however, his mind clung to it. He stepped to one side, hoping a different angle would help. Cosimo tracked him out of the corners of his eyes as warily as Sebastian's armed and grizzled father had once watched sons and foes alike. "Here, too, old fellow?" Sebastian asked from his new position. Then to Corwyn he whispered, "I think I see my father."

"Where?" Corwyn asked, looking about the room.

"In my mind's eye," Sebastian replied. "Dressed just as he lived. How he glares at me!"

Cosimo frowned with distaste, shifting so he could see past Gwen to where Sebastian now stood. Gwen brought de' Medici's attention back with a graceful wave of her hand, dismissing the interruption. *"Oui, monsieur."* She spoke loudly to be heard over Sebastian. "You're very perceptive. I am indeed French."

Corwyn stood so he blocked his apprentice from Cosimo's view. "Sebastian, are you mad?" he muttered.

Sebastian sidestepped Corwyn and moved to the other side. To his relief, the vision vanished. Only Cosimo remained, although that in itself was more than sufficient cause for alarm. Suddenly self-conscious, Sebastian grabbed his cap from his head and looked around for Oliver. He hoped the broom wouldn't cause another fiasco like the one at the banquet in Genoa.

"Some of the finest wines are French as well," Cosimo continued to Gwen, pressing his point delicately. "And are you also, like them, from the southern region?"

Sebastian saw Oliver near the doorway, poking at one of the tapestries. Sebastian hissed as the creature lifted a corner of the fabric and peered underneath. Oliver released the corner, but refused to respond when Sebastian gestured for the broom to come stand by him. Instead, Oliver gazed up at the woven image with an air of innocence.

Gwen, her back stiffened against the ruckus behind her, nodded in response to Cosimo's question. "We are from the small, independent duchy of Gardenia in southernmost France, nestled in the very foothills of the Pyrenees."

Sebastian tried to focus on their conversation, but Oliver distracted him. When the broom attempted to peer beneath the tapestry again, Sebastian snapped his fingers at the little creature, causing Corwyn to gesture for silence.

A startled look spread across Cosimo's features at Gwen's response, and de' Medici glanced briefly at Corwyn. The expression was short-lived, however, and Sebastian would have missed it if he hadn't happened to be watching. When Cosimo turned back to Gwen, his smile had returned. "The duchy of Gardenia," he mused. "Where you are"—he shrugged—"who?"

Gwen matched his smile. "No one of importance, *signore*."

Sebastian squirmed. Gwen should set their status as high as possible. Cosimo wouldn't be impressed by people of no consequence.

Cosimo snorted softly and peered at each of them. Sebastian grew hot under the old man's stare. In some ways, Cosimo so resembled his father. At last de' Medici jerked a chin in the apprentice's direction. "I think your servant needs to relieve himself, *signorina*. He's been restless since you arrived."

Indignantly, Sebastian held himself still.

"He'll be all right," Gwen said without looking, her tone grim.

"He's an Englishman, I'd venture," Cosimo said to her, his attention still on Sebastian. A malicious twinkle sparked the old man's eyes.

Gwen nodded.

"I thought so, from his accent and behavior." Cosimo rose and came around from behind his desk. "Put your cap to its proper use," he ordered Sebastian. "It was made for your head, not your hand."

"Thank you, *signore,* but it's very warm," Sebastian replied, still holding his cap.

"No, believe me, it's cold," Cosimo insisted. "The wind is northeasterly, and brings a chill from the snow that lingers on the Apennines."

Sebastian hesitated. Finally, not wanting to antagonize the man further, he put on his cap. "I suppose it is rather cold, *signore,* indeed."

"And yet it's sultry for this time of year," Cosimo continued, wiping his brow.

Sebastian whipped off the cap, wishing Cosimo would make up his mind. Perhaps the old man was senile, in which case it would be best to humor him. "Exceedingly, *signore*. It is sultry, as if it were . . . I can't say how." His words sounded lame, and he let them trail away.

"Please, remember your bare head," Cosimo went

on, sounding solicitous. He guided Sebastian's hand up
to replace the cap.

Suspicious now, Sebastian let the cap remain on his
head. De' Medici was beginning to irritate him, and
Sebastian felt an anger that might have been directed
against either Cosimo or his own father.

Cosimo returned to his seat and spoke to Gwen. "This
man is a fool and should be sent back to England."

"Why back to England?" Corwyn asked, cutting Sebastian off as the latter stepped forward to protest Cosimo's words.

"Why, because he *is* a fool. He'll either recover his
wits there; or if he doesn't, at least it won't matter."

Corwyn grabbed Sebastian, restraining him. "How so,
signore?" he grunted.

"His manner won't be noticed there," Cosimo replied,
"for in England, all men are fools as much as he."

In an instant, the old man again became the gloating
figure of Sebastian's father. His insult rang through the
room like echoes rising from the well of time, setting
off a cascade of memories. Sebastian flung off Corwyn's
hands and drew back to strike the specter for its insolence.
"Sebastian, no!" Gwen cried. "Stand back." Sebastian
hesitated. "Do as I say!" she snapped.

The specter shimmered, became Cosimo once more.
Sebastian lowered his hand reluctantly, feeling betrayed.
How dare Gwen speak to him like that, as if he really
were a mere servant! Cosimo wasn't a ghost, but he
wasn't a real nobleman, either; he was only a merchant,
little better than a fishmonger.

Corwyn pulled Sebastian away from Cosimo's desk,
then cleared his throat. *"Signore,* what are you getting
at?"

"Only that the age has grown presumptuous," Cosimo
told the alchemist with a shrug. "The toe of the peasant
treads so near the heel of the courtier that he galls his
own corns."

Through his outrage, Sebastian sensed sudden fear
emanating from Corwyn and Gwen. The room fell silent,

except for a slight rustle as Oliver tugged again on the corner of the tapestry. When the cloth failed to budge this time, Sebastian wondered vaguely at its sudden resistance, too preoccupied to give the matter full attention. Oliver cocked his stick head at the tapestry, then scuttled over to Corwyn.

"Are you suggesting we're not what we seem?" Corwyn asked at last, his voice a whisper in the quiet chamber. He waved Oliver away as the broom yanked on his sleeve and pointed to the tapestry.

Cosimo chuckled. But when he spoke, it was to Gwen. "Just as your servant"—he nodded at Sebastian—"obviously isn't nobleborn, so you cannot hope to hide your true breeding behind the guise of nondescript nobility, *signorina.*"

Sebastian's stomach cramped as anger gave way to growing dread. Gwen sat rigidly erect. Corwyn's face paled above his beard, and he pushed Oliver away again without looking.

"I don't know the real purpose of this masquerade," Cosimo went on, "but a masquerade it is. *Che vero è, signorina?*"

Dumbly, Gwen nodded her head. Sebastian tried to swallow and found he couldn't.

"Doubtless you have reasons for traveling *incognito,* and I need not know what those reasons are to respect them," Cosimo said. "But at least allow me the honor within the privacy of these walls of properly addressing the duchess of Gardenia." He bowed to Gwen. "Your grace."

Sebastian's jaw dropped. Cosimo thought Gwen was royalty—not just a noblewoman, but the ruler of a sovereign realm! For a moment, Sebastian felt triumphant. He had made good on a hasty boast by transforming Gwen into a duchess. His success was marred only by a twinge of jealousy at not being held of equal status.

Then all sense of triumph collapsed. Cosimo's mistake, however flattering, made the game Sebastian and his companions were playing infinitely more dangerous.

Gwen reached a hand to Cosimo. "Oh, no, you don't understand. I'm not—"

"That's all right, your grace," Corwyn interrupted, thrusting himself between Cosimo and Gwen. "We needn't worry about his knowing. I'm sure we can count on Cosimo for discretion."

"Of course," Cosimo said. Sebastian thought the old de' Medici's voice fairly dripped with calculated sincerity.

Gwen looked dazedly at Corwyn. "But—"

The alchemist must have shared Sebastian's sense of danger. He pulled Gwen to her feet even though she hadn't shown any intention of rising. "For now, your grace, let us determine how best to inform Cosimo of the real nature of your plans, so that this knowledge might work to your mutual advantage." He bowed to Cosimo. "Thank you, *signore,* for your time. And for the onion." He turned back to Gwen. "Shall we retire to your quarters, your grace, to discuss this?" He propelled her toward the door, indicating for the others to follow.

"Dr. Tox," Cosimo called out.

Corwyn froze. Sebastian looked around wildly for the real duchess's physician and personal adviser, wondering how the man had followed them here from Gardenia.

Cosimo nodded to Corwyn. "A word with you, Dr. Tox, if you please."

Corwyn dragged Oliver away from the tapestry, where the broom was motioning frantically for the alchemist's attention. "Wait for me at the Piazza San Lorenzo," Corwyn whispered, turning the broom over to Sebastian. "If I'm not there in fifteen minutes, the three of you flee the city."

"That Cosimo's a shrewd devil," Sebastian whispered to Gwen as Maddalena led them back through the palace to the entrance. "I'll bet he knows Dr. Tox isn't the duchess's adviser anymore."

Ahead of him, Gwen said nothing, making Sebastian uncomfortably aware of the void between them. He cleared his throat and tried again, anxious to direct attention away from the humiliation he'd suffered. It discouraged him to find himself still haunted by his father. "Cosimo must have found out Dr. Tox was caught embezzling."

There was no hesitation in Gwen's step to show whether she even heard.

Oliver, pulled reluctantly behind Sebastian, pried the apprentice's grip loose from his skinny stick arm and replaced it on the sleeve of his monk's robe. Without looking, Sebastian let Oliver make the substitution, too concerned with his own problems to do more than drag the broom along. The rough cloth of Oliver's robe jerked against Sebastian's hold a couple more times, then the broom seemed to relent to Sebastian's authority.

Maddalena reached the entrance and held the door for them, her normally impassive face quizzical as Sebastian followed Gwen into the hot Florentine sun. Sebastian wondered at this, then dismissed it.

From the outside, it was clear that Michelozzo, the architect for the de' Medici palace, had tried to conceal the fortresslike nature of the three-story building by giving an elaborate design to the upper stories. But the palace's defensive nature, intended as much to withstand assault from Cosimo's fellow citizens as attack by foreign invaders, was revealed in the rough-cut stones and windowless solidity of the ground floor. Sebastian shivered, feeling he had escaped from the building rather than having been freely let out.

"That whole business about Dr. Tox was probably just a trap," he muttered, no longer expecting a response from Gwen. "And Corwyn fell right into it."

They had emerged at the corner of Via Larga, the widest street in Florence, and Via dé Gori, which led to the church of San Lorenzo, a stone's throw away. Gwen headed for the church, with Sebastian a half step behind and still holding Oliver's sleeve. People on the street paused to snicker, infuriating him. Hadn't they ever seen an Englishman before?

When they reached the piazza in front of the church, Gwen turned. Sebastian knew she couldn't pretend not to hear him this time and continued his grumbling. "Cosimo has probably imprisoned Corwyn in there and we'll never get him out."

He waited for her to say something, but Gwen only stared past his shoulder. Finally, she looked at him. "Sebastian, where's Oliver?"

"Huh?" He turned to where he had been pulling Oliver by the sleeve, only to discover he'd been dragging an empty monk's robe behind him. No wonder people were laughing. His eyes traveled back to the impregnable mass of the de' Medici palace, rising from the earth as if thrust up by the very stones upon which the city stood.

Slowly, Sebastian swung back to Gwen, heartsick over his latest failure. "He's somewhere in the palace, with Corwyn."

"You're in a precarious position, Dr. Tox."

Cosimo's words filled the counting room with their veiled threat. Corwyn struggled to breathe the heavy, tainted air.

"Very precarious," Cosimo continued. "If the duchess ever learned about the funds you diverted from her husband . . ."

All at once, Corwyn realized where Cosimo had learned about the duchy of Gardenia, and why de' Medici had mistaken Corwyn for the duchess's one-time personal adviser, Dr. Tox. The year before, Dr. Tox had been enlisted by a man named Hydro Phobius to help with a scheme Phobius was conducting in the duchy. Phobius's plan called for bribing the then-duke, with payments to be delivered through Dr. Tox. Instead, however, Dr. Tox had deposited the payments into his own account in the de' Medici bank, where the amounts must have been substantial enough to warrant Cosimo's attention. Eventually, the scheme in Gardenia had been detected, along with Dr. Tox's indiscretions, and Phobius had escaped after taking revenge on the doctor by exposing him to demonic possession. For the past year, Dr. Tox had been an unwilling guest of the Inquisition, no more capable of using the money in his account than he was of scratching his own nose.

Somehow, Cosimo had figured out that Dr. Tox was a thief. But what else did the wily old man know? Apparently he hadn't heard about Dr. Tox's subsequent fate or he wouldn't have mistaken Corwyn for him. Did Cosimo know where the stolen money had come from or about the role Dr. Tox had played in Hydro Phobius's scheme?

Sudden doubt passed like a shadow through Corwyn's mind. Had Cosimo been involved with Hydro Phobius as well? But that was preposterous. Surely even Cosimo de' Medici wouldn't represent two thieves simultaneously, knowing one was stealing from the other. Nevertheless, Corwyn's skin turned cold at the possibility.

"As your banker, you can count on me for complete discretion, of course," Cosimo went on smoothly. "After all, what good would it do for the duchess to learn of your misdeeds?"

Corwyn almost smiled, although the thought behind the impulse was grim. With Dr. Tox out of the way, the bank could quietly help itself to the funds in the doctor's account. Since the money had been stolen to begin with, no one would be the wiser.

"However, there's always the danger of the duke or duchess finding out, as long as you remain employed by them." Cosimo smiled, further lowering the temperature. "Why live under that uncertainty, Dr. Tox, when you could be well rewarded here, providing a service to me?" He took a heavy leather purse from his desk, then stood. "But come, let's go somewhere more suitable for our conversation."

Acting the gracious host, Cosimo led the way back through the *cortile*, where Corwyn had noted the fine sculptures gracing the courtyard and gallery. He'd been impressed by these works on his previous trips to the palace, especially Donatello's *David*. In their unabashed celebration of the human form, such works approached the aesthetics of pre-Christian antiquity. Even the design of the *cortile* itself, as well as the surrounding palace, incorporated principles from Greek geometry, emphasizing the circle and the square. The effect was almost enough to make tangible that cultural resurrection Corwyn sought. Almost, but not quite—for something was missing. Corwyn had felt it since his first visit to the de' Medici palace two days earlier.

Apparently, there was more to this Renaissance than he'd dreamed of with his alchemy.

"Lovely, isn't it?" Cosimo asked, indicating the courtyard with a sweep of his arm. Coins jangled in the purse clutched in his hand. Corwyn nodded, lips tight. Cosimo beamed, and this time his satisfaction seemed genuine. "I will admit you've been a surprise to me, Dr. Tox. And I'm not a man who is easily surprised. From our earlier correspondence, you hadn't impressed me as much of a scholar, yet your arrival here has proven otherwise."

"Thank you," Corwyn said, unhappy at having his scholarship attributed to that wretched fool, Tox. "I'm afraid you mistake me for my better. But where is this leading?"

For answer, Cosimo took the alchemist from the courtyard and down a familiar corridor, to a door Corwyn recognized as that of the library. Cosimo flung the door wide. The coin purse in his hand thudded heavily against the wood. Startled scribes and scholars looked up, scowling at the intrusion, then, recognizing their benefactor, quickly returned to work.

"As you can see, I'm a great supporter of learning and the arts," Cosimo said. "I have assembled the greatest library since Alexandria, with thousands of works by Greek and Latin writers."

Corwyn looked where he was directed, his gaze sweeping the library he had first entered two days earlier. Everything Cosimo claimed was true; it was indeed the most extensive collection of books Corwyn had seen since his youth, many of them lost during the intervening centuries. Here were manuscripts by Sophocles, Aeschylus, Virgil, and Pliny, as well as more recent works by Dante and Petrarch. In some cases, the manuscripts were the only known copies left in existence. A few of the books had been printed with the new movable type which was quickly becoming popular. But all were traitorous works, it now seemed to Corwyn—intellectual witchcraft with the power to seduce.

Most significant, and the greatest concern for Corwyn, was the original copy of the Pandects of Justinian, a book which embodied the whole of Roman law. Its discovery had influenced the rebirth of civilization throughout Europe, and Florence regarded the book as the republic's most valued treasure.

Corwyn felt the weight of his years as he stared at the book's rich, gold-embossed binding. How useless the knowledge of the ancient world suddenly seemed to him. No, not *seemed*, he corrected—his search had proven that. The perfect, cultured civilization he remembered from his youth was only an old man's fantasy, constructed over the distance of too long a time.

Drawn to an inner summit where he teetered, Corwyn stared beyond the precipice into a flood of recollections he had suppressed for centuries, and that threatened now to drown him in despair. "What do you want of me?" he whispered. "Tell me, or I'll go no farther."

"Dr. Tox, scarcely a shipload of spices sails from the East without also carrying manuscripts collected by my agents," Cosimo said. He bounced the purse in the palm of one hand, making the contents jingle. "All of this collected learning, I offer to you, for I need someone to oversee the continued growth of my library, and ultimately the founding of an institute dedicated to the study of Plato."

Corwyn reeled at what Cosimo was offering him, a prospect he previously would have embraced. But an old man's memories could color the past, he now saw, enhancing its strengths and overlooking its weaknesses. The law alone left an indelible record of what values a former age had upheld, what crimes it had punished. Corwyn, abruptly thrust by the pandects into full remembrance, recoiled from the abuses he once had witnessed but had long forgotten. In his youth, the world had enjoyed learning and greatness, but had also turned blind eyes on misery and despair. The Roman Empire, victim of its own excesses, had been crumbling for more than a century by the time Corwyn was born. In its decadence, it had demonstrated a savagery unsurpassed by later barbarians. Even the great library of Alexandria had stood upon the achievements of enslaved peoples. In the end, it was Rome itself as much as any outside forces that had destroyed the empire and the library, killing the last and greatest of the library's directors—Hypatia, the only woman Corwyn had ever truly loved.

All the learning in Alexandria had not prevented the abuses of that bygone age, any more than it could now blunt the ruthlessness of Cosimo de' Medici, an acknowledged man of culture. So what good, Corwyn wondered, did Cosimo's library represent?

It was a question for which he no longer had an answer.

Corwyn stumbled back from the door. Cosimo watched him with a wry, bemused expression. "I . . . I must think this over," the alchemist said.

"By all means," Cosimo replied, smiling. Corwyn, seeing it, thought one could smile endlessly and still be a villain—at least, here in Florence. "Think it over," Cosimo went on. "But don't take too long. In the meantime, perhaps this will help you reach your decision." He took Corwyn's hand and laid the purse in it, wrapping the alchemist's fingers around the taut leather. The purse was heavier than Corwyn had realized. Before he could pull it to him, however, Cosimo grabbed his wrist. "Just be certain you make the right decision," de' Medici hissed, and let go.

Released, Corwyn fled toward the entrance of the palace, trying once again to outdistance the past. Cosimo's laughter pursued him, echoing through the corridor. *"Addio,* for now, Dr. Tox. Remember me."

Corwyn knew that as long as he had any memory, he would remember Cosimo. He hurried around a corner, then another. Near the counting room, he paused to catch his breath. He was leaning over, his hands on his knees, the coin purse dangling by its thong, when a movement up ahead caught his attention. There stood Oliver without his monk's robe, his stick form displayed for anyone to see.

Before Corwyn could say anything, the counting room door opened. A small, thin boy slunk out, then froze when he saw Corwyn. His black eyes looked large in his tightly sculpted face. Without a word, he bolted away from the alchemist, only to collapse in a tangle of arms and legs when Oliver jumped into his path and tripped him. The boy stared up at the broom from the floor and whimpered.

"Oliver," Corwyn panted, trotting over to them. "What are you doing?"

Oliver pointed from the boy to the counting room, then made motions as if lifting a curtain to peer underneath. The alchemist stared while the broom repeated the gesture. Finally, Corwyn's eyes widened and he turned to the boy, who lay huddled against the alchemist's legs to get as far from Oliver as possible. "Were you watching in the counting room from behind the tapestry?" Corwyn demanded.

The boy whimpered again and nodded.

"Who are you?"

"Niccolò." The boy's voice was a whisper. "Niccolò Machiavelli. Oh, please, you won't tell Cosimo I was there, will you?"

"Why shouldn't I?"

The boy considered this. After a moment, a sly smile brought a look of cunning to his serious face. "Because you're not who you claim to be. I could see it by your actions in the counting room." He looked at Oliver again and shuddered. "You're more of Hydro Phobius's agents, aren't you?"

Corwyn staggered back, stunned. Hydro Phobius? The man who had seduced the real Dr. Tox into betraying the duchy! The man who had taken Gwen hostage when Sebastian and Corwyn were hunting him in the Pyrenees!

Niccolò got slowly to his feet, his eyes on the purse in Corwyn's hand. "You came to get more money from Signor Cosimo for the destruction of Venice."

"Agents of Hydro Phobius?" Corwyn gasped. Niccolò started to turn away. With his free hand, Corwyn grabbed the boy's *lucco*. "The destruction of Venice? What are you talking about?"

Niccolò scowled at Corwyn's hand on his clothes and shook his head. "Don't think I don't know. I watched when your master's other agent, that simulacrum or whatever it was"—he shot a distasteful glance at Oliver— "demanded money last time. Signor Cosimo said then that he wouldn't pay any more until the job's finished." The boy sneered. "Better hurry. You've only got till Ascension Day." He paused to peer at Corwyn, suspicion narrowing his eyes. "You're not like that other agent, are you?" Suddenly, he pinched the alchemist's arm hard.

"Ow!" Corwyn cried, letting go of Niccolò to clutch his bruised skin.

For a moment, Niccolò stared. Then, before Corwyn could grab him again, the boy darted down the corridor. Oliver gave chase, but soon returned empty-handed. The broom shrugged apologetically at Corwyn.

"It's all right," Corwyn muttered, rubbing his sore arm. "Wretched child—I think he was trying to pluck the flesh from my bones. Well, we must go to Venice, and quickly." Corwyn slapped his thighs, wincing from the renewed pain that brought to his arm. "We can't let Hydro Phobius destroy so magnificent a city." He looked back toward the library and added under his breath, "Besides, it's better than what I've been offered here."

* * *

In the ballroom of his palace on the Grand Canal in Venice, Antonio Nessuno slouched in a chair, a letter from Jessica dangling from his fingers. The cavernous room was dark save for an eerie glow from the six-foot glass sphere mounted on a dais in the center of the floor. Staring into the pale light of the sphere like a man seeking comfort might peer into flames, Antonio could almost shut out the creatures frolicking around it and pretend he was alone.

They were a bizarre lot, these creatures who shared his quarters, from shambling, half-fleshed skeletons to goblins, wraiths, and sprites of magic—all drawn by the enchantment radiating from the sphere, dancing to its tune. An aging mermaid with pendulous breasts slapped her tail on the marble floor, keeping the beat and smelling like a fish too long out of water. Immature wyrms, not yet bound to treasure hoards that would keep them from the song in this room, writhed and wriggled to the rhythm. Mangy werewolves shifted between human and animal forms, pausing occasionally to scratch at fleas or to gnaw on their neighbors. And crowding everywhere were the sheeted dead—former tenants of Venice's now-empty graves.

Outside, pealing clock bells echoed over the canals, tolling midnight. A cadre of Germanic kobolds answered the call by scrabbling out of the hole they were digging in a far corner of the ballroom. Squat and muddy and bristling with superiority, they jostled the other creatures aside to march in formation around the sphere.

At the sound of bickering, Antonio's eyes focused on his houseguests. "Now is the very witching time of night," he murmured, "when churchyards yawn and hell breathes forth contagion, and we are engaged in such bitter business as would make the day quake to look upon."

Actually, the business Antonio was engaged in didn't require most of these creatures, nor was it limited to this time of night. The real work went on in shifts around the clock, except at midnight when the kobolds insisted on parading around the dais. The rest of the creatures in the room were here as a mere by-product of the force generated by the sphere, and they spent their time in its vicinity. Like a lodestone or siren, energy leaking from the sphere overflowed the vast hall, spilling out into the world to summon the dead and things supernatural. Once here, they quarreled and cavorted and got in the way of the kobolds, who had been brought in to excavate the final stage of Hydro Phobius's project.

The power of the sphere pulled at Antonio as well, for as a creature of magic, he was subject to its lure. But he also had been given strength of will in his creation, that he might resist temptation long enough to complete his tasks. Since his arrival in Venice, it had become a matter of pride to him never to stoop to the base veneration of the sphere exhibited by his fellows. It was an achievement without significance, he knew, but it was all he had of honor.

His hands sought the armrests of the chair now, as if to raise him to his feet of their own volition and propel him into the center of the room. The letter from Jessica, smuggled to him earlier in the day by her servant, fluttered to the floor. Antonio clenched his teeth and forced his hands back into his lap, where he toyed with the turquoise ring Jessica had sent him as a parting gift, trying to distract himself with its hardness. But the ring only reminded him of her. She'd told him to pawn it because she couldn't give him any more money; her father had confined her to the house and had cut off her clothing allowance. That was why she'd been unable to meet him several days earlier. Shylock would rather have Jessica enter a nunnery than allow her to marry Antonio and become, as he put it, "a breeder of fools."

Evidently, Shylock had known about Antonio's relationship with Jessica on the day Antonio had suggested a pound of his own "flesh" as bond for a further loan, and it had been this knowledge which had goaded Shylock into accepting the contract.

Suddenly restless beyond bearing, Antonio shoved himself upright and lurched across the floor. He pushed between two patchwork chimeras, cobbled together for some nefarious purpose long ago and left to wander the earth ever since. The pair scarcely noticed his rudeness, so obsessed were they with exchanging ill-fitting body parts while they danced, forever trying to remake themselves into paragons of beauty.

With effort, Antonio veered away from the sphere and staggered over to survey the kobolds' hole. Seepage from the canals obscured the bottom of the shaft, but Antonio gauged the creatures' progress by the amount of new mud heaped on the marble floor next to the opening. In a couple of days, he judged, the hole would be deep enough. The *Magdalen* should arrive by then. If he could hold Shylock off a little longer, Antonio's debt would be canceled when Venice and Shylock and Antonio all plunged into the sea together in a series of brief, momentous blasts.

Blasts that would also be the end of Jessica.

Tightness gripped Antonio's chest. On impulse, he squatted and thrust his hand into the oozing mound beside the hole. His was a form, he knew, upon which God had seemed to have set His seal, giving the world the assurance of a man. But the devil also had the power to create a pleasing shape, and in Antonio's case, that devil was his maker, Hydro Phobius. Antonio, even more than the descendants of Adam, was the very quintessence of dust. He withdrew his arm and stared at the dirty streaks on his skin as if seeing into his soul, wishing the clay from which he was made would melt, dissolving back into mud.

Something wet trickled down his cheek. He wiped it, only to leave a telltale smudge on his arm, and Antonio wondered whether even his tears gave forth soiled evidence of his guilt.

The tramp of booted feet at the door of the ballroom

intruded on Antonio's melancholy. He daubed again at the dampness on his cheek, then jerked around as another squad of kobolds arrived from one of the half-dozen other sites Hydro Phobius had set up within the city. Energy generated by the sphere was distributed to these sites, where it was used to pump massive quantities of groundwater from beneath the floor of the Venetian lagoon. The fresh water was then dumped into the city's canals. The pumping weakened the seabed under the lagoon, causing it to settle. In time, this alone would submerge Venice, but Phobius wanted a quicker, more dramatic climax to the city's destruction. The kobolds were therefore digging shafts at each remote site as well as here in Antonio's palace. When the *Magdalen* arrived with its cargo of Turkish detonators—enormous bronze casks filled with black powder—they would be placed in the shafts, where the explosions would crack the weakened lagoon floor, and Venice would disappear beneath the waves.

Antonio's first task after his creation had been to oversee construction of the sphere which was at the center of this plot. The sphere had been a technical impossibility until a local glassblower had rediscovered the secret of making clear glass. Soon, Antonio's final task would involve setting off the detonators which would destroy the sphere, himself, and Venice.

The squawk of a cockatrice, accidentally stepped on by a kobold in hobnailed boots, shattered the air of concentration in the room. For a moment, several of the figures dancing around the sphere hesitated, wondering whether this might be the dawn cock crow signaling them to return to their graves. Then the power of the sphere won out over uncertainty, and they resumed the ghoulish procession as they had at every dawning since their arrival. After a while, the offended cockatrice also went back to circling the sphere, going in the wrong direction as it invariably did, darting among the other creatures on spindly chicken legs and glowering, unable to comprehend why its deadly stare had no effect on corpses and immortals.

The sphere's purpose was to generate thaumaturgical flux, the force responsible for all acts of magic. It was this energy, produced on a scale never before attempted, which powered Hydro Phobius's pumping stations. In order to generate the high densities of flux needed, the outer surface of the sphere had been covered with an amalgam of mercury and tin, which turned the device into a large, spherical mirror, reflecting back upon itself the image of anything that occupied the interior. Inside the sphere was a captive fire elemental—one of the huge, homophobic "salamanders" whose abhorrence for their own kind kept them forever isolated from one another. Faced with its own reflected image in every direction, the enraged elemental sought escape by collapsing upon itself in the center of the sphere, thereby giving off energy that corresponded with its supernatural character.

Ideally, of course, thaumaturgical flux produced in such densities should have been shielded to prevent leakage. This would have kept unwanted creatures from cluttering up Antonio's quarters and would have protected Venice from the side effects of exposure. Phobius, however, wasn't concerned with Antonio's comfort or the safety of his neighbors. As a result, people near the sites who had never shown any magical talents suddenly found themselves capable of unusual skills, and the resulting charges of witchcraft had filled Venice's jails.

In the ballroom, a commotion broke out as several creatures began teasing one of the skeletons, tossing the figure's skull from one tormentor to another while the rest of the bones felt anxiously about the room for it. The skull snapped its jawbone angrily, trying to bite its persecutors. Then a willowy young wood nymph missed a catch and the skull rolled to a stop against Antonio's boot.

Antonio picked the relic up, careful to keep his fingers

away from the clacking teeth. What a piece of work was
man, Antonio reflected—of which he himself was but a
poor imitation. This skull had had a tongue in it once,
and could speak. Perhaps it had been the head of a pol-
itician or a courtier or even a lawyer, hiding its emptiness
behind fine words. Now that emptiness had been made
visible, the cranium devoid of anything but a bit of sand
spilling into the air. Antonio wrinkled his nose. Sand,
and a residual smell. He lobbed the skull to the feet of
the searching skeleton. "Alas, poor fellow," he said with
a grimace. "I never knew him."

Even a lawyer's bones remained, Antonio thought.
When he himself was gone, there would be nothing at
all to mark his passing.

When he was gone . . . There wasn't any question in
his mind whether he would continue to exist or not—
he'd known since his first awakening what his end was
to be. Everything he'd done since then had been on Hydro
Phobius's behalf, and had helped advance that end.
Everything, that is, except loving Jessica. Now, for the
first time, Antonio tasted the full bitterness of his fate,
and wished it could be otherwise. He hadn't expected
this final irony. Life as Phobius's minion was torment,
but the release offered by the destruction of Venice would
take even Jessica from him.

Would he dream when he was dead? he wondered.
If so, perhaps he would dream of her. Or did creatures
that left no bones behind leave nothing of consciousness
either? What right did he have to believe he had a
soul? In sudden fury, Antonio spun on the sphere,
seeing in it the spectral face of his maker, his diabolical
"father."

"Leave me alone!" he shrieked, startling the other
creatures in the room. "Let me go, or by heaven I'll
make a proper ghost of you. I should have fed you to
the crows by now."

He clenched his fists in a silent appeal for strength to
carry out his vow. Yet already his rage was turning im-
potent, draining away like sand trickling from an up-

turned, ancient skull. The sphere wove a mocking refrain in his head. When honor was at stake, how then could he stand, who had no honor? Defeated, Antonio trudged back to his seat across the room, where Jessica's letter lay upon the floor. "I remain constant to my purpose," he murmured to the fallen sheet, "and follow my maker's pleasure."

Tomorrow, he would pawn Jessica's ring. After all, he told himself, it was what she had intended.

ACT 11:

The Tempest

WHEN CORWYN DREW UP JUST BEYOND RAVENNA, EAST of Florence on the Adriatic coast, Sebastian breathed a sigh of relief. He and his companions were soaked from a cold drizzle that had been falling since they'd crossed the Apennines, the mountains that ran like a backbone down the length of Italy. They had ridden for hours, and now Sebastian's horse was limping. Sebastian didn't know what was wrong with it, but the animal's gait had become increasingly off rhythm for several leagues, and Sebastian doubted the beast could travel much farther.

Neither, for that matter, could he. Bad enough being on a good horse when he was unaccustomed to riding, but a halt one was worse. He groaned as he slid from the saddle, then steadied himself against the animal's side. For the next few days, his own gait would be as lame as his mount's.

They sought refuge in a small tavern on the waterfront. The smoke-filled common room overflowed with sailors waiting out the rain, which was expected to worsen. Sodden rushes covered the floor. Strings of dried herbs—thyme, marjoram, and coriander, as well as the ubiquitous garlic and onions—hung from low rafters, mingling their spicy odors with the smells of cheap wine, wet

wool, and mildew. Corwyn directed Gwen toward a pair
of empty stools in a corner of the room, and Sebastian,
wrinkling his nose against the stench, scrounged around
until he found a third, then dragged it over to join them.
The three stools were as dilapidated as the tavern itself,
but—like it—would have to do for now. Oliver could
stand.

As Sebastian huddled on his seat, he wondered dully
why Corwyn was in such a hurry to reach Venice. He
understood their abrupt departure from Florence after the
audience with Cosimo de' Medici: there was too much
chance Cosimo would discover they weren't who they
pretended to be. Sebastian also had personal reasons for
putting the encounters with Cosimo and Lorenzo behind
him. Cosimo in particular had resurrected memories Sebastian wanted laid to rest. Sebastian was through with
ghosts from the past, content to be under Corwyn's tu-
telage.

Even after they were out of the city, however, Corwyn
had kept urging them on. He did say something about
Venice being in danger, although it had been difficult to
talk on the road, what with the rain and the need to ride
single file over narrow, mountainous trails. Besides, Corwyn hadn't been very communicative lately. If anything,
he was more withdrawn than ever. This worried Sebastian, and he wondered whether he had disappointed Corwyn (again!) and whether his master was purposely
shutting him out. That seemed in danger of becoming a
trend; since the audience with Cosimo, Gwen had treated
him to silence as well.

In the tavern, a grizzled old man won a place for
himself near the fire by producing a small hurdy-gurdy.
Sebastian had seen such instruments before, of course,
though usually they were square and boxy. This one had
the deeply rounded look of a lute. The old man turned
a crank at one end, creating a steady drone from four
fixed strings. With his other hand, he varied the pitch
on two additional strings by means of keys mounted
above the soundboard. The melody he played was simple

but lively, and evidently familiar to the other patrons.
Soon most of them were singing what Sebastian gathered
was a sailing song, although it might have been about
tubs of marinating pickles—he wasn't sure of his trans-
lation.

Corwyn, who had been staring off with a glum expression, got up abruptly and pushed his way through the
swaying, bellowing throng to the tavern owner. The pro-
prietor listened to Corwyn while ladling stew into bowls,
occasionally wiping his hands on a greasy leather apron.
Then he pointed to a dark, hairy figure hunched against
a post across the room. More like an animal than a man,
the stranger surveyed the crowd with the feral look of a
predator. Corwyn made his way over to him and soon
they were deep in conversation.

Sebastian grimaced and turned his attention to Gwen.
She was peering through the haze with a wistfulness he
hadn't noticed when they had stopped at taverns previously. "Are you missing the Reluctant Virgin?" he
asked, thinking of her parents' tavern in Pomme de Terre.

Slowly, she focused on him, staring. Even in rough
traveling clothes, she looked regal, and Sebastian felt
disoriented when he tried to picture her serving wine
again in the Reluctant Virgin. "I'm missing my home,"
she said at last with peculiar emphasis. "I thought it was
your home as well."

Sebastian shifted, suddenly uncomfortable. He
glanced around for Oliver. Behind Gwen, two sailors
began a clog dance in the center of the room, while the
crowd roared its approval. "Pomme de Terre *is* my
home," he said. "I suppose."

"I don't think so," she replied, shaking her head.

The sea chanty—or pickling song, whichever it was—
ended and the hurdy-gurdy player began a mournful song
about love gone wrong. For a moment, Sebastian's heart
froze as he thought he spotted Oliver without his robes,
then realized it was only the tavern's broom propped in
a corner. Someone had draped an old cleaning rag over
the top of the broom's handle, and it looked as though

the broom were wearing a scarf. "If Pomme de Terre's not my home, what is?" Sebastian asked.

Again Gwen shook her head. "I don't know. I wish I did."

Her answer stabbed deeper than Sebastian wanted to admit. He continued searching the crowd for Oliver as if the broom's whereabouts were important.

"What are you turning me into?" Gwen asked, leaning forward, her voice a tense whisper.

Suddenly, Sebastian realized there were two brooms in the corner—Oliver, fortunately still dressed in his monk's robes, and the ordinary tavern broom used for sweeping. "Huh?" he answered, distracted.

"What are you trying to make of me?" Gwen asked again. "Isn't it enough for me to be who I really am?"

Sebastian's face went hot. "Of course it is," he insisted, his eyes still on Oliver, who was approaching the tavern broom with hesitant, bashful gestures. "You are enough, Gwen—for me."

The love song ended on a long, quavering note and was replaced by another rollicking tune. A one-eyed man with a recorder played accompaniment. Across the room, Oliver gestured toward the middle of the floor as if inviting the tavern broom to join him.

"You don't show me that," Gwen said quietly, oblivious of what was happening behind her.

Sebastian started to object, then choked off, half rising from his stool as Oliver gathered the other broom to him and swirled across the floor in a madcap dance. The tavern erupted in laughter. Someone began clapping to the rhythm and soon the other patrons were clapping and stomping while Oliver, looking like a midget monk, danced with his ragtag partner.

Sebastian took a step forward. "Damn Oliver," he swore. "He'll ruin everything!"

"Leave him alone," Gwen hissed. "You're just angry because he refuses to be anything but himself." She eyed Sebastian in bitter appraisal. "Poor Sebastian. Does Oliver, too, shame you with his humble origins? He's the only one of us you haven't reshaped in your own godlike image.''

''What have I done?'' Sebastian asked. ''You said yourself you were lending a hand. What about the phoenix, aiding in her own transformation?''

''I didn't realize I'd be losing myself in the ashes that remained behind.'' With that, Gwen spun and crossed the room to Corwyn, who was returning toward them.

Sebastian stood, stunned. How could Gwen accuse him of such a thing? He wasn't trying to make his companions like himself. Far from it. He was simply sparing them the anguish he had suffered from not fitting in. And as for being ashamed of Oliver—well, that just wasn't true . . . was it?

He strode over to Gwen and Corwyn to tell her so, but the alchemist cut him off before he could begin. ''I've been talking to Caliban, the mate on a ship bound for Venice, carrying wine from Spain.'' He shouted to be heard over the roar of the crowd. ''The captain plans to leave with the tide. He's overdue in Venice now and only put in here for repairs. Caliban assures me the captain will grant us passage the rest of the way—apparently, he never passes up a chance to increase his profit—so we won't have to ride overland. The coast north of here is marshy at best, but it'll be impassable from the rain. The tavern keeper is buying our horses.''

Sebastian glanced at Gwen, saw his reluctance mirrored there. ''Corwyn,'' he began, ''maybe if you told us what this is all about—''

''We'll talk about it on the way,'' Corwyn interrupted, ushering his apprentice toward the door. ''Right now, we don't have time. Where's Oliver? The tide is changing.'' Behind them, a cheer rose as Oliver cut an elaborate caper with his wood and straw partner. ''Oh, Oliver, there you are. Come here. Sebastian, get moving. We've got to get to the dock with Caliban before the captain shoves off.''

Sebastian stole another look at the ship's mate who looked like a beast impersonating a man. The hairy fellow caught his gaze and grinned savagely, then sauntered toward the door. Sebastian shuddered again, reluctant to leave the security of the tavern. But even as he hesitated, Corwyn gave him another shove from behind, pushing him after Caliban. Gwen and Corwyn followed, with Oliver firmly in tow. "I'm sorry, Oliver," Corwyn said, "but we have to leave right now."

Sebastian half expected Oliver to answer, but of course he didn't. Nevertheless, Sebastian glanced over his shoulder, puzzled by the broom's silence. Oliver, torn from his newfound friend, was struggling mutely with Corwyn, his thin arms stretching past the alchemist toward the other broom, now lying abandoned on the tavern floor.

Sebastian hurried out into the rain, feeling terrible and wishing he hadn't looked.

Corwyn stood by the railing of the *Magdalen,* staring into the storm that had overtaken the ship. He was remembering again how much he hated travel by water. For someone who specialized in this particular element, seasickness left him remarkably unsuited for traveling on it, especially with the waves and the rain vying for the chance to drown him. Unfortunately, it was too late to change his decision now. Besides, if Hydro Phobius was behind a scheme to destroy Venice, Corwyn had to get there and stop him.

The alchemist groaned and gripped the railing tighter, seeking to allay the swells through force of will. From the dock, the two-masted, lateen-rigged caravel had looked like a plump little dove riding out the rain, an image Corwyn had found encouraging. He imagined that such a ship would bob lightly on the waves, and so it had—bobbing and bobbing, up and down, tossed by the storm. . . .

Sebastian lurched across the deck toward Corwyn in what the alchemist assumed was a misdirected attempt by the youth to lift his master's spirits. Corwyn wished Sebastian would spare them both the effort; the last thing he wanted right now was a witness to his misery. Sebastian, however, unaware of being slighted, hunched beside his master, saying nothing for a time as he shielded himself from the slanting rain. "Quite a storm," he called at last.

The words came out muffled by the wind, and it took Corwyn a moment to figure out what his apprentice had said. Then the obviousness of the statement seemed to make a reply unnecessary.

Across the deck, Gwen stood with Oliver, and Corwyn wondered why Sebastian didn't go over and bother them. But Gwen and Sebastian had scarcely spoken to one another since they'd left the tavern, and Oliver apparently needed comforting after being forced to leave his dancing partner behind. Corwyn knew he'd feel bad about having dragged Oliver away—as soon as he felt well enough to feel bad about anything.

After a while, Sebastian shouted again, "God's will be done, but I'd rather die a dry death than drown."

This statement also was too self-evident to require an answer. Of course Sebastian was afraid of drowning; he couldn't swim. But something else roused the alchemist's curiosity. The words had sounded indistinct, even considering the noise of the storm, like a man talking with his mouth full. With morbid fascination, Corwyn peered more closely. In Sebastian's hand was a pickle—huge, grotesque, revolting. Corwyn's stomach reeled. Sebastian thrust out his hand, offering a bite. Corwyn shook his head and pressed his lips together.

"You sure?" Sebastian yelled, chewing another mouthful. "It's pretty good."

Corwyn groaned through clenched teeth and edged along the railing away from his apprentice. Obviously, Sebastian could stop worrying about a watery grave, he decided grimly. As the old proverb said, a man that's born to hang needn't fear drowning. All Corwyn lacked to prove this in Sebastian's case was a length of rope. He glanced about the deck.

"It's funny, I've been wanting a pickle since we

stopped at the tavern outside Ravenna,'' Sebastian went on, following his master along the rail. ''When the other patrons started singing, I couldn't tell whether the song had to do with sailing ships or tubs of pickle brine, but it got me remembering the kitchen on my family's manor when I was growing up. I used to hide in the pantry as a boy, despite the stink when the pickles were fermenting. I still recall how stifling it would be, huddled in the darkness, listening to the crocks bubble as their contents churned, the aromas of stored foods and pungent spices overlaid with the smells of vinegar and brine, all of it filling the air of that little room. . . .''

Corwyn lunged over the railing, cutting off Sebastian's story and almost toppling himself into the sea. To the alchemist's dismay, Sebastian prevented him from falling with a tight grip on his robes. Then Corwyn lost interest in anything but the need to relieve his stomach of every meal he'd eaten in eleven hundred years. It was the price he paid, he told himself miserably, for daring to live so long.

Gradually, the crisis subsided to a more tolerable level of agony. Corwyn hung—cold and bedraggled—over the closely fitted wooden planks of the ship's hull and watched the grey swells rush by, rising toward his face as if to engulf him and then dropping away again. When physical discomfort ceased to demand his full attention, remorse took over. Regrets accumulated during the equivalent of several normal lifetimes weighed on him, but none more heavily than the ones acquired on this trip. Not only had he failed to identify the philosopher's stone which would transform Gardenia, but he himself had misremembered the past, recreating his own Alexandria into a dream that had never existed.

Somehow, despite ignorance and superstition, the Renaissance was taking place throughout Italy. The transformation was flawed, of course, yet the fact that it was occurring at all led Corwyn to doubt his conclusions. Ultimately, it forced him to question his abilities as an alchemist.

Now, his powerlessness over the storm threatened a complete collapse of his faith. What was the good of neglecting worldly ends and dedicating himself to the betterment of his mind for all these centuries if he couldn't use what he'd learned to save the people who mattered to him?

Corwyn struggled to right himself, floundering helplessly until Sebastian pulled him backward onto the deck like some wretched creature fished up from the depths of the sea. He flopped onto his back, his robes awash in the waves that increasingly crested the ship. Lightning briefly lit up the world. Peering through a blur of rain and salt spray, Corwyn studied his three companions: Gwen, whose carefully constructed regal facade couldn't quite hide the price she was paying for her transformation; Sebastian, an unwitting sorcerer's apprentice whose efforts to prove himself, combined with Corwyn's inattention, had wreaked this havoc on Gwen; and Oliver, driven throughout the journey to seek the company of corpses and inanimate objects because his creator had been too distracted to spend time with him.

Was it right for Corwyn to be placing them in peril without even telling them of the danger? Not that there had been time to warn them, he told himself. Yet the real problem, he knew, was his own longevity. It left him insensitive to the ephemeral nature of others' lives. Long stretches of Corwyn's life had been devoted to contemplation and seclusion. He tended out of habit to think in terms of epochs, eras, and centuries, forgetting that those around him were bound to shorter spans. It was both the advantage and the curse of living such a long time.

Now, he had inadvertently allowed his friends to hurt one another, leaving the fragile vessels of their beings to founder in the uncharted waters of human experience.

A huge wave crashed onto the deck, inundating Corwyn. Only Sebastian's grip on the alchemist's robes kept him from washing away. He sat up, spluttering and choking, determined to quit thinking in nautical metaphors.

Better to say he had allowed his friends to become lost amid the burning sands of uncharted personal deserts—images of aridity were much more appealing right now than anything related to the sea.

The ship's mate shouldered his way across the deck, lithe as a panther despite the storm. *"Vivace,* you men there," he shouted to the sailors. "Yare, yare. Take in the top sail. Tend to the master's whistle."

"Caliban," Corwyn yelled from where he lay sprawled on the deck, "where is your master? I still haven't seen him."

The mate scowled down at the bedraggled figure. Lightning flashed again, and Caliban waited until the thunder died away before he replied. "What are you doing up here? Get below."

"But where is your master?" Corwyn insisted. He staggered to his feet, hoping to present a more forceful appearance.

"Don't you hear him? Now get below. We're nearing the Venetian lagoon and you're in our way. All you can do out here is assist the storm."

"Now, be civil—" Corwyn began.

"When the sea is," Caliban snapped.

Another wave crested the ship, emphasizing his words. Corwyn choked as water swirled over him, and he decided it might be well to remain close to Sebastian after all. A man destined to hang might be the only anchor in such a storm.

"If you don't get below," Caliban continued when the water subsided, "I'll throw you into the sea myself." He started to turn away, but a violent lurch from the ship threw him to the deck. The ship shuddered and listed precariously. Suddenly, the main mast tore loose and thundered down next to Corwyn and Sebastian. "Mercy on us; we split, we split," came shrieks from the sailors. Caliban jumped to his feet, swearing. "Lay her ahold, ahold," he shouted. "She's run aground."

"Oh my God," Sebastian wailed. "Corwyn, look!"

The alchemist stared along the length of the toppled

mast to where Sebastian was pointing. Another flash lit
the scene in harsh relief despite the rain. Across the deck,
next to Oliver, the end of the mast jutted out over the
water, having smashed the railing in its fall. Fortunately,
the mast hadn't fallen on Oliver. Then the significance
of the broom standing alone at the shattered railing struck
Corwyn. Gwen had been hurled overboard!

Sebastian grabbed Caliban, who was hurrying toward
the high aft deck. "Hurry! You have to rescue Gwen."

Caliban shook him off. "Save her yourself. Would
you have us all drown?" He ran after a pair of sailors
who were crying that all was lost and were making for
the ship's boat.

"But I can't swim!" Sebastian shrieked into the gale.

Corwyn and Sebastian tried to climb the sloping deck
to where Gwen had stood in hopes of spotting her, but
the ship's cant was increasing and they couldn't gain
purchase on the slippery wood. Oliver motioned frantically to them from across the ship, pointing over the side
where Gwen had fallen. Then, when Corwyn and Sebastian failed to reach him, the broom turned back to the
sea. Helplessly, Corwyn watched Oliver leap into the
waves after Gwen.

Corwyn grabbed Sebastian, who was still struggling
to climb the deck, and pulled him to the fallen mast.
"But, master," Sebastian protested, "what about
Gwen?"

Corwyn shook his head. "Whatever her fate, we can't
help her now. But if I don't tie you to this mast, you'll
drown." He snared a rope that had torn loose from the
rigging and bound Sebastian to the toppled beam, aware
of the irony in a length of rope being the means of saving
Sebastian from drowning after all.

For good measure, Corwyn fastened himself as well.
He had just tied off the end of the rope when the night
was rent with a blast like a dozen bolts of lightning
striking simultaneously. The vessel lit up in a hideous
flash even as it was torn asunder. The explosion lifted
the mast free and flung it into the waves. When it rose

heavily to the surface, Corwyn and Sebastian emerged with it, choking and spluttering, but alive. Thunder and a horrible sulfurous stench engulfed them. It was as if, Corwyn thought, the lowest regions of hell itself had erupted beneath the ship to swallow the entire Venetian lagoon.

ACT 12:

Two Gentlemen from Barcelona

BY THE TIME THE TEMPEST PLAYED ITSELF OUT, SEBAStian was nearly senseless from the constant dunking. The rain slackened and the swells diminished, though the sea remained uneasy. With the approaching dawn, Sebastian was finally able to distinguish between up and down, between air and water. He took deep breaths of the one and quit trying to inhale the other, then looked about for Gwen. But it was still too dark, he decided, because he couldn't see her. Nor could he see his blue cap, which had washed away during the storm.

Choppy, slate-grey waves lapped against the mast at his back—the one to which he was tied—leaving him as queasy as the aftermath of a drinking bout. He regretted the pickle he had eaten hours earlier, and shivered with cold and exhaustion. Beneath the surface, something nibbled at his shoe. Sebastian kicked in alarm, hampered by the rope that bound him. The nibbling ceased, only to resume a moment later.

A groan reminded him that he wasn't alone. He twisted against his bindings until he could just make out Corwyn behind him, on the opposite side of the mast. The two of them were tied back to back, with the mast crosswise between them. Corwyn glanced over his shoulder at Sebastian with a wry smile. "Lucky for us we weren't killed by the blast that destroyed the ship. I doubt anyone else survived."

"Oh, yes . . . the blast," Sebastian said, the memory slowly coming back to him. He frowned. "What happened? Did we get struck by lightning?"

Corwyn snorted and shook his head. "No, not lightning. Whatever it was came from the ship itself. I suspect the cargo on the *Magdalen* was something more potent than wine."

Sebastian puzzled over this while Corwyn turned away again. "The ship must have gone down near one of the inlets to the lagoon," the alchemist said. "Apparently, the storm washed us on in." His voice sounded husky with inner emotion, or maybe just fatigue, but his words reassured Sebastian who took them to mean that Gwen and Oliver had probably been swept into the lagoon as well.

Corwyn jerked his chin in the direction he was facing. "Look, there's Venice."

Sebastian strained to see, but could turn no farther than to glimpse the distant mainland, a grey smudge slightly darker than the water and veiled in mist where the shoreline rose toward the mountains beyond. "If only the waves had cast us a little closer," he said, uncomfortably aware of the nibbling sensation at his foot. He kicked again, forestalling a fate that began to seem inevitable.

"The waves were more generous with us than with the others," Corwyn said sharply. Then his voice softened. "I think if we untie ourselves, we can paddle the mast right into the Grand Canal."

To Sebastian, who couldn't swim, the thought of casting loose from the one thing that kept him afloat was alarming. He started to say so, but was interrupted by a cry of *"Finito!"* from Corwyn who had been struggling with the rope. The alchemist flung the loose end aside and promptly dropped beneath the surface, his cry of victory turning to a gurgle. Panic surged through Sebastian. He fumbled at the rope which still held him. Before he could undo it and attempt some kind of rescue, however, Corwyn's head and shoulders burst free of the water. "I forgot this gold from Cosimo is tied around my waist," he spluttered. "It weighs a ton!"

Sebastian watched his master enviously, admiring the way he swam in place without apparent effort. Then Corwyn reached both hands up to loosen Sebastian, the alchemist's chest rising further from the water. Sebastian frowned. "How do you do that?"

Corwyn paused, looking puzzled. "Do what?"

"How do you float so high out of the water without moving?" Sebastian said. "Especially with all that, gold."

"Oh, that." Corwyn came around the end of the mast, chest deep in water and looking sheepish. "I also forgot the lagoon is so shallow. You can stand upright in most of it." He finished untying Sebastian. "See for yourself."

Sebastian's legs dropped the short distance to the bottom, then sank several inches into mud before coming to a rest. The nibbling sensation intensified, moving up both legs. Sebastian kicked violently and flailed his arms, terrified of the unseen danger threatening him from the lagoon floor. Water flew everywhere. Corwyn grabbed Sebastian and held him until Sebastian stopped. When the alchemist finally let go, it was to wipe the water from his ancient face and beard. "Are you all right?" he asked.

Sebastian felt himself go hot as he realized the tickling was from marsh grasses submerged by high tide. They drifted back and forth against his legs like a kelpie caressing her victim. Sebastian shivered, then pretended it was from the cold. He glanced at Corwyn, but the alchemist's face showed only concern. "Fine," Sebastian lied, surveying the watery expanse around him suspiciously. "I'm fine now."

Corwyn nodded and licked water from his lips. His expression became thoughtful. He licked again, then bent over to lap at the water of the lagoon. Sebastian grimaced.

"That's odd," Corwyn said. "The water's fresh." He shrugged and pointed eastward to where the rising sun had burnished the mist with gold. "At last, it's day. This has been the longest night I've ever watched, and the heaviest." He shook his white head ponderously. "Spring's too uncertain a season for travel. I should have known better. But who'd believe a glorious April morning could follow yesterday's clouds, after they seemed to have stolen all sunshine away?"

The alchemist's words conveyed a sorrow that Sebastian couldn't comprehend. At a loss as to how to respond, he said nothing, looking about instead for Gwen and Oliver. It bothered him that they still hadn't been seen.

Corwyn started toward Venice, breasting the water in long, slow strides and pointing out sights like some waterborne tour guide. Sebastian struggled in Corwyn's wake, hampered despite longer legs by his determination to push the broken mast ahead of him, just in case.

Gradually, the spires and towers of the city took shape as they approached, revealing not the splendid goddess Sebastian had imagined, raised up from the deep in virgin purity on a bed of oyster shell, but a bedraggled Venice that seemed awash in a drunken stupor, sprawling on the waves like a faded courtesan after a night of debauchery. They passed several smaller islands and finally entered the basin of San Marco, where debris from the storm littered the waterway. Off to the right, toward the Arsenale, ships lay mired in muddy shallows, their masts and spars awry, their rigging tangled like uncombed hair. Directly ahead, the Piazza San Marco looked disheveled with its hodgepodge of artifacts looted from all parts of the world. The rain-streaked marble facades of the Doges' Palace and other buildings gave the city's face a tawdry, painted appearance. Even the piazza itself was flooded, betraying a grey, rheumy harlot beneath Venice's public exterior.

Sebastian sniffed. "This is the great city we were in such a hurry to save?"

Corwyn's lips tightened, but he kept his reply sur-

prisingly mild. "You're not seeing Venice at its best."
He regarded Sebastian closely. "I realize, however, that
no city could possibly offset the loss you've sustained
in reaching here. I'd rather now that we hadn't encouraged Gwen to accompany us to see the wonders of the
world. Truly, Sebastian, I'm sorry."

Sebastian grunted, uncomfortable with Corwyn's sudden solicitousness. Besides, why shouldn't Gwen get to
see Venice, if it really was the rare, noteworthy object
of their travels that Corwyn maintained?

He jerked his head to indicate the nearest ships, where
crews labored to free the listing vessels from the mud.
"If the lagoon is so shallow, how did those ships get in
here to begin with?"

"Deeper channels," Corwyn said, pointing to a merchant galley being rowed from the Grand Canal ahead
and to the left of them, past its less fortunate brethren
on its way to the inlets that connected the lagoon with
the open sea.

Sebastian clutched at the shattered mast, which had
begun to drift away, and tested his footing more cautiously. Indeed, the channel was deepening. Corwyn
rested a hand on Sebastian's shoulder. But if this was
meant to comfort him, Sebastian found the gesture lacking. Eager as he had been throughout this journey for
Corwyn's acceptance and attention, something about the
alchemist's present manner irked him, though he couldn't
say exactly what.

They reached the quay on the southeast side of the
piazza and walked up the broad, white marble steps that
led right into the water. On either side of them rose a
tall pillar, one topped by the winged lion of St. Mark,
the other by a statue of St. Theodore with his foot on a
dragon.

Sebastian was grateful to be on firm land again, although with the piazza ankle deep in floodwater, it was
hard to regard anything as truly *terra ferma*. An old man
trundled by with a barrowful of household goods soaked
from the flood. Across the canal, workmen emptied dam-

aged bales of Egyptian cotton and Persian pepper from the first-floor, warehouse level of one of the palaces, carrying what could be salvaged to the living quarters upstairs and discarding the remainder in the lagoon. A well-dressed matron shuffled by in a pair of *chopines*— pedestal shoes over a foot high that kept the wearer's hem from dragging in mud and water. So treacherous was her footing in the cumbersome devices that she had to be supported by a man on either side to maintain her balance.

Sebastian looked around for something familiar, hoping his cap had washed up on the quay. "I wonder where Gwen and Oliver came ashore?"

Corwyn's only response was to clap Sebastian on the back and embrace him in a fierce, impetuous hug. Sebastian endured it stiffly. The alchemist's behavior was beginning to grate on him. "I suppose we'd best look for an inn where we can stay," he ventured, watching Corwyn in case the old man tried any more impulsive gestures.

"Mmmmm," Corwyn replied, peering around. He leaned close, then looked puzzled when Sebastian quickly backed away. "I think we should keep quiet about our coming here from Pomme de Terre," he whispered. "Since the ship we traveled on was sailing from Spain, perhaps we should claim to have come from there as well."

The whole time he spoke, his eyes darted about restlessly, so that Sebastian wondered if his master had suffered some mental affliction from exposure to the weather. "If you say so," he said.

Corwyn's eyes were still on the Venetians around him. "We'll claim we're from Barcelona," he whispered. "That should do it."

"Ah, yes." Sebastian nodded sagely. "Barcelona— of course."

"Shhh!" Corwyn hissed, irritation showing in his features. "Do you want Hydro Phobius to find out?"

Slowly Sebastian shook his head. Poor Corwyn, he thought. The old alchemist had gone quite mad.

"Hydro Phobius," Corwyn repeated, his eyes again scanning the strangers around them. "And an agent of his, a simulacrum. I learned about them in Florence from one Niccolò Machiavelli, who likes to eavesdrop on Cosimo de' Medici. Phobius and his agent are the ones Cosimo has hired to destroy Venice by Ascension Day."

Sebastian shuddered despite the fact that his clothes were now drying in the warm Venetian sun. Hydro Phobius had made a fool of him the year before. If Corwyn was right, and Phobius really was in Venice—

"We've got to find Gwen and Oliver," Sebastian burst out, tugging on Corwyn's robes. "We've got to warn them!"

Corwyn resisted Sebastian's efforts to drag him along. "There's no need to worry about them now," he said, and rested a hand on Sebastian's arm.

Sebastian gritted his teeth against Corwyn's attempt at comfort. "But Gwen and Oliver—"

"Have perished," Corwyn interrupted.

Sebastian jerked free of his master's grip. "What!"

Corwyn nodded. "Gwen was probably killed when the mast struck her. But even if she was still alive when she hit the water, she would have either drowned in the storm or died along with Oliver in the explosion of the *Magdalen*, as close to the ship as they were."

Sebastian had difficulty understanding Corwyn's words. Gwen dead? "I don't think so," he answered aloud. "We'll find her in Venice."

Corwyn's head swung slowly from side to side. "We must accept it—Gwen and Oliver are dead." His voice was soothing, but a ragged breath betrayed his feelings. He reached for Sebastian.

Sebastian leaped away. To accept comfort now would be to accept the need for it, and that he could not do. What light would there be without Gwen? What joy if she wasn't near him? "But not buried," he answered, his voice hard. "And if not buried, then perhaps not dead. After all, we survived."

Corwyn shrugged, and for a moment Sebastian pitied him, he looked so withered. Having Gwen and Oliver thus taken from him threatened to embitter the alchemist's old age, for their deaths—had that really happened—would weigh heavily upon him. "We were lucky," Corwyn said. "How many, do you think, shared our good fortune?" He paused, as if Sebastian might answer, though the question sounded rhetorical. "Now, we must go on," he continued. "I propose we start our search for Hydro Phobius in the business district, where we can find out whose cargo was on the *Magdalen*."

"You search for Phobius," Sebastian snapped. "I'll search for Gwen and Oliver."

Corwyn opened his mouth as if to say something, then shook his head. "As you will." He started down the street, his shoes sloshing at every step.

Sebastian followed a short distance behind, fearful of losing Corwyn in the crowd, yet not wanting to appear in need of consolation, either. It would be dreadful, he told himself, to think Gwen dead. Without her, he was but a shadow. Gwen had transformed him; when he had sought to alter her. Now he regretted having tried. Gwen rose above such petty masquerades. Truer stars governed her birth, and her heart was as far from fraud as heaven from earth. Without her, he wasn't truly alive.

Everything Corwyn had said was crazy, Sebastian concluded, but the part about Gwen being dead was craziest of all.

It had to be.

By the next day, the damage to Venice was being repaired and the face of the city began to change. Flooding receded, and this latest *acqua alta*—storm waters combined with unusually high tides—was banished to hazy memory by the Adriatic sun. Venice again became a city of self-confident splendor and unrivaled power. From decrepit harlot, her appearance youthened into that mature but elegant queen of Renaissance cities for which she was famed, neither virginally innocent nor yet corrupted by cynicism—worldly wise, majestic, imperial.

For Sebastian, one fact alone marred this rejuvenation, and that was his failure to locate Gwen and Oliver. As Corwyn had predicted, he and Sebastian appeared to be the only survivors from the *Magdalen*—or, indeed, from any of half a dozen ships that had been caught outside the lagoon by the storm. Yet Sebastian refused to give up hope and took grim satisfaction from Corwyn's inability to uncover any evidence of Hydro Phobius's presence or activities. If Corwyn could be wrong about Phobius's plotting against Venice, perhaps he could also be wrong about the fate of Gwen and Oliver.

So they mingled with merchants and financiers whose cargoes had been lost, posing as Spaniards for security, each one hoping for information that would lead them to their separate ends.

Early on the first morning after the storm, Antonio hurried through the narrow, twisting labyrinth of streets to the little *campo,* or square, where Shylock did business in good weather. Although the pavement was still awash from combined rain and tide so that Antonio's boots sloshed at every step, the blue sliver of sky visible between the buildings promised fair weather ahead. Venice would once again earn its reputation as La Serenissima.

Antonio's mood was anything but serene. Somehow, he had to convince Shylock to flee Venice with Jessica, but without compromising either his true nature or his master's purpose.

Duty versus love—Antonio felt trapped between them, unable to pursue one without forswearing the other. Of course, even the rashest vows could be heedfully broken, perhaps, if one had the wit to exchange bad for better. And Antonio wasn't sure of his moral obligation to fulfill a role programmed into him without his consent. Yet if he abandoned the purpose for which he'd been constructed, what would he be then—an inconstant, changeable creature, shifting with every wind?

As an artificial being who lacked a soul, he shouldn't be plagued by attacks of conscience. But loving Jessica had altered him, so that he even thought of setting her above his commitment to his master. Not that he had the right to love her—but he did, anyway.

He neared the *campo* and paused, hearing voices. "How now, Shylock," a stranger said. "Have you heard the news among the merchants?"

"What news?" Shylock growled. "And what of it, unless it concerns that merchant, Antonio, who has profaned my daughter? Two hundred thousand ducats gone in these past few months, Tubal—yet I could forgive him even that. But now he robs me of my most precious jewel."

Antonio had crouched behind the carved marble head of a cistern to listen. Poor Shylock, he thought. Jessica's deception had heaped one too many trials upon him, pressing him down into the lonely depths of an old man's sorrow.

"That my own flesh and blood would rebel!" Shylock went on. "Loss upon loss. And no satisfaction, no revenge against the thief who steals from me. No ill luck stirring but what lights on my own shoulders."

"Other men have ill luck, too," Tubal replied. "Antonio, as I've heard—"

"What, what?" Shylock interrupted. "Antonio, suffering ill luck?"

"Antonio had a ship, richly laden, which wrecked on the seas in yesterday's storm," Tubal continued.

"I thank God," Shylock exclaimed. "Is it true?"

"I spoke but half an hour ago with some passengers who escaped the wreck," Tubal said. "A pair of Spanish gentlemen, one young, one old, who've come here from Barcelona." He laughed. "They looked like they'd swum the whole way and had just dragged themselves out of the canals. They were asking whose cargo was aboard the ship, but I didn't tell them for fear it would help Antonio receive compensation for his loss.''

Antonio smiled grimly to himself at the thought of being compensated for the loss of the detonators that had been aboard the *Magdalen*. Not only hadn't the cargo been insured, but Antonio had actually been pleased at first to learn the ship had gone down, thinking this would foil Hydro Phobius's plans. But Phobius was determined to receive his final payment from Cosimo de' Medici, and would undoubtedly come up with some means of replacing the detonators before Ascension Day. In the meantime, Antonio stood in even greater danger than before of being revealed as a result of Shylock's claim against his flesh.

Suddenly Antonio frowned. Tubal spoke of meeting passengers from the *Magdalen*, but there were to have been no passengers aboard the ship. That was one of the terms he had made with the captain—the same captain whose drowned corpse and crew now cavorted with the other enchanted creatures in the hall of Antonio's palace. Then another thought struck him, leaving him even more mystified. The *Magdalen* hadn't really sailed from Spain at all. That was a lie to cover the ship's actual route from Genoa to Venice by way of the Ottoman Empire. So how could two gentlemen from Barcelona have reached here on the *Magdalen?*

"Thank you, Tubal," Shylock said, bringing Antonio's attention back to the *campo*. "That's good news, good news."

"I've also recovered—at considerable expense—a portion of your daughter's jewelry," Tubal said. "Someone pawned her ring for four score ducats."

"You stab me, speaking so lightly of my daughter's infidelity," Shylock cried. "Four score ducats for her ring. And well I know who benefitted from the money!"

"Several of Antonio's creditors swear he can't help now but break," Tubal went on. "He owes too much to ever repay his debts on time."

"And I'm the creditor to whom he owes the most,"

Shylock said, "the one from whom he's taken more than money. But, oh, I'm glad to hear this, Tubal. I'll plague him; I'll torture him. I'm glad of it."

Antonio clenched his fists at Shylock's threat, knowing how vulnerable he was to the moneylender's fury.

"It was one of his creditors who showed me the ring that belonged to your daughter," Tubal continued, extending his open hand. "Antonio pawned it."

"Out upon her!" Shylock cried, taking the ring and cradling it. "Why are you torturing me, Tubal? This was my turquoise; my departed Leah—she was a saint—gave it to me when I was a bachelor. I wouldn't have sold it for a chest of ducats."

"But Antonio's certainly undone, now that he's suffered this loss at sea," Tubal said.

"Oh, that's true," Shylock gloated. "That's very true. I made a bad match, Tubal, loaning money to Antonio— a bankrupt, a prodigal who scarcely dares to show his head on the Rialto, a beggar who used to deal with me so smugly. But he made a worse match when he took my daughter from me. I could have forgiven anything but that. Now, let him look to his bond. I'll have the heart out of him if he forfeits!"

Faced with the revelation that cutting his flesh would bring, Antonio sprang forward. He sauntered haughtily into the *campo*, forgetting his purpose in coming, scarcely bothering to veil his anger. "Shylock, what's this? Surely if I forfeit you won't take my flesh. What's the good in that?"

"Go, Tubal," Shylock whispered. "Meet me later." He waited until the other man had gone, then turned to Antonio, hatred showing in his expression. "What good? Why, I'd use it to bait fish with," he replied. "If it'll feed nothing else, it'll feed my revenge."

Antonio stepped closer, feigning surprise, and reached for the ring Shylock held. "Why, what trinket of mine is this? How'd you come by it?"

"I might ask you the same," Shylock snarled, clutching the ring in his fist.

Antonio shrugged indifferently. "I had it from Jessica," he said, wielding truth like a weapon. "She's a virtuous gentlewoman, your daughter—mild and beautiful."

"Beautiful, yes," Shylock growled. "But virtuous only till you led her astray. My fallen daughter since. But it seems you didn't love her after all, to have pawned her token. She's dead to you, perhaps?"

"Not so; she lives forever in my heart."

Shylock grunted. "Even if I grant that you do love her, to you, be assured, she's dead."

Antonio shook his head. "If she were, I'd be lying with her in her grave."

"It would be worth any lesser price to see you dead and buried," Shylock said. "Bad enough that you've hindered me of a quarter of a million, but now you've disgraced my child. And for what reason?"

"The reason?" Antonio said, suddenly reminded of his purpose. "Shylock, listen to me. As you love Jessica, even if not for yourself, regard your danger. Heed what I say."

"For what reason, I say?" Shylock went on, oblivious of Antonio's plea. "Why, only that I'm a Jew! But doesn't a Jew have eyes? Isn't he fed with the same food, hurt with the same weapons, subject to the same diseases as a Christian? If you prick us, don't we bleed? If you poison us, don't we die?" Shylock leaned close, hissing in Antonio's face. "And if you wrong us, shall we not be revenged?"

Antonio wiped spittle from his face. "You think I did this because you're a Jew? Shylock, you don't understand."

"Shall I not be revenged, I say?" Shylock went on. "The villainy you teach me I'll execute; and it'll go hard, but I'll better the instruction."

"Shylock, listen to me."

"Look to your bond. Don't plead with me for mercy, you who took my daughter and showed her none. Look to your bond."

"Hear me, Shylock. I'm not asking for mercy."

"I'll have my bond. No more talk. I've sworn an oath that I'll have my bond. You've treated me like a dog. Well, if I'm a dog, beware my fangs. The doge will grant me justice when you forfeit."

"I pray you, hear me speak!"

"I'll have my bond; I won't listen to you speak! And don't follow me; I'll hear no pleading. I'll have my bond." Shylock hurried from the *campo*, shielding his ears from any parting words.

Antonio started to pursue him, then stopped. Why follow? Antonio understood all too well why Shylock wanted his life. Now, only the doge might alter the course of the law to save him—and even that was in doubt.

But come Ascension Day, even Shylock's bond must be denied. Ah, sweet Jessica, Antonio thought—without her, he was but a shadow, lacking substance. Yet he had to be false even to her. Honor to his creator had to remain his highest purpose, even though in doing so he proved untrue to himself. Without that constancy, there'd be nothing of perfection in him!

Yet as these thoughts troubled Antonio's mind, another rose unbidden, strangely reassuring. If Shylock pressed him, and the doge decreed the bond should be collected in public, all of Venice would learn at the first cut what sort of creature Antonio really was. His masquerade would be considered a crime against the state deserving quick punishment for himself and his maker. Without Antonio ever having actually to betray Hydro Phobius, Venetian justice—known for its ferocity—would descend upon them both.

Antonio wouldn't survive, of course; if he was lucky, he would fall to Shylock's knife at once rather than be imprisoned to await formal execution. But whatever his end, and however shameful, it might save Jessica.

ACT 13:

What She Will

GWEN AWOKE THE MORNING AFTER THE STORM TO A grief that felt inconsolable. Sebastian and Corwyn were surely dead from the mysterious blast that had destroyed the *Magdalen*, while she had been cast up by the sea, penniless and alone, onto the shores of a foreign land.

For a long time, she could do nothing but cry, scarcely caring that she lay half in the water, half in the reeds of a marshy strand. Each time her sobbing seemed about to wane, the image of Sebastian would rise unbidden in her mind, appearing as he had in the tavern outside Ravenna when she'd berated him, a hurt look in his eyes, and her tears would start afresh. How she regretted her sharp words now.

Between bouts of crying, she dozed fitfully, exhausted and desolate, finding little solace even in sleep.

Gradually, however, she became aware of the sun on her back, and the screech of swifts overhead. Tiny wavelets lapped at her legs where they dangled in the water, tugging at the hem of her gown. A dry branch—nudged by a gusting breeze—brushed her shoulder.

Except there was no breeze.

She opened her eyes, able to see again without tears obscuring her vision, and found Oliver sitting on a sea chest beside her, looking like a bedraggled monk. His hand was on her shoulder. Dim memories came back to her of Oliver guiding her onto the chest when it had bobbed to the surface after the wreck of the *Magdalen*, then helping her stay afloat throughout the night. That chest and Oliver had saved her life.

With a sigh, Gwen heaved herself the rest of the way out of the water and sat up. She pushed damp strands of hair from her face and surveyed the world into which she had been reborn. Before her, water stretched for leagues like a vast, burnished sheet, broken occasionally by small islands. In the distance, fishing boats with orange and red sails trolled the waters. Closer in, masses of dark seaweed separated and rejoined under the surging of tidal swells. Seabirds moaned and swooped against an azure sky or squabbled noisily along the shore, fighting over tidbits cast up by the storm.

A bit of blue cloth awash among the nearby reeds caught her attention. With cold premonition, she picked it up. It was Sebastian's cap from Pomme de Terre. Gwen hugged the sodden cloth to her, crying over it like a drowned child.

When her tears stopped this time, she turned away from the sea, afraid of what else she might find washed up on the shore. She looked inland, to where the land rose in a sea of reeds, climbing into hazy foothills and mist-shrouded mountains beyond, their jagged, snow-capped peaks glistening in the morning sun.

Gwen inhaled deeply, the air tinged with salt and rank with the smells of plant growth and decay. She let out her breath in another sigh, then began considering what to do.

She was a woman alone—except for Oliver—in an unknown land, without friends or means of support, and she felt painfully vulnerable. Of course, her own escape encouraged the thought that Sebastian and Corwyn might also have survived, despite the evidence of Sebastian's cap. But even as she thought it, she knew she was only comforting herself with the vagaries of hope.

Her shoulders sagged. Then Oliver rested his twig hand on her arm sympathetically and Gwen shook off her doubts. First, she needed warm, dry clothes. Everything else would follow.

She dragged the sea chest higher onto the shore and opened it. Inside, she discovered a young nobleman's clothes, mostly untouched by water, protected by the chest's seaworthiness. A small, jeweled dagger with a thin blade, a sword of Italian styling, and several personal items completed the contents.

At first, Gwen was disappointed that the chest didn't contain a woman's clothing. But after she thought about it, she decided it would be better this way, appearing as a man in a strange country where it might be dangerous to be recognized as a woman without companions.

She settled on a hip-length cloak of silk brocade, a green silk doublet with slashed sleeves, a slashed velvet hat, silk hose, and velvet shoes. She checked to be sure no one was watching, then stripped off her wet clothes. To better disguise herself, she bound her breasts with a long sash, then covered that with the bulky doublet and cloak. The hose, more revealing than any article of woman's clothing, left her feeling exposed. But the greatest difficulty was the codpiece.

Gwen had often chuckled over the huge codpieces popular here in Italy, and over Sebastian's discomfort at wearing one. Now she recalled his feelings with more sympathy. But it was essential that others think she possessed what she lacked, and lacked what she actually had. So Gwen gritted her teeth and donned a codpiece, stuffing it with strips of cloth torn from her discarded gown.

She tried unsuccessfully to hide her long hair, then finally gave up and cut it. Oliver helped, using the dagger. The results were ragged, but would do until she either abandoned her disguise, or could finish the task properly with scissors.

She looked down where the curling auburn locks lay spilled among the reeds, and for a moment Sebastian's face loomed again in her mind. She was certain he would disapprove of her masquerading as a man, and that troubled her. Her vision swam at the thought of him. She fought back the tears. Sebastian wasn't here, damn him! She still had to survive. Angrily, she belted the sword at her waist, tucked Sebastian's cap inside her doublet, and set off inland. From the angle of the sun, she guessed it was now early afternoon. She was hungry and needed food, but was even more concerned about finding somewhere to spend the night.

As she walked, she recalled Sebastian's stride and mimicked it, abandoning the mincing steps he had taught her. After a while, she added a swagger.

Oliver tried to pull her back to the water. Every few steps, he tugged on her arm and gazed toward a grey smudge on the horizon. Gwen guessed he was looking for Corwyn and wanted to return to where the ship had gone down. Sadly, she urged him on.

Soon they were overtaken by a man on horseback. Gwen debated a moment, then waved for him to stop.

The stranger started to gallop past, then drew rein and waited impatiently for Gwen and Oliver to catch up. His clothes were similar to Gwen's, except that he wore an embroidered cloth mantle with gold buttons over a brocade tunic, and the predominant color of his clothing was scarlet. A dark-haired man of medium height and stature, he'd have been handsome, Gwen thought as she ran to him, if it weren't for the worry lines creasing his face. As it was, he looked like someone who had shouldered a burden heavier than he could bear.

"What country is this?" Gwen asked breathlessly as she reached his stirrup.

He looked taken aback. "Why, this is the Veneto. Out in the lagoon there is Venice itself." He pointed across the water toward the smudge.

Gwen was dismayed to learn that the *Magdalen* had reached the lagoon, that Corwyn and Sebastian had perished so near their destination. "What'll I do in Venice now?" she asked herself. The stranger shrugged and made as if to ride on. "Do you know this country?" Gwen asked quickly, reluctant for him to leave.

"*Sì*. I was made—that is, I was born—not three hours from here."

"And is that where you ride? Are you returning to your estate?"

The stranger scowled. "What business, boy, is that of yours?" Gwen felt herself blush. She started to stammer out an excuse, but he relented and waved her discomfiture aside. "In Belmont there's a lady, richly endowed. La Bella Donna, and as noble as her name." His voice sounded oddly mocking. "Suitors come here from every coast, like so many Jasons after her fabled fleece. I'm on my way to her villa."

With surprise, Gwen remembered that one of the pilgrims from Canterbury had mentioned this woman. "I've heard of her. She's an heiress, I believe." Gwen tried to remember what else she had heard—something about how the woman was to choose a husband. She shook her head, unable to recall the details.

The stranger nodded. "A virtuous maid, whose father died some twelve months ago, only days after moving here with his daughter." His voice still held its mocking tone.

"And are you, then, one of her suitors?" Gwen asked.

The stranger's face darkened. "No," he said, his voice cold. "I have business there."

Gwen struggled with herself. She was tempted to trust this man, for his manner seemed in keeping with a gentleman of honor. Of course, she knew what could be hidden by appearance, but she needed help and decided to believe that his character was truly reflected in his looks. Besides, she felt drawn to him.

"Please, *signore*," she asked, "I'd like to serve this lady, if you'll present me to her. I'll repay the favor when I can." Irritation clouded his face, and she continued impulsively. "I can wait on her at table and . . . and do many sorts of things that will make me worth her service."

Her appeal sounded lame in her own ears, but the stranger smiled as if he found it amusing. "You'd rather serve her, someone you haven't seen, than me?"

Gwen dropped her eyes. "I meant no affront, *signore.*" Quickly, she sought an excuse to explain why she should serve a mistress rather than a master, knowing that the real reason—her gender—had to remain secret. "It's just that I seem to have been orphaned by last night's storm and need employment, at least until I can determine my estate."

"Ah, another casualty of the storm," the stranger said, soothing his horse's restlessness. "I, too, suffered from it, although my loss was only cargo. Were you on a ship, then?"

"Yes," Gwen said. "The *Magdalen.*"

The stranger started, then frowned. "There seem to have been any number of passengers aboard the *Magdalen.*"

"Why?" Gwen asked. "Have you heard of others?"

"Only a pair of Spanish noblemen," the stranger replied, watching Gwen. "From Barcelona, they said. Do you know them?"

Gwen shook her head, disappointed. "That monk over there"—she indicated Oliver, who was straying back toward the shore—"and I boarded in Ravenna with two companions, but they were French. I fear they may be drowned."

"Most likely," the stranger said. "It's a wonder you survived." He continued studying her. "What's your name, boy?"

"Cesario," Gwen blurted without thinking. "My name is . . . Cesario."

"Well, Cesario, if I introduce you to La Bella Donna, can you be discreet?"

"I'll be my lady's mute, as voiceless as that monk." Gwen pointed again to Oliver.

"So?" The stranger laughed. "Well, then perhaps La Bella Donna can use your services after all." He patted his horse behind the saddle. "Climb up here, boy, and I'll give you a ride."

Gwen shook her head and backed up a step, afraid that such close contact might lead to her being discovered. "I'll walk," she said, "with my remaining companion."

The stranger shrugged again, the laughter gone from his face. "As you wish." He urged his horse forward.

"What's your name?" Gwen puffed as she trotted alongside. She motioned for Oliver to catch up with her.

"Antonio," the man answered. He half turned and bowed to Gwen, his manner once again mocking. "Antonio Nessuno, merchant of Venice, at your service."

"I thank you, *Signor* Nessuno," Gwen panted, trying to act as though the effort to keep up were nothing. "Lead on. My friend and I'll follow."

Oliver did follow, as Gwen ordered him to, but he did it unhappily, lagging farther behind with every step. Didn't Gwen know she was going the wrong direction, leading them away from the song of enchantment that called to Oliver from across the lagoon? Although wordless, the song promised Oliver the very things he'd longed for most on this trip—a chance to play and friends to play with. It bewildered him that Gwen refused to heed the song, walking away as if she couldn't hear. Only his devotion to her kept him following in her footsteps.

Yet even that devotion wasn't enough to prevent him from turning frequently, harking to a call that became ever harder to ignore.

A short distance inland, the landscape changed. Copses of sycamore, beech, and elm trees became common, with occasional stretches of woodland. Grass replaced the reeds. Villas and gardens dotted the low hillsides, blending formal architecture with stylized natural settings. Although the brilliant expanses of flowers Gwen had seen elsewhere on her journey were notably lacking, architects here had achieved a particular grace in their combinations of sunlight and shade; of red marble structures, pooled or running water, and green plant life.

They reached the outskirts of a village, where the villas were more thickly clustered. Antonio entered a broken gate to one of the estates, stabled his horse near an abandoned gatekeeper's cottage, and led Gwen and Oliver down a weedy, ilex-lined path toward the building that dominated the grounds. Occasional cul-de-sacs opened off the main path, and peering into them, Gwen saw cracked marble benches, a rusted sundial, or crumbling statues around a silted pond. Except for a pervasive sense of decay, as if the villa had stood untended for several years, the setting was idyllic, and it had Gwen missing Sebastian more than ever.

La Bella Donna had guests when Antonio directed Gwen onto a terrace outside the villa, with Oliver straggling behind. A tall Moor, darkly resplendent in his white turban and caftan, towered over the woman Gwen guessed must be the heiress, then stooped to kiss her gloved hand. Across the gravel path, the white teeth and eyes of the Moor's retinue shone against a sea of sun-darkened, grinning faces. A mixed cluster of European noblemen—other suitors, Gwen judged from their annoyed expressions—watched from benches nearby.

Off to one side, Oliver fidgeted, clearly bothered by something. Gwen wondered what was disturbing the broom, but could only hope he stayed out of trouble for now. She'd ask him about it later, when she could spare the attention.

"By my troth, Antonio," La Bella Donna gushed when the Venetian merchant arrived, "my little body is weary of this great world." She heaved her bulky frame around Antonio, placing him between herself and the Moor.

Gwen stared at the woman in disbelief, for her body was anything but little. Of course, it was difficult to be sure because La Bella Donna had draped herself so thoroughly in the black garb of mourning. Even her face was heavily veiled, so that nothing of her showed save a squat, round outline. From this, however, and the woman's shrill, grating voice, Gwen concluded that La Bella Donna wasn't the fair young maiden Antonio had implied.

The Moor glowered at Antonio and circled him to move in on La Bella Donna. "Don't dismiss me because of my complexion," he insisted, taking her gloved hand again. "It's only the shadowed livery of the sun, to whom I am a neighbor. But compare my blood with the fairest northerner's, and mine will prove as red. *Signorina*, this face strikes fear into valiant men, yet the most favored virgins of the desert have also loved it, and I wouldn't change its hue except to steal your heart, my queen."

Gwen felt weak-kneed at the fervor of the Moor's suit, so handsome and poetic was he. But La Bella Donna appeared less affected. "In terms of choice, I'm not led solely by the direction of my gaze." The heiress clapped the Moor on the shoulder. He staggered, then righted himself. "But if my father hadn't hedged me in with his method for determining a husband," La Bella Donna continued in her nasal voice, "then you'd have stood as fair as any comer for my affection." She patted him again.

The Moor grunted under her blows and rubbed his shoulder, narrowing his eyes at his intended. "For that assurance, I thank you."

La Bella Donna curtsied and led Antonio aside, where she let out a heavy breath. "I no sooner shut the gate upon one wooer than another knocks at the door," she whispered. "This game is more trouble than I expected." Her veiled face stopped abruptly, directed at Gwen. Her voice became hostile. "Antonio, who's this waif?"

There was something uncomfortably familiar about La Bella Donna. Gwen wasn't sure what—they couldn't possibly have met before—but something about the woman haunted her. She wished she could see La Bella Donna's features without the veil. But Antonio had warned Gwen on the way to the villa that La Bella Donna had resolved on her father's deathbed to remain in mourning until one of her suitors won her hand. Since her father had enjoined her before his death to some absurd system of choosing a husband, La Bella Donna's period of mourning didn't appear likely to end anytime soon.

Embarrassed to find herself staring, Gwen tore her eyes away and looked around the terrace. Several statues leered from the sides of the open area, horrible grotesques that made Gwen shudder. She almost broke down crying, she missed Sebastian and Corwyn so. Then she saw Oliver, shifting fitfully near the path by which they'd arrived, and Gwen felt somewhat reassured. At least she wasn't completely alone. And Oliver, fortunately, was still wearing his monk's robes.

Meanwhile, out of the corner of her eye, Gwen noticed La Bella Donna's veiled face studying her as if trying to connect her with some memory as well.

"This is Cesario, my lady," Antonio said, indicating Gwen.

"And what do I want with a Cesario?" La Bella Donna demanded.

"I thought you might need him for carrying your suit to the doge, my lady," Antonio replied.

"Ah, the doge." La Bella Donna sighed, fanning air upon her veil as if the mention of him warmed her. "Antonio, I asked you to press that suit. What news do you bring from him?"

"So please you, my lady, I couldn't get admitted," Antonio said. "I was told by his page that the doge intends to mourn the death of his wife for seven years, and won't consider marriage during that time."

La Bella Donna dropped the hand with which she'd been fanning herself. "That's ridiculous, remaining in mourning for so long," she snapped. "Donna Maria's been dead for months now. Foscari's children need a mother. Venice needs a dogaressa. The council can't allow the doge to remain unmarried."

Antonio nodded. "They're already pressuring him to

choose another wife, threatening to pick one for him.
Yet still the doge resists.''

"The idiot! Doesn't he know he's making a fool of
himself?''

Gwen eyed the heiress, wondering if La Bella Donna
realized how extravagant her own terms of mourning
sounded. "Are you in love with him, my lady?'' she
asked, surprised at a woman so brazenly pursuing a man,
especially a woman already surrounded by suitors.

"What, Cesario?'' La Bella Donna replied, sounding
distracted.

"The doge's heart,'' Gwen said. "Are you hunting
it?''

"Ah, his heart!'' La Bella Donna exclaimed. "The
noblest heart there is.'' She fanned herself again. "Oh,
that I might be his hart, and he the hunter. When I first
saw him, I thought he purged the air of pestilence. In
that instant I became his prey, and have desired ever
since that he, like a fell, cruel hound, would pursue me.''

"That won't happen any time soon,'' Antonio muttered.

"What's that?'' La Bella Donna demanded, dropping
her hand again and turning on him.

"I said, Cesario could convey your suit,'' Antonio
amended evenly. He glanced at Gwen and continued, his
words becoming guarded. "The cargo of Spanish wine
I awaited was lost in last night's storm. Other arrangements will have to be made to replace the loss. Until
then, I won't be able to carry your suit to the doge.''

"What!'' La Bella Donna's veiled face stared at him.
"*Signor* Antonio, you'd better hope someone takes my
suit to him, and successfully, too. Shylock is probably
hounding Foscari at this very moment about the forfeiture
of your bond. If we don't distract the doge in time from
hearing Shylock's demands, or if the loan isn't otherwise
nullified . . .'' Her voice trailed off.

"So I forfeit,'' Antonio said airily. "What of it? Let
him try to collect his pound of flesh.''

"This attitude is new in you,'' La Bella Donna replied.

"One might almost think you wanted Shylock to try. Need I remind you what that attempt would reveal?"

Antonio clenched his jaw so hard the muscles stood out. He and La Bella Donna stared at each other, locked in private struggle. Finally, La Bella Donna turned away. "We'll talk about how to replace the lost cargo later. Meanwhile, Cesario, I guess I need your services after all. You've heard me tell of my love for the doge. Already, I've unclasped the secrets of my soul to you."

"Yes, my lady," Gwen said, thinking that La Bella Donna's intentions appeared to have less to do with love than with business. But Gwen needed employment and the security it would bring. She started to curtsy, then remembered in time to bow. "But what of your promise to submit to your father's means—whatever those are— for choosing a husband?"

"The brain may devise laws for the blood, but a hot temper leaps over a cold decree," La Bella Donna said breezily, dismissing Gwen's objection with a flick of her hand. "Go to the doge. Don't be denied. Stand at his gate and say your feet will grow roots there unless you're granted an audience."

"But if the doge has abandoned himself to sorrow as Antonio says, he'll never admit me," Gwen objected.

"Make a ruckus," La Bella Donna said. "Ignore the bounds of decency rather than return unsuccessful."

"And if I do speak with him, my lady. What then?"

"Where did you find such a thickheaded oaf?" La Bella Donna asked Antonio. She turned back to Gwen. "Unfold the passion of my love, of course. Tell him of my desire. He'll listen to you more readily than to a graver messenger." She looked pointedly at Antonio.

"You know why I'm grave," Antonio muttered. "And it's not over a cargo of Spanish wine."

La Bella Donna glared at him.

"I don't think the doge will listen to me," Gwen interrupted at last. "I'm too young."

"Dear boy," La Bella Donna replied, "true, you're not yet a man. A woman's face couldn't be smoother or more lovely, and your voice still sounds like a maiden's.'' La Bella Donna's own voice—shrill and irritating—took on a caressing tone. She reached out to stroke Gwen's cheek with a gloved hand. Gwen cringed. Suddenly, La Bella Donna shook herself, realizing what she was doing. "Still, I know you're right for this," she continued huskily. "Prosper well in it, and you'll live as freely as if my fortunes were your own."

Antonio snorted softly.

"Then I'll do my best to woo him for you," Gwen said, the words emerging through clenched teeth. If La Bella Donna weren't so rich, she thought, the heiress wouldn't stand a chance of attracting a husband. As it was, the fact that she had so many suitors merely confirmed Gwen's suspicions about the foolishness of men—noblemen in particular.

As if to confirm her thoughts, a muffled cough from the Moorish prince interrupted them. "Lead me to the caskets. I'll try my fortune," he said with a terrible scowl. "By this scimitar"—he placed his hand on the hilt of a blade so wickedly curved that it made Gwen shiver—"I'd rather face wild animals and slay fierce enemies to win you, my lady, and to acquire your inheritance as a dowry. But, alas, in this I must trust chance to lead me to what bravery can't attain. *Inshallah*, then. As Allah wills it. Lead on."

La Bella Donna raised her hands, then let them fall helplessly to her sides. "Oh, was ever the will of a living daughter so curbed by the caprice of her dead father?" she lamented. "Isn't it hard, Antonio, that I can neither choose one suitor nor refuse another?"

"Your father was very virtuous," Antonio said, speaking loudly enough for all to hear. "Such men at their deaths often have good inspirations. The lottery he devised will, no doubt, never be chosen correctly except by the one you should rightly love."

Gwen shook her head and struggled to make out the meaning in Antonio's words, uttered like a speech that was well rehearsed.

"Well, there you are, then," La Bella Donna told the Moor. "To win me, you must take your chances. But before you do, swear that, if you choose wrong, you'll never speak to any woman again about marriage, you'll never tell anyone what choice you made here, and you'll promptly leave Venice forever."

La Bella Donna skimmed through the terms as quickly as a mountebank reciting a shady contract. The other suitors in the room grumbled at the severity of the agreement, although they had evidently heard the terms on other occasions. Gwen, who had heard them only once before—and then as a roadside tale scarcely to be believed—stood rooted in astonishment. The Moor swallowed hard. "I swear. Come, let's get on with it."

La Bella Donna waddled from the garden, followed by the Moor. Antonio shrugged and motioned Gwen after them. Gwen glanced about for Oliver, too terrified to move when she discovered him gone. Antonio took her firmly by the arm and led her into the villa. They entered a small room, richly decorated as a chapel or shrine and apparently dedicated to the memory of La Bella Donna's father. A banner, possibly the family coat of arms, draped from a pole on one side of a curtained alcove, while a polished suit of armor stood guard on the other. Above the alcove hung a portrait of an ordinary-looking man whose splendid attire outweighed his features. He was dressed in a luxurious velvet gown, with a heavy gold chain over his shoulders. Jeweled rings flashed on his fingers. His mouth quirked up at one corner as if his wealth embarrassed him.

La Bella Donna and the Moor were waiting in front of the curtain. La Bella Donna scowled at Gwen, obviously displeased at her presence. But when she spoke, it was to Antonio. "Draw the curtain and let this noble prince see the caskets," she commanded. Antonio did so, displaying a niche which held three small chests—one of gold, one of silver, and one of lead. "Now," La Bella Donna continued, addressing the Moor, "make your choice."

Gwen glanced around, hoping to see Oliver in a corner. But there was no sign of him.

The Moor hesitated. "How'll I know if I choose the right one?"

"One of the chests contains my portrait," La Bella Donna said. "If you choose it, then I'm yours."

"Allah guide my judgment!" the Moor whispered. He stepped forward to examine the three small chests. "Why, there are inscriptions," he said. He peered at the casket made of lead. "'Whoever chooses me reveals all that he is.' Well, what risk is there in that? I'm sufficient. Yet it sounds impertinent, threatening. Bah! I won't stoop to a worthless metal." He turned to the silver chest. "'Whoever chooses me gets what he deserves.' That would be the lady, for I deserve her and more. Yet why set so rich a jewel in anything less costly than gold? So what does the gold chest say? 'Whoever chooses me gains what many desire.' Ah, that's the lady for certain; the whole world desires her—and her fortune with her, of course." He turned to La Bella Donna, holding the gold chest before him like a sacred relic. "Give me the key, and may I thrive by my choice!"

Gwen shook her head in disbelief. Beyond a doubt, this was the most ludicrous method of choosing a spouse she'd ever heard of.

La Bella Donna took a key from a ring hooked to her ample girdle. The Moor grabbed it, unlocked the casket, and flung open the lid. Eagerly, he reached inside. Then his expression fell. "A death's head!" he hissed, gingerly withdrawing a portrait of a grinning skull. "And underneath, another inscription. 'What many men desire.'" He stared at the painting in silence a moment, then replaced it and relocked the casket. "Everything lost," he murmured, handing the key to La Bella Donna. "*Addio*. I won't take my leave tediously." He straggled from the room.

"Good riddance." La Bella Donna sighed after he had gone. "I hope he takes the others with him. I dote on the absence of every one of them, and pray for their swift departure." From behind her father's portrait, she withdrew a parchment sheet decorated with the horse-head outlines of perhaps a score of chessboard knights, neatly arranged in columns. Nine of the silhouettes had been crossed out. La Bella Donna took a quill and ink pot from a small drawer and crossed out another knight, then returned the sheet to its hiding place. She turned and was visibly startled when she encountered Gwen. "Well, what're you doing still here? Haven't you been told what to do? Go to the doge with my suit."

Gwen bowed and hurried out, anxious to leave more so she could look for Oliver than so she could carry out this strange woman's command. Compared with La Bella Donna, Sebastian's antics seemed trifling. Yet so alone and helpless did Gwen feel that she knew she would comply with the heiress in order to remain in her employment, at least until she found Oliver.

But what, she wondered miserably, was she to do without Sebastian and Corwyn?

ACT 14:

Measure by Measure

"WE'VE BEEN GOING ABOUT THIS ALL WRONG," COR-
wyn announced to Sebastian on the morning of their third
day in Venice. "We've been wasting time with merchants and moneylenders, trying to find out whose cargo
was on the *Magdalen*. Obviously, the owner isn't coming
forward to file a claim. If the cargo was contraband, it
might not even have been insured."

Sebastian scratched irritably at the stubble on his chin
while his master lapsed back into silence. Corwyn was
still working through the puzzle posed by the loss of the
Magdalen and its crew, although Sebastian suspected this
was just the alchemist's way of distracting himself from
the far more personal and more devastating loss of Gwen
and Oliver. As a result, Corwyn's manner had been
strained, almost desperate these past three days. Sebastian longed to help, but felt too weighed down by his
own grief to pretend concern for the *Magdalen*. He
wished he could find his cap; it was like a talisman that
had linked him with Gwen.

He and Corwyn sat on the marble parapet of a quay
bordering one of the small squares, or *campi* as the Venetians called them, in the heart of the business district
near the Rialto. In the center of the *campo*, a fountain

stood silent, its flow of water cut off. Around it, sunlight beat on the paving stones until even the dust lay motionless, too lethargic to rise in the sultry air. The parapet, however, enjoyed a modicum of shade and was nearer the water. From here, Sebastian could look up and down the canal, watching women gossip on a nearby bridge and listening to the gondoliers' cries of *"A premì!"* and *"A stalì!"* as they approached the narrow junctions. An occasional swallow skimmed the water at his feet, feeding on mosquitoes. Swifts screamed overhead as they crossed the narrow patch of open sky.

Sebastian understood his master's fascination with Venice, for water was present everywhere, caressing the senses. There was the soft hiss of gondolas gliding along the canals and the gentle lapping of waves against the marble steps of a quay. There was the delicate play of light flung back from the water's surface against the rose-colored facades of the buildings, and the mirrored doubling of the city reflected in the emerald depths. And there was the damp smell of water, sometimes fresh, sometimes fetid, permeating everything.

La Serenissima was worthy of its name, Sebastian thought, and he would have been contented with it if only Gwen had been there, too. Since she wasn't, Venice could be only tedious, distracting.

Next to him, Corwyn stroked his beard, deep in thought. "If Hydro Phobius is using an agent who can pass for a Venetian, as Niccolò claimed, then we're not likely to find either of them."

Across the *campo*, a pair of masons repaired one of the buildings bordering the canal. High water had crumbled the marble facade, exposing a brick foundation. Sebastian watched the masons the way he might stare at the toiling of a spider or cicada, without real interest. Over the past three days, he had seen numerous craftsmen working on the buildings surrounding the *campo*, and still more damage would have to be dealt with before all evidence of the recent storm was erased.

"It's hard to believe Hydro Phobius planned to destroy

Venice with the paltry explosives on the *Magdalen* alone,'' Corwyn went on.

Sebastian grunted, disturbed from his misery by the suggestion that whatever blew up the *Magdalen* had been a ''paltry'' force. A trickle of sweat dripped down his cheek and made the stubble itch again. He scratched absently.

''Even if Phobius smuggled several shiploads of explosives into Venice, I don't think he'd be so naive as to think he could blow up the whole city that way,'' Corwyn said. ''Although enough to sink a ship, or even a fleet, they would be inadequate against the city.''

Across the *campo,* one of the masons wiped his face with his leather apron. Mortar dust streaked his skin. ''This storm alone will keep us busy through summer,'' he grumbled to his partner. ''Before then, we could get another storm or two and several more high tides. We'll never catch up.''

''Ah, quit complaining,'' his companion said. ''It keeps us in work and our families fed.''

The first man muttered to himself, then went back to chiseling away salt-weakened marble. Sebastian turned to Corwyn. ''Is it true that there's been an unusual amount of water damage in the city lately?'' he asked, rubbing furiously at his itchy chin.

Corwyn snorted. ''The Venetians love to complain about the city's gradual settling. Each generation claims it's worse than before. The truth is, it's been going on since the first refugees from the mainland escaped Attila, the Hun by fleeing here a thousand years ago. People grumble about it, but they've learned to live with it, building on pilings and continuously repairing any damage that's done.'' Corwyn pursed his lips and tapped them idly with a finger. Sebastian turned back to the masons.

''You have raised an important point, however,'' Corwyn added after a while. ''Venice is dependent on water for everything, from food and defense to its merchant empire. No other city is so intimately allied with this most noble of elements. If Hydro Phobius is out to destroy the Venetian republic, what would be more likely than to attack it through its water? And what better way for me to prove the worth of my alchemy than by foiling him?'' He slapped his thighs and stood up, groaning more than was his custom. ''Time for us to get moving.''

Sebastian got to his feet. ''What're we going to do?''

''Why, survey the canals and lagoon for contamination, of course,'' Corwyn said. ''I think we'll find what we're looking for in one of those places, if this threat is real.''

Sebastian stopped. ''You don't mean we've got to get into one of those little dragon ships, do you?'' He shuddered at the thought of being in any kind of craft after their narrow escape from the *Magdalen*.

''Gondolas,'' Corwyn replied. ''And, yes, I do. We can't see what we need to on foot.''

''We've done all right so far.''

''We haven't really been anywhere except the business district,'' Corwyn said, pulling Sebastian by the arm toward the quay. ''We've been sitting here, waiting for Hydro Phobius's agent to come to us. Now we're going to go find him. Besides, we'll need a boat to take samples from the canals and the lagoon.''

Sebastian wondered whether he might change his specialty to some element other than water—say, earth or fire. Anything that wouldn't require him to set foot in another boat. He let himself be dragged along, hoping his dissatisfaction showed in his face.

It must have, because Corwyn abruptly halted, peering up at his apprentice. ''All right, what is it?''

''Huh? I just don't like getting into boats.''

Corwyn shook his head. ''I don't either as a rule, but that's not what I meant. What's on your face?''

''Oh.'' Sebastian scratched at his stubble in embarrassment. ''It's a beard.''

''Hmmm,'' Corwyn snorted, unconsciously stroking his own whiskers as he studied Sebastian. ''Not yet it isn't. Maybe in a couple of years. But why are you starting a beard in this heat?''

Sebastian shrugged, unwilling to admit that he was growing it to be more like Corwyn. "I'm tired of barbers breathing garlic on me." He felt himself flush. "A man can only take so much."

Corwyn pursed his lips and nodded, apparently satisfied. "Well, just don't trip over it," he quipped dryly. "And don't let it dangle in your plate." He let go of Sebastian's arm to hail a passing pair of gondoliers.

Sebastian followed, struggling to suppress a sheepish grin. Maybe a gondola ride on the canals with Corwyn wouldn't be so bad after all.

From dim, narrow canals where even whispers echoed, Corwyn and Sebastian sailed out of the city and onto the brilliant, tranquil expanse of the lagoon. Near the horizon, the umber sails of fishing boats stood in sharp contrast against the green water and the azure sky. Corwyn, reassured by the water's stillness, watched with amusement as Sebastian gripped the sides of the gondola, terrified of sinking.

But the alchemist's amusement died when he realized Sebastian's fear stemmed from the wreck of the *Magdalen*. It was just one more brick added to the edifice of Corwyn's guilt.

He shifted on his velvet cushion, suddenly uncomfortable under the silk awning of the gondola's *felze*. If he hadn't been in such a hurry, Gwen and Oliver would still be alive. After the storm, Corwyn had made quiet inquiries into their fate, not wanting to raise Sebastian's hopes. Their bodies hadn't been found, but the only other survivor from the *Magdalen* appeared to be a young nobleman who had washed up somewhere in the Veneto. Gwen and Oliver must have perished, and it was all Corwyn's fault. The only way he knew to atone for their deaths, however, was to push himself harder. Even more than before, he had to stop Hydro Phobius and save Venice.

As if to emphasize his morbid frame of mind, the gondola glided by the watchful silence of San Michele, the cemetery island where the Venetian dead lay buried. Dark green cypresses peered mournfully over the somber, ivy-covered wall encircling the island. The two gondoliers, who had chattered amiably the whole way, paused.

"It's a small place, but there's room enough for all of Venice on it," the forward gondolier commented after a moment.

The aft gondolier nodded. "It's the one place where we poor folk become landowners at last."

Corwyn muttered under his breath.

"What was that?" Sebastian asked.

"I said, the time'll come when gondolas will only require a single gondolier—and it won't happen soon enough, either!"

They sailed on to Murano, a wealthy suburb of Venice and the center of the Venetian glass industry for the past hundred years, from the time when fire danger to the city had forced the glass manufacturers out of Venice itself. Here Corwyn planned to buy the bottles he would need for his alchemical tests. The chemicals would come from local apothecaries.

Built on nine islands like a smaller version of Venice, Murano boasted its own Grand Canal and coined its own money. The significance of the latter occurred to Corwyn when he had to exchange ducats for *oselle*. He was convinced he always lost in these exchanges, and he made a mental note to find another dice game for Oliver. They were running short of funds.

Then, remembering that Oliver could no longer help him, he felt guilty for having such thoughts.

He wasn't allowed to see the glass being blown, of course; Venetian glassmakers could be executed for revealing the secrets of their craft. But he was shown an assortment of finished wares from which to choose: goblets and vases, bowls and bottles, ranging from opaque glasses in vivid colors to the newly invented Venetian crystal with its amazing clarity.

Corwyn marveled at it all, but was most impressed by the crystal. The manufacture of clear glass was an art that had been lost since the Roman Empire—even in Alexandria, Corwyn had never seen glass of such clarity. It was yet another sign of the reawakening in Italy, Corwyn concluded, frustrated by his inability to fully grasp this awakening so it could be conveyed to Pomme de Terre.

He selected some bottles, regretting the cost, and was waiting for them to be crated when he caught sight of his reflection in a mirror. Made from the same colorless glass, this mirror lacked the smoky quality of mirrors he had seen before. Corwyn frowned, discouraged by how old and tired he looked. There were advantages to imperfect mirrors after all, he thought, ones which softened the truth.

Then he straightened, recalling the story one of the pilgrims from Canterbury had told—the pardoner, if he remembered correctly—about a large, spherical mirror made of clear Venetian glass. Corwyn asked the shop foreman if he'd ever heard of such a mirror.

The foreman, previously garrulous, quickly turned laconic. Yes, he had heard of such a mirror, he admitted when pressed. It had been made by a renegade glassmaker who was later punished for revealing secrets to a foreigner and then trying to escape. Everything to do with the glass industry in Venice, he said, from techniques and equipment to the workers themselves, belonged to the state. And, no, the foreman didn't know what had happened to the strange mirror afterward; it had never been found. Perhaps it was just a legend after all.

Corwyn puzzled over this for a while, deciding at last that it was just one more example of the Venetian tendency to romanticize everything connected with the city. In Venice, any object or event could be recast to support the city's grandiose view of itself, from the stolen bronze chimera on the piazza that had been transformed by popular consent (and the addition of a pair of wings) into the lion of St. Mark, to the adoption of St. Mark as the city's patron, thereby ousting St. Theodore, the previously reigning saint. Even the past could be altered, turning Venice's questionable involvement in the Fourth Crusade into a glorious victory for Christendom; that this victory also brought tremendous wealth and advantage to the republic was an unexpected outcome, of course.

Despite his cynicism, Corwyn took grim satisfaction in all of this, for it mirrored what he had done in reshaping his memories of Alexandria. The only difference was that the Venetians seemed untroubled when they passed their wishful thinking off as truth, while Corwyn's past had caught up with him when he'd tried to do the same with the Renaissance.

Back in the gondola with the crate of bottles, the chief gondolier confirmed Corwyn's impression by launching into a series of stories that underlined Venice's uniqueness. He told of local midwives who claimed to have witnessed bizarre births in recent months, and monks from the cloister on San Michele who had abandoned their vows and left the order after the graves there began to disgorge their dead. Corwyn smiled and watched Sebastian, who looked strangely bereft without his blue cap. The apprentice listened awestruck, his knuckles white where he gripped the gunwales. At least the stories took Sebastian's mind off the water, Corwyn thought. And they gave the lad something to do besides hovering around Corwyn.

Corwyn sighed. He knew he'd been ill-tempered since Gwen and Oliver were lost, but Sebastian made him even grouchier by crowding so close, needing comfort like an abandoned pup, yet flaring up whenever Corwyn's efforts to console him became too obvious. It seemed he wanted Corwyn to be a father to him as well as a master, and that Corwyn wasn't prepared to do.

Suddenly, Corwyn realized that the gondolier had abandoned Spanish, which he'd spoken when Corwyn and Sebastian claimed to be from Spain. Now he was speaking English instead, evidently having recognized

Sebastian's true native tongue. Corwyn felt a moment of
panic, then relaxed. Anyone who tried speaking Spanish
with Sebastian soon realized the apprentice didn't know
the language. And Corwyn, busying himself with water
samples and other alchemical tasks, wasn't likely to be
mistaken for a gentleman. Clothes hadn't altered what
he and Sebastian were. Maybe it was time to abandon
their disguise as noblemen from Spain.

Then the gondolier told about fish catches in the lagoon
that consisted of nothing but schools of long-dead bones,
the skeletons still miraculously intact and swimming. At
least with Ascension Day coming up, the gondolier went
on, and with it the ritual Marriage of the Sea, Venice's
dominion over the water would be restored. Soon, he
said, all would be well again. And he crossed himself
anxiously.

Corwyn jerked upright. The gondolier was obviously
embroidering his tale with the part about the bones still
swimming—trying to impress a pair of gullible foreigners. But fish kills themselves provided a clear indication
of how Hydro Phobius planned to destroy Venice. He
was poisoning the lagoon!

In the rooms they had rented for their combined living
quarters and laboratory, Sebastian tiptoed nervously
around Corwyn. The alchemist was setting up bottles for
the last procedure they would perform—the breath of
demons test. Around him, dirty vials, spilled chemicals,
and shards of glass littered the tables and stools. Most
of the debris resulted from finished work; the rest was
evidence of Sebastian's assistance. Since the gondola
ride, when they'd collected samples of water from the
canals and the lagoon, Corwyn had become so frenzied
that it flustered Sebastian and he'd made repeated mistakes. In his hands, glassware became slippery, reagents
spilled from their containers, and water samples dribbled
to the floor on their way to rejoin the sea.

So far, the analyses had established nothing more ominous than an influx of unusually fresh water into the

canals and lagoon. Corwyn had looked perplexed. "Well, that explains why fish catches are down," he'd said. "Saltwater fish have been driven from the lagoon, while freshwater fish haven't caught up with the change. In time, a new stability will develop. But I can't imagine that Hydro Phobius thought he could endanger Venice this way, even if it were possible for him to alter the salt content of the lagoon." Then he'd laughed. "Maybe he was planning to further disrupt fish catches with the explosives aboard the *Magdalen*. How pathetic! Hydro Phobius must have seriously underestimated how hard it would be to destroy a city. It would serve him right if we let him proceed so the whole world could watch him fail."

Corwyn had decided, however, to confirm these initial results with the breath of demons test. Although it took five days to complete, this test—combined with other findings—would prove beyond doubt whether slow-acting poisons were contaminating the lagoon.

The breath of demons test measured the amount of life force, the *spiritus* or *pneuma* so central to all alchemy, which was present in a sample of water, and how much that amount diminished over the five-day period. This life force was essential to all living things, Corwyn had told Sebastian at their first meeting; streams gurgled and waves beat against the shore for the sole purpose of infusing this force into the waters of the earth, so that the creatures of those waters could breathe it and live. These creatures included not only the fishes and other things visible to the eye, but also the naiads and sprites and other benign demons present in all waters. They, too, took life force from the waters, and if present in unusually large numbers, they could deplete a water's ability to support ordinary forms of life. The breath of demons test measured the effect these minor demons exerted on a given body of water.

Corwyn lined the bottles up in front of him in two rows. He placed a pair of minnows in each bottle of one row, resealed the bottles, and began timing how long the minnows survived as they used up the life force in their respective bottles. The second row consisted of identical bottles, but they would be left sealed for the five days, after which the procedure with the minnows would be repeated. The difference in times that the minnows survived would tell Corwyn how much effect the naiads and sprites and such had exerted on each water sample during incubation.

Corwyn fidgeted while he waited, hastily jotting down each time as the pairs of minnows expired, then quickly dumping out the finished bottles. Indeed, so hurried did he seem that Sebastian wondered whether his master was really waiting long enough to be sure the minnows were dead. He considered saying something when one pair appeared to flop weakly again just as Corwyn poured the contents of the bottle out, but thought better of it. He'd learned not to cross Corwyn when the alchemist was in this state.

While Corwyn watched the first row of bottles and recorded survival times, Sebastian dripped sealing wax over the corks of the second row of bottles. Then he carried the bottles outside to the canal and lowered them beneath the surface in a wicker basket. Here, each bottle would be bathed in the essence of the canal environment during the five-day incubation period, keeping conditions inside the bottles as near as possible to those of the waters their contents represented.

When Sebastian returned to their rooms, Corwyn had finished. He was leaning back, looking pleased with himself. "What I like about aquatic alchemy is that it's so dependable," the alchemist said. "Everything can be measured, quantified. By conducting these tests, we can show what the state of a given water is and whether it's been poisoned or corrupted. You always know exactly where you are." He waved a hand expansively at the mess in the room. Sebastian suppressed a groan as he realized whose job it would be to clean it up. "Today, for instance," the alchemist went on, "we've proven conclusively that the waters in the canals and the lagoon have turned fresh. If we traced this fresh water back to its source, we'd probably find that natural artesian wells in the city are flowing more heavily than usual, and that saltwater from the Adriatic Sea is being flushed from the lagoon at a faster rate than can be offset by the tides.''

Sebastian frowned to himself, recalling the various fountains he'd seen throughout the city. Some were barely dribbling, if water flowed in them at all. Water sellers with jugs brought over from the mainland were doing a brisk business keeping the city's cisterns supplied. That didn't seem consistent with what Corwyn was saying. Maybe they weren't looking at this the right way. He opened his mouth to say as much, but the alchemist went on. "Obviously, all Hydro Phobius has accomplished is to inadvertently drive stagnant water out some of the smaller canals, much to the relief of local citizens. And fishermen are having to get their catches from the Adriatic instead of the lagoon. Actually, if it weren't for the explosive charges on the *Magdalen,* I'd be inclined to doubt that Phobius is here.'' For a moment, some private thought cast a shadow over Corwyn's face. Then he brightened. "Well, the *Magdalen*'s gone and Ascension Day will arrive in another week. Whatever Hydro Phobius planned, it's too late for him to do any damage now.''

The alchemist slapped his thighs and stood. "I don't know about you, but it's time for me to resume wearing my normal clothes. *Cucullus non facit monachum.*''

"Cuckold us what?''

Corwyn shook his head. "It's Latin. It means the hood doesn't make the monk, or in this case a pair of noble Spaniards. I'm tired of acting like a worn-out old Spanish nobleman. I'd rather be a worn-out old aquatic alchemist instead.''

Sebastian frowned and considered this. He'd gotten the impression lately that people didn't believe he was the Spaniard he claimed to be, though he couldn't understand why his disguise had failed. On the other hand, he didn't want to go back to wearing the clothes he'd worn in Pomme de Terre. And trying to keep up with changing styles here in Italy had completely frustrated him—not to mention having to wear those embarrassing codpieces.

An alchemist's robe would be the perfect solution. He could become a younger version of his master.

Corwyn put an arm around Sebastian's shoulder, standing on tiptoe to reach. "We have five days to wait before we get the results on the breath of demons test," he said. "Let's use this time to find a tailor, then see what damage the Venetians themselves are doing to their city with this Renaissance business." He chuckled, evidently pleased with his joke. "You know, it's too bad there aren't ways of measuring social changes like in aquatic alchemy. The Renaissance will never reach the level of a true alchemical science until we can measure it objectively."

Sebastian stooped so his master could reach his shoulder, and let himself be led awkwardly to the door. Despite Corwyn's apparent enthusiasm about seeing what the city had to offer, Sebastian thought his master's words rang hollow. After all, there were only the two of them now. Gwen and Oliver left a void which Corwyn and Sebastian tried unsuccessfully to ignore. Also, Sebastian couldn't shake the feeling that Corwyn, in his distracted state, was overlooking something important about the water of Venice. And finally, it irritated him to hear his master dismiss the Renaissance so casually. Sebastian found the spirit of rebirth in Italy infectious. He only wished Gwen could be here to share his excitement.

A stray thought crossed his mind, and he wondered whether a lack of objective measurements might explain the difficulties he'd encountered in transforming Gwen. Perhaps that had limited his own success at social alchemy. But how would one measure the amount of nobility in another person?

ACT 15:

Twelfth Knight

EVEN WITH PERSISTENCE, GWEN HAD TROUBLE GETTING an audience with Francesco Foscari. Each time she went to the Doges' Palace, she worked her way through layers of clerks and bureaucrats on the first and second floors, only to be stopped at last outside the doge's chambers by an impudent young page. "State your name and business," the boy invariably demanded, as if he'd never seen Gwen before.

After a week of this, Gwen sighed. "By now, you know who I am and why I'm here."

"You've come to see the doge?" the page asked haughtily.

"You know I have."

"And you represent La Bella Donna of Belmont?"

"Just as I did yesterday and the day before and the day before that."

"And you still insist your business with the doge is private?"

"For his ears alone, from my mistress to him."

The page sneered. "The doge isn't. here today. Not for you."

"Then I'll stand here like a post, but I will speak to

him,'' Gwen said. She remained rooted this time, staring back at the page.

It was a role she adopted, a person separate from herself that she had constructed in order to survive, while the real Gwen huddled somewhere inside, lost to grief and despair. If this outer person sometimes acted mechanically, at least it—''he,'' she reminded herself firmly; this person she played was a ''he''—at least he went through the motions of being alive. For now, that was more than the real Gwen could do.

So this person, unimpressed by the spectacle of Venice, dealt with the ducal bureaucracy through braggadocio and bullying, and even patience when need be.

On this particular day, the page made the mistake of trying to stare her down. Gwen stood before him, eyes unfocused, unblinking. After a while, the page began to fidget. Finally, he shuffled away, mumbling excuses. He returned to tell her that the doge would see her now, and looking none too happy about it.

Gwen was admitted into a room gaudy with velvet hangings, gilt carvings, and huge paintings on the ceiling and walls. Across the room, a pair of windows with elaborately carved moldings overlooked the Rio di Palazzo, with the boatyards of the Arsenale visible some distance away. Across the lagoon lay the Lido, white in the sun, and the Adriatic beyond.

At the far end of the room, several old, beady-eyed men—their ancient, parchment-covered bones draped with scarlet robes and the gold chains of office—stood around a table, examining a large map. One of the men, a handsome, gray-haired individual, younger than the rest, quickly folded the map over, obscuring Gwen's view. ''Plans for the *Festa della Sensa*,'' he told her with an easy smile.

Gwen nodded. It was a reasonable explanation—Ascension Day was one of the most important celebrations in a Venetian calendar thickly set with civic and religious festivals. But Gwen had glimpsed enough of the map to see that it was of the neighboring mainland, where Venice had been waging a series of wars in a *terra ferma* policy designed to protect the city from land-based attack. Could it be these men were making plans that would harass the Duke of Milan through the summer?

But neither domestic affairs nor foreign policy were Gwen's concern. She approached the man who had spoken to her. "The doge, *signore*, which one is he?"

"I'll answer for him," the man replied with the same warm smile. "What do you want?"

"*Signore*, please tell me if you're the doge, for I never saw either of you before. I'm reluctant to waste a good speech that I've taken pains to learn."

The man's smile broadened. "Your accent's foreign. Where are you from, boy?"

"Your pardon, but I can only tell you what I came here to say, and that isn't part of it," Gwen said. "Please tell me if you're the one I seek, so I may proceed."

"Are you an actor?"

"No, definitely not. And yet, I'm not the part I play. But are you the doge?"

The man sighed, his smile gone. He waved a hand at the room. "Can't you tell the canary by the cage they keep him in? Yes, I'm the doge."

There were grumbles from the men at the table while Gwen inspected the doge. Three years earlier, at fifty-one, he'd been one of the youngest men ever elected to his position, and the most controversial.

Gwen took a deep breath and pushed on. "Why do you keep your subjects and your children from having the dogaressa they deserve?" she asked. "It's your civic duty to remarry, *signore*."

Francesco Foscari looked startled. Then he shrugged and indicated the other men. "So the council frequently tells me. But I'm resolved to seven years of mourning before I'll marry again." There were protests from the councillors at this, but Foscari restrained them with an upraised hand. "Thus do I forestall remarriage, not prevent it. It's a burden I'll eventually have to bear again." For a moment, his shoulders sagged and he added softly,

"A burden as well for the woman I take to wife, who will also have to endure it." Then he straightened. "The council would limit my mourning if they could. But come, what's the point of your speech? Leave out the frivolous parts and get to the heart of it."

"But I worked hard to memorize it," Gwen said. "It's very poetical."

"Then it's all the more likely to be untrue," the doge replied. "Keep it for yourself." He drew back to study her. "I heard you were disrespectful to my page, and I allowed you in more to wonder at you than to hear you. This message must be something hideous, since your lack of courtesy is so frightful."

"Your pardon, *signore*. My name is Cesario, and my business concerns your ears alone." Gwen glanced pointedly at the others present, then noticed again the upturned map. "I'm not bringing an overture of war from Filippo Maria Visconti or a demand for submission. I carry an olive branch, and my message is peaceful."

"Yet you began rudely, Cesario. Who are you? What do you want?"

Gwen drew herself up. "The rudeness I learned from my reception. Who I am doesn't matter, and what I came for is for you alone to hear."

The doge chuckled and motioned to the others. "Leave us. I'll hear this saucy boy's secret." Again there were protests, but he waited them out. When the councillors had gone, he asked, "Now, boy, what's your message?"

"The heart of it is simply that—a heart, and nothing more," Gwen said, falling back on a message learned by rote. "The heart of my mistress, La Bella Donna. She sends me to tell you that she loves you and begs your love in return."

"Ah, La Bella Donna," the doge replied. "Yes, I've heard of her late father's strange injunction, and the banishment it brings to those who seek her hand. The republic has lost a half dozen leading citizens this past year, including high-standing officers of the state. But never mind that now. I've told your mistress before, I cannot love her.''

''Yes, but I'm commanded to press her suit,'' Gwen said. ''She says I'm to write sonnets to you on her behalf, to sing them from a gondola beneath your windows in the dead of night, and to make the air reverberate with your name. I assure you, *signore,* you'll find no rest until you heed my plea.''

''You might do much, Cesario,'' Francesco said, his lips a tight smile. ''Especially if you did all this on your own behalf.'' He took a step toward her, then walked away instead. ''Tell me, boy, what's your parentage?''

''As you see, I'm a gentleman.''

Francesco snorted, his back to Gwen. ''One without manners, I think. Yet captivating, nonetheless.'' His voice became stern. ''Return to your mistress. I can't love her. Bring no more messages''—he turned, his voice softening—''unless perchance you yourself come again to tell me how she takes my refusal. Until then, Cesario, farewell.'' From a purse at his waist, he produced a coin. ''Thank you for your trouble. Spend this for me.''

Gwen brushed his hand aside indignantly, knowing this was called for by her part. ''Keep your money. It's my mistress, not me, who lacks repayment. May you come to love someone with a heart of flint, so that your entreaties, like my mistress's, will suffer the same contempt you now show. Farewell, *signore.*''

Gwen strode from the room, pursued by a chuckle from Francesco. In the hall, the page also heard his master's response, and glared at Gwen malevolently.

Arriving back at La Bella Donna's villa in Belmont, Gwen made her habitual check for Oliver. She no longer expected to find him, but was reluctant to let go of the last remnants of hope. Part of the reason she remained in La Bella Donna's service was because this was where she had seen him last, and she told herself he might eventually come back here.

But Oliver still hadn't returned. Gwen reached into

her doublet and touched what remained of Sebastian's cap to assure herself that her companions had existed, then went on.

The usual cluster of suitors waited on the terrace. Gwen wondered if they were always there, even in the rain, struggling between prudence and greed in their eagerness to win La Bella Donna's hand. The price of failure was high, yet so was the lure of her inheritance. As a result, they idled away their days in endless boasts, lacking the courage to either commit to the gamble or withdraw from the field without trying. Gwen heard the stridency in their voices as she entered the villa, and she shook her head. In the past several days, she'd begun to suspect that La Bella Donna's fortune was an illusion. For one thing, there was a shortage of servants at the villa; and most of the rooms remained closed, despite the normal practice of opening them for circulation. Also, the gardens were run-down except near the main path and the terrace where the suitors congregated.

All in all, Gwen decided, La Bella Donna lived much more modestly than the impression she gave. But it was also obvious why she tried to appear wealthy—without an inheritance, such a woman had little chance of attracting a husband.

Gwen found her mistress in the shrine containing the three caskets. It was the second time La Bella Donna had escorted one of her suitors there since Gwen had arrived, and Gwen marveled anew at the wealth implied by the room's furnishings. Attending La Bella Donna this time were the Prince of Aragon and Antonio Nessuno.

Besides Oliver, there were other reasons why Gwen stayed in La Bella Donna's service. For one, Gwen found herself perversely fascinated by the woman, and she hoped the sense of mystery surrounding the heiress would be resolved before it came time for her to leave.

Then there was Antonio. Withdrawn yet always polite, Gwen felt in him a kindred spirit who knew what it was to suffer in silence. Wounded in her own heart, she was drawn to the pain she sensed in his, and found in him comfort for her anguish.

La Bella Donna scowled when Gwen entered the shrine, apparently angry at the intrusion. She covered her irritation with a curt command. "Quick, open the curtain. The prince has taken his oath and comes to choose."

Gwen drew back the curtain, revealing the caskets. La Bella Donna turned to the prince and warbled, "There they are, my sweet! I'm locked in one of them. If you love me, you'll find me out. Antonio and Cesario, stand back while he makes his choice."

The prince grunted, his attention on the caskets. Gwen thought he looked more pale than usual, though it could have been the light. He read the inscriptions, stretched out his hand toward one of the chests, then drew back. At last he reached again, selecting the silver casket. "'Whoever chooses me gets what he deserves,'" he read. "Very well, I deserve good fortune. Give me the key for this one at once, so I may learn my fortune."

La Bella Donna handed him the key, and he threw open the casket and looked inside. For a time, he was silent.

"That's a long pause for whatever you find in there," La Bella Donna coaxed at last.

Gwen frowned, thinking her mistress sounded strangely unconcerned about the outcome of the attempt. Perhaps other suitors had tried the silver casket previously, so that she already knew its contents.

"All that's here is the portrait of a fool," the prince replied miserably, removing a picture of a jester's head. He held it up and compared it to La Bella Donna's veiled face. "I don't suppose it much resembles you?" he asked, hope sounding fragile in his voice. La Bella Donna huffed indignantly. "Ah, no," the prince answered himself before she could respond, "I don't suppose so. The text beneath the portrait assures me of that. 'Herein lies as much as fools like you deserve.' Or so it reads." He replaced the picture in the casket, locked it, then addressed La Bella Donna. "I'll keep my oath, my lady, and leave at once." He turned and left the room.

"Thus has the candle singed another moth," La Bella Donna gloated under her breath, marking this latest victory on her tally sheet. "Oh, these fools, displaying their lack of wits. I only wish I'd known how many foreigners would be drawn to this flame—I might have chosen a different candle."

Gwen didn't understand what La Bella Donna meant. All she knew was that eleven men of noble birth—eleven of La Bella Donna's knights—had now been sent into exile. Gwen shivered, more certain than ever that she, like the departed Prince of Aragon, had once endured this woman's gloating, but unable to recollect when or where. Perhaps it had been somewhere else in Italy, while Gwen and her companions had been on their quest.

The thought made her long for her friends all the more.

La Bella Donna jolted Gwen from her reverie. "You've been to see the doge?"

"Yes," Gwen answered slowly, wondering how much of the audience to relate.

"Well?"

"So please you, my lady, he told me that he won't remarry for seven years out of courtesy to his departed wife."

"That sounds more like cowardice than courtesy," Antonio interrupted, his voice casual. "He's as much a fool as the others. Why bother with him?"

"*Signore*," La Bella Donna said softly, "may I remind you that Shylock's been crying out against you in the streets, complaining that his daughter has been seduced by a thief? He swears he'll have vengeance."

Antonio snorted. "Perhaps we should let him try."

La Bella Donna's veiled face stared at him. "Let him try? Surely I haven't heard you right." When Antonio failed to answer, she turned to Gwen. "Come hither, boy."

Gwen wondered what the moneylender's loan to Antonio had to do with La Bella Donna and the doge, but did as she was told.

"If you ever fall in love," La Bella Donna cooed, "in the sweet pangs of it, remember me. Mine is the way of all true lovers: unsettled and skittish in everything except the constant image of my beloved's face."

Even if the doge were interested in La Bella Donna, Gwen thought, he wouldn't be able to dwell upon her face. Who knew what it looked like?

Antonio snorted again. La Bella Donna glared at him in a way that was withering despite the veil, then went on. "Go back to him, Cesario. Tell him that my love, more noble than anything, has nothing to do with lands or power. Tell him it's only that miracle of nature—himself—that attracts me."

The thought of the doge believing such tripe struck Gwen as humorous. She choked back a laugh. "Perhaps he fears the terms your father set for winning your hand," she suggested.

"I could teach him how to choose correctly," La Bella Donna trilled. "Although then I'd be forsworn."

And I could teach him to choose correctly as well, Gwen suddenly realized, for the correct casket, the one with La Bella Donna's portrait, could only be the one made of lead. She'd seen the contents of both the others. Yet she was sure the doge would never need such instruction, because he'd never be fool enough to try for La Bella Donna's hand. "What if he can't love you, my lady?" she asked, drawing out the game.

La Bella Donna drew her dumpy figure upright. "I won't accept such an answer!" She waved at Gwen with disdain. "But you're a man—or a boy, anyway. What can you know? A man's heart couldn't hold the passion that I feel, for men lack the capacity. Their love is mere appetite. No, Cesario, you can't understand what a codpiece prevents you from feeling."

"But I do know." Gwen sighed, thinking of Sebastian. "And I can love as deeply as any woman."

"What do you mean? How can you know?" La Bella Donna snapped, her voice shrill at being contradicted.

Gwen thought quickly. "My father's daughter once loved a man, yet her love wasn't any stronger than mine."

"Hmmph," La Bella Donna snorted. "Yes, well, you understand the general theme, at least," she said, abruptly dismissing Gwen. "Go to him quickly, Cesario. My love can't be denied."

Gwen started to leave, but the heiress called her back. "I almost forgot," she said, reaching into a fold in her gown and producing a letter, set with Antonio's seal. Antonio, seeing the letter over La Bella Donna's shoulder, grimaced and turned away. La Bella Donna had had Gwen deliver such letters on previous occasions, but this was the first time Antonio had witnessed it. La Bella Donna handed the letter to Gwen, unaware of his reaction behind her. "Take this. Deliver it here in Belmont on your way, giving it only into the hand of the person to whom it's addressed."

Gwen accepted the parchment and left, thinking more about her mistress than about Antonio or the letter. Why did La Bella Donna seem so uncomfortably familiar? If only Gwen could see her face!

Gwen delivered the letter to an attractive but bored looking noblewoman whose husband's business often kept him in Venice—the fate of many wives and mistresses in Belmont, Gwen reflected. This one sized Gwen up, evidently considering whether the "boy" before her might offer an afternoon's diversion, then changed her mind when she recognized Antonio's seal. To Gwen's relief, the woman quickly dismissed her and began opening the letter.

From there, Gwen rode to Mestre where she stabled her horse (La Bella Donna's horse, actually) and picked up the *traghetto*, or ferry, which ran between the mainland and Venice. Soon, she was again at the Doges' Palace. Foscari's page made clear his displeasure at seeing Gwen back again so soon, but Gwen reminded the boy that the doge had asked Gwen to come and tell how his message had been received by La Bella Donna.

"Your servant, *signore*," Gwen said with a bow when she was admitted.

"Please leave us," Foscari said to the councillors, who were again grouped around the map as if unable to agree on a plan. The councillors scowled at Gwen. When they were gone, the doge turned to her. "My servant, boy? You're the servant of La Bella Donna."

"And she is yours," Gwen said formally, "so all that's hers must therefore be yours as well. Your servant's servant is your servant, *signore*."

Foscari frowned. "She's most forward. I'd rather her thoughts were empty, instead of filled with me. I certainly don't think of her—not if I can help it."

"I didn't imagine you did," Gwen said with a grin. "But I'm charged to come and whet your thoughts on her behalf."

"I told you not to speak of her again," the doge snapped. Then he softened, smiling at Gwen. "Instead, I wish you'd undertake another suit, one I'd rather hear than music from the spheres."

"*Signore?*"

"Let me hear you speak on your own behalf."

Confused, Gwen turned away. "My mistress would have me press her suit with as much passion."

"Then I'm talking to a heart of stone," Francesco said. "I've said too much too hastily." He squinted at her. "Young though you are, there's already someone you love, isn't there, boy? What kind of person is she?"

"Much like yourself." Gwen dropped her gaze in embarrassment.

"Then she isn't worthy of you. How old?"

"A little older than me, but not as much as you."

"Too old, by heaven, in any case," the doge said. "Take a younger woman." Outside, the campanile bells rang the hour. The doge started. "The clock upbraids me for wasting time." He smiled. "Don't be afraid,

Cesario, I won't press you. I'll leave you to this mistress of your heart."

"No woman will ever be the mistress of my heart, except me," Gwen mumbled, feeling suffocated by her masquerade. It hadn't occurred to her before that playing this role might hurt another's feelings.

The doge's brow furrowed. "What do you mean? Cesario, if I thought I might persuade you . . ." He stared, then shook himself as a scuffle sounded outside the chamber.

Suddenly, the moneylender, who had been waiting when Gwen arrived, burst through the door, followed by the page.

"Grant me justice!" the moneylender cried as the page tackled him. "Let me have my bond. I'll have my bond!"

The doge frowned. "What is this?"

"Your pardon," the page panted, trying to drag the moneylender back out the door. "It's Shylock. He insists on being admitted. I've never known a creature who so resembled a man, yet was so keen to confound one."

"It'll go hard on the reputation of the state if I'm denied justice," the moneylender cried. "Hear me out, your lordship, I beseech you."

Gwen tensed, realizing this was the man who threatened Antonio.

"Very well," the doge said. He sighed and turned to Gwen. "The state's the only mistress I'll ever serve, and she bids me return to my proper duties. Your pardon, Cesario."

"And so, *addio, signore,*" Gwen said with a bow. "I won't bother you again with my mistress's entreaties." She hurried to the door, anxious to warn Antonio.

"Yet do return," the doge added with a slight smile, "for perhaps you'll yet move this heart, which now abhors her, to something more to her liking. So gentle a fiend as you might bear my soul to hell, if you wanted."

The page glanced from one to another of them suspiciously, while Shylock snorted and shuffled with impatience at the delay. Gwen let herself from the room and ran down a staircase with a lavishly molded and painted barrel vault. She reached the paved *cortile*, pushing past a water seller with his cartload of jugs. The water seller had made his rounds each day Gwen had been at the palace, finding buyers for his water now that the two bronze wellheads in the palace courtyard had mysteriously run dry. From there, Gwen made her way to the piazza, startling pigeons into sudden, thundering flight, a grey cloud that swirled quickly to the pavement again after she passed. She hurried on, her sword slapping awkwardly at her thigh, threading her way among the workmen who were constructing booths for the upcoming *Festa della Sensa*.

Halfway across the crowded piazza, Gwen heard running footsteps behind her. "*Signore*, wait," someone called. "Aren't you *Signore* Cesario, who was just now with the doge?"

Gwen turned, surprised to find the page overtaking her. "Yes?"

The page frowned in recognition, puffing laboriously. "My master returns this ring to you, *signore*," he gasped. "You might have saved me the effort by taking it away yourself. He adds, moreover, that you should tell your mistress he'll have nothing to do with her." The boy paused to wheeze, then continued with a scowl, "One more thing. You're never to come again . . . unless it's to report how your lady takes this response."

He looked pained at having to add this qualifier that invited Gwen's return.

"But I didn't give the doge a ring," Gwen said, puzzled.

"Come, *signore*, he says you threw it at him peevishly. I'm sure he'd want me to return it the same way." The boy hurled something at Gwen. She ducked and it clattered to the pavement. "There it lies," the page continued. "If it's not worth stooping for, let it belong to whoever finds it." Haughtily, he strode back to the palace.

Gwen retrieved the ring—an emerald surrounded by

smaller diamonds—and slipped it on her thumb. The fit was loose. If the doge's fingers had been any thicker, the ring would have fallen off Gwen's hand. But what did Foscari mean by sending it to her? She hadn't given him anything from her mistress.

Apparently, this wasn't intended for La Bella Donna, but was actually a gift for Gwen, delivered by an unwitting messenger. Yet it wasn't for Gwen either, but for "Cesario," an invented creature who bore only the outward shape of a man. And not much of that, Gwen added to herself, glancing at her rag-stuffed codpiece. Better to chase a dream than to fall in love with her disguise.

Time would have to untangle this mess, she decided. It was too hard a knot for her to untie.

It was night by the time Gwen crossed to the mainland again and arrived at Belmont. She made her way through darkened lanes to La Bella Donna's villa, walking her horse, not having anticipated the need for a lantern. She stabled the horse near the entrance to the estate and had just reemerged when the familiar shape of La Bella Donna waddled from the shadows ahead. Moving stealthily, the heiress entered the deserted gatekeeper's cottage, half hidden under a stand of cypress trees. Gwen frowned, wondering again where she had seen La Bella Donna's peculiar gait.

Inside the cottage, the yellow glow of a candle moved around for a while, then went out. Gwen waited for it to be relit, but nothing happened. Gwen shrugged. La Bella Donna often disappeared at night; maybe this was where she went, although Gwen couldn't imagine why.

Gwen was about to leave when someone approached from the lane, passing close to Gwen. The newcomer carried a veiled lantern, but for a moment Gwen could see the person's face. It was the noblewoman to whom La Bella Donna had written earlier that day. At the cottage, the woman hesitated, then blew out her lantern, knocked softly, and went inside.

Gwen crept closer. Through an open window, she heard the noblewoman fumbling across the room. "Antonio?" she called in a loud whisper. "Antonio, where are you?" Suddenly, the woman gasped. "Is that you?" She giggled. "Oh, Antonio, you're so impetuous!"

A hiss shushed her, and all talking ceased. Gwen frowned, puzzled. Clothes rustled as they were torn off and flung aside. The sounds from the cottage became guttural, instinctive, rising in urgency. Gwen eased away from the window, embarrassed to be eavesdropping. For a moment, she wondered how La Bella Donna was able to act like Antonio with such intimacy. Gwen had found it difficult enough to appear as a man while dressed. Automatically, she checked the padding in her codpiece. What the heiress did with her neighbors in the dark was her business, however, not Gwen's. Still, Gwen couldn't help feeling sorry for the suitors who risked exile for La Bella Donna's hand—among other of her parts.

Gwen started up the path to the villa, then stumbled as she suddenly realized where she had seen someone move with La Bella Donna's gait before.

It wasn't possible, she told herself. Yet more than ever, she wanted to see the face behind La Bella Donna's veil. Then she thought of the three caskets inside the villa. The answer was within reach, in the form of La Bella Donna's portrait inside the third casket, the one made of lead.

The villa was silent, La Bella Donna's suitors gone to wherever they went at night. Gwen tiptoed into the shrine where the caskets were housed. She shut the door and lit a candle. Light gleamed from the polished armor and the gilt frame of the portrait. It glittered off the gold and silver caskets. Only the lead casket seemed immune—dull, aloof, sinister. Gwen reread the inscription. "Whoever chooses me reveals all he is." Nearby lay La Bella Donna's tally sheet, with eleven of its chessboard figures crossed off for the eleven noblemen sent into exile after they failed to choose correctly. Gwen smiled to herself, smug in the knowledge that she would be the twelfth such "knight" to try—the one who would finally succeed.

It took a while for her to pick the lock with the tip of her dagger, fumbling at the mechanism without experience and guided only by candlelight. At last the lock fell open. Eagerly, Gwen flung open the lid and peered inside.

A spectral face floated in the depths of the casket. Gwen almost dropped the candle as she sprang back. The image jumped away too. Finally, Gwen gathered her courage and looked again. Her own face stared back at her. Cautiously, she reached inside the casket and withdrew a small, oval mirror in an inlaid frame. Beneath the mirror was an inscription: "Herein is revealed all that you are—no more will you receive."

It took a moment for Gwen to absorb the significance of the message. When she did, rage replaced bewilderment. Not only had La Bella Donna tricked her suitors with a test that couldn't be passed, but she'd drawn Gwen into this web of deception as well, using her in an attempt to lure the doge into exile. "The cheat! The fraud!" she cried.

But the worst of it was that Gwen still didn't know what La Bella Donna looked like.

Then she noticed the silk banner draped upon its stanchion near the alcove. Cautiously, Gwen unfurled the cloth. A familiar crest greeted her—a fish floating belly-up in a stylized body of water. Above the image arched the Latinized motto: *"In pollutis profitum est."*

Gwen dropped the cloth as if it burned her and hurried from the room. More than ever, she wished Sebastian and Corwyn were here, for she knew beyond question now where she had seen her "mistress" before.

Not in Genoa or Florence, but in the Pyrenees the previous summer!

ACT 16:

The Cook's Tale

FIVE DAYS AFTER SETTING UP THE BREATH OF DEMONS test, on the eve of Ascension Day, Sebastian and Corwyn sat in their rented rooms, preferring to stay inside rather than venture out into the city. Everywhere in Venice, people were preparing for the following day, for *Sensa* as the Venetians called it, when the city's dominion over the sea would be reestablished. Sebastian and Corwyn, however, found the excitement elusive without their companions. Even the brilliant Adriatic sun failed to dispel their mood, just as the book publishers and libraries of Venice couldn't capture their attention.

Nonetheless, Sebastian had begun to fidget after two or three days of this. Now he stroked his chin, wondering whether the straggly growth there had become any heavier. He tried to make himself sit still, then smoothed his new black gown, its simple lines modeled after Corwyn's. It had been a relief when he'd quit trying to keep up with Renaissance styles—and the codpieces! He lifted his chin, reminding himself that he had more important things to do than to slavishly follow the latest fashions. After all, he was an alchemist, like Corwyn.

Part of Sebastian's frustration lately stemmed from the conceit the Venetians had for themselves and for the advantages they felt were theirs by right of birth. "So you're from Spain," natives often said to him and Corwyn in the first few days after their arrival. (Now the same comment was made about England, where they had since relocated their origins.) A consoling tone would enter the speaker's voice. "Ah, well, you're in Venice now," as if mere presence was enough to convert them to the true faith of cultural reawakening as perfected here in Venice.

In fact, the self-absorption of Genoa and Florence reached a pinnacle in Venice's obsession with itself. Sebastian had to admit, however, that there was something contagious about the city. As ephemeral as the foam flecking her lagoon, Venice was nonetheless as vast and enduring as the sea itself. If only the Venetians weren't so arrogant about it, Sebastian thought, so condescending!

In their rooms, Sebastian finally tired of listening to his master's sighs. He practiced standing up a few times, imitating Corwyn's manner of slapping his thighs and jumping to his feet, until the old alchemist grumbled at him to stop. Sebastian sulked quietly a while, then wandered out to the canal, where he fished the wicker basket out of the water. The bottles shifted, clunking against one another dully. Sebastian carried the basket inside, where he lined up the bottles on one of the tables and broke the wax seals. Quickly, he put a pair of minnows in each bottle and replaced the corks. Using a series of hourglass-type timers, he noted how long it took before the pairs of minnows began to die. He marked the times on a parchment sheet, next to the numbers of the respective bottles.

He had just finished and was about to dump out the contents of the bottles when a faint motion in one of them caught his eye. He waited, puzzled. After a moment, one of the "dead" minnows started swimming. It was lethargic, and something about its motions didn't seem quite right, but the minnow was definitely circling inside the bottle. Soon the minnows in the other bottles were swimming as well. Sebastian called Corwyn over.

"What is it?" the alchemist asked, sounding irritated at being disturbed. He leaned over Sebastian's shoulder to peer at the bottles, where the minnows now swam with undiminished energy, then at the timers, the sands of which had all run out. "Sebastian, what have you done?" he demanded. "The minnows are lasting longer than they did with the first series of bottles."

"That's what I wanted you to see," Sebastian said, stung by his master's words. "Something's wrong."

Corwyn grunted. "Something's wrong, all right. You've contaminated the test."

"Huh? What do you mean?"

"I mean that these results are impossible, and you know it." Corwyn turned away, disgusted. "Somehow, you compromised the integrity of the bottles."

Sebastian sat, stunned, watching the minnows swim vigorously in their bottles.

"Well, it's too late to set up another test," Corwyn growled. "Ascension Day is tomorrow. According to Niccolò Machiavelli, Hydro Phobius has to destroy Venice by then if he's going to do it at all." He grabbed his conical alchemist's hat and strode to the door. "I'm going out for something to eat. You can come along or not, as you like."

Sebastian remained seated, not speaking, while Corwyn waited for an answer. Finally, Sebastian heard the door close. He turned, but his master was gone. Wasn't it enough, he wondered, that he had to endure Gwen's death; did he have to be subjected to this as well? Even Corwyn could be wrong sometimes—about the water in Venice and maybe even about the Renaissance.

Angrily, Sebastian swept the bottles off the table. They shattered, spilling water and flopping minnows onto the floor. Corwyn would be displeased, of course, but Sebastian was used to that. For now, he felt better. He snatched up his own conical alchemist's hat, purchased the day before to replace the cap he'd lost in the storm, and hurried after his master.

In a nearby shop where they had started eating when their funds ran low, Sebastian pulled up a stool at a small table, opposite Corwyn. He glanced at his master, but Corwyn wouldn't acknowledge him. Sebastian drew a little away from the table, pretending it didn't matter, and listened unhappily to the conversations around him. Normally, the topics concerned Ascension Day and the recent floodings, or the problems caused by some heiress on the mainland whose method of selecting a husband was sending Venetians into exile. Today, however, everyone was talking about the doge's decision to hear a moneylender's suit against a Venetian merchant, with the trial set to begin in a couple of hours.

The eccentric local dialect was difficult to follow. The pronunciation and rhythm of speech was soft and liquid, and many of the words themselves were altered or short-ened. Sebastian worked at following the conversations, however, telling himself he was trying to improve his understanding of the language. At least it kept his mind off Corwyn's disappointment.

Sebastian also tried to keep his attention away from one of the tables across the room, where two courtesans sat dressed like men. Although cross-dressing was offi-cially banned, many of the city's thousands of registered courtesans adopted it, presenting an ambiguous sexuality that Sebastian found both provocative and repelling. He lifted his chin and turned away, yet glanced back at the pair frequently, reminding himself how strongly he dis-approved. It reassured him to know that Gwen would have found their behavior appalling as well.

They ordered their meal, Sebastian choosing one of the pork pies for which the shop was noted. Corwyn ordered something called *fegato alla veneziana,* together with a plate of pasta, then launched into a long expla-nation of how Marco Polo had brought noodles back to Venice from Cathay, and how they had swept through northern Italy since then. The unfortunate thing was that

Corwyn himself hadn't thought to introduce noodles into
Europe after his own travels to Cathay, he said, before
Marco Polo was born. The alchemist, too, seemed to be
avoiding the undercurrent of tension between them, Sebastian noted grimly.

When their meals were served, Sebastian was disappointed to discover that Corwyn's dish with the exotic
name was nothing more than calf's liver fried with onions. He wrinkled his nose, then attacked his pork pie
hungrily, finding relief in the diversion of eating.

They had just started on their meals when the cook
and owner of the shop emerged from the back to chat
with some of his customers. Like most Venetians, he
seemed ebullient today, reassured no doubt by the arrival
of *Sensa* on the following day.

"Hey, Giuseppe," someone called to him, "let's see
that leg."

The cook plunked a foot atop a stool and lifted his
dirty gown. Sebastian craned his neck along with the
other patrons, and was rewarded with the sight of a running sore on the man's shin. Sebastian swallowed hard
and turned back to his meal, his appetite diminished.

He resolved to mind his own business from then on,
just as the same person called out to the cook again, too
loudly to ignore, "How many customers would you
have, do you think, if they knew where you get that
white sauce you're so famous for?"

Sebastian froze, a bite of pork pie halfway in his mouth
and dribbling sauce down his chin. He spat out the bite,
aware of several customers at an adjacent table who were
pointing and laughing at him. Maybe he'd misunderstood
the Italian. But no, across the table from him, Corwyn
too looked green behind his beard, and seemed to have
lost interest in his liver and onions. For once, Sebastian
had understood correctly.

Abruptly, one patron left the shop, accompanied by
further jeering.

Giuseppe, who had been laughing as heartily as anyone, frowned in sudden doubt at the retreating customer.

"Ah, don't take it in earnest," the heckler called to him. "It's only a game, a jest. Besides, your wife'll make up the loss. She earns more with her one pie than you do with all of yours put together—and without ever getting off her back!"

"*Sì*, and she sells the same pie over and over again, which is more than Giuseppe can get away with," another patron called.

There was renewed laughter, with Giuseppe joining in. Sebastian noticed, however, that the two courtesans were disgruntled by this talk of competition from an amateur.

"Ah, that's funny," Giuseppe choked out at last, wiping his sweating face. "But a cook can sell the same pie over again, if he's smart." He laid a finger alongside his bulbous nose and grinned, cutting off several derisive snorts. "It's the truth, as I'll tell you. Judge for yourself."

Sebastian winced, wondering if this was to be another tasteless joke. But he listened as the cook told about a baker whose pie crusts were thick enough to stand on their own. Once cooked, the baker would remove some of the filling from each pie and use it over again. Meanwhile, the crusts still looked full to bulging, so he was able to sell the adulterated pies at full price.

This went on undetected for some time. One day, however, the baker's greed pushed him too far and he tried selling a pie which was nothing but crust, the entire filling having been removed. But a fly landed on the pie while the baker was displaying it to a crowd, and the added weight caused the empty crust to collapse, revealing the man's dishonesty. He was promptly beaten out of town and never returned.

"*Sì capisce!* And I'll bet you carry the marks of that beating to this day, don't you, Giuseppe?" another heckler cried when the cook had finished his story.

Once again, the patrons of the shop erupted in laughter, led by the cook who was the butt of their jibes.

Sebastian laughed as well, preferring this story to the

one about the cream sauce. When he looked over at Corwyn, however, the alchemist was grim. "What is it?" Sebastian asked, thinking that he'd done something to further irritate his master.

"All that fresh water," Corwyn mumbled. He reached across the table and gripped Sebastian's arm. "It's not flowing out of the ground naturally. It's being pumped."

Sebastian grimaced and shook his head. "I don't understand." He tried to pry off Corwyn's hand.

Corwyn shook himself, becoming aware of his apprentice. "Oh, sorry." He let go of Sebastian.

"Corwyn, what's the matter?" Sebastian asked, rubbing his arm.

"The lagoon. It's just like one of those pies the cook was telling about." Corwyn pointed to where the cook was laughing at another tale. "I don't know how Hydro Phobius is managing to pump so much water out of the ground, but he is. He must be. As he depletes the aquifer beneath the city, the lagoon floor begins to settle."

"So Venice really is sinking." Sebastian thought about all the rumors they'd heard in the city. "That's why there's been so much flooding."

Corwyn nodded, his eyes on the ceiling, his thoughts further away. "But that isn't the worst of it. If he pumps enough water out, the lagoon floor will be in danger of collapsing. Just a slight disturbance, properly applied, would be sufficient to trigger that collapse. A disturbance like"—the alchemist squinted as if seeking an answer among the rafters—"like a series of black powder charges."

"The *Magdalen*," Sebastian whispered.

Corwyn nodded again, then pursed his lips. "We have to find Phobius's pumping operation and stop it, or this *Sensa* will become Venice's 'descension' day, and the city will do more than symbolically join with the sea. But how could Phobius be removing so much water from under the lagoon?" He thought a moment, then his gaze swung around to bore into his apprentice, making Sebastian squirm. "I owe you an apology," the alchemist said at last.

Sebastian glanced behind him to see who Corwyn was speaking to. "You do? What for?"

But Corwyn was already leaping up from the table, his expression fierce. "The minnows! Come on, Sebastian, we haven't any time to waste."

Perplexed, Sebastian ran after his master, who was evidently returning to their rooms. Then he faltered, thinking about the bottles he'd broken. Corwyn didn't know about the mess in their rooms. Suddenly, Sebastian felt guilty about it, and about having left the minnows on the floor to die. What if they were vital to Corwyn's plan for saving Venice?

Sebastian continued after his master, hurrying more slowly than before.

ACT 17:

The Merchant of Menace

THE MORNING AFTER DISCOVERING LA BELLA DONNA'S secret, on the eve of Ascension Day, Gwen was awakened by the sounds of an argument. She emerged from her room to find La Bella Donna blocking the entrance to the villa, preventing a jailer from leaving with Antonio in his grip.

"I'm sorry, *signorina*," the jailer said as he tried to dodge around La Bella Donna's bulk with his captive, "but Shylock has been plaguing the doge morning and night, threatening the reputation of the state if the doge denies him justice. No one can shake him from his course. Antonio, he claims, has forfeited, and he says he'll have justice, he'll have his bond."

La Bella Donna shifted to block the jailer's way again. "I don't care. You can't take him. You brought him here to tell me this; let him go and claim he escaped."

The jailer shook his head. "I came here as a favor to Antonio, but I must return him to Venice."

"The doge will never allow this forfeiture to hold."

Antonio shook his head, a strange half smile on his lips. "The doge can't deny the course of the law. The business foreigners have with Venice will be badly affected if justice is denied."

Gwen, listening from her doorway, was startled. Antonio sounded almost pleased by his arrest.

The jailer, still trying to escape around La Bella Donna, nodded at Antonio's words. "I've heard Shylock swear he'd rather have Antonio's flesh than twenty times the value of the loan, that his daughter's reputation can't be purchased. For his part, the doge wants to finish this business before the *Festa della Sensa* tomorrow, so he'll hear the case this afternoon." The jailer shook his head. "If the law doesn't stop Shylock, I pity Antonio." He indicated the merchant with one hand while holding him captive with the other.

"Let us go," Antonio told the La Bella Donna, moving her aside. "It's over. I'm no longer of any use to you." He smiled fully this time. "Worry has so wasted me that I hardly have a pound of flesh left for Shylock to take. I just pray Jessica comes to see me before I pay my debt to her father. After that, I don't care."

"Antonio, you fool!" La Bella Donna screeched as the two men left, her veil fluttering out from her face with the fury of the blast. "Just remember you'll die like anyone else if Shylock cuts deep enough. Do you hear me? You're not immune to his knife." She raised herself on tiptoes to better hurl her invective. "Do you understand me, you miserable creature? Your beloved Jessica will see what you're really made of if you go through with this! What'll she think of you then?"

Antonio stiffened, but continued walking. La Bella Donna slammed the door and stalked back into the villa. "The ungrateful wretch!" she hissed. "He'll ruin everything. And I still need him, damn his nonexistent soul!" She stopped short when she discovered Gwen watching. "What're you doing here?" she snapped. She leaned forward, seeming to peer at Gwen intently from behind her veil. "What did you overhear? Did I say anything?"

Gwen shrugged, purposely casual. "Only that Antonio's been arrested, and that you'd stop Shylock if you could." It was hard to control her revulsion now that she knew the truth about her "mistress." But Gwen was concerned about Antonio; if La Bella Donna could free him from the moneylender's grip, Gwen was prepared to help rather than lose the one friend she had in Belmont.

"Hmmph!" La Bella Donna sniffed, but let Gwen's explanation stand. She held an elbow in one hand while tapping her teeth with the fingers of the other, apparently unaware of the intervening veil. "There may be a way out of this yet," she said after a while. "Cesario, you've been honest and true so far; remain so now. Take another letter to the doge. Perhaps I can convince him to allow, uh . . . a cousin of mine from . . . from Padua, a man well learned in the law, to act as judge when this case is tried. Things may yet be resolved in a way that'll satisfy both my interests and those of Venice." Suddenly, she stopped talking and grabbed Gwen's hand. "What's this?" She pointed at the gift the doge had given Gwen.

"A ring."

"I can see that, fool! But these are valuable gems, and you didn't have the ring before. Besides, it's much too large for you. Who's it from?"

"The doge." Gwen considered saying it had been given to her by the doge's page, since that was the literal truth, but decided against it. Such an excuse was unlikely to satisfy La Bella Donna's suspicion.

"So that's the way the wind blows, is it?" La Bella Donna purred, studying Gwen. She reached a hand to stroke Gwen's face, her touch conveying a malevolence that hadn't been there when she'd brushed Gwen's cheek once before. "Such a pretty boy, too."

Gwen repressed a shudder. On impulse, she took the ring from her finger and offered it to the heiress, more to protect the doge from La Bella Donna's machinations than to save herself. "I wore it merely to convey it safely to you, my lady," she said. "You were out when I arrived." Gwen stared pointedly at her, recalling La Bella Donna's secret assignation of the night before.

"Ah, yes, well . . ." La Bella Donna's words trailed off. With a snort, she grabbed the ring and pulled off her glove, jamming the band onto the smallest finger of her plump hand. Then she held out her hand to admire the effect.

It was the first time La Bella Donna's hand, or indeed any part of her, had been exposed to Gwen's view. Seeing the blunt, warty fingers, their knuckles tufted with reddish hairs, Gwen repressed a shudder. How well she remembered that hand from before, but not as the hand of an heiress.

La Bella Donna drew the glove back on, concealing hand and ring alike. "Well, you're forgiven, I suppose," she told Gwen. "This time. Just don't let it happen again." She sighed, sounding like a smithy's bellows. "It's too late for the casket routine to save Antonio now, anyway. We must resort to different tactics. Come with me, Cesario."

La Bella Donna led Gwen to a desk, where she hastily penned a letter, then folded it and sealed it with wax. "Give this to the doge, since you seem to have such ready access to him," she said, her voice dripping innocence. She raised a palm to fend of any response, though Gwen hadn't planned on making one. "Waste no time in words, dear boy, but get to the ferry and thence to Venice."

"With all convenient speed, *signorina*," Gwen replied with mock formality, bowing as she headed for the door.

"I don't care whether it's convenient or not," La Bella Donna snapped. "Get that letter there immediately!"

"Ah, Cesario," the doge said when Gwen was admitted, surprise lightening his normal severity.

"I'm sorry, *signore*," Gwen said, extending La Bella Donna's letter, "but I'm here only to deliver this from my mistress."

The doge turned without taking the letter, his face darkening. "I told you, your mistress's suit is pointless. Be gone, if that's all you came for. I won't be bothered with her."

"La Bella Donna has given up her earlier intentions,"

Gwen said. "This concerns the case against the merchant, Antonio Nessuno."

The doge turned back to her, raising his eyebrows. "In that case, perhaps I'll read it after all. I'm eager for a solution to this miserable case. The Jew has bound Venice in a Gordian knot, endangering the republic's reputation on the one hand and threatening the life of a merchant on the other." He took the letter and broke the seal, then frowned as he read. "Why, she urges me to allow a stranger to preside over the trial in my place," he said, striking the sheet with the back of his hand. "Some lawyer from Padua."

"A cousin of hers, I think she said," Gwen murmured.

"Hmmm, yes. A man named Balthazar. It seems your mistress recommends him highly." The doge began pacing. "Perhaps this isn't such a bad idea at that. If I don't like his finding in the case, I can always overrule him. On the other hand, he might solve this riddle in a manner that will preserve the reputation of the state, yet without requiring the death of one of its citizens." The doge grinned at Gwen. "Come, Cesario. You shall witness this trial as a clerk of the court."

Gwen protested, but the doge was insistent. He had her wait while his page dressed him in the cloth-of-gold robe and ducal bonnet worn on state occasions, then he motioned for the page and Gwen to follow him from his chambers. The page, clearly annoyed, turned up his nose at Gwen.

In the corridor, they were met by a procession of squires, stewards, and councillors, the latter dressed in crimson robes and the gold chains that bound them to their offices like royal prisoners. Gwen squared her shoulders self-consciously and stayed close to the page's side near the rear of the assembly.

They climbed the stairs, holding the pace to a funereal march for the sake of the wheezing, aged councillors. On the third floor, with its official halls and rooms of state where the Council of Ten, the Senate, and the other ruling bodies of Venice convened, they proceeded solemnly to the judicial chamber where the case was to be heard. The chamber was garish with self-importance: paintings, banners, and gilt dazzled the eye, so that Gwen found it difficult to focus on any one element but rather was assaulted by everything at once.

Officials and merchant noblemen already crowded the room, seated facing a lavish table at the far end. Around the sides of the table were arranged the ornately carved chairs of the doge's councillors and advisers, while the massive ducal throne dominated the center.

To one side of the room was the prisoner's dock. Gwen noticed Antonio standing there under the watchful eye of the jailer who had accompanied him to the villa that morning. How fearful his fate seemed, Gwen thought; yet Antonio appeared undisturbed by the prospects of the trial.

The doge was seated with great fanfare, followed by the councillors. The doge motioned for his page to stand behind his throne on one side and Gwen on the other.

When the official delegation had been seated, several more people entered the chamber, including a heavily bearded man dressed in gaberdine and yarmulke. Lest these marks prove insufficient to identify him, he also wore the required saffron circle of a Jew on his breast. A hiss sounded from the crowd, and people drew back as the man strode into the room. Gwen also tensed, recognizing him as Shylock the moneylender, the man who had interrupted her in the doge's chamber the day before. A dark-haired young woman with a matching circle and a tear-streaked face accompanied him. The woman glanced at Antonio, then lowered her gaze despondently, rousing Gwen's curiosity.

"Make room," the doge told the officials grouped before the table. "Let the moneylender stand before us." This done, the doge continued. "Shylock, the world thinks—and I think, too—that you're simply carrying your threat to its final hour before showing mercy. Before exacting the penalty—a pound of this poor merchant's flesh—it's believed you'll not only yield the forfeiture,

but touched with human gentleness, you'll forgive a portion of the principal as well, in view of the severity of
Antonio's recent shipping losses.''

"I've told your grace what I intend," Shylock said.
"If you deny me his bond, let the danger alight upon
your city and its charter.''

An angry growl rose like the sea and spread through
the room. "That's no answer," the jailer snapped from
the prisoner's dock.

Shylock folded his arms against the resentment flowing
around him. "I'm not bound to please you with my
answer.''

"Signore," Antonio said to the doge before the jailer
could respond, "I beseech your grace, make your judgment. Let Shylock have his will.''

Gwen frowned, studying Antonio. He seemed anxious
for the case to be decided against him.

"Your grace," said the dark-haired woman who had
entered with Shylock, stepping forward, "for the thirty
thousand ducats Antonio borrowed, here is sixty thousand.'' At her motion, a servant came from the back of
the chamber and dumped the contents of a small chest
onto the table before the doge. Gold coins spilled across
the surface and rolled onto the floor. For a moment, a
scramble to reclaim the escaping coins interrupted the
proceedings.

"Jessica, where did you come by that?'' Shylock demanded over the confusion.

Jessica lifted her chin. "I borrowed the money from
Tubal. Not a ducat of it comes from you, father.''

"But your standing with him comes from me, and
thereby his willingness to loan you the sum.'' Shylock
dismissed the mounded coins with a sweep of his arm.
"Not that it matters. If these sixty thousand ducats were
worth six times sixty thousand, still I wouldn't take them.
A daughter's reputation is beyond price. I'll have my
bond!''

"How can you hope for mercy, Shylock," the doge
asked, "if you'll render none?''

"What judgment should I dread, having done no wrong? I demand justice. Shall I have it?"

Again the angry murmur rose, and Francesco waited for it to subside. "Upon my power, I could dismiss this court," he cried when the room quieted again. "And I might, were it not that a certain Balthazar, a learned doctor of the law from Padua, has come here today."

Gwen, noticing Antonio's look of wariness, wanted to let him know that La Bella Donna had arranged for this Balthazar to come on Antonio's behalf, but was afraid if she did, Shylock would object.

The officer who had admitted Shylock earlier now approached the doge. "My lord," he whispered, *"Signore* Balthazar awaits outside."

"Bring him in," the doge replied.

Moments later, a squat, pop-eyed toad of a man in judicial robes waddled into the room and approached the table. Terror pinned Gwen where she stood, for she had seen the "doctor's" face before. It was Hydro Phobius, the man who had once captured and tormented her, until she had managed to escape. Now he was here, dressed up like a doctor of law. Gwen's knees went weak and she was afraid she might slide to the floor. She slipped behind the doge's throne, keeping it between herself and her former captor. Phobius, apparently unaware of her, advanced until he stood before the table.

"Give me your hand," the doge said. "Are you Balthazar, from Padua?"

"I am, my lord," Phobius rasped, extending his hand with a bow.

Gwen scarcely heard Phobius's answer, for her attention was caught by the ring on Phobius's little finger— the same ring the doge had given Gwen the day before, and that she in turn had given to La Bella Donna. So it was true, she thought—La Bella Donna was actually Hydro Phobius and not a woman at all. And the man standing before the doge was also Hydro Phobius, not Balthazar, doctor of law. Gwen leaned forward to warn the doge, then stopped. In telling what she knew of

Phobius, she would reveal herself. Besides, there was Antonio to think of. She crouched behind the throne, uncertain what to do.

The doge, too, apparently recognized his ring, for he glanced over his shoulder at Gwen and clucked with reproach. "You are welcome," he told Phobius, the words sounding more formal than sincere. He waved to a chair at one end of the table. "Take your place. Are you acquainted with the case before this court?"

"Oh, I'm thoroughly informed of it," Phobius said airily. "Which one is the merchant here, and which one the Jew?"

The doge hesitated, staring at Phobius. Gwen wondered if he was having doubts about this stranger, who recognized neither prosecutor nor defendant. Maybe Francesco would dismiss the case after all. Then the doge motioned to Shylock, whose saffron badge and clothing clearly marked him, and to Antonio, who stood bound beside the jailer in the prisoner's dock. "Antonio and Shylock, both of you, stand forth."

For the first time, Gwen felt uncomfortable in the presence of Antonio, and she wondered about the merchant's connection with La Bella Donna. Antonio had looked surprised when Hydro Phobius entered, and had been regarding the "learned doctor" suspiciously ever since, seemingly wary of Phobius's intentions on his behalf. Did Antonio know this man was also his "mistress," the heiress of Belmont? More importantly, did he know Balthazar and La Bella Donna were both really Hydro Phobius?

Suddenly, Gwen caught Antonio staring, as if he was wondering the same things about her.

"Is your name Shylock?" Phobius asked the moneylender.

"It is."

"It's a strange suit you pursue," Phobius said. "Yet such is the law that Venice cannot oppose you if you proceed." He turned to Antonio. "You stand endangered by his suit, do you not?"

"*Sì,*" Antonio replied, his voice guarded.

"And you admit to having agreed to this bond?" Phobius asked.

"I do," Antonio said.

Phobius raised his hands, palms up. "Then the moneylender must be merciful."

The doge sighed in exasperation. Gwen's lips twisted cynically at the thought of Hydro Phobius—who knew no mercy—urging others to show it.

"Why must I be merciful?" Shylock demanded with a baleful glare at the doge.

"The quality of mercy isn't to be strained by compulsion," Phobius replied, "but falls like gentle rain from heaven. It blesses him that gives, and him that takes. I say this to mitigate the justice of your plea, which if you insist on pursuing, this court must grant, giving sentence against the merchant there."

Her old adversary's words—so reasonable to the ear—left Gwen nauseous. She wondered what was at stake that would cause Hydro Phobius to abandon his masquerade as La Bella Donna and risk another, potentially more dangerous disguise. Phobius wanted Antonio freed, but why?

"My deeds upon my own head!" Shylock cried. "I crave the law, the penalty, and the forfeit of his bond."

Phobius looked around the room. "Is the merchant able to repay what he owes?"

Gwen snickered under her breath. Hydro Phobius knew the state of Antonio's finances better than anyone present, except perhaps the merchant himself.

The doge turned to Gwen and shushed her while the jailer leaned toward Phobius. "The moneylender's daughter offered to pay twice the sum on Antonio's behalf"—the jailer nodded at the gold heaped on the table—"but her father wouldn't take it. *Signore,* I beseech you, use your authority to twist the law a bit, doing a great good by committing a small wrong against this devil." He jerked his chin to indicate Shylock.

"I can't do that," Phobius said. He spoke to the jailer,

but his eyes were fixed hungrily on the gold. "There's no power in Venice that can alter an established decree. It would be recorded as a precedent, and many similar errors would take place as a result." He shook his head emphatically, as if to assure himself. "No, it cannot be."

The doge nodded, his face grim.

"I pray you, let me look at the contract," Phobius said, rubbing his warty chin thoughtfully. Shylock handed Phobius the parchment sheet and Phobius read it, pursing his thick, rubbery lips. "Shylock, there's twice the money Antonio owes you." He indicated the table with a wave of his hand, lingering on the gesture as if his fingers longed to grasp so much wealth.

"No," Shylock replied, "not for all the wealth of Venice."

Phobius shrugged and addressed the room. "Why, then this bond is forfeit. Lawfully, Shylock may claim a pound of flesh, to be cut by him from Antonio." He turned again to the moneylender. "Be merciful. Take twice the money, as offered by your daughter. Have me tear up the contract."

Gwen, still hiding behind the doge's throne, peeked at Antonio and was surprised to see him squirm, as if uncomfortable with the delay. Was he so eager for a verdict against him? She shook her head, unable to comprehend why Antonio would be anxious to lose this case, and thus his life, while Phobius seemed equally determined to save the reluctant merchant.

"I'll tear up the contract," Shylock said warily, "when the bond it calls for has been paid. You appear to be a worthy judge, *Signore* Balthazar; you know the law, and your comments have been most sound. I charge you by that law, of which you are a pillar, to proceed. There's no power on earth that can sway me. What Antonio took from my Jessica can't be repaid. I stand on my bond."

"What he took, I willingly gave," Jessica muttered from her seat, clutching her face in her hands.

Phobius opened his mouth, but before he could speak,

Antonio stepped closer. "I also beg the court for judgment."

Phobius scowled and motioned for the jailer to draw Antonio back. "Why then, here it is," he said at last, speaking to Antonio rather than Shylock. "Prepare yourself for his knife."

"No!" Jessica shrieked, rising to her feet. The doge shifted on his throne, apparently uneasy about the way the case was progressing. Antonio unlaced his doublet and blouse, baring his chest.

The doge half rose and turned to Phobius, but Phobius motioned him back down. "Do you have a balance to weigh the flesh?" he asked Shylock.

"I have it ready," Shylock replied.

"And have you brought a surgeon to stop the wound, lest he bleed to death?" Phobius continued.

Antonio snorted, earning him a glare of reproach from Phobius.

"Is that called for in the contract?" Shylock asked, examining the document.

"It isn't specified, but what of that?" Phobius said. "It would be good of you to show that much charity."

Shylock shook his head. "I can't find it. It isn't in the contract."

The doge interrupted, turning to Antonio. "You, merchant, have you anything to say?"

Antonio shook his head. "I'm prepared." He turned toward the room, where Jessica had been forced to resume her seat. "Give me your hand, Jessica." She looked at the officers who stood over her. After glancing to the doge for his nod, the officers let go and she went to Antonio. "Farewell," he told her when he had her in his arms. "Don't grieve. I do this willingly, for my own sake as well as yours. Think well of me in death, regardless what you are about to learn of me. I'm indebted to you, and if your father will but cut deep enough, I'll repay that debt instantly, with all my heart."

He motioned for the officers to take her away again, and they led her sobbing back to her seat. Gwen shook her head, puzzled by the daughter's opposition to her father's suit.

"We waste time," Shylock growled to Phobius, his expression shifting from anguished love as he looked at Jessica to open hate as his gaze swung to Antonio. "Proceed with the sentence."

Phobius nodded. "A pound of the merchant's flesh is yours. The law awards it, and the court agrees."

Gwen frowned, wondering if Hydro Phobius was indeed yielding to Shylock's claim. That didn't sound like him. A glance at Antonio told her that he, too, was suspicious, although why he should be, Gwen couldn't begin to understand. She felt sick with confusion, disoriented by loss. Even Sebastian's cap, tucked inside her doublet, failed to comfort her.

"Most righteous judge!" Shylock exclaimed, brandishing his knife in Antonio's direction.

"And you must cut this flesh from his breast," Phobius said with a trace of a smile. "The law allows it, and the court concedes."

"Most learned judge," Shylock cried. He moved in on Antonio. "A sentence! Come, Antonio, prepare yourself."

Phobius raised a hand. "But wait a moment. There is something else. This contract doesn't give you the right to a single drop of blood. The words are 'a pound of flesh.' In cutting it, if you shed one drop of Antonio's blood, your lands and goods are, by the laws of Venice, to be confiscated by the state."

Antonio's face clouded. "What?"

"Oh, upright judge!" the jailer exclaimed, clapping his prisoner on the back. "Mark him, Shylock—a learned judge, indeed!"

Shylock held motionless, his knife extended before him. "Is that the law?"

Gwen noticed that Francesco's frown was asking the same question.

"I'll show you the act for yourself," Phobius said.

"For, as you urge justice, be assured you'll have it, and more than you desire."

"No," Antonio groaned, shaking his head. "No, no."

"Oh, learned judge." The jailer laughed, gloating.

Shylock quickly collected himself. "I take the offer, then, of sixty thousand ducats." He looked from the table to Jessica. "But only if Antonio pays it."

Phobius shook his head. "You'll have justice, and that alone. Nothing but the bond. Cut off a pound of his flesh, but shed no blood."

To Gwen's surprise, Antonio lunged forward, his eyes bright. "No!" he hissed at Phobius. "You think to fool him. You think to fool them all and deny Shylock his rightful bond. Well, I relinquish all rights to my blood." He smiled, but it was a grim, twisted expression. "How much of it do you think he'll spill from me?" Then he turned away and ripped his blouse open wide. "Do your worst, Shylock, but do it now, so everyone present may learn the truth."

"Antonio, no!" Jessica shrieked. She turned to Phobius. "Don't let him do this."

Phobius shrugged, but Gwen thought the motion looked calculated. "Very well," he told Shylock, "do as the merchant says. But cut neither more nor less than exactly a pound. If you err by a single grain, you die and your goods will be confiscated."

Shylock hesitated. Antonio stepped toward him, still baring his breast. Shylock shook his head and backed away.

"Antonio, why are you doing this?" Jessica wailed. Behind the doge's throne, Gwen wondered the same.

"What are you waiting for?" Phobius asked, his manner exuding sincerity. "Take your forfeiture, Shylock."

"Give me my principal, and let me go," Shylock pleaded, backing up another step as Antonio continued to advance on him.

"I'll get it for you," the jailer said, turning to the gold on the table. "Here it is."

Phobius held up a hand. "Wait! He refused it in open court. He'll have nothing but justice and his bond."

Antonio spun on Phobius, his face contorted with rage. "You! You know if he cuts me, what he'll find. You scare him off with idle threats to prevent them from learning the truth." Abruptly, he leaped at Shylock and grabbed the knife. Shylock let go with a shriek and jumped away. Antonio raised the weapon with both hands, aiming the blade at his own body. Jessica screamed; officials shouted. Gwen knew Antonio was about to die by his own hand, but to what purpose?

Before Antonio could drive the blade home, however, the jailer and two other officers tackled him and wrestled him to the floor, pinioning his arms behind his back. The knife clattered away.

Phobius, ever calm, turned to the doge. "He talks madness, your grace. I believe these proceedings have affected his senses."

The doge nodded sadly. "I believe you're right. What else could account for this behavior? Pray, continue, Balthazar. Antonio will undoubtedly thank you when he regains his proper mind."

Phobius nodded and turned back to Shylock, who stood uncertainly, his attention divided between Phobius and Antonio. "Shall I not even have my principal?" the moneylender asked.

Phobius shook his head. "You'll have nothing but the forfeiture, and that to be taken at your peril."

Shylock grunted and made an abrupt gesture of dismissal. "Why, then the devil give him the good of it! I'll stay no longer." He started toward the door. "Come, Jessica!"

"Wait, Shylock," Phobius said softly. "The law still has a hold on you. The laws of Venice state that if an alien—which any Jew must be, being denied the rights of citizenship—if such an alien, I say, attempts to take a true citizen's life, then that citizen is to be awarded one-half of the offender's goods. The other half goes to the state, and the offender's life lies at the mercy of the doge. That's the predicament in which you stand, for it appears you've conspired against the life of Antonio. Kneel, therefore, and beg mercy of the doge.''

"Beg for leave to hang yourself," the jailer snarled, still gripping Antonio. "For the harm you've done to this innocent man, hanging is all you deserve."

The doge held up his hands for silence. "So that you'll see the difference between us," he said to Shylock, "I pardon your life before you ask it. But half of your wealth is Antonio's; the other half now belongs to the state."

Phobius nodded with satisfaction, and Gwen suddenly realized that he had managed to enlarge his own funds by bestowing half of Shylock's wealth on Antonio. In spite of the feeling in the room, Gwen felt sorry for the old moneylender and his daughter, now reduced to poverty. From Corwyn, she had learned tolerance of other faiths.

"*Anzi*, take my life as well," Shylock begged, going to his knees before the doge. "Don't pardon that. You take my house when you take the foundation upon which it stands. You take my life when you take the means whereby I live. I sought only to avenge my daughter for the disgrace Antonio caused. If this is justice, better that I should die."

When the doge shook his head, Shylock slowly turned on his knees to Antonio, his face a mask of anguish.

"What mercy do you expect Antonio to render you?" Phobius asked smugly. "You, who would have taken his life."

"A rope for his neck," the jailer responded for Antonio. "Nothing else, for God's sake!"

Antonio, having collected himself, motioned for the jailer to let go of his hold. The jailer did so, but remained close by. "So please my lord the doge and all the court," Antonio said, "I relinquish the fine of one-half Shylock's goods." Phobius spluttered and waved frantically at him, but Antonio pretended not to notice. "I'm content for Shylock to retain my half for his own use, to be rendered to his daughter upon his death."

Shylock stared at Antonio, dumbfounded, while Gwen looked on, equally surprised.

"But you can't do that!" Phobius shrieked, finding his voice at last. He turned to the doge. "Tell him he can't do that."

The doge shrugged, looking unhappy about Antonio's announcement. "It's most unusual, I admit, but I can't prevent him from giving the money to whom he will."

"No," Phobius cried, rising. "Oh, no, no! It's mine . . . I mean, it's Antonio's!" When the doge shrugged, looking at Phobius strangely, Phobius glared at Antonio, his face showing all the hatred Shylock had displayed earlier. "Now see what you've done?" he hissed. "You haven't heard the end of this. Just you wait."

The doge, apparently sensing that things were getting out of hand, rose to eclipse Phobius. "Are you content, Shylock? What do you say to this?"

Shylock tore his bewildered gaze from Antonio to stare at the doge. At last, he shook himself. "I'm content," he mumbled.

"Clerk, draw up the deed to this effect," the doge ordered one of the petty officials present.

Antonio hurried to Jessica, but Shylock pulled her toward the door, evidently still distrustful of the merchant. "Please, let me go," he asked the doge. "I'm not well. Send the deed after me, and I'll sign it."

The doge grunted. "Then go. So long as you do sign it." He turned to Phobius. "*Signore,* please accompany me to my chambers for dinner. There are questions I'd like to ask you about this case."

For a moment, Gwen wondered about Francesco's intentions, recalling his interest in her as "Cesario." But a quick look at the doge's face revealed utter seriousness.

Phobius's attention, however, was on Gwen. "You!" he whispered. "Now I remember." He tossed an answer to the doge, moving around the throne after Gwen. "I ask your grace to pardon me, but I must leave for Padua tonight."

Gwen bolted. Behind her, the doge ordered Hydro

Phobius to stop, but Gwen knew he wouldn't. She ran down the aisle and into the corridor. But before she could catch her breath, Antonio burst through after her, with Hydro Phobius close behind. Gwen hurried down the stairway and out of the palace, swiftly reaching the piazza, where she scattered pigeons and pedestrians. Her sword slapped at her side, and she steadied it with one hand to keep from tripping. Workmen, interrupted from building booths for the Ascension Day fair, swore at her as she careened by, then kept on cursing as other footsteps pounded after her.

From the piazza, Gwen darted down a side street, turned quickly onto another, and then a third, hoping to lose her pursuers in the bewildering twists and turns of Venice's streets and alleys. But the passage she'd chosen turned out to be a dead end, stopping abruptly at a small, deserted quay where waves lapped placidly against the bricks. She lurched to a halt and stared about her, seeking escape. The footsteps closed in from behind. She was about to dive into the canal when someone struck her around the waist, driving her to the pavement. Gwen struggled, her doublet tearing open as Antonio straddled her and grappled for a hold. He grabbed at her roughly, then froze, one hand on her breast, a perplexed look on his face. Gwen, too, held still, terrified of discovery. Antonio felt her breast as if assuring himself of what he held. Gwen slapped his hand away. Antonio grinned, but the expression held no humor.

"So, Cesario is a woman," he said.

ACT 18:

Odd Fellows

BACK IN THEIR ROOMS, SEBASTIAN SHOWED CORWYN the shattered remains of the breath of demons test. His face burned while the old alchemist surveyed the minnows—now quite dead from exposure to the air, lying among the shards that had once been bottles.

"Perfect!" Corwyn exclaimed. Sebastian flinched, thinking he was being sarcastic. But the alchemist looked genuinely pleased as he peeled a drying minnow off the floor. He handed Sebastian a bucket. "Go out to the canal and fill this, then hurry back."

Mystified, Sebastian did as he was told. When he returned, Corwyn dropped the tiny corpse in the water. Sebastian felt a pang of sympathy at witnessing this pathetic behavior. "Master, I'll go find some more minnows," he offered. "Some live ones."

Corwyn waved him to silence, staring into the bucket. After a moment he smiled, though it was an expression lacking in humor. "Come look," he said.

Reluctantly, Sebastian complied. When he looked into the bucket, however, instead of a dead minnow, he saw one apparently resurrected, swimming sluggishly in circles. "How'd you do that?" he gasped, awed by his master's powers.

Corwyn shook his head. "I didn't. It's still dead, but the thaumaturgical flux in the water gives it the appearance of life."

"Thaumaturgical what?"

"Flux. The energy responsible for all forms of magic." Corwyn put up his hands to fend off further questions. "As an alchemist, I deal with natural phenomena, solving pragmatic problems. I don't dabble with magic." He added in a barely audible mutter, "That is, not anymore."

Sebastian could see little difference between studying the energy behind acts of magic and measuring the life force consumed by demons, but he kept his opinion to himself. Corwyn tended to be touchy about such distinctions. "Venice must be a great place for doing magic," he ventured instead.

Corwyn glared. "This much thaumaturgical flux doesn't occur in the water naturally."

Sebastian, dismayed, tried to figure out what his master was driving at. "I didn't think it occurred naturally," he said. "There must be a supernatural reason."

"This is hardly the time to joke," Corwyn snapped. Sebastian started to object, but Corwyn cut him off. "The flux is contaminating the water that Hydro Phobius pumps out of the ground." Sebastian's confusion must have shown on his face, for Corwyn went on. "Phobius is using the flux to power his pumping operation. That's the only thing powerful enough to raise so much water. I've known it was theoretically possible, of course, but it's never actually been done before. For one thing, flux isn't safe at the high densities required." He frowned. "There are other problems, technical ones. I wonder if Phobius is using an elemental to generate the flux?"

That question didn't bother Sebastian nearly as much as the thought of being around magical energy after it was generated. A shiver ran up his spine, like the touch of a phantom hand. Maybe there was some truth after all to the stories they'd heard about empty graves and other strange happenings in the city. A force that brought dead minnows back to life might be capable of anything. He looked around for the short sword he'd brought from Pomme de Terre.

"We have to find where he's generating the flux," Corwyn said, breaking into Sebastian's search. "By stopping that, we can stop the pumping. But it has to be done safely."

To Sebastian, nothing about this sounded safe anymore, except the idea of leaving Venice right away. He was reluctant to suggest it, however. "So much for objective measurements always giving the right answers," he grumbled instead. As he waved an arm at the broken bottles, he spotted his sword under a pile of rags. "The breath of demons test didn't tell us anything."

Corwyn, who had still been watching the dead minnow, straightened indignantly. "Objective measurements do give reliable answers," he said angrily. "Provided we use the measurements, or tests, to ask the right questions in the first place."

"Huh?" Sebastian buckled on the sword. It fit awkwardly over the bulky alchemist's robe, but appearances didn't matter as much as they had moments earlier. "But, master, the tests didn't tell us there was theological flux in the water—we figured that out by accident. And they haven't told us the source of the flux. We aren't really any better off than we were with the question of how to conduct a renaissance. Aquatic alchemy's no more reliable than the social kind."

Corwyn drew his lips tight. "Thaumaturgical flux," he said, "not theological. And the tests didn't fail. If they didn't answer the right questions, it's because we didn't ask them. The fault lies with us, not the tests— and certainly not with aquatic alchemy."

"But—" Sebastian bit his lip; the look on his master's face didn't encourage argument. Besides, Sebastian suspected Corwyn might be right. But if he was, might not the same problem hold true of their attempts at social alchemy as well? Could they have gotten the wrong answers to the Renaissance only because they hadn't asked the right questions?

"In fact," Corwyn went on, pressing his point, "I think a slight modification in the breath of demons test might lead us straight to the source of the thaumaturgical flux."

"A slight modification?" Sebastian asked, bewildered, his mind still occupied with questions and answers.

"Well, a significant modification, perhaps." Corwyn paused, looking exasperated. "Oh, all right, a major modification, an enormous one." When Sebastian continued to stare, the alchemist sighed. "Just go to the fishmonger's and get a half-dozen fish."

"What kind?"

"Any kind, as long as they're dead. The more dead, the better."

Sebastian jumped to comply. At least this was an order he understood, even if its purpose eluded him.

Twenty minutes later he was back, holding a string of fish well in front of him to avoid the smell. Corwyn reached for them, then shrank back instead, clutching his nose.

"The fishmonger tried to convince me these were fresh this morning," Sebastian said. "Then, when I told him what I wanted, he said he'd meant that they were *ripe* this morning, that they'd actually been caught yesterday." Sebastian wrinkled his nose and tried to stretch his arms out further. "I think he was still lying. These fish have to be at least two days old. He just couldn't believe anybody would actually want such a thing." Sebastian paused. "Why do we want them?"

Without taking time to answer, Corwyn motioned for Sebastian to set the fish on a table, next to six bottles left over from the breath of demons test. The bottles were empty, although the alchemist had corked them and sealed them with wax. Around the neck of each bottle he had tied a length of cord. He indicated for Sebastian to pass the other end of one of the cords through the gills of one of the fish and then tie it. Soon, each fish was connected to a bottle by a long cord. Then Corwyn had Sebastian carry cords, fish, and empty bottles outside. Once in the open, the two of them gulped lungfuls of fresh air. "Wait here," Corwyn gasped as he led Sebastian to the nearest quay, then hurried off along the canal.

Sebastian waited uneasily, standing upwind of the fish and ignoring the glares of passersby. Soon Corwyn arrived in a gondola. "Hey, he can't come aboard with those," the lead gondolier protested when Corwyn waved Sebastian onto the boat. The two gondoliers nudged the craft away from the quay, holding it at a safe distance with their long oars.

"He's not bringing them aboard," Corwyn responded. "Just be ready to follow those bottles. Now, move closer."

Hesitantly, the gondoliers allowed the boat to drift back toward the quay. When it was close enough, Corwyn had Sebastian drop his burden in the water and step aboard. The fish sank in an oily cloud of peeling scales, pulling the bottles after them. Then the bottles bobbed to the surface, still connected to the fish by the cords.

For a moment, nothing happened. Then the dead fish began swimming up the canal, dragging the makeshift buoys behind. As the corpses swam faster, the bottles gained momentum. The gondoliers stared in disbelief. "After them!" Corwyn shouted, breaking the men from their trance.

The gondola rounded a turn and came upon the sounds of a commotion ahead. Sebastian rested his hand on his sword, thinking they had reached the source of the magical energy. But the noise was only an old man's shouting. Dressed in gaberdine and wearing the yellow emblem of a Jew, he railed at the buildings like someone possessed.

"Thieves, thieves!" he cried, while a young woman guided him down the street. "Look to your houses, Venice, look to your daughters and your money! Oh, what's to become of me?''

The woman tried to hush him, but he shook her off. "Who would be a father? Never trust your daughters except in what you witness for yourselves," he shouted to the echoing walls. He turned to the woman who was pulling him. "Jessica, he must have used magic charms to weaken your will, or you'd never have loved him. I'll have him arrested as a witch!''

People on the quay glanced at the pair, then looked away, hurrying their steps.

"Oh, my daughter," the man moaned as he was dragged along, "corrupted by the spells of a mountebank, in love with a villain.''

"Serves him right," one of the gondoliers muttered to Sebastian as the vessel rounded another corner, leaving the pair behind. "That's Shylock, the moneylender who was pressing the doge for a pound of Antonio Nessuno's flesh. The doge's decision must have gone against him.'' He spat into the water.

"Keep your mind on your task," Corwyn growled, pointing to the bottles that were drawing further ahead.

Sebastian shivered, strangely unsettled. Much as he disliked dealing with magic, even that seemed preferable to whatever troubled the moneylender, and Sebastian was glad his own course took him elsewhere.

So the gondola glided through the waterways, a gruesome parody of the holy processions that carried sainted relics through the canals of Venice. Finally, outside one of the lesser palaces along the Grand Canal, the bottles stopped, bobbing against the building's foundation.

The dead fish had reached their destination.

ACT 19:

The Merchant's Tale

"DON'T BE AFRAID," ANTONIO SAID. "I WON'T HURT you."

Gwen didn't believe him, but stopped struggling and lay still, letting him think she did. "What do you want?"

Antonio sat back, giving her enough room to breathe, too little to escape. "I want you to deliver a message for me."

"You have a strange way of asking." Gwen snorted.

Antonio glanced nervously around the quay. "This is no ordinary message. I must have your word that you'll deliver it."

"All right," Gwen said slowly. "Let me up and I'll deliver it. What's the message?"

Antonio shook his head. "I don't trust you. If I let you go, you'll escape."

"Then we're at an impasse," Gwen said. Eventually, someone would stumble upon them and she could cry out for help. Until then, she had to keep Antonio talking.

Antonio studied her. "Do you know the penalty for women dressing in men's clothes?"

Gwen didn't want to admit that she didn't. "The courtesans do it all the time. You see them in gondolas of

271

an evening often enough, dressed like men and surrounded by admirers.''

"Yes, they do," Antonio agreed. "But there are still laws against it, nonetheless, laws which they choose to flaunt. Perhaps the doge would make an example of you, to discourage such disdain for the law in other women.''

"The doge wouldn't do that," Gwen flared. "He likes me.''

"As a man, no doubt. But what would he think if he knew you were a woman?'' Antonio waited. When Gwen failed to respond, he went on. "Even so, perhaps the council would choose to force his hand, if they were to find out. Francesco Foscari has powerful enemies who'd relish the opportunity to hurt him through someone he cares about. Besides, are you prepared to be revealed as a woman in any event, and to be considered no better than a courtesan? An unlicensed one at that.''

Gwen listened, dismayed. She knew courtesans were held in high regard in Venetian society, yet she couldn't bring herself to be considered one of them. Besides, what Antonio said was true: she couldn't afford to be exposed as a woman. "What do you want me to do?'' she asked, her voice dulled with defeat.

Antonio nodded to himself, apparently satisfied, then let her up, keeping a hand on her wrist. While she brushed herself off and tucked Sebastian's cap back inside her doublet, he glanced around again uneasily. "This isn't safe. *He* might find us here.''

Gwen didn't need to ask who Antonio meant.

"We'll go to my palace," Antonio went on. "It's one place my master wouldn't think to look for you. I'll explain everything there.''

He led her through side streets and alleys to the entrance of an impressive—if somewhat dilapidated—palace on the Grand Canal. The doors and windows were surrounded by the elaborate rope-carved stone moldings typical of many Venetian buildings, but the rivets holding the marble facings to some of the walls had rusted, al-

lowing the slabs to pull loose and expose the brick core
of the structure.

Hurriedly, Antonio unlocked the door and pushed
Gwen in. The vast hallway they entered was dark and
bare, and the building looked to have been vacant for
years. Cobwebs hung in strands from the ceiling. Dust
lay thick on the floor, undisturbed except for a trail made
by the passing of many feet between the outer door and
an archway across the hall. Beyond the arch, the trail of
footprints disappeared into the unlit depths of the palace.
Gwen peered at the gloom near her feet and saw where
something had stepped briefly outside the usual path,
leaving a few prints distinct from the rest. She shuddered
and drew closer to Antonio. Whatever had made those
three-toed, clawlike marks clearly hadn't been human.

Antonio followed the path through the archway, dragging Gwen after him. She stumbled along unwillingly in
the near dark. Fleeting glimpses of the rooms beyond
left a series of disjointed impressions: a row of graceful,
spiral columns that vanished into obscurity overhead; a
Byzantine mosaic showing dimly through the dust on the
floor; and ornately carved cornices high on the walls,
their gold leaf dulled by age and grime. As Antonio
hurried her along, their footsteps echoed back from the
vaulted expanse of the chambers. The little light that
penetrated this far was quickly swallowed up by distant,
shadowy corners. Even the air was tainted with the musty
smell of ancient tombs.

Finally, Antonio veered onto a lesser path, his boot-
prints faint in the dust underfoot. With relief, Gwen
noticed that his seemed to be the only prints coming or
going from this direction.

Antonio took her to a small side room, where he lit a
candle. Though sparsely furnished, this room possessed
a feeble domesticity which Gwen found appealing after
what she had seen of the rest of the palace. A narrow
bed stood in one corner, next to a stand which held a
pitcher, a wash basin, and a chamber pot. Across the
room in the opposite corner was a table supporting a

bowl of overripe fruit. A pair of mismatched chairs had been drawn up to the table.

The only other furnishing was a large wardrobe. One door stood ajar, and inside, Gwen caught sight of bright silks, cloth of gold, and rich velvets—garments which suggested wealth far beyond anything else in the room. This was the apparel in which Gwen had always seen Antonio dressed and which defined him socially. She looked at him, inviting an explanation.

Antonio closed the wardrobe sharply, as if embarrassed by it, and motioned Gwen to a chair. When she was seated, he dragged the other chair closer to the door, then apparently changed his mind and crossed instead to the nightstand by the bed. "Would you like some water?" he asked, holding up the pitcher. "I'm afraid I can't offer any wine."

Gwen shook her head.

"How about something to eat?" He returned the pitcher to the stand with a thud and hurried to the table. "Some fruit perhaps?" With a stroke of his dagger, he sliced a withered melon in half. The two portions fell away, rank and discolored inside. Gwen recoiled from the smell. Antonio frowned at the offending fruit, looking puzzled. "I'm sorry," he said. "I didn't know. I only keep it to pretend."

"Then what do you eat?" Gwen asked.

"I don't." Antonio turned away. "Not . . . not very often."

It was Gwen's turn to frown. She had been kidnapped and brought here against her will, but now her captor seemed suddenly intent on proving himself a good host, trying desperately to please her. Then she smiled. Whatever his purpose, she knew how to turn a man's attentions to her own benefit.

Antonio faced her and waved an arm that took in his surroundings. "It's not mine, you know. The palace is only leased, and that on borrowed money. Even my name on the city's registers belongs to someone else—a minor merchant without friends or family who was returning here after several years on Cyprus. When the ship he traveled on was found adrift, overcome by plague, I was quietly substituted in his place. You saw in court today how my carefully constructed facade is beginning to unravel. But in the next day or so, this masquerade will finally bear fruit''—he stared unhappily at the rotting melon—''and I won't have to pretend any longer.''

He stopped, and the silence grew oppressive. ''Who are you?'' Gwen whispered at last.

''No one.'' He shook his head. ''No one at all.''

''But why are you doing this?'' Then Gwen remembered what she had seen in the courtroom. ''Hydro Phobius,'' she hissed. ''He's up to something, isn't he?''

Antonio nodded.

Gwen shivered in an unseen draft. ''What do you want with me?''

Antonio crossed the room and toyed with the silver knobs of the wardrobe as if they fascinated him. He pulled one of the doors open, ran a hand down the sleeve of a yellow silk blouse. ''I need you to warn someone,'' he said. Abruptly, he spun on her, his face struggling with itself. ''I've done something Hydro Phobius never counted on, the one thing he thought impossible. I've fallen in love. Now, you must warn her to flee Venice before the city's destroyed.''

''Who?'' Again the scenes from the courtroom replayed themselves in her mind. ''The moneylender's daughter.''

''Jessica,'' Antonio said, her name like a prayer on his lips.

''But . . .'' Gwen fussed with her hands in her lap. Despite everything she'd learned from Corwyn, she was unprepared for this. ''But she's a Jew.''

Antonio's face took on a caged, wary look. ''Yes?''

''God's blood, Antonio, you're a Christian!''

''Ah.'' His voice was as smooth as the silk he again caressed, and as cold as the distant Alps. ''Is that what I am?'' One corner of his mouth quirked up in a wry expression. ''And you are an honest woman.'' He looked pointedly at her clothes. "Or so you say." He shrugged. *"Non importa."*

Gwen trembled a little. "Why do you need me? Why don't you warn her yourself?" She shook her head, her attention again on her hands. Some vital piece in all of this was missing. "You aren't going ahead with Phobius's scheme, are you?"

When Antonio failed to answer, Gwen jerked upright, peering at her captor. "Antonio, you can't!"

His laugh was so harsh it frightened her. "Can't I? And how should I avoid it? Would you have me disobey my master, my maker"—his voice dropped to a coarse whisper—"my god?"

Gwen drew back in her chair, trying to make herself small, frightened by this heresy, so casually committed. "What do you mean? I don't understand." Her voice sounded strange in her ears, and she found she was crying.

Antonio didn't seem to have heard. "A second Adam," he laughed, pacing the room. "Another Lucifer." Then he sobered. "Except that, unlike them, I might rise to grace by rebelling, where they could only fall." He looked at Gwen, his expression mildly startled as if he had forgotten her. "What do you say—have I a soul?"

She blinked back tears and stared at him, too confused to respond.

"You asked who I am," Antonio said, his flat voice belying his tortured features. "Well, I'll show you." He bared an arm, then drew his dagger. Gwen, suddenly realizing what he intended, leaped to her feet, toppling her chair. Too late! Before she could grab the knife, he slashed his arm with the blade. Gwen gasped and threw her hands over her face, staring through spread fingers, grimly fascinated by the wound he was inflicting.

Nothing happened.

Slowly, Gwen lowered her hands. An icy cold gripped her stomach as she watched, the gash made more horrible somehow than if it had been spilling blood. But there was no blood, no gaping flesh. Only the infinite malleability of common clay, gradually reforming itself into the semblance of an arm.

Gwen screamed.

Antonio kneaded the clay with his other hand until the gash disappeared, then smoothed away the seam. Had it not been for his tightly clenched jaw, Gwen would have thought he was unaware of her. She choked back her cry, ending on a series of broken sobs.

"As you can see, I'm not a true member of the flock," Antonio said calmly, still staring at his arm. He chuckled without humor. "They say a good wife should be as pliable as warm wax in her husband's hands—perhaps my master should have made me in the shape of a woman." He pulled his sleeve down and buttoned it. "Of course, what Shylock had in mind would have cut me beyond repair. But at least my death in the courtroom would have served as a warning." He looked at Gwen and frowned. "You're pale. Here, let me get your chair."

He stepped toward her, but stopped when she cringed, her hands up to ward him off. As she watched, his shoulders stiffened, his lips pressed together in a hard, thin line. "I'd thought you might understand," he said bitterly. Then he turned away, a man of unutterable sorrow.

But that was just the problem, Gwen thought guiltily. He wasn't a man at all. She shuddered, recalling how attracted to him she had been. Although she knew and liked several creatures of magic, especially Oliver, none of them had pretended to be a man, summoning her innate responses as a woman. That she had reacted toward Antonio that way shocked and frightened her.

She lifted her hands to him, thinking to call him back—

Just then, two figures in black robes burst into the room. Gwen blinked, her outstretched hands frozen in surprise. The intruders looked like two Corwyns, one the alchemist she knew, the other a younger version, his beard still straggly. She looked again, her heart leaping. "Sebastian?"

The younger figure squinted back at her, his attention torn between Gwen and Antonio while he held the latter at bay with his sword. "Gwen? Is it really you?" His blade wavered, then steadied menacingly as Antonio shifted his weight. "Don't move," Sebastian growled. He edged toward Gwen. "Gwen, thank God you're alive! We thought you'd drowned. Are you all right? Did he hurt you?" Suddenly, he paused. "What in heavens are you wearing? And your hair! Gwen, you look like a . . . a . . ."

Antonio had grabbed for his own weapon when the two swarmed in, then stopped when confronted with the bared tip of Sebastian's blade. He held out his hands, palms exposed. "A courtesan?" he prompted, sounding overly casual. Sebastian scowled and waved his blade, but Antonio ignored him, addressing Gwen over his shoulder. "I gather you know these two."

"They're my friends," Gwen said through clenched teeth. She had started eagerly toward them, but now she held back, smiling briefly at Corwyn, uncertain how to act toward Sebastian. Antonio's earlier words about men wanting wives they could shape like warm wax echoed in her head. "Is that what you meant?" she demanded of Sebastian. "Are you saying I look like a courtesan?"

Sebastian flushed behind his sparse beard. He stepped closer.

Gwen moved back, letting her eyes rake him. "Well, if you're going to bring up appearances, I might ask you the same. What are you wearing, Sebastian? And what's that on your face?"

"I'm an alchemist," he mumbled, scratching his stubbly beard. "And all I meant was that you didn't have to look like a common . . . a common . . ."

"A common what?" Her voice was low, threatening.

"Well, like a man, Gwen. After all, that is what the courtesans wear."

"How dare you burst in here and criticize how I'm dressed," Gwen snapped. "And making such accusations, after I thought you were dead and I was left to shift for myself.''

"But . . .'' Sebastian looked pained. ''Well, you were reaching for him when we came in,'' he said at last angrily. ''It looked pretty peculiar to me, especially you being alone with him in his room.''

Antonio's eyes widened upon hearing that Gwen had been reaching for him, and he looked at her in surprise. She glowered back, feeling her own face grow warm, then turned to Sebastian. But before she could frame a retort, Corwyn interrupted. ''Children, do you think you could postpone your reunion till later? We have urgent business to attend to before Venice sinks into the sea while you argue.'' He turned to Antonio, his expression stern. ''Are you the master of this house?''

Antonio hesitated.

''Be careful, Corwyn, he's in league with Hydro Phobius,'' Gwen blurted. Quickly, she explained about Phobius's La Bella Donna ruse, feeling like a traitor to Antonio as she did.

''Ah,'' Corwyn said to Antonio when she was through, ''so you're Hydro Phobius's agent.'' His voice hardened. ''Show us the thaumaturgical generator.''

Antonio shrugged and started toward the door, followed by a nervous-looking Sebastian, still brandishing his sword. As Gwen and Corwyn fell in behind, Sebastian whispered over his shoulder, ''He's not even a real man, you know. He's just a simulacrum.''

Ahead, Gwen saw Antonio's shoulders stiffen, and he held himself rigidly erect. Gwen felt angrier than ever at Sebastian for hurting Antonio's feelings—though it was an anger tinged with guilt.

They wandered through the dark palace until they rejoined the trail of footprints where Antonio previously had veered away. Now he took them where the path led. He reached a set of towering double doors and threw them open, revealing an immense ballroom beyond. Sebastian, still ahead of Gwen, peered into the room that was lit from within by a strange glow. Abruptly he grunted, his sword dangling, forgotten. "What's that smell?"

Curious, Gwen pushed around him, closely followed by Corwyn. They stopped as the fetid odor in the room reached them. Gwen wrinkled her nose. Now she knew where the odd, musty smell in the rest of the palace had come from. Antonio sneered with disdain, although Gwen noticed that he, too, was breathing through pinched nostrils. Suddenly, Corwyn gripped her arm and pointed. "Look!" he said. "Next to the sylph."

She squinted at the bizarre scene, wondering what a sylph looked like. In the center of the room, swarms of ghoulish creatures danced around a large sphere. Despite a coating over the outside of the sphere, enough light leaked out to create a glow. The glow illuminated a pale blue, nearly transparent figure that Gwen decided must be the sylph, particularly when she recognized the creature's spindly companion. "So this is where he wandered off to!" she cried.

It was Oliver, without his clothes, cavorting happily amid the supernatural and the dead. At last he had found friends who would play with him, here at the base of Hydro Phobius's terrible sphere.

ACT 20:

Imbeciline

ALL OF THE JOY GWEN HAD FELT AT SEEING SEBASTIAN alive she now lavished on Oliver, feeling guilty as she did. The broom tolerated this awhile, then began pulling on Gwen's hand. She was still crouched at his level, but allowed herself to be dragged forward a couple of awkward steps. "What's he want?" she asked Corwyn.

Corwyn pointed toward the creatures cavorting around the sphere. "I think he wants you to join the dance."

Gwen shuddered and wrenched back her hand. Oliver looked hurt at this, making Gwen feel terrible. Without thinking, she glanced at Sebastian for support. He started toward her, his face brightening in a smile he, too, must have repressed, his arms outstretched. Gwen's anger melted.

Then the stench of rotting fish reached her along with Sebastian's arms. She jerked back instinctively, pushing him away. "Sebastian, what's that smell?"

"Fish," he said, staring at his hands in dejection. "I forgot, I was handling dead fish just before we came."

"Again? You reek like a Lenten sacrifice. It's as bad as when we left Pomme de Terre!"

She regretted her words immediately, but it was too late. Sebastian had already turned away. She called his name, and he smiled wanly over his shoulder but wouldn't come nearer.

Which made Gwen angry with him all over again. He could afford to be a little more understanding at times.

Oliver, meanwhile, had danced back to the sphere, drawn—as Antonio explained—by the irresistible lure of its song.

Gwen, being mortal and therefore unable to hear the song, nevertheless stared at the sphere, covering up hurt with a show of fascination. Beside her, Corwyn stared as well. "A fire elemental! I knew it was theoretically possible," he said, "but I never expected to see such a generator built." He paused. "Of course, it couldn't have been done without the recent advances in Venetian glassmaking."

Gwen had no idea what he was talking about and didn't care enough to ask.

Off to one side, Sebastian shook his head in disapproval. "Only Hydro Phobius would create something so foul that it attracts creatures like those," he said, nodding at the figures around the sphere.

Gwen edged back as a griffin in the throng screeched and snapped its beak in their direction, although most of the creatures seemed unaware of their arrival.

"Magic!" Sebastian snorted, smoothing his black robe and looking from Gwen to Antonio. "Such a disgusting practice. Not at all like the true science of alchemy."

Antonio gave him a baleful glare, which Sebastian pretended not to notice.

"There's so little shielding," Corwyn said, still sounding awestruck. "Aren't you concerned about side effects?"

Antonio shrugged. "That doesn't seem to bother Hydro Phobius."

"No," Corwyn agreed. "I guess it wouldn't." After a moment he asked, "What safeguards have you used to prevent a thaumaturgical gulp down?"

When Antonio didn't answer, Corwyn turned to stare

at him. Gwen, who wasn't comprehending any of this, frowned at them both.

"What's a thaumaturgical gulp down?" Sebastian asked.

"If a fire elemental becomes sufficiently excited, it'll begin swallowing its own tail," Corwyn said, his attention still on Antonio. "Theoretically, it could devour itself."

Sebastian shrugged. "So?"

"So, when an elemental drops out of existence, it can take part of the surrounding world with it."

"Oh." Sebastian backed up several steps. "How big an area would be affected?"

Corwyn shrugged. "Who knows? Enough certainly to cause the Venetian lagoon to collapse." He peered more closely at Antonio, who had begun to fidget. "That's it, isn't it? That's how Phobius plans to trigger the collapse without the detonators from the *Magdalen?*"

Although Gwen didn't understand any of this, Antonio evidently did; she could see it in the way he refused to meet the alchemist's eyes.

Sebastian strode across the room toward the sphere, holding his sword by the blade to smash the hilt against the glass. "I'll put an end to it."

"No, Sebastian, don't!" Corwyn cried.

Sebastian hesitated. "Why not? We want it destroyed, don't we?"

"Not that way," Corwyn answered. "You'll release those creatures from their enchantment to wander loose in the city. That is, if anything in the room survives the blast of freeing a captive fire elemental so abruptly."

Sebastian eyed the creatures ahead of him with evident distaste. "I certainly wouldn't want to unleash that loathsome lot on Venice. Ugh! Supernatural creatures are so disgusting!"

Antonio bristled. Gwen knew Sebastian's anger was really directed at her, and she turned to the merchant to apologize. But what should she say to this man who was not a man, yet who appeared as deeply affected by emotion as anyone she knew?

Before she could think of anything, Antonio bounded across the room, grabbing up a pickax left by one of the kobolds as he ran. He pushed past Sebastian and on through the dancing creatures, knocking them aside, then leaped onto the dais beside the sphere. "Of course, as a creature of magic myself, I'm not subject to the refined sensibilities you display," he told Sebastian bitterly, hefting the axe to smash the glass. "One way or another, I'll be freeing myself."

"Antonio, no!" Gwen cried.

He hesitated. "Why not? It's only what my master would have me do."

Gwen thought frantically, knowing she couldn't ask for pity after granting none herself. Antonio waited a moment, then drew back the axe, ready to strike. "Not for us, then," Gwen said on sudden inspiration, "but for Jessica." Antonio stiffened. The axe trembled as he struggled with himself. "Would you turn these things loose," Gwen went on, gesturing at the creatures, "knowing they might harm her?"

For an agonizing time, Antonio stood there, racked with indecision, the axe poised above the glass. His face twisted in agony. After a while, he began to shake. Slowly, he lowered the axe and let it rattle to the floor. To Gwen's amazement, a tear trickled from his eye. "Oh, Jessica," he said, his voice barely audible across the room. "I can't destroy my master's vile creation, knowing you would thus be harmed. And yet, by not destroying it I leave you and all of Venice doomed."

Pity rose unbidden in Gwen—the same pity she had denied him earlier. She wondered whether Jessica knew the truth about Antonio, and what that truth had cost them.

Antonio climbed down from the dais and walked back toward Gwen and her companions, moving slowly with defeat.

"Well, so much for that," Sebastian said. He turned to Corwyn. "What do we do about the generator?"

"I'm not sure," the alchemist said. He looked at Antonio as the simulacrum trudged up to them. "But whatever we do, we're going to need help. *Signore* Nessuno, will you help us?"

Antonio squinted at Corwyn suspiciously. "You just saw how unsuccessful I was in overcoming this cursed thing, and yet you ask my help?"

"We can't proceed without you," Corwyn said with a bow.

"Then you're a bigger fool than your companion," Antonio said, indicating Sebastian.

"But you'll help?" Corwyn asked, restraining his apprentice.

"Very well," Antonio said wearily. "I'll be a fool as well."

"Why're you being so formal with him?" Sebastian objected. "Master, you're not going to trust him, are you? He's only a simulacrum, and one made by Phobius at that."

Antonio's eyebrows rose in mock surprise. "Why, aren't we brothers, you and I? So two men should be. But perhaps there's a difference between the clay your god made you from, and mine—though both will return to dust when we're dead."

Sebastian looked too startled to respond. Then Corwyn took him aside for a private conference, the subject of which was obvious from Sebastian's repeated glances in Antonio's direction. Antonio moved closer to Gwen. "You think he's so superior, just because he's real?" he whispered. "Well, I'll make you a wager."

"What kind?" she asked guardedly, still uncertain how to respond to him.

Antonio looked over at Sebastian. "One that it'll benefit you to lose, because it'll open your eyes. And in return, you'll agree to deliver my message to Jessica."

Gwen considered telling him that she would take a message to Jessica for him in any case; all he had to do was ask. Then she changed her mind, annoyed by his manner. In some ways, he was a lot like Sebastian. "What's the wager?"

"Simple," he said. "Before the day's out, I'll have your friend"—he jerked his head to indicate Sebastian—"believing you were unfaithful to him while the two of you were separated."

Gwen gave Antonio a hard look, angrily aware of how attracted to him she had been. "You mean you'd claim to have—?"

"No, no, not me." He put up his hands, then slowly grinned. "The doge."

"The doge? But he's—" Gwen bit back her objection. Antonio clearly needed a lesson in humility. Afterward, she would decide whether to deliver his message anyway. "You'd have him believing what he said earlier, about me looking like a courtesan?"

Antonio shrugged. "I make my wager against your confidence rather than your reputation."

Gwen tossed her head in annoyance. "Very well, I accept."

Antonio's grin became sardonic. "A most delicate fiend," he murmured, looking her over as if taking her measure. "Who is it that can read a woman?"

Gwen frowned, uncertain of his meaning, but not liking it in any case. Antonio only chuckled and sauntered toward Sebastian, a hunter closing in on his prey. Gwen chewed her lip as she watched, telling herself she really was confident of Sebastian. She touched his cap inside her doublet, seeking reassurance. After all, she'd already seen all of his faults—or hoped she had—and loved him anyway.

Nevertheless, she wished he knew the doge as well as she. This wouldn't be a good time for Sebastian to surprise her.

"Sebastian, we need Antonio's cooperation," Corwyn said when he had drawn his apprentice aside. "Can you understand that?"

Sebastian looked with cold fury at the figure hovering next to Gwen. Although Antonio looked like a man, Sebastian knew he wasn't. The simulacrum possessed no more humanity than the creatures around the generator. Sebastian turned back to his master, wanting to tell him so, but was stopped by the intensity of Corwyn's gaze. "I guess so . . . maybe." He shrugged, noncommittal. "What do we need him for?"

Corwyn, too, looked across the room, although Sebastian knew his master was staring not at the simulacrum but at the sphere. "Sebastian, I'm not your father, I'm your master." He indicated Sebastian's robe and hat, so much like his own. "Sometimes, however, I'm not sure which you need more."

Sebastian flushed but didn't answer.

Corwyn went on. "Only Antonio, as a creature of magic, can remain close to the generator long enough to stop it. The rest of us risk thaumaturgical poisoning if we stay here any longer."

"But what about Oliver?" Sebastian asked. "He's magic. Couldn't he stop it?"

Corwyn pointed to the dancing creatures. In their midst frolicked Oliver, looking like a besotted sapling bereft of leaves. "Would you turn the fate of Venice over to him?"

Sebastian scowled. "I don't see why Antonio isn't out there, too. After all, he's one of them."

"Perhaps," Corwyn said. "And yet . . . Sebastian, have you looked at him closely?"

Sebastian glanced again at the handsome figure Gwen had been reaching for when he and Corwyn had burst into Antonio's room. As if to further irritate him, Antonio chose that moment to whisper something to Gwen. "Close enough," Sebastian said, gritting his teeth.

"No, I mean really looked at him," Corwyn insisted. "At his face, his stance, his gestures."

Sebastian looked again, struggling to see beyond his disapproval. To his surprise, he discovered that Antonio had a tic in one eye and cheek. Sebastian wondered why he hadn't noticed before, then decided it was because Antonio kept his jaw clenched, possibly to suppress the twitch. But even that didn't account for the tension in Antonio's shoulders or the careful way he had of moving, as if he thought out every gesture in advance. "What's the matter with him?" Sebastian asked. "Is he wearing out?"

"No, he's resisting the pull of the sphere," Corwyn said. "Seldom have I seen such self-control in a human being."

"But he's *not* human!" Sebastian snapped. "That's the point."

"It doesn't matter," Corwyn answered equably. "It takes self-control, just the same. And that control is why only Antonio can deactivate the sphere."

"But can we trust him?"

Corwyn shrugged. "Can we afford not to?"

Sebastian didn't have an answer for that or anything else, for that matter.

Corwyn clapped him on the shoulder. "Just don't antagonize him, all right?"

Sebastian nodded. As Corwyn started to turn away, Sebastian added, "It just seems strange that we have to rely on a creature of magic to stop a device from generating magical energy." He shook his head. "But why should this be different from anything else on this fool quest? Nothing makes sense anymore."

"Fool quest?" Corwyn frowned. "All I said was that we need Antonio."

Sebastian waved away his objection. "Oh, it's not just Antonio. It's everything." He began ticking off specifics on his fingers. "We took a practical alchemical test and modified it to detect something as absurd as thaumaturgical contamination in water."

"But—"

"Of course, that was only after we three adults had traipsed halfway across the known world, posing as wealthy nobles while living off booty stolen by Oliver, the world's oldest child."

"Now see here—!"

"And then there's my attempt at social alchemy," Sebastian continued, waving at Gwen. "I tried to transform her from a serving girl into a noblewoman, and instead I seem to have created a man—or a boy, at least." He snorted. "A boy with a codpiece!"

Corwyn huffed himself up to respond, but Sebastian hurried on. "Finally, there's your effort to find the key to the Renaissance, the philosopher's stone which would let us take what's happening in Italy and transplant it to Pomme de Terre. We've looked for an answer; but the key to the Renaissance isn't an answer at all, it's a question, or a whole lot of questions all bound together." He threw up his hands in despair. "See what I mean? Nothing's working out the way it should."

Sebastian started to turn away, his point made, but Corwyn stopped him with a hand on his arm. "No, I don't see," he said gruffly. "And I especially don't see what you mean by this nonsense of yours about the Renaissance."

"Oh, that. It's just that we've looked all over northern Italy for ancient knowledge that either doesn't exist any longer or that doesn't mean anything now, all in an attempt to reconstruct a way of life that died long ago. We were so busy looking for another Alexandria that we failed to notice what's going on around us."

"I understand that," Corwyn said irritably. "I've known it since I first set foot in Cosimo de' Medici's library. What I want to know is what you mean about the key to the Renaissance being a lot of questions."

"That's just it," Sebastian said, palms up. "The Renaissance isn't about rediscovering old answers, it's about rediscovering the fact that there are questions to be asked. Our answers have to be new ones. Forgive me, master, but what the world lived by in your youth doesn't necessarily matter anymore. The basic questions may be the same, but the answers to them differ. Look at Genoa or Florence or Venice. Each one represents a different set of answers. Until people began to look at the past, however, we didn't know that we'd forgotten to ask the questions."

Corwyn stared. After a few moments of being on the receiving end of this, Sebastian began to fidget, wondering what blunder he'd made this time. He smoothed his robe and straightened his hat—the tip was inclined to droop—all while chiding himself for having opened his mouth. When would he ever learn!

Antonio walked over, adding to Sebastian's discomfort. Corwyn mumbled something and wandered off, pretending to study the thaumaturgical generator more closely. But Sebastian could tell by the way the alchemist's mouth was working that he was holding a conversation with himself. Occasionally, he glanced back at his apprentice, a strange expression on his face.

Suddenly, Sebastian realized he was alone with Antonio, the man who wasn't a man, but who had nevertheless attracted Gwen's attention. At a loss as to how to talk with this creature, Sebastian watched Gwen instead, occasionally checking on Antonio out of the corner of his eye.

Antonio, too, was looking at Gwen. "Quite a woman," he said.

Sebastian pretended he hadn't heard, but Antonio waited, watching him now, until finally Sebastian nodded, wondering what Antonio meant.

Antonio returned his gaze to Gwen. "So full of life," he murmured. "Such a passion for living."

Sebastian nodded again.

"And of course, she thought you were dead," Antonio continued.

Sebastian's nod came more slowly.

"I'm sure things would have been different had she known you were alive."

Sebastian thought about this a moment. "What things?"

Antonio shrugged. "You know, things that happened. That probably explains them. After all, if you were dead . . ."

Sebastian stared at Gwen without answering, wishing Antonio would go away. The creature was being ridiculous, of course. Gwen was much too sensible for what he was suggesting, if that was really what Antonio meant.

"Ah, *signore*," Antonio went on, his attention still on Gwen, "I might be tempted to envy you, if I thought I could keep up with the needs of such an attractive, healthy woman." He shook his head. "But I'm only an artificial creature, and although designed for stamina, I know my limits. You must be quite a man indeed to keep such a woman satisfied."

Sebastian frowned, recalling how Gwen had resisted his advances since their betrothal, urging him to wait until they were married. Who was this woman of insatiable appetite Antonio was discussing?

"Of course, the men she encountered all knew she was a woman," Antonio said. "Her costume was much too provocative to hide her sex or to conceal her passionate nature." He turned to Sebastian. "You're familiar with the practice among courtesans of dressing in men's clothes, are you not?"

Sebastian nodded involuntarily, his head moving like a marionette's.

"And she was around so many handsome, virile men while you were away," Antonio said.

Sebastian glared at this creature whose suggestions were so absurd, yet so impossible to ignore.

"Oh, no, not me, *signore*." Antonio laughed. "As I said, I know my limits, and besides, there is another who has my attention. But she kept company with powerful men. The doge in particular is known for his generosity."

"I don't believe you," Sebastian said.

"Then ask her about the ring she's wearing, the one from the doge."

Sebastian peered at Gwen's hand. "She's not wearing a ring."

"No?" Antonio looked, then shrugged. "Well, maybe she gave it in turn to another. After all, the doge is very occupied with civic matters. Even he can't expect to fully satisfy her, not alone.''

"You're lying," Sebastian hissed.

"Am I?" Antonio smiled, full of innocence. "No matter, then. Dismiss what I've said and think nothing of it."

Sebastian was fuming, wondering how to respond, when Corwyn came back over, interrupting his thoughts. The alchemist gave Sebastian another peculiar look. "I think I know how to dismantle the sphere," he said at last. "If we gradually remove the reflective coating from the outside of the glass, the fire elemental's excitement should diminish. When the thaumaturgical flux it gives off drops low enough, we can tow the sphere safely to the mainland, while still keeping the creatures around it sufficiently enchanted to follow. Once on the mainland, we'll let the elemental go, taking these other creatures with it." He looked at Antonio. "What do you think? Will it work?"

A strange light warmed Antonio's face. Sebastian, watching him, realized it was the look of hope. Antonio's shoulders lifted. "Yes," he whispered. "Yes, I think it will. But you'll need me to remove the reflective coating." His expression took on a mischievous gleam, and he winked at Sebastian. "Mere mortals couldn't stand that much thaumaturgical flux."

Corwyn nodded. "I'm feeling dizzy as it is. Come on, Sebastian, we have other work to do." He motioned to Gwen and started for the door. "Let's see if we can get an audience with the doge to warn him about what's happening. We'll need help catching Hydro Phobius, and Venice isn't safe while he's loose."

"You want to see Francesco?" Gwen asked as she joined them. "I can get us in." She smiled. "We're old friends."

Sebastian tried not to attach any particular significance to this, but he couldn't ignore Antonio's knowing grin as the simulacrum watched them leave. Sebastian wished they at least had time for Gwen to change into more suitable clothes.

"You again," a page sneered at the outside the doge's chambers. To Sebastian's dismay, the page was addressing Gwen. "Well, you can't see him this time. He's gone to the mainland to talk to La Bella Donna."

"La Bella Donna," Corwyn gasped. "Oh, no! Right into the spider's web!"

"Yes, he wanted to find out more about that lawyer La Bella Donna recommended for the moneylender's case. Among other things, it seems my master was quite annoyed when the judge showed up at the trial wearing the ring my master had given you yesterday." Again the page looked at Gwen.

"A ring?" Sebastian exclaimed. "The doge gave you a ring?" He, too, gave Gwen a searching gaze. "What's the meaning of this? Why'd he give you a ring? And who's this judge you gave it to?"

"So many questions," Corwyn said with peculiar emphasis. "But I forgot, you're the man who believes everything is a matter of questions."

Gwen sighed, sounding exasperated. "Not now," she told Corwyn. Then she addressed Sebastian. "So Antonio made you doubt me after all."

"I don't doubt you, Gwen," Sebastian insisted. "It's just that . . . well, why *did* the doge give you a ring?"

Gwen rolled her eyes without answering.

The page's eyes, meanwhile, had grown very round. "Gwen? That's your real name?" He laughed, a mixture of hilarity and relief. "So Cesario's a woman. Won't my master be surprised!"

Sebastian scowled, wondering what this boy found so amusing.

"We must warn the doge," Corwyn said, hurrying to leave. "Tomorrow is Ascension Day, when Venice renews its dominion over the waves. Hydro Phobius has until then to exert his own dominion by destroying the city."

Dominion . . . the word evoked images of gratefully submissive brides, Sebastian thought, eager for guidance from their all-knowing husbands. Perhaps Venice's marriage of the sea gave Sebastian a chance to renew his own authority. Of course, he didn't really believe what Antonio had insinuated. Rather he was dismayed on Gwen's behalf because she had unwittingly made those insinuations possible. Not that she'd known any better—she was so innocent, so unaware of proper manners. It was Sebastian's fault that she'd strayed, dressing like a man. If only he'd been there to advise her! But that was a fault he was willing to take responsibility for now, one he would willingly correct.

He glanced again at Gwen's sword and codpiece, so excessive in their proportions. It was a good thing he was here to reassert his dominion, Sebastian concluded—before Gwen got herself into serious trouble.

ACT 21:

Taming the Shrew

GWEN TURNED AWAY FROM THE PAGE, ONE HAND ON her sword to keep it from swinging, and strode after Corwyn.

"Gwen," Sebastian hissed at her elbow, "you're walking like a man. Remember, you're supposed to be a noblewoman. And for heaven's sake, leave that sword alone!"

Gwen stopped, rigid. Did he think she was nothing more than a creature like Antonio to be shaped however he desired?

Corwyn continued down the corridor, unaware of leaving his companions, still talking to them over his shoulder. Gwen gritted her teeth and took a slow, deep breath. She reminded herself that she had tried to correct Sebastian's behavior back in Pomme de Terre (though not to this degree—had she?) and she resolved never to do so again once they returned, regardless how much it might be for his own good.

Meanwhile, however, something had to be done about his efforts to reshape her here in Italy.

Then Gwen remembered Dame Alice, the widow from Bath on the pilgrimage to the Holy Land. Alice had boasted of gaining control over each of her five husbands, arguing that this was what every woman wanted. It was, she'd claimed, the key to a peaceful marriage.

Gwen smiled and grew relaxed. Not just relaxed; she went absolutely limp inside. This time, she would cure Sebastian of his nagging once and for all. She would be everything he wanted her to be, and more—until he couldn't stand it any longer.

Dame Alice would be proud of her.

"Of course, milord," she said demurely to Sebastian, her eyes lowered, her hands clasped in front of her. "Whatever you say, milord. Thank you for reminding me."

Sebastian grunted and resumed walking.

Gwen didn't move.

"Well," Sebastian said, pausing to let her catch up, "what are you waiting for? Let's get going."

"Yes, milord." Then, still without moving, she added, "Would you show me again how to walk properly?"

From under lowered eyelashes, Gwen saw Sebastian glance hesitantly around the corridor. "What, here?"

"Yes, milord. If you would, please."

"Oh, all right." Sebastian took a half dozen mincing steps, sliding his satin slippers along the carpeted floor.

From behind them erupted the sound of the page's laughter. "Ho, *signore,* maybe you should take lessons from the *signorina,* instead of the other way around."

Sebastian spun toward the page, fumbling in his robe for his sword. "Damned garments were never intended to be worn by noblemen," he muttered, finally locating the hilt among the heavy folds.

Gwen laid a hand on Sebastian's arm. "He's only a boy, badly versed in manners. Ignore him, milord. Now, how did that walk go?"

Sebastian stared. "You want me to show you again?"

"I want to be sure I get it right, milord."

Grumbling and glancing backward, Sebastian once more adopted the simpering step he'd insisted was appropriate for a noblewoman. The page guffawed so hard that Sebastian's face turned crimson. Gwen nodded. "I think I have it now, milord." She hobbled down the corridor, further exaggerating the gait Sebastian had shown her. Behind them, the page shrieked with laughter.

Chortles from other officials followed. "Maybe it's the clothes," Sebastian muttered to Gwen as they reached the ornate stairway that descended to the main floor. "That walk doesn't look right when you're dressed like a man."

Gwen paused between floors and looked around. For the moment, they were unobserved. "You're right, of course, milord. These clothes are offensive." She took a breath and stripped off her doublet, blouse, and hose before Sebastian could stop her, halting when she was left wearing only her short undergown. Reaching inside that, she undid the sash that bound her breasts.

"What are you doing?" Sebastian cried, scrambling after her clothes as quickly as she discarded them. He paused, clearly startled, when he discovered his water-stained cap among them. "Gwen, put these back on."

"Milord," Gwen said, affecting a shocked tone, "would you have me appear in public inappropriately dressed? Better, I should think, to wear nothing at all than to wear something beneath my station." Summoning her courage, she started down again, remembering to limit her stride. Sebastian hurried after her, mumbling and trailing bits of her clothing as he ran. She let him catch up, then turned on him, widening her eyes as if startled by what she saw. "Milord, surely you're not content to dress like that, either." She rolled a pleat of his outer gown between her fingers, then flicked the fabric away disdainfully. "It's so plain and shapeless and . . . and so common. Here, let me help you out of it." She reached up to pull his robe over his head, knocking off his hat in the process.

Sebastian flailed his arms and backed away. "Stop it, Gwen! Think what you're doing!"

She let her shoulders sag. "Very well, milord. Whatever you say. It's just that I thought we were supposed to look the part of nobles together. I didn't realize your concern was for me alone, that you were content to appear as a commoner while passing me off as a lady." With a show of effort, she straightened her shoulders and started down the stairs.

"But Gwen," he cried, "the only part we're going to look without clothes is foolish."

She turned on him with a level stare. "Are you saying I look like a fool? Milord, I'm doing everything I can to avoid embarrassing you by appearing as your inferior. After all, what commoner would presume to appear like this?" She indicated her thin gown, which clearly revealed her gender. "Only a noble would dare to be so immodest, preferring humiliation to loss of status. Besides, it's only until we can find more appropriate clothes." She frowned. "But if you're unwilling to share the trials of noble life with me, as my equal . . ." She let the words trail off, heavy with unstated significance. Without waiting for a reply, she turned away again.

"I don't believe this," Sebastian wailed. "If I don't go along with you, you'll condemn me. If I do go along, we'll both be condemned by the Inquisition."

She pretended not to hear, holding her head high and continuing down the stairs. On the floor below, a passing official staggered to a halt and stared open-mouthed as Gwen came into view.

"Oh, all right," Sebastian growled. "But wait up. At least when they come for us, they'll cart us off together."

Gwen paused, holding herself as regally erect as if she were fully clothed. The man on the floor below stumbled into the wall as he stared at her, then rounded a corner, only to peek back again for a final look. A moment later, Sebastian caught up with her, stripped down to his long, white undergown, holding their bundled clothes in front of him to shield himself from view. He had rebuckled his sword around the waist of the billowing gown, making it look more absurd. Gwen took his blue cap from the pile of clothes and placed it on his head, completing the picture. Sebastian swallowed hard. "All right," he said, "lead on."

She widened her eyes. "But that, too, would be unseemly, milord. You lead, I'll follow."

He shook his head and muttered, then began descending the steps, his face a mask of resolution. Smiling, Gwen followed a half step behind his right elbow.

"Gwen? Sebastian?" Corwyn's voice drifted to them as they reached the bottom of the stairs. "Where are you? When I reached the *cortile*, you weren't with me." The alchemist appeared in the corridor ahead, retracing his steps. Suddenly, he froze. *"Bon dieu!* What have you done?"

Around her, Gwen heard sounds of strangled surprise as the ducal staff and various officials noticed Sebastian's and her condition. Sebastian faltered, then headed for Corwyn. "Don't ask," he hissed to the alchemist. "Let's just get out of here while we can."

Corwyn raised his bushy eyebrows at his apprentice, noting the stained, dilapidated cap. "The man who claims the Renaissance is all about questions doesn't want me to ask any? Well, I've lived long and seen many things. I suppose I should be grateful that anyone can still astonish me." Without another word, he led off the way he'd come.

Gwen was relieved when they made it out of the palace without being stopped, though whether this was due to their imperious bearing or to the unexpectedness of their state, she couldn't be sure. When she'd decided to do this, she hadn't thought out the possible consequences. Yet she didn't regret her decision, not if it cured Sebastian of his criticizing. She'd be so meek that he chafed from her devotion.

The three of them crossed the piazza, which was more crowded than normal with the completed booths and stalls for the *Sensa* celebration. People drew away in shocked silence ahead of them, then closed in behind, pointing and chattering in a dozen tongues. Even the pigeons made way for them, as if, among all the transgressions committed in Venice over the centuries, theirs alone had the ability to scandalize. Yet perhaps their behavior wasn't as scandalous as all that, for no one tried to stop them.

Corwyn headed toward the Molo, the quay bordering the waterfront. "You'll be less conspicuous in a gondola," he said over his shoulder, then rolled his eyes. "At least you'll be sitting down."

Before they could board, however, two guards from the palace caught up with them. But before Gwen and Sebastian could be dragged away, the doge's barge approached the Molo from the canal, and all activity on the piazzetta stopped in anticipation of his arrival. The barge drew closer. Despite her concern for herself and Sebastian, Gwen shook her head sadly as she spotted Francesco enthroned on the deck under the golden umbrella reserved for him, dressed in the heavy robes of his office and bearing the scepter of state, alone in a crowd of courtiers and retainers. So completely did the doge embody the state's concept of itself that he couldn't venture out for any purpose without the event being turned into a formal occasion, recorded in the annals of the city. No cage was ever so gilded as this, she thought, nor so confining.

The crowd on the Molo scarcely knew whether to watch the arrival of the doge or continue staring at Gwen and Sebastian. A sea of faces flitted between the events like spectators at a game of badminton. Even the doge, vigilant as an eagle guarding his domain, spotted the pair from the gold and velvet sedan in which he was being carried over a carpeted gangplank to the quay. The doge raised his eyebrows at them and started to turn away, surprised but tolerant, then his eyes widened even more at Gwen, evidently recognizing her. He leaned over and spoke to one of his liveried stewards. A moment later, the steward approached with a summons for Gwen and her companions to appear in the doge's chambers.

"Oh, no," Sebastian groaned. "This is it. We'll be imprisoned for sure."

They retraced their steps, held by the guards and with the steward clearing a path through the crowd. The steward ushered them into the palace in the wake of the ducal procession, then up a private stairway at the north end of the palace wing directly to the doge's chambers. The guards were dismissed and Gwen and her friends were shown inside. Francesco was already there, his expression a blend of annoyance and bemused humor. Gwen introduced herself and her companions, using her real name. Francesco studied her in silence while the page they had spoken with earlier removed the ducal bonnet and cape and other trappings of state. "Gwen," Francesco repeated at last, testing the sound of her name. "Then there is no Cesario?"

"No, *signore*," she said. "I'm sorry."

She started to explain, but Francesco held up his hand. *"Non fa niente,"* he told her with a wry smile. "It doesn't matter."

Behind him, the page smirked. He caught Gwen watching and sniffed, moving closer to the doge.

Francesco's attention, meanwhile, shifted between Gwen and Sebastian, studying their lack of attire, his eyes lingering on Sebastian's cap. Sebastian shuffled and blushed. The doge opened his mouth as if to speak. Gwen, standing erect, eyed him steadily, anticipating his question. Francesco's gaze found hers and held it. After a moment, he chuckled softly and turned away, leaving his question unasked, apparently satisfied to wait for an answer. "I was about to have dinner," he said instead over his shoulder. "Will you join me?"

Sebastian stepped forward, shaking his head. "But of course," Gwen blurted out before he could decline, encouraged by Francesco's silence. "We'd be honored." Then she turned to Sebastian. "That is, if my lord approves."

Sebastian stammered, finding it more difficult now to refuse. He turned to Corwyn, but the alchemist looked away. Sebastian shrugged. "I guess so. Why not? We haven't eaten since our meal at the pie shop was cut short." He grimaced at some private memory.

Francesco nodded. "Inform the staff," he told his page.

The page scowled at the intruders and left the room. When he returned a few minutes later, the doge led his guests to an elegant dining room. On the table were four place settings, including linen napkins, porcelain plates, crystal goblets, and gold utensils for each person. Everything bore the winged lion of St. Mark. The page held his master's chair at the head of the table, then waited while servants seated the others. Corwyn sat at the end opposite the doge, Gwen on the doge's right, and Sebastian on the left. If the servants found Gwen's and Sebastian's appearance unusual, they were careful to conceal it.

With studied nonchalance, Sebastian handed his bundle of clothes to the servant who had seated him. The servant took the bundle gingerly and dumped it in a corner of the room, while Sebastian studied the utensils at his place suspiciously.

When they were seated, Gwen scrunched up her face and squirmed in her chair. Finally, she stood. "This chair isn't comfortable."

Sebastian and Corwyn rose.

"Oh, please," Gwen said to Corwyn, "don't get up." Then, when Sebastian started to sit back down as well, she added, "It's enough that my lord and master keeps me company." She smiled sweetly at Sebastian while he scrambled to his feet.

"I think I'm beginning to understand," Francesco murmured. He motioned for his servants to bring another chair, his eyes twinkling when it proved equally unsatisfactory.

Gwen made a show of trying two more chairs, finding fault with each, then spoke to the doge. "I'll stand, as undoubtedly my lord will likewise. But please, don't let us interfere with dinner. We'll be all right this way."

She turned to Sebastian, catching his puzzled frown. "Won't we, milord?"

He forced his expression into something like a smile. "Of course, Gwen. If you're really that uncomfortable . . ."

While they waited to be served, Corwyn told the doge about the plot to destroy Venice and Hydro Phobius's disguise as La Bella Donna. Francesco nodded. "That explains why she evaded me when I went to Belmont to ask about the judge she'd recommended for the trial. I couldn't understand why she wouldn't see me, especially after she'd tried so hard to entice me into becoming one of her suitors." He grinned at Gwen, who acknowledged him with a nod. Gwen was beginning to feel self-conscious, standing at the table in her underclothes. But if her plan was to work, she mustn't let Sebastian know it embarrassed her.

"On the way back to Venice, we discovered La Bella Donna had hidden from us in a cartload of garbage," Francesco went on. "So anxious was she to avoid discovery that she remained hidden even when the cart was hauled away, apparently not realizing that the contents were to be dumped in the lagoon. The driver of the cart realized his mistake as soon as the refuse hit the water, with La Bella Donna shrieking curses from its midst. He tried to help her, but she knocked him in the water and ran away. The driver was most unhappy when we encountered him later, wet from the lagoon and stinking from having been pushed into his own garbage." Francesco laughed. The others joined in, although Gwen noticed that Corwyn was fidgeting, apparently anxious to check on the dismantling of the magic generator.

The doge sobered. "But why did La Bella Donna encourage all those suitors? She couldn't have married any of them since she was really a man."

"She never intended to," Corwyn explained. "The purpose was to destabilize Venice politically by sending influential men into exile, especially anyone who posed a threat of discovering her scheme."

"But what if one of them had chosen the right casket?"

"There wasn't a 'right' one," Gwen said. "I looked. None of them contained her picture."

Corwyn nodded as if he'd expected as much. Francesco glared and slammed a fist on the table, causing a servant who was placing a tray of tiny octopus or squid in front of him to jump. Before continuing, Francesco waited for the flustered servant to move on around the table and begin serving the others. *"Bene,* at least this Hydro Phobius has fled now and the danger to Venice is over, even if we didn't catch him."

The servant set another tray of the tentacled creatures in front of Gwen. She bent to sniff them, making sure Sebastian saw, then straightened with a look of distaste.

Corwyn shook his head in answer to the doge. "I doubt Hydro Phobius has left. He may be nervous about your sudden interest in him, especially if he recognized Gwen at the trial. But he can't be sure how much we know. Until the *Festa della Sensa* is over, he'll stay close by, seeking to finish the destruction of Venice."

Cautiously, Sebastian smelled his own tray. He looked puzzled, then shrugged. "Is it the fork that's bothering you?" he whispered across the table to Gwen.

Gwen shook her head.

Although Sebastian's voice carried like a stage whisper through the room, Corwyn and Francesco acted as though they hadn't heard. "I think you underestimate Venetian security," Francesco replied to Corwyn. He paused for a bite from his tray. "We have soldiers patrolling Belmont for La Bella Donna. Others will be stationed on the *traghetti* as well, so she can't sneak over from the mainland. Our agents will find her—or rather, him."

"But will you catch him in time?" Corwyn grumbled, picking through his utensils.

Sebastian speared an octopus—or squid, whatever they were—showing improved skill with a fork since Genoa. Gwen waited. Sebastian paused with the bite at his lips, its tentacles dangling. "What's wrong?" he whispered when he saw her watching him, her food untouched. "Aren't you hungry?"

"They're not fresh," she said, lifting her nose as if to remove it from an offensive smell.

"Uh, oh," Corwyn groaned, glancing at the doge. "Gwen, you're going too far."

Francesco motioned as if smoothing the air with his hands. "Not at all." He gestured to a servant, indicating Gwen's and Sebastian's trays, which were quickly removed. "I'm sure this humble fare is adequate for you and me," he went on to Corwyn. "But these two, having such obviously refined sensibilities, can't be expected to stomach it." He turned to Sebastian. "I trust you agree with the *signorina* and wish to share the privileges of her position?"

"Oh, of course," Sebastian replied miserably, his eyes on the servant who was disappearing from the room with the two trays of food.

With the doge's help, Gwen found something wrong with every course she was served, from the *bronzino* to the veal and even the strawberries. Francesco played his role with enthusiasm, relishing the game. Each time, Corwyn shook his head as if disavowing any part in it, looking increasingly anxious to leave. Once embarked upon this sport, however, Francesco wasn't to be rushed. His page, on the other hand, who obviously didn't understand, became increasingly outraged at Gwen and Sebastian. But it was Sebastian's expression which almost weakened Gwen. He looked so pitiful after a while, staring at each plate hungrily, no longer expecting to be allowed to eat from any of them, waiting for each new item that was brought to be abruptly withdrawn.

Then she'd remind herself of what he'd put her through while teaching her to act like a noblewoman, and she'd find the strength to send yet another dish back to the kitchen untasted.

"For tonight, milord, we'll fast together for company," she whispered to him, full of innocence. "Maybe tomorrow's fare will be better."

It was dark by the time dinner was over. Corwyn, unable to convince the doge that Phobius remained a threat, was almost apoplectic with anxiety. Before they left, however, Francesco announced that Gwen and Sebastian would need something more to wear, not only to protect them from the cool night breeze off the sea, but also to preserve the dignity of the state. He whispered something to his page which sent the boy scurrying from the room with a smirk.

The page soon returned carrying a pair of coarse, moth-eaten cloaks, holding them out as if they offended him. Gwen understood the boy's reaction when he handed her one, for it reeked of pigsties and stables. Sebastian stumbled back, a hand over his nose, when the page presented him with the other.

"I'm sorry we don't have anything appropriate for you to wear," Francesco said with a straight face. "These simple garments, so clearly beneath your station, will have to do until you find something more suitable."

Gwen held herself like a queen being readied for coronation while the doge helped her on with her cloak. Sebastian gagged and tried to shy away as the page threw the other garment over him.

Gwen thanked Francesco and they left, with Corwyn keeping to the lead, upwind of her and Sebastian. "I can't believe that in the midst of the world's greatest Renaissance city, we've been reduced to this," Sebastian grumbled over his shoulder to Gwen. "It's a high price for nobility."

Despite hunger and discomfort, Gwen allowed herself a private smile, wondering how much more he'd be willing to pay.

ACT 22:

The Merry Wives of Belmont

SEBASTIAN SANK WEARILY TO THE BALLROOM FLOOR OF Antonio's palace after trudging back with Gwen and Corwyn. Faint with hunger, he watched Corwyn (evidently refreshed by his meal with the doge) hurry over to examine the glass sphere, its glow much diminished from when Antonio had first brought them to see it a few hours earlier.

Antonio, true to his word, had been industrious in their absence, and Sebastian regretted having doubted him. The merchant, who'd been stripping the reflective coating from the sphere when Corwyn and the others returned, was even sweating, which surprised Sebastian. He hadn't thought an artificial creature could sweat.

Then Gwen drew Antonio aside, dissolving Sebastian's remorse in a fit of renewed jealousy. The merchant might be only a simulacrum, but with his tousled hair and his jerkin and blouse unlaced from working, he cut too dashing a figure to ignore. Sebastian felt justified in listening to their conversation.

"I apologize for what I said earlier," Gwen told Antonio, looking as tired as Sebastian felt. "I was wrong. I'll carry your message to Jessica."

Antonio hadn't commented on her or Sebastian's appearance, but now his eyebrows rose. "So I won my obscenity?"

Sebastian puzzled over this before realizing the word Antonio had used meant "wager," not "obscenity." He started to chuckle at his mistake, then frowned. What wager?

He let it go. At least this wager had nothing to do with him.

Meanwhile, Gwen had stiffened, and Sebastian started to drag himself to her defense even though he still didn't know what was at issue. But Antonio put out a hand to Gwen. "I'm sorry, I shouldn't have made that bet. I was angry." The merchant glanced over at Sebastian, who pretended innocence by staring across the room at the sphere. "He means well, I suppose," Antonio went on.

"Yes, he means well," Gwen repeated, also looking in Sebastian's direction. "Sometimes, that's the problem."

Sebastian felt himself blush and hoped the room was too dark for them to see. He wondered what Gwen meant by that. And what did this have to do with a wager?

Gwen sighed and turned back to the simulacrum. "Sometimes meaning well is the best that can be said of me, too. Maybe that's why I want to deliver your message to Jessica in spite of what I said at the time."

Antonio nodded. "I think I understand." He withdrew a sweat-stained, folded sheet of parchment from inside his jerkin and handed it to her. "Thank you."

Gwen studied the sheet where it had been folded over and secured with wax. "So many messages I've delivered for La Bella Donna bearing your seal, yet this is the first to have actually come from your hand."

"Hydro Phobius's intrigues." Antonio snorted. "In the dark, each of his mistresses thought she was meeting me. I can't pass through Belmont without strange women giving me knowing glances and lecherous winks." Suddenly, Antonio's eyes widened and he stared at Gwen. "Hydro Phobius's mistresses!"

Gwen lifted her gaze from the letter to stare back at

him, then motioned anxiously to Corwyn. Sebastian edged closer, made uneasy by an excitement he didn't understand.

"We think we know where Hydro Phobius is hiding," Gwen blurted as the alchemist approached. "In one of the other villas in Belmont—"

"With one of his mistresses—" Antonio interrupted.

"He's probably blackmailing them—" Gwen went on.

"Because they didn't know it was him—"

"They thought it was Antonio they were seeing—" Gwen said, pointing to the merchant.

"But it was dark, and they couldn't really see at all—" Antonio explained.

"So he's probably using his knowledge of their affairs to force them to hide him—"

"And all the while, they still think he's La Bella Donna."

Antonio and Gwen both stopped for breath, apparently finished, while Corwyn peered at each in turn, his expression bewildered. Sebastian, who was thoroughly confused, gave up pretending that he wasn't listening and joined them. "Slow down," Corwyn told the pair, holding out his hands. "Now what's this about Hydro Phobius having mistresses in Belmont?"

"And why didn't they know it was him?" Sebastian asked, glancing sideways at Antonio.

"And why would they shelter Hydro Phobius in any case?" Corwyn asked. He silenced Sebastian's next question with a wave, then went on, "But, please, only one of you answer at a time."

So Gwen and Antonio, still interrupting each other but talking slower this time, explained about Hydro Phobius's late-night liaisons with the neglected wives of Belmont, telling how each woman thought it was Antonio she was meeting in the dark. Finally, Corwyn nodded. "But what good does that do us?"

"Don't you see? I know where those women live," Gwen said. "I delivered the letters."

"So we can send our own letters to each of them, explaining how they've been deceived," Antonio added.

"When the women find out La Bella Donna is really a man, and that it was him they were with, not Antonio, maybe they'll turn him in to the doge's soldiers," Gwen concluded.

Corwyn nodded again. "It's worth a try." He looked over his shoulder at the glass sphere, where the creatures around it were becoming restless as its influence over them waned. "We may have stopped the immediate danger, but Venice isn't safe as long as Hydro Phobius is loose. He could still come up with a way to trigger the lagoon's collapse."

So Sebastian soon found himself again threading his way through Venice, accompanied by Gwen and bearing letters which the two of them were to deliver in Belmont. He was grateful for darkness, for the night helped hide their undergarments and the cloaks from the doge that— except for Sebastian's cap—were their only clothing. Sebastian shook his head as he considered the strange twists of logic Gwen had used to get him to appear in public again dressed like this, arguing as she had that anything better was beneath them. At the time she'd sounded convincing. Now that they were actually on the streets once more, Sebastian wasn't so sure. He sighed, perplexed by the changes in Gwen since she'd been in Venice. Maybe working for Hydro Phobius had affected her thinking.

Suddenly, Sebastian realized Gwen was no longer following him. He backtracked and found her in front of a wealthy residence some distance behind. She'd been waiting, he gathered, for him to discover her absence, reluctant to intrude on his thoughts. Sebastian felt he was supposed to be grateful, but it irked him. "Gwen, what are you doing?"

"Milord, I need to speak with someone who lives here," she said.

Sebastian, unwilling to be seen and anxious to finish

in Belmont, started to walk away. "We can stop on the way back."

"Yes, milord." But she made no move to follow.

Sebastian sighed, knowing it was pointless to argue. She'd simply agree with everything he said until they somehow ended up doing exactly what she wanted. He looked at the building, which was surrounded by a protective wall, without recognizing it. "Who lives here?"

"Jessica, milord, the moneylender's daughter. I have a letter for her from Antonio."

Sebastian shivered. So this strange journey had now linked him with the moneylender's problems as well as magic, he thought, recalling Shylock and his daughter from the quay earlier in the day.

He started to cover his reaction with a nod, then realized the gesture was useless in the dark. "Ah, Antonio," he said, angry at Gwen for mentioning him. Sebastian wasn't ready to forgive Antonio for misleading him about the doge's relationship with Gwen, nor Gwen for her apparent friendship with the simulacrum. "You don't sound very happy about this task. Could it be you don't want to deliver Antonio's letter to another woman?"

"What?" Gwen sounded startled, and more than a little annoyed, making Sebastian regret his words. "Milord, Antonio can send letters to whomever he pleases. It's no business of mine."

"Then what's the matter?" Sebastian asked, his voice softening.

In the dim light, Sebastian could just make out Gwen studying the wall around the building. "She's Jewish," she said after a while.

"Oh." It was Sebastian's turn to be startled. When Gwen didn't continue, he pressed her gently. "So?"

"So, I can't pretend that doesn't bother me, and I'm ashamed to find it does."

"Huh?"

After a moment, he became aware of her peering at him in the gloom. "It really doesn't matter to you, does it?'' she asked. Before he could respond, she answered for him. "No, I suppose not. Why did I think it would? Sometimes, Sebastian, you can be very refreshing—when you're not being aggravating instead.''

She went to the door and knocked while he tried to think what to say. "Does it bother you that he's a simulacrum?'' Sebastian asked at last.

"It did, but I'm getting over it.''

Sebastian started to nod, then remembered the futility. "Me, too.''

"Are you?'' Gwen asked.

Sebastian didn't know how to answer that.

Through the door, he heard someone unlock the shutter of a small grille which allowed visitors to be inspected. "I'll only be a few minutes,'' Gwen called back to Sebastian. She held a brief, whispered conversation at the grille, then the door opened and a servant admitted her.

Sebastian, weak with hunger, paced the empty street outside with only his worries about the changes in Gwen for company. She was proving as extreme in her submission as she had been previously in her independence. And she was imposing her whims on Sebastian as well, taking for granted that he shared her views.

Yet Sebastian had to admit that he himself had quickly fallen back into his role as a nobleman when Gwen had challenged him with it in the Doges' Palace. But if Gwen's current dissatisfaction with life was what the Renaissance led to, he wanted none of it. The only problem was to convince her to abandon this extravagance and accept something more reasonable.

Sebastian's thoughts were interrupted by women's voices, one of them Gwen's, on the other side of the wall that separated the moneylender's house from the street. Looking up, he saw the boughs of a lemon tree rising above the wall, lit by flickering torches from below. Apparently, Gwen and Jessica were talking in the garden. Sebastian listened, but couldn't make out the words. Their laughter, however, was unmistakable. Sebastian wondered at this latest extreme in Gwen, who'd been reluctant to enter only a short time ago.

He shook his head, perplexed by what was happening to himself and his friends. The whole world was changing; Italy was proof of that. And Sebastian had embraced that change, seeking salvation in the promised new order. But he hadn't anticipated the chaos that went with change or the uncertainties which would lead him to question everything he'd taken for granted. The very things he'd come to Italy to find were now the things he held most in doubt.

Questions and change—lately everything seemed reduced to that. Gwen, whom Sebastian had tried to transform, had indeed been altered, but not the way he'd intended. And Corwyn, searching for the right answers to everything from the Renaissance to his alchemical tests, had been too obsessed to realize that the real dilemma lay in the questions themselves and in the changes those questions brought about.

From the other side of the wall, laughter again rippled over the city, soft as wavelets on a canal or a sea breeze fragrant with distant blossoms. Sebastian ached, feeling excluded, and he wondered why contentment always seemed to lie on the other side of some wall he couldn't climb.

Suddenly, he thought again of his father, and of his father's father before him—specters recalled from their graves perhaps by a trace of thaumaturgical energy still lingering in the city. Sebastian knew this time, however, that the figures existed only in his mind. Yet he was unprepared for seeing his own doubts mirrored in them, where he expected only certainty. They, too, had searched for something in an alien land. Sebastian's Saxon grandfather, foregoing an England ruled by Normans, had gone to France to find new hope for his family. Yet his son, Sebastian's father, had lived in Gardenia as an outsider, trapped between pride in his own ancestry and the resentment of a people his father had come to conquer.

Sebastian bowed his head before this revelation, humbled in his own search for security. He'd thought he alone faced the terror of not belonging, and that this was due to some lack within him. Now he saw it as a legacy handed down from father to son, a struggle he shared with his ancestors as far back as his grandfather and possibly beyond.

The closing of a door jarred him from his reverie. When he looked up, the ghosts of his forefathers were gone. In their place was Gwen, a spectral shape in the gloom, reemerging from Shylock's house and coming toward him. She too had chosen to face a new and potentially frightening world by loving him, accepting the disruption this brought to her life in Pomme de Terre. His chest tightened at the thought, and he reached for her.

She rushed past him, possibly unaware of his arms in the dark. "We must reach Belmont quickly, milord. I hadn't planned on staying here so long."

He hurried after her to regain the lead, frowning at her renewed energy. For a moment, he wondered if Jessica had fed her, while he went hungry. Perhaps guilt explained Gwen's avoidance of him. He was so starved, fatigue made him stagger. Then he dismissed his suspicion as unbecoming. Nevertheless, he was hard pressed to remain ahead of her.

"It sounded as though you enjoyed your visit after all," he panted, still resentful at having been on the wrong side of the wall, whether she'd eaten at Jessica's or not.

"I saw this as a duty, not expecting to like her. But Jessica and I have much in common."

"Does she know about Antonio?"

"Yes. He told her in his letter." Gwen paused. "She already suspected."

"And?"

"She loves him anyway."

Sebastian snorted, then regretted the waste of breath. "I don't see what that gives you two in common."

"We're both in love with difficult men, milord."

This stung Sebastian more than he cared to admit. "But Antonio's not a man," he objected, evading the point. "He's a simulacrum!"

When Gwen didn't respond, he looked back over his shoulder, unable to read her expression in the dark. Then he stumbled over a loose paving stone and decided to keep his attention on his feet.

A *traghetto* conveyed them to Mestre on the mainland, where they roused the ostler for Gwen's horse. *"Sì, signore,"* he mumbled to Gwen, eyes wide at the change that had come over her since she'd left the horse earlier in the day. He brought out a spirited gelding. Sebastian, recalling Gwen's previous trouble with horses, cleared his throat. "This is yours?" he asked dubiously.

Gwen gave him that strange, penetrating stare he was beginning to dread. "You're right, of course, milord. It would be unseemly for a lady to ride such an animal."

"Gwen, I didn't mean—"

But she was already scolding the ostler for having brought the horse. He cringed, peering up at her as if hoping for a sign. *"Sì, signore . . .* uh, *signorina,"* he said.

He led out one horse after another, and Gwen faulted each of them. Sebastian tried to intervene a couple of times, but she twisted his objections in ways he didn't intend, using his words to fuel her own ends. Finally, the ostler produced his last horse—or rather, nag. It was a broken-down, swaybacked, windgalled, spavined animal, possessed with the glanders, afflicted with the staggers, gnawn with bots, shoulder shot, and near legged. Its tack was equally decrepit, for Gwen had refused the gear from her former mount with arguments as specious as those she'd used to reject the horse. Two mismatched stirrups hung from a moth-eaten saddle, the halter was knotted from frequent repairs, the bit was cracked, and the girth had been sewn back together a half-dozen times with bits of velour from a woman's crupper.

Sebastian winced. Gwen studied the animal with contempt, then nodded. "It's obviously beneath us, mi-lord," she explained, "but the ostler doesn't have a proper mount. We'll have to make do with this."

Sebastian wondered why they couldn't make do with one of the other horses the ostler had shown them, but was reluctant to ask. This new aspect of Gwen unnerved him. She was so demanding, so severe, that she deprived them both of the slightest luxury.

The ostler looked dubious, glancing about as if he might be arrested for so lopsided a trade. Hastily, he helped them mount, then waved the nag clear of the yard.

Soon, they were plodding up the road to Belmont, with Sebastian in the saddle and Gwen seated crosswise before him. The night breeze blew off the lagoon. Se-bastian's undergown had ridden up embarrassingly high, exposing his bare legs to the chill. He shivered, then used that as a pretext for drawing Gwen closer. She resisted at first, holding herself rigidly erect as she had since their visit to the Doges' Palace long hours earlier. Then she relented and leaned against him. Her touch sparked fire, but Sebastian held her gently, fearful of disrupting the spell which enveloped them. Despite the cold and hunger, the late hour and the painful, jolting gait of the nag, Sebastian had never known such contentment.

The nag collapsed on the way back from Belmont, and they had to walk the remaining league to the shore, where they were to meet Corwyn and Antonio.

Sebastian grumbled, wondering whether to lie down in the road with the dead horse or to continue on with Gwen. It was a choice he had to think about, for his earlier contentment had evaporated while hurrying to deliver the letters and return to the rendezvous on time. Gwen too was short-tempered as they stumbled along the dark, rutted path. If she had eaten at Jessica's, Se-bastian reflected, the meal had worn off long ago.

Their mood had soured when the letters they had delivered produced no observable effect. Hydro Phobius's

mistresses, surly at being roused from sleep, had accepted the messages with irritation, then slammed the
doors on Gwen and Sebastian before reading them. Since
then, no one had alerted the doge's soldiers to Hydro
Phobius's whereabouts.

The land turned marshy as the two of them approached
the shore, and the breeze, blowing across the lagoon from
the Adriatic, smelled of seaweed and salt. The footing
became treacherous, with muddy, reed-covered bogs that
sucked at their feet. Only the grey predawn light enabled
them to keep to the path at all.

They reached the water's edge to see two torchlit gondolas gliding toward them across the lagoon. Finally, the
vessels drew close enough to make out Corwyn and
Oliver in one, while Antonio and a boy with a torch rode
in the other. Behind the gondolas floated the glass sphere,
towed in a fishnet and glowing very faintly now.

"Poor Corwyn," Gwen murmured.

"Poor Corwyn!" Sebastian repeated indignantly, his
teeth chattering with the cold. "Why poor Corwyn? He's
still wearing his proper clothes. He ate dinner with the
doge. He didn't have to walk a league to get here because
his horse dropped dead beneath him. Poor Corwyn, indeed!"

"Sebastian, surely you don't mean it's my fault you've
had to put up with these hardships? You weren't forced
to accept them simply because I did—you could have
chosen otherwise. Of course, I'm only trying to live up
to what you taught me, and those lessons would be seriously weakened if you didn't abide by them yourself.
Nevertheless, you have to make your own decisions,
milord; it wouldn't be my place to make them for you,
nor yours to allow me to."

Sebastian opened his mouth angrily, then closed it
again. Anything he said would come out sounding
wrong. "I just don't see anything pitiful about Corwyn,
that's all," he grumbled at last.

"Why, Sebastian, how can you be so heartless! Don't
you see the world is changing on him?"

"It's changing on me, too."

"Yes, but not to the same degree. He's an old man, Sebastian. He came here hoping the Renaissance would bring back the world he knew in his youth—his lost Alexandria. Instead, that world is slipping ever further from his grasp. Living so long has left him very much alone."

There it was again, Sebastian thought, stunned—the problem of living in a changing world. He'd believed it was a problem unique to him; now he realized it afflicted everyone. He felt reassured by this, and humbled as well. So Corwyn, too, was troubled by change. No wonder the alchemist had been obsessed with finding answers rather than with looking at the questions—answers implied a certainty which questions denied.

The prows of the gondolas slid among the reeds at the water's edge. Sebastian and Gwen scrambled to join Antonio and the alchemist as they dragged the sphere to shore, then rolled it onto higher ground. Sebastian jerked back after touching the thick glass for the first time, unprepared for its warmth or its soft vibration against his fingertips. Then he gritted his teeth and threw himself into the task. Antonio's torchbearer stood by to illuminate their work while Oliver stayed aboard one of the gondolas. The gondoliers, too, remained at their posts, casting uneasy glances at the lagoon behind them.

"What's the hurry?" Sebastian gasped, slumping down among the reeds while Corwyn unsealed a circular section of the sphere.

Corwyn jerked his head at the lagoon without pausing to answer. Sebastian peered into the distance, where the growing light was offset by rising mist. Still, there seemed to be something on the horizon . . . a cluster of shapes that churned the water as they headed this way. Sebastian squinted to see them better.

He almost choked when they finally took form. They were the creatures from Antonio's palace, wading through the shallow lagoon, throwing up wakes as they breasted the water in an effort to overtake the sphere.

Sebastian jumped to his feet, his energy restored by fear. He helped Corwyn lift out the circle of glass the alchemist had unsealed, then Sebastian and Antonio rolled the sphere over to tip its contents out through the opening. A slimy, sluglike creature about five feet long spilled onto the wet reeds—a fire elemental or "salamander," Sebastian knew, though he'd never seen one before. The ground hissed and steamed where the elemental touched it, leaving a blackened trail as the creature crawled away. The salamander headed inland in a curving path that would eventually take it down the length of Italy.

"Hurry, let's rinse this out to remove any last traces of thaumaturgical flux caught in the slime," Corwyn said, pointing to the sphere.

They rolled it back down to the lagoon and let water spill in through the opening. The water sizzled as it touched the slime coating the inside of the sphere, sending up great clouds of steam to mix with the mist from the lagoon. Presently, the hissing stopped. They sloshed the water around a bit more to be certain they'd removed all the flux, then rolled the sphere back onto the reeds and drained the water out. Antonio, working next to Sebastian, moved with stiff determination.

They finished just in time. With much splashing and shoving, the creatures from Antonio's palace arrived, already swinging southward to intersect the elemental's path. They thrashed their way out of the lagoon less than a hundred yards from where Sebastian and his companions stood. Sebastian shuddered as a werewolf at the near edge of the cluster paused to shake the water from its fur, casting a hungry gaze at the humans. The torchbearer gasped and moved closer to Antonio, though the simulacrum was staring so intently after the salamander that he seemed scarcely aware of the boy's presence. Then the werewolf loped after its fellow creatures as they headed inland. Sebastian let out his breath, discovering that he'd been holding it.

"That salamander's still pretty vexed after its captiv-

ity," Corwyn said. "With luck, having those other creatures swarming around it will keep it annoyed all the
way back to Mt. Aetna. It'll give off enough thaumaturgical flux to lure the whole lot of them with it."

"But what about Oliver?" Gwen asked, looking over
at the gondola where the broom, dressed again in monk's
robes, was gazing sadly after his newfound friends, now
vanishing in the distance. "Why didn't he follow, too?"

"He would have," Corwyn replied softly. "That's
why we tied him up. Until the elemental's a safe distance
away, Oliver will have to be restrained."

Sebastian, noticing Oliver's rope bonds for the first
time, felt sad for the little broom. He and Oliver seemed
to share a tendency to chase after things they couldn't
have.

Then another thought struck Sebastian, and he glanced
at Antonio. The simulacrum stood rigidly, fists clenched
at his sides, his attention—like Oliver's—fixed on the
retreating elemental. But whereas Oliver needed ropes
to restrain him, Antonio was relying only on strength of
will. Grudging admiration filled Sebastian as he watched,
sensing the simulacrum's struggle. Here, too, Sebastian
found he had something in common with another being
where he hadn't expected it, and the realization troubled
him.

A far-off clamor on the road from Belmont distracted
him. In the waxing light, he saw another crowd running
toward them in the distance. Their yells drifted to him,
tenuous as the mist from the lagoon. For a moment,
Sebastian wondered if these were yet more creatures of
magic hastening after the elemental. But this time, the
creatures appeared to be human, and the figure they were
chasing was a short, heavyset woman in black. The fugitive, well ahead of her pursuers, ran with a peculiar
hopping gait and was headed directly toward the group
on the shore. For an old lady, Sebastian thought as she
drew rapidly closer, she moved with surprising speed—

—but not, he added as she bowled him over and

slammed into Antonio's torchbearer, with much attention to where she was going.

"Save me," the woman cried in a shrill, nasal whine. "Save a helpless old woman. They think I'm a witch!"

As if to confirm this, the shouts of the still-distant mob rose to a thin but triumphant roar.

"Of course," Corwyn said smoothly, taking the woman's elbow and leading her to the water's edge. "Don't worry, we'll save you."

Sebastian, angry at landing on his back in the reeds, started to complain. "Shhh!" Gwen whispered, helping him up and brushing at the muddy splotches on his gown. But her attention was elsewhere, and all she did was spread the mud around. She seemed to be averting her face from the squat old woman.

"Quick, climb in here," Corwyn went on, handing the woman into the glass sphere.

"Oh, thank you," the woman screeched. Her veil had been knocked askew and Sebastian could see her staring with large pop-eyes at the advancing mob, aware of nothing else. The shouted threats from her pursuers were clearer, the individual faces—mostly women, Sebastian noticed—distinct in their fury.

Halfway into the sphere, the woman stuck. "Ooph! Say, what is this thing?" She glanced down for the first time, and her eyes widened further. "Hey, I know what this is!"

Sebastian frowned, puzzled over her deepening voice. He had the feeling he'd heard it before.

Corwyn and Gwen lunged for the woman and began pushing her into the sphere. She shrieked and clawed at them, drowning out the cries of the approaching mob. The suddenness of the attack startled Sebastian, and he considered going to the old woman's aid. Antonio, however, having moved aside with his torchbearer when the old woman arrived, now joined the assault. When she saw him, the old woman froze. "You!" she gasped in a raspy, masculine voice. Her face twisted in rage.

Just then, Corwyn, Gwen, and Antonio shoved to-

gether, and the old woman who was not a woman popped
into the sphere like a cork pushed too far into a bottle
of wine. The captive's bellows emerged from inside the
sphere with a muffled, distant sound that belied the force
with which they were uttered.

The bellows of the mob, however, were growing
louder. "Hurry!" Corwyn called. "Into the water!"

Sebastian, understanding at last who the fat, toadlike
person in the sphere really was, helped slide the makeshift prison into the lagoon. Inside, Hydro Phobius cum
La Bella Donna flung himself against the walls of his
cell, rocking the sphere. He stopped abruptly as the
sphere tipped too far and sloshed several inches of water
in through the opening. After that, he huddled at the
bottom without moving, apparently realizing that if the
sphere sank, he'd be unable to escape through the narrow
opening before he drowned.

The fishnet was still strung between the two gondolas.
Corwyn and Antonio threw it over the sphere, then Corwyn clambered onto one of the vessels. Sebastian and
Gwen started for the other, but Antonio held Gwen back.
"Sweet lady, you've given us life," he told her, indicating the torchbearer at his side. "Thanks to you, like
two ships we have come safely to a single harbor."

Sebastian started to ask what he meant, but Corwyn
shouted at them to hurry. Sebastian led Gwen to the
second gondola and they quickly climbed aboard. The
gondoliers leaned on their oars, sending the two craft
skimming over the water. The vessels jerked to a stop
as the fishnet snapped taut around the sphere, then proceeded more slowly, dragging Hydro Phobius's glass
cage through the water behind them.

Hydro Phobius, crouched inside, looked relieved to
be underway despite any concerns about sinking. That
relief was understandable, Sebastian thought; no sooner
had the sphere cleared the shore than the mob from Belmont (which seemed to consist primarily of Phobius's
unwitting mistresses) reached the water. They splashed
into the lagoon a ways before giving up the chase, forced

to content themselves with hurling curses after the retreating captive.

"Maybe we should have let those women have him," Corwyn called from the first gondola, watching the mob milling on the shore.

"What!" Sebastian exclaimed, appalled at the idea of anyone—even Hydro Phobius—suffering that fate. "Master, they'd have torn off parts of his anatomy."

"Exactly," the alchemist replied. He swiveled to stare over his shoulder, past the gondola's bow. "Ah well, maybe turning him over to the doge is the right thing after all. Venetian justice isn't known for mercy."

Not sure what to say, Sebastian glanced at the gondola his master was riding. He started to turn away, then wrenched his gaze back again. Except for Corwyn and Oliver and the two gondoliers, the second vessel was empty. "Oh, no! We've got to go back!"

"Why?" Corwyn asked, his expression mystified.

"We left Antonio and that torchbearer of his behind," Sebastian cried. He stared at the shore, trying to distinguish them among the crowd.

"Sebastian, you sound worried," Gwen said with a smile. She rested a hand on his arm.

"Aren't you?"

"It's all right, Sebastian," Corwyn called. "Antonio intended to remain behind. He's on his way to Verona, to become a real merchant there. That mob isn't after him."

"And the torchbearer?" Sebastian asked.

Gwen's smile broadened. "Jessica. The torchbearer costume was my idea to help her sneak away."

"I thought he looked a bit effeminate," Sebastian grumbled, wondering why everyone knew these things but him. "Well, where to now?"

Corwyn pointed across the lagoon to the glow that heralded the coming dawn. For a terrible moment, Sebastian thought the alchemist meant they'd simply follow the sun wherever it led. After a night without food, sleep, or adequate clothing, that sounded like more adventure than he could endure.

"It's the beginning of *Sensa*," Corwyn explained. "Vessels are probably already assembling for the procession. If we hurry, I think we can catch up before the doge's barge leads them across the lagoon to the Lido, for the ritual Marriage of the Sea." He grinned and pointed at Phobius in the sphere. "He'll make a suitable wedding present, don't you think?"

ACT 23:

All's Well That Ends

WITHIN THE HOUR, THE TWO GONDOLAS TOWING HYDRO Phobius were assigned a position of honor alongside the Bucintoro, the doge's ceremonial barge. Accompanied by a fleet of several hundred gaily festooned gondolas, fishing boats, and pleasure craft, the great barge was being rowed from the Molo past San Giorgio Maggiore and the island convent of Sant' Elena toward the Lido and the open waters of the Adriatic.

To the east, the sun rose, setting a wide swath of the sea on fire—a highway of gold forming a direct path to heaven for the inhabitants of the lagoon.

From her gondola, Gwen watched Francesco, lit by the newly risen sun, enthroned on his glittering barge beneath the banner of St. Mark. The banner shone with the inevitable winged lion standing against a crimson background, its paw on an open book. Yet for all its majesty, there was pathos in the image as well. Gwen shook her head, struck again by the sense that Francesco, embodying as he did the Venetian state, was a prisoner of the republic, a caged lion on public display. He wasn't a man—he was a living emblem, a political myth. Hydro Phobius in his glass prison was no more thoroughly confined.

Gwen had to admit, however, that the cage in which Francesco rode was spectacular. A golden figure of Justice dominated the prow of the ducal barge, resplendent in the morning sun. The top deck sloped up toward the stern, where two carved figures held a curving shell as a canopy over the doge's throne. The entire upper deck formed a gallery roofed in crimson velvet and hung with tassels, rich in carved woodwork overlaid with gilt, and lined with the highest officials of the state: the Procuratori, councillors, foreign ambassadors, the Senate, and the Great Council, all robed in crimson or scarlet and wearing the stoles of the knightly orders to which they belonged. So great was the honor of this occasion that each oarsman on the lower decks, working four men to an oar, were chosen from volunteers at the Arsenale.

Gwen and her companions hadn't been invited to travel with the doge aboard the Bucintoro, of course. Gwen's friendship with Francesco notwithstanding, every position on the craft was precisely determined, a jealously guarded privilege earned or inherited by its occupant. Not even a doge dared to challenge that order. Indeed, the decision allowing the two gondolas to travel adjacent to the barge had in itself disrupted the time-honored positions established among the craft accompanying the doge, leading to considerable grumbling from the lesser officials aboard those boats whose traditional prerogatives had been usurped.

Beyond Sant' Elena, another vessel approached, a flatboat or *piatto* only slightly less ostentatious than that of the doge. The new vessel drew alongside the Bucintoro, and the white-mitred patriarch of Venice, with his company of bishops, canons, priests, and chapter of his church at San Pietro, crossed from the *piatto* in a cloud of incense to join the officials aboard the doge's barge. The patriarch moved up the center of the gallery and took his seat below the steps leading to the ducal throne. Behind him, three acolytes carried golden basins filled with roses, which they gave to the doge to be distributed

among the members of his company in memory of this
Ascension Day.

Then the Bucintoro resumed its stately voyage, passing
between the towered fortresses of Sant' Andrea and San
Nicolo to the open sea beyond the Lido. Behind the
procession, church bells rang on islands scattered
throughout the lagoon. Sackbuts and trumpets on many
of the boats heralded the doge's coming. Overhead, sea-
gulls swooped and cawed like impudent angels.

Gwen, awed by the spectacle in which she was a par-
ticipant, however minor, glanced at Sebastian and was
surprised to find his eyes on her instead of the unfolding
ceremony. His expression was distant, wistful. He looked
haggard with lack of food and sleep, causing Gwen to
wonder if she looked as bad. "What's wrong?" she
asked.

Instead of answering right away, he took off the bat-
tered blue cap and gazed at it a moment, his expression
unreadable. Then he flung it out over the water. The
shapeless cloth dropped into the waves, where it quickly
filled and vanished as the gondola sailed on. Gwen felt
an unexpected twinge of loss.

"It's no use continuing this masquerade," Sebastian
said softly, as if speaking to himself. "I'm not a wealthy
nobleman any more than I'm from Spain. Neither am I
another Corwyn." He fixed Gwen with a steady gaze.
"But I'll be a good alchemist someday. In the meantime,
however, I've done you a grave disservice, and I apologize."

"Oh?"

"Yes." He hesitated, seeming unsure of his words.
"I set up false standards for you to follow, and now I
must rescind them, for myself as well as you."

He paused again, perhaps hoping for a response, but
she waited. "Gwen, you have to lower your expectations
a little," he blurted finally. "Or else you'll never find
any real happiness in life." He leaned toward her, im-
passioned. "Believe me, Gwen, I know. Regardless how
lofty the rewards you deserve, it's important to also rec-

ognize the simpler joys, the humble pleasures, and to delight in them. Otherwise, there'll be nothing along the way but disappointment and misery." He sighed. "I made that mistake, Gwen. I don't want you to suffer from the same error."

She nodded slowly, as if contemplating an idea she hadn't thought of before.

The flotilla of boats had moved out well beyond the Lido now, leaving many of the smaller vessels behind. From the objections being raised by the occupants of these smaller craft, it was apparent that the doge was taking the Bucintoro farther out to sea than usual for the marriage ceremony. The complaints carried over the water like angry, disembodied spirits. In her gondola, Gwen put a hand on one of the gunwales to keep from being pitched about by the Adriatic's higher waves. She glanced at Corwyn in the second gondola, wondering why they were going out so far. Corwyn, gripping both sides of his craft and looking green, shrugged back at her, then broke off abruptly to lean over the gondola's side.

Finally, the oarsmen on the ducal barge interrupted the steady rhythm of their oars. They swung the vessel around so the stern faced out to sea. The patriarch rose on uncertain legs and, with the help of two younger priests, emptied an ampulla of holy water onto the waves. In a voice cracking with age, he pronounced the *benedictio*, or blessing of the sea. Then the doge took his place at the stern, vitality showing in his step and bearing despite the formality of the ritual. He dropped a gold ring made for this purpose into the sea and called out the traditional words of the marriage in a clear, commanding voice: "We wed thee, O sea, as a sign of true and perpetual dominion."

Gwen's lip curled cynically. Here, then, was the true purpose of the ceremony—to reestablish Venetian dominance over the sea. As the wife of the doge, the sea could be regarded as chattel.

Gwen didn't want the kind of marriage Francesco was

proclaiming over the sea, but neither, she'd decided, did she want a marriage like those of Dame Alice, who had dominated each of her five husbands. The first kind required too great a submission, the second too great an arrogance.

She turned back to Sebastian. "Thank you for this advice, milord. Although it contradicts what you've told me before, I think perhaps it deserves much credence, and I'll do my best to heed your words. Still, it won't be easy," she added, "and I may forget from time to time."

Sebastian's brow wrinkled as he considered this, and Gwen allowed herself a private smile. "I trust you'll help remind me if I forget?"

He nodded solemnly.

"Thank you, milord. But there is one other thing." It was her turn to hesitate. "Milord, when we're married, do you intend dominion over me?"

He looked perplexed by this sudden shift in topics and shook his head. Then a slow, sheepish grin spread over his face like a second dawning. "Ah, I think I begin to see. And if I understand correctly, I suppose I've deserved all the things that've happened to me since yesterday in the Doges' Palace." He laughed and plucked at his tattered cloak for emphasis. "Believe me, Gwen, I've had a taste of dominion—from both sides now— and I want nothing more to do with it. When we're married, it'll be as equals."

Gwen nodded again, more contented than she'd felt in a long time.

On his barge, Francesco caught her attention by adding a new twist to the traditional marriage formula. "In token of this espousal," he proclaimed, "we offer up this wedding gift into the keeping of our wife, the sea."

Everyone within earshot looked puzzled, including, Gwen noticed, Corwyn and Sebastian. Francesco ignored the buzz of questions around him and signaled to the gondoliers piloting Gwen and her companions. Quickly, the gondoliers unlashed the fishnet which had towed the

sphere. The net fell away, leaving the sphere bobbing
on the surface of the sea. Inside, Hydro Phobius rose to
a half crouch, his pop-eyes widening as he realized his
fate. Slowly, the Bucintoro began rowing away, followed
by the other vessels, returning in stately grace to Venice.

"With Hydro Phobius for a wedding gift, Venice will
be lucky if the sea doesn't sue for annulment," Gwen
muttered, watching the sphere until it was lost in the
distance. Even for Hydro Phobius, this seemed harsh
punishment, but there was nothing she or her companions
could do. Besides, she was relieved at knowing Phobius
no longer endangered them or the city.

She returned her attention to Sebastian. "Milor—"
she began. He frowned and she caught herself. "My
husband," she corrected, smiling, "for such I would
have you be, help me begin learning this new lesson as
soon as we're back in Venice. Let's find a quiet little
chapel and get married today."

Sebastian stared at her in surprise. "I suppose you
know of just such a place?"

"I found one that might serve." She shrugged. "From
the beginning of this journey, I've often strayed to holy
places, to kneel and pray for a happy marriage. But if
you'd rather pick a place yourself . . . ?"

He shook his head. "No, I'm sure the one you found
would be fine. But what about your parents and the wedding they've planned for us in Pomme de Terre?"

"We can repeat the ceremony when we get home,"
she said, her words breathless as they tumbled from her.
"But today, I'd like to make the real commitment with
you, before God and in the company of Corwyn and
Oliver. Just a simple ceremony, without fanfare." She
halted abruptly, holding her breath while she waited for
an answer. Her words sounded forward in her own ears,
and she wondered if he might refuse.

The tightness around Sebastian's mouth eased into a
smile. He took her hand. "I'll wed thee, O Gwen," he
said, paraphrasing the doge's marriage vow to the sea,
"as a sign of true and perpetual love, foregoing any claim

to dominion." He sobered. "But you have to promise the same, Gwen—foregoing dominion."

She started to flare at him, then chuckled instead. "Agreed, no dominion. But, Sebastian, no more masquerades, either."

He nodded, looking sober. Then he gave her a mischievous grin. "As for masquerades, you stopped being Cesario when you gave up his clothes. Now, you're just a pretty wench again." He pulled the covering of the gondola's *felze* closed, shutting out any prying eyes from the other boats. "Come over here, wench." He drew her to him, and she came willingly. "Now kiss me, Gwen."

They sealed their vows with a deep, lingering kiss that lasted all the way to Venice.

Two weeks after the Marriage of the Sea, the *Festa della Sensa* came to a close and Venice, sated at last, stumbled back to a semblance of normalcy. Sebastian, two weeks married as well and feeling smug about life in general, returned one afternoon to the Foscari family palace on the Grand Canal where he and his companions were staying. He found Oliver (whom he was looking for) in the company of Corwyn (whom he'd been avoiding). Ever since Sebastian's comments to the alchemist on Ascension Day eve about the Renaissance and the importance of asking questions, Corwyn had been giving his apprentice strange, glaring looks.

Today was no exception; when Sebastian entered the room, Corwyn glanced up from a crate he was packing with books and straw, and scowled. Sebastian's careful smile evaporated and he started to slink back through the door. Then he remembered his purpose in coming and went over to Oliver, who was going through the stacks of books before Corwyn packed them. Sebastian felt sorry for the broom, who'd been despondent ever since the thaumaturgical generator was dismantled and the other creatures had left without him.

"Here, Oliver," Sebastian said. "I have something for you."

In his outstretched hand was a small whisk broom. Two days earlier, he'd seen the palace steward use it to brush the clothes of the Foscari family. Since then, Sebastian had altered the whisk broom, adding a tiny skirt and scarf made for him by the Foscari seamstress. The resulting doll now resembled a smaller version of the tavern broom Oliver had danced with outside Ravenna.

Oliver reached for the doll, his stick fingers protruding from the monk's robe Corwyn again had him wearing. But he stopped short, stroking the air around the miniature broom without daring to touch it.

"It's all right," Sebastian coaxed, moving the whisk broom closer. "You can touch it."

Oliver cocked his stick head at Sebastian and slowly pointed to himself.

"Yes," Sebastian said, "it's yours."

Oliver took the doll hesitantly, as if still unsure of his good fortune. Then he scurried off to a corner of the room, where he cradled the whisk broom and rocked it like a sleeping child.

While Oliver hovered over his gift, Sebastian squatted to examine the litter on the floor. Suddenly, he grunted, eyes wide as he realized what he was seeing. Pages torn from Corwyn's books lay strewn around the room. Apparently, Oliver was angrier with his maker than any of them had realized, for the broom was destroying the books Corwyn had so carefully selected during the past two weeks.

As unobtrusively as he could, Sebastian began matching discarded pages with the books they'd come from, slipping the torn sheets back inside the covers in the hope that Corwyn wouldn't notice the damage.

"Sebastian, what are you doing?" the alchemist demanded.

Sebastian, feeling guilty despite his innocence, dropped the book he was working on. "Uh, the binding's not very good on some of these. The pages are falling out.'' He picked up the fallen volume and continued replacing pages, knowing as he did the futility of his explanation. The mass of sheets on the floor couldn't have come from one book, or even a handful of them. "You know how it is with these cheap books printed on paper with movable type,'' he went on. "They just don't hold up like hand-copied, parchment editions.''

"Those pages aren't falling out because of poor binding,'' Corwyn snapped, grabbing the book and dumping the loose sheets on the floor. "They were ripped out on purpose.''

Sebastian glanced at Oliver, still bent over his doll, oblivious of everything else in the room. "Oh, I'm sure he didn't mean any harm,'' Sebastian ventured.

"Harm?'' Corwyn sounded incredulous. "What are you talking about? Of course he didn't mean any harm. I told him to do it.''

"You did?'' It was Sebastian's turn to be incredulous.

"Of course,'' Corwyn said, obviously pleased with himself. "These books are central to my plan for introducing the spirit of the Renaissance in Gardenia.''

"But . . . ?'' Sebastian stared in disbelief at the pages on the floor. "But why'd you have Oliver tear pages out? You spent a lot of time picking these books. Don't you care what's in them?''

"Certamente.'' Corwyn tilted his head as if this gave him a clearer view of Sebastian. "For someone who claims the Renaissance is all about asking questions, you seem doubtful about the idea of my posing them. Perhaps you like the certainty of definite answers more than you'd have me believe.'' He held up the book whose pages he'd discarded. "When I get back to Pomme de Terre, in addition to setting up trade relations with Venice, I plan to open a school of alchemical and Renaissance arts. Now, when a student reads this book and reaches the end, only to discover the book didn't originally stop there, or that part of another book has been substituted for this one, what's going to happen?''

"He'll want his tuition back?'' Sebastian suggested.

Corwyn looked disgusted.

"Well, he won't be able to finish the book," Sebastian said belligerently. "That much is certain."

"Yes, but what else?"

Sebastian considered this. "I suppose he'll wonder what the text actually said or how it ended. It'd be frustrating not to know, especially if the book seemed important."

"Exactly!" Corwyn beamed. "And then what?"

"Oh," Sebastian said, beginning to understand. "He'll have to reason the rest out for himself. Or look through other books for the missing pages or for clues as to what else those pages held." Sebastian regarded his master with admiration. "He might correspond with other scholars, or even travel to Italy personally to find the answers, if he can afford it."

"He or she," Corwyn said. "My students will include both men and women."

"Ah," Sebastian said. "That's daring."

"Remember, when I was at the university of Alexandria, the head of that institution was a woman." Corwyn waved his hands. "But you've gotten me off the subject. For students needing to travel abroad for further study, I'll set up scholarships to help pay the expenses. The knowledge a student brings back will always far exceed whatever was in the missing or scrambled portion of the book that sent him."

"Can you afford to pay for scholarships?"

"When it comes to education—which this is in the truest sense—can anyone ever afford not to? Besides, Francesco has offered to underwrite several such scholarships in return for our having saved Venice. The cost is insignificant to him, and will result in the greatest possible benefit to Gardenia in the long run."

"But will this be sufficient to bring about the Renaissance in Gardenia?" Sebastian asked.

Corwyn shrugged. "It'll help. The Renaissance will happen in Gardenia anyway, if it's going to happen there at all. But this may hurry it along a little. Now, I have to get back to work. Business calls me and I must return to Pomme de Terre.''

Sebastian's heart sank while Corwyn went back to packing. Sebastian watched him unhappily for a while, then finally blurted out, ''Are you planning on leaving without me?''

Corwyn straightened. ''Eh?''

''You're talking about leaving right away, and how you're going to do this or that when you get back—well, what about me? Don't you want me to be your apprentice anymore?''

''I didn't think you wanted to come back,'' Corwyn said slowly. ''I thought this''—he waved a hand that took in the palace and Venice beyond—''was what you wanted, and that you intended to stay. You could, you know. I'm sure you'll always be welcome here.''

Sebastian looked at his feet. ''I know. And I hadn't intended on going back, not originally. But now, I want to go home.''

''And is Pomme de Terre your home?''

''As much as anyplace is,'' Sebastian replied, remembering when he'd spoken similar words to Gwen in the tavern outside Ravenna. But now, his meaning had deepened.

Corwyn nodded and stared off absently for a time, lost in thought. Finally, he noticed Oliver playing with his whisk broom doll and smiled. ''You're quite something, Sebastian, more so than you may realize, and often very likable as well,'' he said. Then he added quickly, ''although you do make it difficult sometimes.''

Sebastian frowned, not daring to look up. Hadn't Gwen said something like that, too? ''So what does that mean?'' he asked. ''Can I go back with you or not?''

''Of course you can. I want you to. And I assume Gwen wants to go back as well. How soon can the two of you be ready to leave?''

''As soon as possible,'' Sebastian said, brightening. ''We're both anxious to start.''

''*Bene*.'' Corwyn surveyed the disarray of the room.

"In the meantime, you can help me pack." He sighed a little, sounding wistful. "I think it's time we stirred up the pace of change in Pomme de Terre, and brought Gardenia into the fifteenth century, don't you?"

"Yes," Sebastian said, understanding the eagerness in his master's words as well as the reticence in his sigh. "Yes, I do."

"Then what are you waiting for?" Corwyn demanded. "Start mixing up the pages of those books and handing them to me to pack. We have a renaissance to see to."

"Yes, master." Sebastian smiled. So things were ending well after all—and if they each had tasted a little bitterness getting here, perhaps that just made the present more sweet.

He stooped to his task, happy to have found his place at last in this new era of a changing world.

Author's Note

MOST OF THE FIGURES AND SITUATIONS IN THIS NOVEL
have been portrayed with strict regard for historical ac-
curacy, including Cosimo dé Medici's distrust of Venetian *terra ferma* policy long before this became a concern
to his fellow citizens. After the death of Filippo Maria
Visconti, Cosimo openly backed Milan despite opposition within Florence, and attempted to enlist the support
of Rome and the Papal States against Venice.

For dramatic purposes, however, certain details have
been altered, one of the most notable being the date of
Niccolò Machiavelli's birth. Although Machiavelli ad-
mired Cosimo dé Medici and urged Cosimo's grandson,
Lorenzo, to be more like him, Cosimo actually died five
years before Machiavelli was born. The present book
rectifies this oversight of history, allowing the two to
meet.

As for the plot to destroy Venice and construction of
the thaumaturgical generator, readers will have to decide
for themselves. But it should be noted that the lagoon
experienced unusually severe flooding and earthquakes
around the time of this story. And La Serenissima con-
tinues to sink.

Mr. Clark earned his B.S. in biology at the University of New Mexico, but after a brief foray into graduate school, found himself back in the "family business" as a laboratory technician at the local sewage treatment plant. Eventually he began publishing technical articles and founded a newsletter, *The Bench Sheet*, for laboratory analysts involved with water and sewage. It was on the pages of that newsletter that Corwyn, the world's only aquatic alchemist, was born. Though he has since sold the newsletter, Mr. Clark has continued to write about Corwyn's adventures in short stories and in two novels, *Alchemy Unlimited* and *Rehearsal for a Renaissance*, which you are holding.

The Epic Adventure

THE OMARAN SAGA
by
ADRIAN COLE

"A remarkably fine fantasy…
Adrian Cole has a magic touch."
Roger Zelazny

BOOK ONE:
A PLACE AMONG THE FALLEN
70556-7/$3.95 US/$4.95 Can

BOOK TWO: THRONE OF FOOLS
75840-7/$3.95 US/$4.95 Can

BOOK THREE:
THE KING OF LIGHT AND SHADOWS
75841-5/$4.50 US/$5.50 Can

BOOK FOUR: THE GODS IN ANGER
75842-3/$4.50 US/$5.50 Can

Three Wondrous Stories
of Adventure and Courage by
B R I A N
J A C Q U E S